I0634822

Rouletabille
and the
Mystery of the Yellow Room

*also by **Gaston Leroux***
Chéri-Bibi
(*stage play by Alevy & M. Nadaud
adapted by Frank J. Morlock*)
The Phantom of the Opera
(*adapted y J.-M. & R. Lofficier*)

*also by **Jean-Marc & Randy Lofficier***
Edgar Allan Poe on Mars
Despair (*screenplay adapted from Marc Agapit*)
Robonocchio
Royal Flush (*original screenplay*)

anthologies
Tales of the Shadowmen:
1. The Modern Babylon - 2. Gentlemen of the Night
3. Danse Macabre - 4. Lords of Terror
5. The Vampires of Paris

translations
Arsène Lupin vs. Sherlock Holmes: The Hollow Needle
Arsène Lupin vs. Sherlock Holmes: The Blonde Phantom
(*adapted from Maurice Leblanc*)
Doc Ardan: City of Gold and Lepers
(*adapted from Guy d'Armen*)
Doctor Omega (*adapted from Arnould Galopin*)

non-fiction
Shadowmen: Heroes and Villains of French Pulp Fiction
Shadowmen 2: Heroes and Villains of French Comics
Over Here: An American Expat in the South of France

artbook
If Your Possum Go Daylight (*art by Raven Okeefe*)

Rouletabille
and the
Mystery of the Yellow Room

by
Gaston Leroux

adapted in English by
Jean-Marc & Randy Lofficier

A Black Coat Press Book

English adaptation Copyright © 2009 by Jean-Marc & Randy Lofficier.
Cover illustration Copyright © 2009 by David Rabbitte.

Visit our website at www.blackcoatpress.com

ISBN 978-1-934543-60-3. First Printing October 2009. Pub-lished by Black Coat Press, an imprint of Hollywood Com-ics.com, LLC, P.O. Box 17270, Encino, CA 91416. All rights reserved. Except for review purposes, no part of this book may be reproduced or transmitted in any form or by any means, electronic or mechanical, including photocopying, recording, or by any information storage and retrieval system, without permission in writing from the publisher. The stories and cha-racters depicted in this novel are entirely fictional. Printed in the United States of America.

Foreword

Pierre Reverdy said: "*There is no such thing as love; only proof of love.*" An admirable precept which can be applied to other fields. For instance: "*There is no such thing as genius; only proof of genius.*"

There are also no such things as minor arts. The only thing there is, is the strange marriage of the conscious with the unconscious mind, the exquisite spark generated by the contact between wisdom and the schizophrenic twin whom we all carry within ourselves, and of which we are generally ashamed.

Poetry is the monster born of that strange marriage, that brutal coupling between the extraordinary and the ordinary. Personally, I don't care about the size and strength of said monster. The essential thing is that IT should be born. I ask for nothing else.

What I speak of is very different from the gifts granted to Shakespeare, Hugo, Goethe, Beethoven or Wagner. Instead, IT reminds us of Stendhal who, when talking about a woman descending from a coach, said that *she did it with genius*.

This allows us to respect, adore and applaud that phenomenon known as genius, whether it is manifested in Offenbach or Mozart, or to salute a song by Charles Trenet rather than one of those heavy compositions that modern orchestras inflict upon us, where idiocy is more painful to hear than to see. [1]

The purpose of this foreword is to convince you that *The Mystery of the Yellow Room* deserves compliments far above those it usually receives, and also to acknowledge that, under

---

[1] Nietzsche followed this example by contrasting Wagner's misty tretralogy with the hot-blooded operas of Bizet.

Fantômas' cloak, some writers of popular literature should be unreservedly loved. And if I say "loved," it is because that word isn't understood by intellectuals, and because admiration is nothing but another form of love, a transcendant form of sexuality, as if it came from the soul's very skin, sensitive or insensitive to some forms of beauty, causing or not causing a moral erection, proof that the admiration that one's mind feels towards a work is true and sincere, and not mere diletantism.

Long have I sought refuge from poetic or realistic literature in books whose authors ignore that poetry and truth haunt them, lift them above their station, and even, I might add, above the contempt they claim to feel towards a genre that they deem unworthy of their talents, whereas they err when they try to aim higher.

We found proof of this, Apollinaire and I, when the authors of Fantômas, surprised by our enthusiasm, told us that they could write more sophisticated novels. But these allegedly sophisticated novels turned out to be disconcertingly unsophisticated. They demonstrated, once again, the primality of child-like genius, a genius that a poorly educated person, ignorant of the College of the Muses, may confuse with clumsiness and random luck.

This was not the case, however, with Gaston Leroux. He was always modest, in the true sense of the word, and never pretended to write badly in order to better surprise us with alleged literary masterpieces.

In this family of authors, it is not the plot, nor the cliffhangers, which matter, but the dream-like, dark atmosphere and the sense of foreboding which characterize the world inhabited by their heroes, like a dark orchestra accompanying the story they are telling us without the least derision. From that very lack of disdain springs a marvelous authenticity, a firm balance between the mystery they offer us, and their skill in solving it.

Larsan's long cane... That cane seems to me the very example of a *leitmotif*, like the magical Perfume of the Lady in Black, from Rouletabille's complaint...

The readers who agree with me should study the realm of which Leroux was a Prince, and look back to its King: Edgar Allan Poe; they should reread *The Murders in the Rue Morgue* and, suddenly, enchanted by a world which they thought was only a half-world, they should go looking for its rulers, at the head of which is Gaston Leroux, who triumphs from the indifference which has swallowed up so many more so-called serious writers.

Jean Cocteau [2]

---

[2] (1889-1963) Poet, novelist, playwright and director, the author of *Beauty and the Beast* and *Orpheus*. (*Note from the Publisher*.)

LE MYSTÈRE
DE LA CHAMBRE JAUNE

DEUXIÈME PARTIE
LE SECRET DE Mlle STANGERSON

PAR GASTON
LEROUX

60 f

HACHETTE

Chapter One
In Which We Begin To Not Understand

It is not without some emotion that I begin here to re-count the extraordinary adventures of Joseph Rouletabille. Until very recently, he was so firmly opposed to my telling his story that I had come to despair of ever publishing my ac-counts of some of the most bizarre criminal affairs of the last 15 years. I had thought that the public would never learn the truth about the prodigious "Mystery of the Yellow Room," which provoked many strange and sensational press articles, and in which my friend was closely involved.

It was only when the illustrious Professor Stangerson was recently nominated for the Grand-Croix of the Légion d'Honneur, and, as a result, one of the evening newspapers printed a remarkably bold, ignorant and perfidious article about that terrible affair, that Rouletabille gave me his permis-sion, while confiding in me that he truly wished that this case had been forgotten.

The Mystery of the Yellow Room! Does anyone still re-member this criminal affair, which caused so much ink to flow over our presses 15 years ago?[3] Public events quickly become ancient history in Paris. Have not the very name of the Mar-

---

[3] When Leroux wrote *The Mystery of the Yellow Room* in 1907, he clearly intended the story to take place 15 years prior, i.e.: in 1892. Its sequel, *The Perfume of the Lady in Black*, takes place "a little over two years later," in 1895. However, soon after, Leroux decided to make the Rouletabille saga con-temporary with current events, forcing us to relocate the events of *Yellow Room* to 1902 and those of *Perfume* to 1905, despite the topical references. The original dates have been left unchanged in the text, but should, in light of Leroux's later change in dating more properly, read "five years ago," "1902," etc. (*Note from the Publisher.*)

quis de Nayve, his trial, and the tragic death of little Menaldo, been all but forgotten?[4] And yet, the public was so fascinated by every detail of that trial at that time, that a ministerial crisis went completely unnoticed.

The Mystery of the Yellow Room, which preceded the trial of the Marquis de Nayve by a few years, made an even bigger splash. The entire world spent months trying to solve this seemingly unsolvable enigma—the most baffling, or so it seemed, that had ever challenged the perspicacity of the French police or taxed the minds of our Magistrates. The solution to the problem mystified everyone who tried to unravel it. It was a dramatic puzzle that fascinated Old Europe and America alike. I feel able to say this in all candor, because there is no petty author's vanity at stake here; I am merely a transcriber of the events that happened, and my unique access to Rouletabille has enabled me to cast them in a new light. I believe I do not know of any other similar mystery, whether it be the famous *Murders in the Rue Morgue* or the extravagant cases of the notorious Mister Sherlock Holmes, that can be compared to THE MYSTERY, the "very simple mystery" to quote Rouletabille, of the Yellow Room.

A mystery which no one could solve, Joseph Rouletabille, then merely 18, a junior reporter for a leading Parisian newspaper, succeeded in disentangling. But when, at the Court of Assize, he explained the solution to the whole affair, he did not tell the whole truth. He told only enough to ensure the acquittal of an innocent man. But now, the reasons for his reserve no longer exist, so, the time has come for my friend to speak out. You will learn everything. Without further ado, I am going to lay out before you the Mystery of the Yellow

---

[4] In 1895, the Marquis de Nayve was accused of murdering little Menaldo, the illegitimate son of his wife and spent 18 months in jail. On November 14, he was finally acquitted of the murder, but convicted of cruelty to his wife and children and sentended to six months' imprisonment (time served) and a fine of 200 francs. (*Note from the Publisher.*)

Room, as it unfolded before the eyes of the entire world on the day following the dramatic events that took place at the Chateau du Glandier.

On October 25, 1892, the following article appeared in the morning edition of the newspaper *Le Temps*:

A frightful crime was committed at the Chateau du Glandier, on the edge of the forest of Sainte Genevieve, near Epinay-sur-Orge, at the house of Professor Stangerson. During the night, while the renowned scientist was working in his laboratory, an unknown murderer tried to kill his daughter, Mademoiselle Mathilde Stangerson, who was sleeping in a room adjacent to the laboratory. The doctors have issued no prognostic regarding Mademoiselle Stangerson's possible recovery.

The sensation caused by this news in Paris can easily be imagined. The scientific world was then already deeply interested in the work of Professor Stangerson and his daughter. Their labors—the first attempts at establishing the science of radiography—later paved the way for Monsieur and Madame Curie's discovery of radium. Professor Stangerson was expected to present a report to the Academy of Sciences on his sensational new theory about the *Dissociation of Matter*, a theory that, some said, would overturn the established principles of conventional physics, including that of the Conservation of Energy.

On the following day, the newspapers were full of the tragedy. *Le Matin*, among others, published the following article, entitled: *A Supernatural Crime*:

These are the only details, wrote the anonymous reporter assigned to the story, *that we have been able to ascertain regarding the crime committed at the Chateau du Glandier. Professor Stangerson's state of despair, and the impossibility of obtaining any first-hand information from the victim herself, have made our inquiries and those of the police so difficult that, at present, we cannot accurately tell what actually took place inside the Yellow Room, where Mademoiselle Stanger-*

11

son was found, in her night-dress, lying on the floor, gravely wounded.

We have, however, interviewed Jacques-Louis Moustier, an old servant of the Stangersons, known in the region as "Père Jacques." He claimed to have entered the Yellow Room at the same time as the Professor. This room is adjacent to the Professor's laboratory. Both it and the Yellow Room are in a small pavilion located at the end of the grounds, about 300 meters from the Chateau itself.

"It happened at 12:30 a.m.," the good man told us. "I was working with the Professor in the laboratory, cleaning and putting away his instruments, waiting for him to be ready to retire for the night. Mademoiselle Stangerson had worked with her father until midnight. When the clock chimed 12, she rose and kissed her father good night. She said to me, 'Good night, Père Jacques,' as she went into the Yellow Room. We heard her lock the door and shoot the bolt. I couldn't help laughing and said to the Professor: 'Mademoiselle's double-locking herself in; she must be afraid of the Holy Beast.' But the Professor was so deeply absorbed in what he was doing that he didn't even hear me. Just then, I heard an awful scream outside, which I recognized as that of the Beast. It sent chills up my spine... 'Is that thing going to keep me awake all night?' I said to myself; for I must tell you, Monsieur, that until the end of October, I sleep in an attic directly above the Yellow Room, so that Mademoiselle is not left all alone here. It is her fancy to spend the summer months in the pavilion, which she probably finds more cheerful than the Chateau. During the four years since it's been built, she's never failed to take up her lodging in the pavilion in the spring. When winter returns, she moves back into the Chateau, because there is no fireplace in the Yellow Room.

"We were alone in the pavilion, then, the Professor and I. We made no noise. He was seated at his desk. As for me, I was sitting on a chair, having finished my work. Looking at him, I said to myself: 'What a man! What intelligence! What science!' I stress the fact that we made no noise, for, because of that, the assassin certainly thought that we had left the laboratory. Suddenly, when the clock chimed half past midnight, a desperate scream came from the Yellow Room. It was Mademoiselle Stangerson's voice, crying out: 'Murder! Murder! Help!' Immediately afterwards, gunshots rang out and there was a great fracas of tables and furniture being overturned, as if in a struggle. Again, we heard the voice of Mademoiselle Stangerson calling: 'Murder! Help! Papa! Papa!'

"You can be sure that we quickly sprang up and that Professor Stangerson and I threw ourselves upon the door. But, alas, it was locked, tightly locked on the inside with both key and bolt by Mademoiselle herself, as I told you. We tried to force the door open, but it remained firm. The Professor was like a madman, and, in truth, what we heard would have been enough to cause any father to go mad. Mademoiselle was still shouting: 'Help! Help!' The Professor struck terrible blows upon the door, weeping with rage, sobbing in despair and helplessness.

"That's when I was struck by an inspiration. 'The assassin must have come in through the window!' I said. 'I'll get there myself!' and I rushed out of the pavilion running as if chased by demons.

"The problem is that the window of the Yellow Room looks out not onto the grounds, but onto the woods outside the estate. Because the outside wall abuts to the pavilion, in order to reach that window, one must first exit the property. I ran towards the main gate and, on my way, I met our caretakers, Monsieur Bernier and his wife, who had been awakened by the gunshots and the screams. In a few words, I told Bernier what happened, and instructed him to go and help the Professor at once. Meanwhile, Madame Bernier opened the gate and no more than five minutes later, she and I stood before the window of the Yellow Room.

"The Moon was shining brightly and I saw clearly that no one had touched the window. Not only were the bars that protect it intact, but the shutters were shut on the inside, just as I had closed them myself earlier that evening, as I do every night, even though Mademoiselle Stangerson, knowing that I'm tired from all the heavy work I've been doing, has begged me not to trouble myself, and leave her to do it. The shutters were just as I had left them, fastened with an iron catch on the inside. The would-be murderer, therefore, could not have passed either in or out that way—but I was unable to gain entry!

"It was an unfortunate turn of events, enough to make one scream! The door of the room was locked on the inside, the shutters on the only window were also fastened on the inside. All the while, Mademoiselle Stangerson was still begging for help!... No! Her screams had stopped. Perhaps, she is already dead, I thought. But I still heard her father, inside the pavilion, trying to break down the door.

"Madame Bernier and I hurried back to the pavilion. The door, despite the Professor and the caretaker's furious attempts to open it, was still holding firm. But it finally gave way before our combined efforts and we rushed into the Yellow Room. What a sight met our eyes! I should tell you that, behind us, the caretaker held the laboratory lamp, a powerful lamp that lit the whole room.

"I must also tell you, Monsieur, that the Yellow Room is small. Mademoiselle Stangerson had furnished it with a fairly large iron bedstead, a small table, a night stand, a dressing-table, and two chairs. By the light of the lamp, we saw everything at a glance. Mademoiselle Stangerson, in her nightdress, was lying on the floor in the greatest disarray. The tables and chairs had been overturned, the sign of a violent struggle. Mademoiselle Stangerson looked as if she had been dragged from her bed. She was covered with blood and there were terrible fingernail marks on her throat. The flesh of her neck was almost entirely torn away. From a wound on her right temple, a stream of blood had run down and made a small pool on the floor.

"When Professor Stangerson saw his daughter in that state, he threw himself on his knees at her side, uttering a cry of despair. He ascertained that she was still breathing. As for

14

us, we searched for the wretch who had tried to kill our Mademoiselle, and I swear to you, Monsieur, that if we had found him, it would have gone badly for him!

"But how can I explain to you that he wasn't there, that he had already escaped? It was beyond imagination! There was no one under the bed, no one hiding behind the furniture! All that we discovered was the blood-stained handprints of a man on the walls and the door; a large blood-soaked handkerchief, without any markings, an old béret, and, on the floor, a set of footprints in some kind of black soot that had been made recently by a man with large feet. How had that man gotten away? How had he vanished? Don't forget, Monsieur, that there was no fireplace in the Yellow Room. He could not have slipped through the doorway, which was narrow, and on the threshold of which Madame Bernier stood with her lamp, while her husband and I were searching every corner of that tiny room, where it was impossible to hide! The door, which had been forced open, had been pushed back against the wall, and as we quickly ascertained, no one could have been hiding behind it. The window was still secured behind the bars, untouched, and the shutters were still bolted. There was no escape possible through there. What then? I began to believe that it was the work of the Devil himself...

"Then, we discovered my revolver on the floor! Yes, my very own gun! That brought me back to my semses! The Devil would not have needed to steal my revolver to kill Mademoiselle Stangerson. The would-be murderer must have first gone up to my attic and taken my revolver from the drawer where I normally kept it. We then determined, by counting the cartridges left inside, that the wretch had fired two shots. Ah! I was lucky that Professor Stangerson was with me in the laboratory when this nasty business took place, and that he had seen me there with his own eyes, because otherwise, with my gun found at the scene of the crime, it might have gone badly for me. Why, I might have been arrested and locked up right away! Justice is always in a hurry to send a man to the scaffold!"

The reporter of *Le Matin* then added the following paragraphs:

We have printed here Père Jacques' entire account of the Mystery of the Yellow Room in his own words, uncut except for some judicious editing of his string of repetitive lamentations. It is clear that Père Jacques is very devoted to Professor Stangerson and his daughter, and that he feels the need to say so repeatedly, especially since it was his gun that was found in the Yellow Room. It certainly is his right, and we see no harm in him doing so in our paper. We should have liked to ask him more questions, but we were prevented from doing so when he was summoned by Monsieur de Marquet, the Investigating Magistrate from Corbeil, who has begun his inquiry at the Chateau. It was impossible for us to gain admission at Glandier later, and the grounds themselves were cordoned off by the police, who were carefully checking all trails leading to and from the pavilion, which might help discover the identity of the would-be murderer.

We also wished to question the caretakers, Monsieur and Madame Bernier, but they were nowhere to be found. Finally, we resolved to wait for Monsieur de Marquet at the Auberge du Donjon, a roadside inn not far from the Chateau.

At 5:30 p.m., we saw him and his clerk leave Glandier. Before he was able to enter his carriage, we had the opportunity to ask him the following question:

"Monsieur, can you give us any information on this mystery, without, of course, hampering your investigation?'

"I'm afraid I can't do that," replied Monsieur de Marquet. "I can only say that it is the strangest case that I have ever investigated. The more we think we know something, the further we are from knowing anything!"

We asked Monsieur de Marquet to be kind enough to explain his last words, and this is what he said—the importance of which no one will fail to recognize:

"Unless we discover some new evidence, I fear that the mystery which surrounds the dreadful assault om Mademoiselle Stangerson may well never be solved. However, one

hopes—if only for the sake of our peace of mind—that the examination of the walls and of the ceiling of the Yellow Room, which I shall conduct tomorrow with the assistance of the contractor who built the pavilion four years ago, will help us unearth such new evidence, and prove that logic always prevails. Our problem is this: we know that the perpetrator entered the Yellow Room through the door and that he hid under the bed, lying in wait for Mademoiselle Stangerson, but how did he leave? How did he escape? If we fail to discover any kind of opening or hidden doorway, or any hiding place or aperture of any sort; if the examination of the walls—even to the point of their demolition—does not reveal any secret passage useable by a human being, or any other kind of being; *if the ceiling reveals no trapdoors; if the floor hides no under-ground passage, then I shall start believing in the Devil, just as Père Jacques said!"*

And the anonymous reporter of *Le Matin* added in his article—which I selected because I thought it was the most complete of all those that had been published on the matter—that the Investigating Magistrate seemed to place a peculiar emphasis on that last sentence: *"Then I shall start believing in the Devil, just as Père Jacques said!"*

The article concluded:

We wanted to know what Père Jacques meant when he mentioned the cry of the "Holy Beast." The landlord of the Auberge du Donjon explained that it is the particularly sinis-ter cry sometimes uttered at night by the cat of a local inhabi-tant, Mère Angenoux, a saintly old woman who lives in a hut in the forest, not far from the grotto of Sainte Genevieve.

The Yellow Room, the Holy Beast, Mère Angenoux, the Devil, Sainte Genevieve, Père Jacques... All these make for an utterly baffling mystery, which the stroke of a pickaxe in a wall might solve tomorrow. Let us at least hope so, if only for our own peace of mind, *to quote Monsieur de Marquet's very own words. Meanwhile, the doctors do not expect Mademoi-selle Stangerson—who remains delirious and utters only one,*

*single word repeatedly, 'Murderer!'—to make it through the
night.*

Finally, in its evening edition, *Le Matin* revealed that the
Head of the Sûreté had sent a cable to the famous Inspector
Frederic Larsan, currently in London for an affair of stolen
bonds, to ask him to return at once to Paris.

Chapter Two
In Which We Meet Joseph Rouletabille

I remember, just as if it were yesterday, the entrance of young Joseph Rouletabille into my bedroom that morning. It was 8 a.m., and I was still in bed, reading the article in *Le Matin* recounting the Mystery of the Yellow Room.

Before going any further, I should introduce my friend.

I first met Rouletabille when he was a young reporter. At that time, I was myself a newcomer to the Paris Bar, and I often saw him in the waiting rooms of the Investigating Magistrates from whom I had requested the permission to talk to clients locked up in the jails of Mazas and Saint-Lazare. Rouletabille had, as they say, a "great mug." His head was round as a marble, which is why, I think, his fellow journalists had given him that nickname which stuck to him and which he made so famous—"Rouletabille."[5] "Did you see Rouletabille?" "There's that scamp, Rouletabille!" they said. He could be red as a tomato, happy as a lark, or grave as a judge.

How could he, being so young—he was only 16-1/2 years old when I first met him—be gainfully employed as a journalist? Everyone who came into contact with him soon learned of his first, triumphant case, now mostly forgotten. The body of a woman had been found dismembered in the Rue Oberkampf. Then, Rouletabille brought her left foot to the editors of *L'Epoque*, which was in a heated competition with *Le Matin* for that kind of story. The police had been vainly looking for that left foot for a week, as it had been missing from the basket in which the gruesome remains had been found, but young Rouletabille had found it in a drain, where

---

[5] In French, a marble is a *bille*, and *roule ta bille* means shooting one's marble into the ring. Likely, this nickname also refers to Rouletabille constantly rushing around. (*Note from the Publisher.*)

no one else had thought of looking for it. To do that, he had hired himself out as one of the temporary sewer-men recruited by the city of Paris to clean up after an unusual overflow of the Seine.

When the editor-in-chief of *L'Epoque* found himself in possession of the precious foot, and informed of the series of clever deductions that the boy who had found it had had to make, he was torn between the admiration he felt for the astonishing detective skills of a lad of a mere 16, and the delight at being able to exhibit the left foot of the victim of the Rue Oberskampf murder in the "morgue window" of his newspaper.

"This foot," he said, "will make a great headline."

After entrusting the gruesome delivery to their medical consultant, the editor-in-chief asked the lad, who was shortly to become famous as "Rouletabille," what he would expect to earn as a reporter-in-training for *L'Epoque*?

"Two hundred francs a month," the young man replied modestly, hardly able to breathe from the surprise he felt at receiving such a proposal.

"You shall have 250 francs," said the editor-in-chief, "but you must tell everyone that you've been working for us for a month. Let it be quite clear that it wasn't you, but the paper itself, that discovered that foot. Here, my young friend, the man is nothing, the paper everything."

Having said that, he asked his newest employee to leave, but before the young man had reached the door, he called him back to ask for his name. The boy replied:

"Joseph Josephin."

"That's not a good name for a reporter," said the editor-in-chief, "but since you won't be signing your articles, it doesn't matter."

The young reporter made many friends immediately, because he was helpful and gifted with a sense of humor that charmed the grumpiest and disarmed the most jealous of his colleagues. At the café of the Paris Bar, where crime reporters gathered before visiting the Criminal Courts or the Prefecture of Police in search of new stories, he began to gain the reputation of being a clever lad, a reputation which spread even to the Head of the Sûreté. When a case was worth the trouble, and Rouletabille—by then, he had acquired his nickname— had been assigned to it, he often produced better results than even the most famous of detectives.

It was at the café of the Bar that I became acquainted with him. Criminal lawyers and journalists are not enemies; the former need publicity, the latter information. We chatted and I soon felt much sympathy for the brave little lad. His intelligence was so keen and original, and he had a quality of thought that I have never found in any other person.

A little later, I was asked to chronicle criminal cases by the *Cri du Boulevard*. My entry into the field of journalism only strengthened my friendship with Rouletabille. Also, Rou- letabille had proposed to his editor at *L'Epoque* the idea of a legal chronicle, which he was allowed to write under the nom- de-plume of "M. Business" and I was often able to provide him with the legal information he sought.

Nearly two years went by, and the better I knew him, the more I liked him, because, despite his joyous extravagance, I found him to be extraordinarily serious for someone of his age. However, a few times, accustomed as I was to seeing him cheerful—indeed, often too cheerful—I suddenly caught him in a state of deep melancholy. I tried to question him as to the cause of this mood, but each time, he laughed and gave me no answer. One day, having asked him about his parents, of whom he never spoke, he left, pretending not to have heard what I said.

It was at that time that the famous Mystery of the Yellow Room burst upon us. It was this case which earned him the reputation of being one of the world's best reporters, as well as one of its greatest detectives. We should not be surprised to find a single man embodying these two sets of skills, because the daily press had already begun to turn into what it's become since, which is not unlike the annals of crime. Some negative minds may disapprove of this; for myself, I regard it as a bene- ficial transformation. After all, society can never have enough weapons, be they public or private, against criminals. The same negative minds will say that, by constantly publishing the details of each new crime, the press only encourages the commission of more crimes. But then, one can never reason with some people...

Rouletabille, as I said, entered my room that morning of October 26, 1892. He was looking more flushed than usual, and his eyes were bulging out of his head, as the saying goes. He was in a state of extreme excitement. He waved a copy of *Le Matin* at me with a trembling hand.

"Well, my dear Sainclair," he said, "have you read the news?"

"The Glandier crime?"

"Yes! The Mystery of the Yellow Room! What do you think of it?"

"By Jove, it's either the work of the Devil, or maybe Père Jacques' Holy Beast."

"You can't be serious!"

"All right, I don't really believe in murderers capable of walking through walls. I think Père Jacques made a mistake when he left his gun behind. Since he lived in the attic immediately above Mademoiselle Stangerson's room, I expect that the architectural survey ordered by the Investigating Magistrate will provide us with the key to the whole mystery. We will soon find out by what trapdoor or secret passage that old rascal was able to slip in and out of the room, and return immediately to the laboratory of Professor Stangerson, who failed to notice his absence. That, of course, is only a hypothesis."

Rouletabille sat down in an armchair, lit his pipe, which never left him, and smoked silently for a few minutes, no doubt to calm his excitement.

"Young man," he said, in a tone of contemptuous irony which I cannot adequately convey here, "you are a good lawyer and I don't doubt your ability to save a guilty man from the gallows, but if you ever become an Investigating Magistrate, you will all too soon send an innocent to the guillotine!

You appear to have a gift for it, my friend!" He continued to smoke vigorously, and then continued: "No trapdoor will be found, and the Mystery of the Yellow Room will become more impenetrable than ever. That's why it interests me. The Investigating Magistrate was right; it is the strangest case that I've ever come across."

"Have you any idea how the would-be murderer was able to escape then?" I asked.

"None at the present," replied Rouletabille. "But I have an idea about the gun. I don't think our murderer used it."

"Good Heavens! By whom, then, was it used?"

"Why, by Mademoiselle Stangerson."

"I don't understand," I said. "Worse, I now feel as if I never understood anything about that case at all."

Rouletabille shrugged.

"Was there anything in that article in *Le Matin* which particularly struck you?"

"No, nothing… Truthfully, I found everything equally bizarre."

"But what about the door, locked from the inside?"

"That seems to be the only perfectly natural thing in the whole story."

"Really? What about the bolt then?"

"The bolt?"

"Yes, the bolt, also pushed from inside. Mademoiselle Stangerson seems to have taken some extraordinary precautions. I think she feared someone. That was why she took such precautions, going as far as borrowing Père Jacques's revolver without telling him. No doubt, she didn't wish to alarm anybody, least of all, her father. What she dreaded took place, and she defended herself. There was a skirmish, and she used the gun to wound the assassin in the hand—which explains the impression, on the wall and on the door, of the large, blood-stained hand of the man who was struggling to find an exit. But she didn't fire soon enough to avoid the terrible blow she received on the right temple."

"Then you don't think that the wound on her temple was caused by a gunshot?"

"*Le Matin* doesn't say that it was, and I'm inclined to think it wasn't because, logically, it seems to me that the revolver was used by Mademoiselle Stangerson against her attacker. So, what weapon did he use to strike her? That blow appears to show that he wished to stun Mademoiselle Stangerson, after having tried unsuccessfully to strangle her. Our villain must have known that the attic was inhabited by Père Jacques, and that's one of the reasons why, I think, he probably preferred to use a quieter weapon, a truncheon or a hammer perhaps..."

"All that doesn't explain how the murderer got out of the Yellow Room," I remarked.

"Of course," replied Rouletabille, rising, "and since we still have to solve that mystery, I'm planning to visit the Chateau du Glandier. I came here to ask you if you'd like to come with me."

"I?"

"Yes, my friend. I need you. *L'Epoque* has assigned this case to me, and I have to solve it as soon as possible."

"But how can I be of any use to you?"

"Monsieur Robert Darzac is presently at Glandier."

"Ah, I see... His distress must be overwhelming."

"Still, I need to talk to him."

Rouletabille spoke that last sentennce in a tone that surprised me.

"Is it because you harbor some... suspicions?" I asked.

"Yes."

And that was all he would say. He retired to my sitting room, pushing me to dress quickly.

I knew Monsieur Darzac, having been of great service to him in a civil lawsuit, when I was secretary to Maître Barbet-Delatour. Darzac, who was then about 40, was Professor of physics at the Sorbonne University. He was intimately acquainted with the Stangersons, and, after seven years of assiduous courtship, was about to marry Mademoiselle Stangerson. She was still remarkably beautiful despite the fact that she was now "of a certain age," as some say. (I personally thought her to be around 35.)

While I was dressing, I called out to Rouletabille, who was impatiently pacing around my sitting room:

"Have you any ideas as to the attacker's identity?"

"Some," he replied. "I think he is a man of the world, or at least belongs to the upper class. But that's only an impression…"

"What has led you to form it?"

"Well, the old béret, the common handkerchief, and the footprints left by dirty boots on the floor," he replied.

"I see," I said. "No one would leave so many clues behind them unless they were meant to mislead the police."

"We shall make a detective out of you yet, my dear Sainclair," concluded Rouletabille.

Chapter Three
"Did He Walk Through the Shutters Like a Ghost?"

Half an hour later, Rouletabille and I stood on the platform at the Gare d'Orléans, waiting for the train which would take us to Epinay-sur-Orge.

On the platform, we saw the Investigating Magistrate from the Tribunal of Corbeil, Monsieur de Marquet, and his clerk. They both had spent the night in Paris, attending the final rehearsal at the Scala of a play authored by Monsieur de Marquet under the nom-de-plume of "Castigat Ridendo."[6]

The Magistrate was starting to turn into what is sometimes referred to as a "grand old man." He was ordinarily very polite and courteous, and he had one passion in life—the dramatic arts. As an Investigating Magistrate, he was only interested in those cases that could provide him with enough inspiration to write a play. With his family connections, he could have aspired to higher posts, but in truth, the only success he sought was at the romantic Porte-Saint-Martin, or at the thoughtful Odéon.[7] His relative lack of ambition had led him to be satisfied with a position at the provincial Corbeil Tribunal, and a somewhat naughty one-act play at the Scala.

Because of its nature, the Mystery of the Yellow Room was bound to fascinate such a theatrical mind. It immediately captured his attention. He threw himself into it, not as much as a Magistrate eager to learn the truth, but as a fan of the theater, a lover of mystery and intrigue, who dreads the coming of the last act, when the curtain falls and all is finally explained.

As we were about to introduce ourselves, I heard Monsieur de Marquet say to his clerk, sighing:

---

[6] *Castigat ridendo mores* is a latin maxim meaning "Comedy criticizes customs by laughing;" it is often attributed to Molière, although it was coined by poet Jean de Santeul.

[7] Famous Paris theaters.

"I hope, my dear Monsieur Maleine, that this builder with his pickaxe isn't going to ruin such a fine mystery."

"Have no fear," replied the clerk. "His pickaxe may demolish the pavilion, but I think it will leave our case intact. I sounded the walls and examined both the ceiling and the floor. I'm something of an expert in these matters and not easily deceived. You can rest assured that he won't find anything new."

Having thus reassured the Magistrate, Monsieur Maleine, drew his attention to us with a discreet movement of his head. The Magistrate's expression grew sterner. As he saw Rouletabille approaching him, hat in hand, he sprang into one of the train's empty carriages, saying, half-aloud to his clerk, "And, above all, I don't want to talk to any journalists!"

Monsieur Maleine replied in the same tone: "I understand!" He then tried to prevent Rouletabille from following the Magistrate.

"Excuse me, Messieurs," he said. "I believe that this compartment is reserved."

"I'm a journalist from *L'Epoque*, Monsieur," replied my friend with a great display of courtesy. "I have a word to say to Monsieur de Marquet."

"Monsieur de Marquet is too busy with his investigation to…"

"Please, Monsieur, let me assure you that I'm not at all interested in his investigation. I'm not one of those yellow journalists who spend their lives scavenging through other people's garbage," he added, his lower lip twisting to express his presumed contempt for such low-lives. "No, I'm a theatrical reporter, and this evening, I have to review the new play opening at the Scala."

"I see! Please, do get in, Monsieur," said the clerk.

Rouletabille hopped inside the train. I followed him and sat next to him. The clerk got in last and closed the door behind him.

Monsieur de Marquet looked at him disapprovingly.

"Please, Monsieur," Rouletabille began, "don't be angry with the good Monsieur Maleine for not following your instructions to the letter. It isn't to Monsieur de Marquet, Investigating Magistrate, that I wish to speak, but to 'Castigat Ridendo.' As the new theatrical critic of *L'Epoque*, please allow me to offer you my heartfelt congratulations…"

Rouletabille, having first introduced me, then introduced himself.

Monsieur de Marquet nervously caressed his beard and told Rouletabille, in a few words, that he was too modest to desire that his real identity be exposed, and that he hoped that my friend's enthusiasm for his work would not lead him to reveal to the public that "Castigat Ridendo" was, in reality, the Investigating Magistrate of the Tribunal of Corbeil.

"The work of the dramatic author may interfere," he said, after a slight hesitation, "with that of the Magistrate, especially outside of Paris where people tend to be more conservative."

"Oh, Monsieur, you may rely on my discretion!" said Rouletabille, raising his right hand as if to take an oath.

The train started.

"We're on our way," said the Magistrate, surprised at seeing us still in the carriage.

"Yes, Monsieur—towards the truth," said Rouletabille, smiling amiably. "Towards the Chateau du Glandier. A fine case, Monsieur de Marquet, a fine case indeed!"

"An obscure, incredible, unfathomable, inexplicable affair… I fear only one thing, Monsieur Rouletabille, that the Press will bungle things by wanting to solve it before the Law does."

My friend didn't flinch.

"You're right, Monsieur," he said simply. "That is a legitimate concern. They meddle in everything. As for me, I mentioned it only because luck—pure, blind luck—brought us together at the same time, in the same train."

"Really? Where are you going, then?" asked Monsieur de Marquet.

"To the Chateau du Glandier, of course," replied Rouletabille, without batting an eye.

"You won't be able to get inside, Monsieur Rouletabille!"

"Would you stop me?" said my friend, always ready for a fight.

"Not at all! I like the Press too much to wish to alienate any *bona fide* reporter, but Professor Stangerson has given strict orders for his door to be barred to everyone, and it's well guarded, believe me. Not a single journalist was admitted through the gates yesterday."

"Excellent," said Rouletabille cheerfully. "I hate crowds."

Monsieur de Marquet's lips tightened, and he seemed ready to lapse into an obstinate silence. He only relaxed a little when Rouletabille told him that we were going to the Glandier to meet an "old and close friend," Monsieur Robert Darzac—a man whom Rouletabille had perhaps seen only once in his life.

"Poor Robert!" continued the young reporter. "This dreadful affair may kill him. He's so much in love with Mademoiselle Stangerson, don't you think?"

"His suffering is indeed truly painful to watch," muttered Monsieur de Marquet, reluctantly.

"One can only pray that Mademoiselle Stangerson's life can be saved."

"Let's hope so. Only yesterday, her father told me that, if she doesn't recover, it won't be long until he joins her in the grave. What a loss to science his death would be!"

"The wound on her temple is serious, isn't it?"

"Absolutely! It was lucky it didn't kill her. That blow was struck with great force."

"So it wasn't the revolver that caused the wound," said Rouletabille, glancing at me triumphantly.

Monsieur de Marquet appeared greatly embarrassed.

"I didn't say anything. I don't wish to say anything, and I won't say anything further," he said. And he turned towards his clerk, as if he no longer knew us.

But it wasn't so easy to get rid of Rouletabille. He moved closer to the Magistrate and, pulling a copy of *Le Matin* from his pocket, showed it to him.

"There's one thing, Monsieur, which I may ask of you without committing an indiscretion," he said. "You must have read the account published in *Le Matin*? It's nonsense, isn't it?"

"Not in the slightest, Monsieur."

"What!? The Yellow Room has but one barred window—the bars of which have not been tampered with—and only one door, which had to be broken open—and still, Mademoiselle Stangersom's attacker was nowhere to be found!"

"That is exactly so, Monsieur Rouletabille. That's how the matter stands."

Rouletabille fell silent and became absorbed in his own thoughts. A quarter of an hour passed. Then, he became animated again, and addressed the Magistrate:

"How did Mademoiselle Stangerson wear her hair on that evening?"

"I don't understand what you mean?" replied Monsieur de Marquet.

"That's a very important point," said Rouletabille. "*Her hair was in plaits, wasn't it? I'm certain that, on that evening, the evening of the crime, she had her hair arranged in plaits.*"

"I'm afraid you're mistaken, Monsieur Rouletabille," replied the Magistrate. "That evening, Mademoiselle Stangerson had her hair drawn up in a bun on the top of her head—her usual way of arranging it, I'm told. Her forehead was entirely uncovered. I can attest to this, because I had to examine her wound carefully myself. There was no blood on the hair, and its arrangement had not been disturbed since the crime was committed."

"You're sure? You're certain that, on the night of the crime, she didn't have her hair in plaits?"

"Quite certain," the Magistrate continued, smiling, "because I remember the Doctor saying to me, while he was examining the wound, 'It's a great pity that Mademoiselle Stangerson wore her hair drawn back. If she'd worn it in plaits, the blow she received on the temple might have been softened.' It seems strange to me that you should attach so much importance to this detail..."

"Oh!" whined Rouletanille. "If she didn't have her hair in plaits, then I don't understand... I don't understand at all.... It doesn't make any sense..." He made a despairing gesture, then asked again: "And the wound on her temple was serious?"

"Very serious."

"With what weapon was it made?"

"That, Monsieur, is a secret of the investigation."

"Have you found the weapon—whatever it was?"

The Magistrate did not answer.

"What about the wound in the throat?"

Here, the Investigating Magistrate was kind enough to share with us the doctor's opinion that, "if the perpetrator had strangled her for a few seconds longer, Mademoiselle Stangerson would now be dead."

"The case, as it's been reported in *Le Matin*," admitted Rouletabille, "appears indeed to be more amd more mysterious. Could you tell me, Monsieur, how many entrances there are in the pavilion? I mean, doors and windows."

"There are five in total," replied Monsieur de Marquet, after having coughed once or twice, but no longer resisting the desire to talk about the whole mysterious affair. "The first is the door to the vestibule, which is the only entrance to the pavilion, which closes automatically, and cwhich an only be opened, from either the outside or the inside, with two special keys, which are always kept by Père Jacques and Professor Stangerson. Mademoiselle Stangerson didn't need a key, since Père Jacques slept in the pavilion and, during the day, she was always at her father's side. When the four witnesses rushed from the laboratory into the Yellow Room, after breaking its door open, the vestibule door remained closed as usual. The two keys were still with Père Jacques and the Professor. As to the windows, there are four: one in the Yellow Room, two in the laboratory, looking out onto the neighboring countryside, and one in the vestibule, looking out onto the grounds."

"*That's the window the perpetrator used to flee the pavilion!*" stated Rouletabille.

"How can you know that?" asked Monsieur de Marquet, looking at my friend strangely.

"We'll deal with how he left the Yellow Room later," replied Rouletabille, "but he must have left the pavilion by the vestibule window."

"Once again—how can you know that?"

"That's easy! Since the attacker couldn't escape through the door of the pavilion, his only way out was through a window—one that wasn't barred. The window of the Yellow Room was secured by iron bars because it looks out onto the open countryside; the same must be true of the two windows in the laboratory. Since our man did get away, it means that he used a window that wasn't barred. The only one left is that of the vestibule, which opens onto the grounds, that is to say, inside the estate. Hence, no bars. Not much magic in that, you see?"

"Indeed," said Monsieur de Marquet, "but what you don't know is that the vestibule window, though it has no bars, as you surmised, was nevertheless closed by two solid iron shutters. *We found those two shutters locked with an iron latch; and yet, we have proof that the attacker made his escape by that very window!* We found traces of blood on the inside wall and on the shutters themselves, as well as on the floor, and also footprints outside, identical to those found in the Yellow Room. All this evidence proves that the man escaped through that window. But, how did he do it, *since the shutters were fastened from the inside? Did he walk through them like a ghost?* What's even more bewildering is that we can't figure out how the villain got out of the Yellow Room in the first place, *nor how he got across the laboratory to reach the vestibule!* Yes, Monsieur Rouletabille, it is, as you've just said, a fine case, the key to which, I hope, will not be discovered for a long time."

"You hope that, Monsieur?"

Monsieur de Marquet corrected himself.

"I do not hope that, I believe that."

"Could the shutters have been closed and refastened after the attacker escaped?" asked Rouletabille.

"That is the most natural explanation, but it would imply that he had an accomplice, or accomplices, inside, and I can't honestly imagine…" After a short silence, the Magistrate added: "Ah, if only Mademoiselle Stangerson was well enough to be questioned!"

Rouletabille, following up his line of thought, asked:

"What about the attic? There must be some kind of entrance there?"

"You're right. I forgot to mention it. So there are, in fact, six entrances in total. There is a small window, a skylight in fact, in the attic. Since it, too, looks out towards the countryside, Professor Stangerson had it barred, like the rest of the windows. Those bars were intact, and the shutters, which naturally open inwards, were also tightly shut. In any event, we haven't found any evidence that would lead us to suspect that the attacker passed through the attic."

"So you're certain that he escaped—in some as yet unknown fashion—through the vestibule window?"

"Everything points to it."

"I happen to think so, too," said Rouletabille gravely. After a brief silence, he continued: "If you didn't find any traces of the perpetrator in the attic, such as the same dirty footprints left in the Yellow Room, you must have come to the conclusion that it wasn't he who stole Père Jacques's revolver?"

"There were no footprints in the attic other than Père Jacques'," said the Magistrate with a meaningful nod. To clarify his thoughts, he added: "The old man was with Professor Stangerson in the laboratory—luckily for him."

"Then, what part did his gun play in the attack? It seems to me that that weapon did less harm to Mademoiselle Stangerson than it did to her attacker."

The Magistrate didn't reply to this question, which probably embarrassed him, but told us that they had found two bullets in the Yellow Room, one embedded in the wall stained with the bloody handprint—a man's hand—the other, in the ceiling.

"Oh! oh! In the ceiling!" muttered Rouletabille. "Really? That's very curious! In the ceiling..."

He puffed for a while in silence, wrapping himself in a thick cloud of tobacco smoke. When we reached Epinay-sur-Orge, I had to tap him lightly on the shoulder to pull him out of his meditation, and encourage him to step out onto the platform of the station.

There, the Magistrate and his clerk bowed to us, making it quite clear that they'd had enough of us, and got into a cab which had been waiting for them.

"How long will it take to walk to the Chateau du Glandier?" Rouletabille asked one of the station employees.

"An hour and a half, or an hour and three quarters, without rushing," the man replied.

Rouletabille looked up at the sky and found it clear enough for his tastes—and mine—and grabbed my arm.

"Come on, Sainclair!" he said. "I need a walk."

"Are things getting clearer?" I inquired.

"Not at all!" he said. "If anything, *it's getting more complicated than before!* But I do have an idea..."

"What is it?" I asked.

"I can't tell at the moment. It might be a matter of life and death for at least two people."

"Do you believe someone helped the attacker?"

"No."

We fell into silence.

"It was a bit of luck, meeting the Investigating Magistrate and his clerk, eh?" Rouletabille went on. "What did I tell you about the gun?"

Rouletabille was walking briskly, his head down, his hands in his pockets, whistling. After a while, I heard him murmur:

"Poor woman!"

"Are you talking about Mademoiselle Stangerson?"

"Of course. She's a noble woman, worthy of compassion! A woman of great, very great character, I imagine. I believe..."

"You know her then?"

"Not really. I've only met her once."

"Why, then, do you say that she's a woman of great character?"

"Because she bravely faced her attacker and courageously defended herself. *And, above all, because of that bullet in the ceiling.*"

I looked at Rouletabille and inwardly wondered whether he was having fun at my expense, or if he had suddenly gone mad. But I quickly saw that he'd never been more serious, and the light in his keen, round eyes convinced me of his sanity. I was used to our disjointed conversations—disjointed to me, because I usually found them incoherent and puzzling, at least until a few clear, quick words from Rouletabille clarified his train of thought. Then, I understood the meaning of what he'd been trying to tell me. What had previously seemed nonsensical became suddenly so logical and easy to grasp that I never could understand why I hadn't succeeded in connecting the dots earlier.

Chapter Four
"Its Very Solitude, Deep in the Woods"

The Chateau du Glandier was one of the oldest chateaux in the Ile-de-France region, where so many medieval buildings still stand today. Originally built hidden deep inside a forest during the reign of King Philip IV, The Fair, it now could be seen from a hundred yards or so down the road going from Sainte-Genevieve-des-Bois to Monthlery. It was a jumble of mismatched structures, dominated by a single, massive tower. When a visitor finished climbing the crumbling steps leading to its top, he found himself on a small platform where, in the 17th century, Georges-Philibert de Sequigny, Lord of the Glandier, Maisons-Neuves and other places, had erected an ugly, rococo-styled lantern. From that platform, one could see, beyond the valleys and the plains, as far as the proud tower of Monthléry, located three leagues away. The two towers still gazed at each other, after so many centuries, and, over the verdant forests and the dead woods, seemed to be sharing the oldest legends in French History.

People from the region knew that the tower of Glandier watched over a heroic and saintly spirit, that of the patron saint of Paris itself, St Genevieve, before whom Attila himself had fled.[8] They claim that the saint's final resting place lies

---

[8] Sainte Genevieve (c.419-c.512). According to her hagiography, when Attila the Hun was preparing to ransack Paris in 451 AD, he was met outside the city by Genevieve, alone, and God-inspired resolve compelled the Scourge of God to turn away and spare the city. (He then attacked Orleans which was obviously unlucky to not have a residing saint.) Genevieve's remains were kept in Paris at the Abbey bearing her name, then publicly burned in 1793 by the French Revolution, then housed at the Pantheon, erected on the spot of the old Abbey. They were dispersed again by the Communards in 1871. The

beneath the Chateau's ancient moat. During the summer, young lovers carrying picnic bags come to plan their lives together or swear undying fidelity before the saint's tomb, always piously decorated with bouquets of forget-me-nots. Not far from the tomb is a well whose waters are reputed to perform miracles. The grateful mothers of the region have erected a statue to St Genevieve, under which hang the tiny slippers and bonnets of the children whose lives were saved by the miraculous waters.

It was in this very place, which seemed to entirely belong to the past, that Professor Stangerson and his daughter had chosen to live, in order to lay the foundations of the science of the future. Its very solitude, deep in the woods, had appealed to them right away. The only witnesses to their hopes and labors were the ancient stones of the Chateau and the grand old oaks of its grounds. Glandier—*Glandierum*, as it was once called—derived its name from the large quantity of acorns which used to be harvested on the estate.[9] The property, which is now famous for all the wrong reasons, had been allowed to revert to its original wild and primitive state, due to the neglect or abandonment of its past owners. Only its hidden buildings had preserved some traces of their various metamorphoses. Every century had left its mark on them; every bit of architecture was connected to some terrible historical event or some bloody adventure. The Chateau, where science had now found a new home, was a place that seemed better suited to be the stage of mysterious terrors and deaths.

That said, I have to make one, final observation:

If I have spent so much time painting a rather gloomy picture of Glandier, it isn't because I'm trying to do so for purely dramatic purposes, in effect "creating" the necessary atmosphere suitable for the tragedy taking place before my readers' eyes. On the contrary, in this matter, my first concern

---

Pantheon had since been reconsecrated to Sainte Genevieve, but the exact location of her relics is still unknown.

[9] Acorn is *gland* in French.

is always be to be as simple and direct as possible. I have no ambition to be a great writer, or a famous novelist. God knows that there are enough real, tragic horrors in the Mystery of the Yellow Room to not need any unnecessary literary effects. I am, and only desire to be, a faithful "reporter." My first duty is to report the events that took place there, and in order to do so properly, I must provide their context, that is all. It makes sense that you should know where the things happened.

I now return to Professor Stangerson. When he bought Glandier, 15 years earlier, the Chateau had been empty for many years. Another nearby chateau, built in the 14th century by Jean de Belmont, was also abandoned, so that part of the country was mostly uninhabited. There were a few small farmhouses on the road leading to Corbeil and one inn, the Auberge du Donjon, which provided meals and lodgings to passing travelers. That was the full extent of civilization in this remote part of the countryside, which was, surprisingly, only a few leagues away from Paris.

The deserted nature of the place had been the primary reason why it had attracted Professor Stangerson and his daughter. The Professor was already famous; he had recently returned from America, where his works had caused quite a stir. The book which he had published in Philadelphia on the "Dissociation of Matter Through Electricity" had generated much controiversy in the scientific community. Professor Stangerson was a Frenchman, but of American origin. Several lawsuits pertaining to a large inheritance he expected to re-ceive had forced him to spend several years in the United States, continuing the research which he had begun in France. He had returned, at last in possession of his inheritance, hav-ing successfully won or settled all the lawsuits. This new for-tune was a great comfort to him, even though he could have made millions by exploiting or licensing two or three of his chemical patents regarding new dyeing techniques. But the Professor found it morally repulsive to use his God-given gift of invention to enrich himself. He thought his genius didn't belong to him, but to the entire human race, so he had become a philanthropist, allowing each of his discoveries to pass into the public domain.

Professor Stangerson had not tried to hide his joy at having at last received that large inheritance, which would enable him to continue his research and devote his remaining years to his passion for pure science. But he was also happy for another reason. Mademoiselle Stangerson was, when her father returned from America and bought Glandier, 20 years old. She was extremely pretty, having inherited the Parisian charm of her mother, who had died giving birth to her, and the strength and splendor of the American blood peovided by her paternal grandfather, William Stangerson of Philadelphia. William Stangerson had been obliged to become a French citizen when he had married the French woman who was to become the mother of the illustrious Professor Stangerson. And thus the Professor had been born French.

Twenty years of age, a charming blonde with blue eyes, a milk-white complexion, radiant and divinely healthy, Mathilde Stangerson was one of the most desirable eligible women in either the Old or New Worlds. It was her father's duty, despite the inevitable pain that a separation from her would cause him, to think of her marriage, and the Professor was therefore happy that his inheritance would make an attractive dowry for his daughter. Nevertheless, they both chose to bury themselves at Glandier, just as their friends were expecting Mathilde to make her debut in society. Some of them expressed their surprise; when questioned, the Professor answered: "It is my daughter's wish. I can refuse her nothing. She has chosen to live at Glandier." As for Mathilde, she replied serenely: "Where could we work better than in this solitude?" For Mademoiselle Stangerson had already begun to assist her father in his research.

Still, at the time, one could never have imagined that her passion for science would lead her to reject all the suitors who presented themselves for over 15 years. No matter how secluded their lives, both father and daughter did make the occasional appearance at various official functions and, at certain times during the year, at two or three friendly receptions, where the Professor's fame and Mathilde's beauty always created a sensation.

The young girl's manifest coldness had not, at first, discouraged potential suitors, but eventually, they stopped pursuing her. Only one man persisted, with an affectionate perseverance that earned him the nickname of the "eternal fiancé," which he accepted with sad resignation—Monsieur Robert Darzac.

Mademoiselle Stangerson was now no longer young, and it seemed that, having found no good reason to marry at 35, she would never find any. But such an argument did not discourage Robert Darzac. He continued to court Mathildre—if one could label as "courtship" the delicate and tender attentions he lavished on a 35-year-old woman who had firmly proclaimed her intention never to marry.

A few weeks before the mysterious events of the Yellow Room, the news—which no one believed at first, so incredible did it seem—suddenly spread around Paris that Mademoiselle Stangerson had at last consented to reward Monsieur Darzac's undying attention and marry him! It took Darzac's refusal to deny this matrimonial rumour to give it the weight of truth. Then, Professor Stangerson himself, as he was leaving the Academie des Sciences, announced that the marriage of his daughter and Monsieur Robert Darzac would be celebrated in the privacy of the Chateau du Glandier, as soon as he and his daughter had put the finishing touches to their report summing up their work on the "Dissociation of Matter," i.e.: the reverse transformation of matter back into aether. The newlyweds would live at the Chateau, and Darzac was expected to assist his father-in-law in the work to which both father and daughter had dedicated their lives.

The scientific world barely had time to digest the news when it then learned of the attempted murder of Mademoiselle Stangerson, under the myster\rious conditions which I have recounted, and which our visit to the Chateau was meant to elucidate.

I have not hesitated to provide my readers here with all the necessary background information, which I had learned from my business relations with Robert Darzac. As we are preparing to enter the Yellow Room itself, I can therefore say with confidence that you now know as much as I did then.

Chapter Five
In Which Rouletabille Says a Few Words
To Robert Darzac To Some Considerable Effect

For several minutes, Rouletabille and I had been walking alongside the outside wall of Professor Stangerson's vast estate. We were approaching the main gate when our attention was drawn to a man, half-bent over, who seemed so completely absorbed in what he was doing that he hadn't seen us coming. He was stooping so low that he almost touched the ground. Suddenly, he drew himself up and examined the wall closely; after that, he looked into the palm of one of his hands, and walked away quickly. Finally, he set off running, and again looked into the palm of his hand. Rouletabille had brought me to a standstill with a gesture.

"Hush! That's Inspector Frederic Larsan at work! Let's not disturb him!"

My friend felt great admiration for the famous Sûreté detective. I had never met Larsan before, but I knew his reputation very well.

He had solved the theft of the gold bullion from the Hôtel de la Monnaie, when everyone else had given up. His arrest of the safecrackers of the Crédit Universel robbery had made his name a household word. At the time, Rouletabille hadn't yet displayed his unique crime-solving talents, and Larsan was widely known as one of the most skilled of detectives, capable of elucidating even the most mysterious and complex enigmas. His reputation had crossed national borders, and the police forces of London, Berlin, and even America, often called for his assistance when their own detectives found themselves at their wits' end.

No one was particularly surprised, therefore, when the head of the Sûreté, at the onset of the Mystery of the Yellow Room, had cabled his most famous subordinate in London, where he was working on a case of stolen bonds, and instructed him to return at once. Larsan who, at the Sûreté, had been nicknamed "Frederic the Great," had obeyed at once, knowing from experience that if his superiors were asking him to drop what he was doing, it was because his services were urgently needed on another, even more important affair. That is why Rouletabille and I found him already at work that morning. We soon found out exactly what he was doing.

The reason that he had been looking regularly at the palm of his hand was that it contained his watch, and he had been timing his movements with great precision. We saw him turn around, and run all the way to the entrance of the park. There, he consulted his watch again, then put it back in his pocket and shrugged in disappointment. After that, he pushed open the iron gate, closed it behind him and locked it. It was only then that, through the bars, he noticed us. Rouletabille rushed towards him, and I followed. Larsan had decided to wait for us.

"Monsieur Larsan," said Rouletabille, tipping his hat and showing the great detective the deep respect and admiration he genuinely felt for him, "could you tell me whether Monsieur Darzac is at the Chateau right now? I'm with one of his friends, Maître Sainclair of the Paris Bar, who desires to speak to him urgently."

"I really don't know, Monsieur Rouletabille," replied Larsan, shaking hands through the bars with my friend, whom he had met several times before during other investigations. "I haven't seen him yet."

"The caretakers will be able to tell us, no doubt," said Rouletabille, pointing to the lodge, which was the home of Monsieur and Madame Bernier. Its door and windows appeared to be shut.

"The caretakers won't be able to give you any useful information, Monsieur Rouletabille."

"Why not?"

"Because they were arrested half an hour ago."

"Arrested!" cried Rouletabille. "Are they guilty then?"

Larsan shrugged.

"When the police can't arrest a murderer," he said wryly, "they can always arrest potential accomplices."

"Did *you* order their arrest, Monsieur Larsan?"

"I? Certainly not! First, because I'm almost certain that they have nothing to do with this case, and also because—"

"Because what?" asked Rouletabille eagerly.

"Because nothing," said Larsan, shaking his head.

"Because there are no accomplices!" said Rouletabille.

Larsan stopped in his tracks and looked at my friend closely.

"Ah-ha! I see that you've already got a theory about this case, young man," said the detective "Even though you haven't seen anything or been anywhere. In fact, you haven't even received the permission to set foot inside the Chateau!"

"Oh, I will."

"I doubt it. The orders are strict."

"I'll gain admission if you let me see Monsieur Darzac. Will you do that for me, please? We're old friends, you and I, Monsieur Larsan. Do you remember the flattering article I wrote about you during the bullion affair? Please?"

At that moment, Rouletabille's face looked quite funny, so eager he was to enter this place where such a great mystery was waiting for him. He was begging for that simple favor so earnestly, with his eyes, his mouth, his entire body, that I couldn't help laughing. Larsan, too, was unable to remain serious. His face broke into a friendly smile.

As he stood on the other side of the gate, I took the time to study him more closely.

He was probably about 50; he was a rather handsome man, with greying hair, a dull complexion, and a strong profile. He had a prominent forehead, and was clean shaven. His mouth was finely chiselled. His eyes were small and round, and looked at you in a manner that was both piercing and unsettling. He was of average height, well proportioned, elegant and, overall, rather likable. He looked nothing like an ordinary policeman. In his own fashion, he was an artist, and one could tell that he was aware of that fact, and had a high opinion of himself. His voice betrayed a certain weariness and cyniscism, however, but why not? His profession had brought him into contact with so many awful crimes and villains that it would have been a miracle if his soul hadn't been hardened, as Rouletabille would have put it.

Larsan turned his head at the sound of a vehicle which was coming from the Chateau. We recognized the cab which had picked up the Investigating Magistrate and his clerk at the railway station at Epinay.

"Ah!" said Larsan, "if you want to speak with Monsieur Darzac, here he comes."

The cab was already at the gate. Darzac asked Larsan to open it, explaining that he was pressed for time to catch the next train for Paris. Then, he recognized me. While Larsan was unlocking the gate, Darzac asked what had brought me to Glandier at such a tragic time. I noticed that he was frightfully pale, and that his face was showing the effects of some dreadful suffering.

"Is Mademoiselle Stangerson getting better?" I asked at once.

"Yes," he replied. "She might be saved. She must be!"

He did not add "or it will be my death" but I heard the implied words on his pale lips.

Rouletabille intervened:

"I see that you're in a hurry, Monsieur Darzac, but I must speak with you. I have something of the greatest importance to tell you."

Larsan broke in

"May I leave you now?" he asked Darzac. "Do you have a key, or would you like me to give you mine?"

"Thank you, Inspector," said Darzac. "I have my own key and I will relock the gate."

Larsan then waved good-bye and rushed off in the direction of the Chateau, the imposing shape of which could be seen only a few hundred yards away.

Robert Darzac was now frowning, beginning to show some impatience. I introduced Rouletabille as a good friend of mine, but, as soon as he learned that my young friend was a journalist, he looked at me disapprovingly, and excused himself at once, restating that he had to be in Epinay in 20 minutes in order to catch his train. As he was about to whip up his horse, Rouletabille seized the bridle and, to my utter astonishment, stopped the carriage with a firm hand. Then, he uttered a sentence which was utterly meaningless to me:

"*The presbytery has lost none of its charm, nor the garden its glow.*"

The words had no sooner left his lips than I saw Darzac tremble. Pale as he had been, he became even paler. His eyes stared at Rouletabille in terror. He was clearly in a state of dreadful distress.

"Come in! Come in!" he stammered.

Then, suddenly, with barely contained fury, he insisted:

"Follow me, Monsieur."

He turned the cab around and, without bothering to relock the gate, proceeded at a slow pace towards the Chateau. Rouletabille was still holding the horse's bridle. I tried saying a few words to Darzac, but he didn't respond. I looked at Rouletabille, looking for an explanation, but his gaze was elsewhere.

Chapter Six
At the End of the Oak Grove

We finally arrived at the Chateau. The old tower was connected to a wing that had been entirely rebuilt under Louis XIV by a new section done in a modern, Viollet-le-Duc style. That was where that the main entrance was located. I had never before seen anything so unusual or so ugly as that bizarre mix of clashing architectural styles. It was as grotesque as it was fascinating.

As we approached, we saw four gendarmes pacing in front of a small door leading into the tower. We later found out that its ground floor, which had once been a prison and was now a tool shed, had reverted to its original use. The caretakers, Monsieur and Madame Bernier, had been confined inside.

Darzac took us into the modern part of the Chateau through the main entrance, a large double-door with an overhanging glass awning. Rouletabille, who had left the horse and cab in the care of a servant, never took his eyes off the Sorbonne Professor. I followed his gaze and saw that it was fixated on Darzac's gloved hands. When we reached a small sitting room fitted with old furniture, Mademoiselle Stangerson's fiancé turned to Rouletabille and asked sharply:

"Speak! What do you want?"

My young friend answered in an equally sharp tone:

"To shake your hand."

Darzac shrank back.

"What do you mean?"

Obviously, he understood, as I did, that Rouletabille suspected him of being the author of the abominable attempt on Mademoiselle Stangerson's life. The impression of the blood-stained hand on the walls of the Yellow Room was in everyone's mind. I looked at Darzac, a man who was normally so proud and so decent, and who now looked so strangely troubled. He held out his right hand and, referring to me, said:

"Since you're a friend of Monsieur Sainclair's, who rendered me an invaluable service in a just cause in the past, Monsieur, I cannot possibly refuse to shake your hand..."

However, Rouletabille didn't take Darzac's extended hand. Lying with the utmost audacity, he replied:

"Monsieur Darzac, I've spent some time in Russia, where I've gotten into the habit of never shaking a gloved hand."

I thought that the Sorbonne Professor was going to respond with an angry outburst, but, on the contrary, he made a strong effort to keep his calm, took off his gloves, and showed us his bare hands. They were unmarked and unscarred.

"Are you happy now?" said Darzac.

"Unfortunately, no," replied Rouletabille. "My dear Sainclair," he said, turning toward me, "I must ask you to leave us alone for a few minutes."

I saluted both men and retired. I was amazed by what I had just seen and heard. I couldn't understand why Darzac hadn't already kicked out my impertinent, insulting, and stupid friend. I was angry at Rouletabille for his suspicions, which had led to this shameful scene with the gloves.

I walked back and forth in front of the Chateau for 20 minutes, trying to connect the various events of the day, but in vain. What was in Rouletabille's mind? Did he really think that Darzac had attacked Mathilde Stangerson? How could he believe that this man, who was supposed to marry her in only a few days, had walked into the Yellow Room and tried to murder his own fiancée? Besides, I still had no idea as to how the perpetrator had been able to leave the Yellow Room. As long as that mystery, which seemed so baffling to me, remained unexplained, I thought it was our duty to not point the figer of suspicion lightly at anyone. And what about that seemingly senseless phrase—"*The presbytery has lost none of its charm, nor the garden its glow*"—which still echoed in my ears? What did it mean? I was eager to rejoin Rouletabille and ask him.

At that moment, my young friend came out of the Chateau followed by Darzac. As incredible as it seemed, I saw, at a glance, that they appeared to have become the best of friends.

"We're going to see the Yellow Room. Come with us, Sainclair," Rouletabille said. "And since we'll be spending the whole day here, we'll have lunch somewhere in the area…"

"Please, allow me to be your host at the Chateau, gentlemen," offered Darzac.

"Thank you, but no," replied Rouletabille. "We'll eat at the Auberge du Donjon."

"I'm afraid you'll fare rather badly there. You won't find anything—"

"Do you think so? Because I do hope to find *something* there," said Rouletabille. "After lunch, we'll set to work again, then I'll write my article. Sainclair, would you be kind enough to deliver it to *L'Epoque* for me?"

"Won't you come back to Paris with me?"

"No. I plan to stay here."

I looked at Rouletabille, but he was quite serious, and Darzac did not appear in the least surprised.

We were walking by the old tower when we heard wailing from inside. It was the caretakers.

"Why have those people been arrested?" asked Rouletabille.

"Well, I'm partly responsible for that," said Darzac. "I happened to tell the Investigating Magistrate yesterday that I thought it was strange that the caretakers had time to hear the gunshots, dress themselves, and run all the way from their lodge to the pavilion in two minutes, which is the time that elapsed between the firing of the shots and when they met Père Jacques."

"That is suspicious indeed," said Rouletabille. "And you say that they were fully dressed?"

"That's what's so strange. They were—warmly even. There was nothing missing. The woman wore clogs, but Monsieur Bernier had had time to lace his boots. Now, they claim that they went to bed at 9 p.m., like every other day. But, this morning, the Investigating Magistrate brought with him a revolver of the same caliber as the one found in the room. He obviously didn't want to use the real gun, which is being held in evidence. He asked his clerk to fire two blank shots inside the Yellow Room, with the doors and the windows closed. We stood with him in the caretakers' lodge, and yet we heard nothing, not a sound. Therefore, the Berniers must have lied, no doubt about it! They must have already been waiting near the pavilion for something! They're not accused of being the authors of the crime, but they could very well be accomplices. That's why Monsieur de Marquet had them arrested."

"Ridiculous! If they'd been involved," said Rouletabille, "*they would have arrived all disheveled*—or better yet, not shown up at all. When people throw themselves into the arms of the Law with such obvious proof of wrongdoing, you can be pretty sure they're innocent. Besides, I don't believe there are any accomplices in this affair."

"Then, what were they doing there, fully dressed at midnight? Why won't they explain themselves?"

"They must have some reason for their silence. We've got to found out what it is, because, even if they're innocent, it might still be relevant to the investigation. *Everything that took place on that night is important*."

We had just crossed an old bridge over the moat and entered the section of the grounds called the Oak Grove. The oaks here were centuries-old. Autumn had already shrivelled their golden leaves, and their high branches, dark and twisted, looked like the horrid hair, made up of writhing snakes, that the ancient sculptors gave to the head of the Medusa. This place, which Mademoiselle Stangerson found cheerful during the summer—her stated reason for staying at the pavilion—now seemed to us sad and funereal.

The grounds were dark and muddy from the recent rains and rotting leaves; the trunks of the trees were just as murky, and even the skies above our heads looked as if they were in mourning, filled as they were with great, dark clouds. It was in this somber and desolate place that we first saw the white walls of the pavilion.

It was an odd-looking building, with no visible windows from where we stood. The only opening was a small single door. It looked like a tomb, a vast mausoleum buried in the midst of a thick forest.

As we got nearer, we were able to make out its surroundings. It received all the light it needed from the south, that is to say, from the open woods on the other side of the grounds. Once that small door was closed, Professor Stangerson and his daughter were ideally secluded to complete their work and their dreams.

I shall now insert here a plan of the pavilion. It had a ground floor, which was reached by a few steps, and above it was a high-ceilinged attic, with which we don't need to concern ourselves. It is only the plan of the ground floor that I unclude here.

This plan was drawn by Rouletabille himself, and I have assured myself that there is nothing missing, not a single line, nor any significant detail that might otherwise help to find a solution to the baffling problem that had been laid out before the police.

With this plan, and the accompanying explanations, my readers will know just as much as Rouletabille and I did when we entered the pavilion for the first time.

They may now ask themselves as we did: How did the perpetrator manage to escape from the Yellow Room?

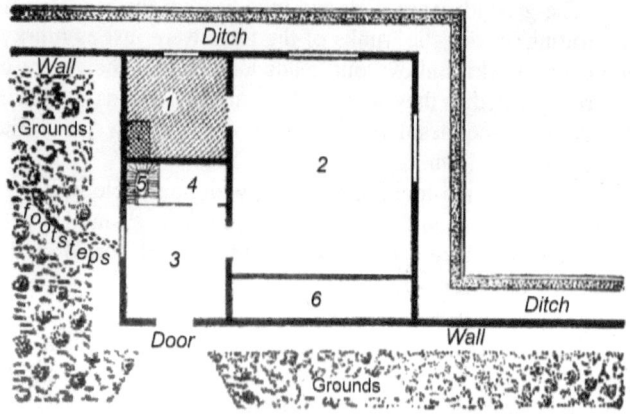

1. The Yellow Room, with its one window and its single door opening into the laboratory.

2. The Laboratory, with its two large, barred windows and its two doors, one leading to the vestibule, the other to the Yellow Room.

3. The Vestibule, with its unbarred window and the door opening onto the grounds.

4. The Lavatory.

5. Stairs leading to the attic.

6. The large and only fireplace in the pavilion, used in the experiments being conducted in the laboratory.

Before climbing the three steps leading up to the door of the pavilion, Rouletabille stopped and asked Darzac point blank:

"What do you think was the motive for the attack?"

"As far as I'm concerned, Monsieur, I have no doubt about that," the Sorbonne Professor replied, showing great distress. "My fiancée's attacker was a savage brute, a blood-thirsty lunatic. The deep scratches on her chest and throat show that he intended to ravage and kill her. The doctor who examined them yesterday concluded that they were from the same hand which left its bloody imprint on the wall; a large man's hand—much too big to fit into my gloves, you will note," he added with a wan and somewhat bitter smile.

"Couldn't that bloody handprint have been Mademoiselle Stangerson's?" I interrupted. "When she fell, she might have leaned against the wall and, sliding down, enlarged the impression?"

"There wasn't a drop of blood on her hands when they found her," replied Darzac.

"Then, that tells us for a fact," I said, "that it was Mademoiselle Stangerson who used Père Jacques's revolver and hit her attacker in the hand. *Therefore, she must have been fearful of something—or somebody.*"

"Very likely."

"Do you suspect anyone?"

"No," replied Darzac, looking at Rouletabille.

Rouletabille then said to me:

"I have to tell you, my dear Sainclair, that the investigation is a little more advanced than our cagey Magistrate, Monsieur de Marquet, chose to tell us. He not only knew that Mademoiselle Stangerson had defended herself with Père Jacques' gun, but he also knew the nature of the weapon that was used against her. Monsieur Darzac told me that it was a sheepbone. Why is Monsieur de Marquet being so secretive about it? Perhaps to facilitate the Sûreté's inquiries? Or he perhaps believes that the owner of the 'murder weapon,' as it were, will be found among the wretches of the Paris underground, because they often use that crude and brutal tool? Who can tell what goes on inside an Investigative Magistrate's mind?" concluded Rouletabille with contemptuous irony.

"So they found the sheep-bone inside the Yellow Room?" I asked.

"Yes, Monsieur," replied Darzac. "At the foot of the bed. But I beg of you to not say anything about it to anyone. Monsieur de Marquet insisted that it should remain totally confidential." (I made a gesture of assent.) "It was a large sheepbone, the top of which, or rather the joint, was still red with the blood of my fiancée. It was an old bone, *which may have been used for other crimes*. At least, that's what Monsieur de Marquet believes. He thinks he saw not only Mathilde's blood on it, but older stains of dried blood, which might be the evidence of earlier crimes. He's sent to the crime laboratory in Paris to be analyzed."

"A sheep-bone in the hand of a skilled assassin is a deadly weapon indeed," said Rouletabille, "more versatile and dangerous than a hammer."

"No more so than in this case," said Darzac, glumly. "That bone was used to hit Mathilde on the forehead, and the joint exactly fit the wound inflicted. I think that the blow would have killed her, if she hadn't shot at the murderer. Wounded in the hand, he dropped the sheep-bone and fled. *Unfortunately, the blow had already been struck*, and Mademoiselle Stangerson was well stunned, after having been almost strangled. If she had succeeded in wounding her attacker with her first shot, she might have escaped that blow, but she used her gun too late. Her first shot went astray and hit the ceiling instead. It was only the second shot that hit her assailant."

Having said this, Darzac knocked at the door of the pavilion. I must confess that I was quite excited at the idea of being able to inspect the room where the crime had been committed. I was trembling with impatience and, despite the interest I felt for the story of the sheep-bone, I couldn't wait for the door to open.

Finally, it did. A man, whom I assumed was Père Jacques, stood on the threshold.

He appeared to be well over 60. He had a long white beard and white hair; he wore a béret, a well-used, brown corduroy jacket, and clogs on his feet. He looked grumpy at first, but his face lit up as soon as he saw Darzac.

"These are friends of mine, Père Jacques," said our guide. "Is anyone else here?"

"I'm not supposed to let anyone in," said the old man, "but, of course, that doesn't apply to you, Monsieur Robert.

Besides, the police have already seen everything there is to see here. God knows they made enough drawings and took enough statements!"

"Excuse me, Père Jacques, but might I ask you a question before we proceed," said Rouletabille.

"What is it, young man? If I can answer it, I shall"

"Did your mistress wear her hair in plaits, that night? You know what I mean, wrapped over her forehead?"

"No, Monsieur. My mistress never wore her hair in that fashion, not on that day or any other. She had her hair pulled up, as usual, so that her beautiful forehead could be seen— pure as that of an unborn child!"

Rouletabille grunted an acknowledgment and began to examine the door, finding that it shut automatically. He determined that it couldn't remain ajar, and that one had to have a key to open it. Then, we entered the vestibule, a small, well-lit room with a red-tiled floor.

"Ah! This is the window through which the murderer is supposed to have escaped!" said Rouletabille.

"That's what they keep saying, Monsieur," said Père Jacques, "but if he had gone that way, we would have certainly seen him. We're not blind, the Professor and I, and neither are the Berniers, who've been arrested. Why haven't they arrested me, too, on account of my revolver?"

Rouletabille had already opened the window and was now examining the shutters.

"Were these closed at the time of the crime?"

"Yes! Fastened with the iron catch, from the inside," said Père Jacques. "And yet, I'm sure the villain just walked through them like a ghost!"

"Were there any blood stains?"

"Yes, on the stones outside… But who did they belong to? That's the question!"

"Ah!" said Rouletabille, "I see some footprints on the path—the ground was very damp and preserved them. I'll look into this later."

"Nonsense!" interrupted Père Jacques. "The murderer can't have gone that way."

"Which way did he go, then?"

"How would I know?"

Rouletabille looked at everything, smelled everything. He went down on his knees and rapidly examined every one of the vestibule tiles. Père Jacques went on:

"Ah! You won't find anything there, Monsieur. No one has found anything so far. And now, it's all dirty! Too many folks have been trampling all over the place. They won't let me wash the floor now, but on the day of the crime, I'd washed it thoroughly, I, Père Jacques, and if the murderer had crossed my clean floor with his big, dirty boots, I'd certainly have noticed it! After all, he left plenty footprints in Mademoiselle's room."

Rouletabille rose.

"When was the last time you said you washed these tiles?" he asked, and he looked at Père Jacques carefully.

"Why—as I've just told you—on the day of the crime, around 5:30 p.m., when Mademoiselle and the Professor were taking a walk before they had dinner here, in the laboratory. The next day, when the Investigating Magistrate came, he could see all the footprints on the floor, clear as ink on paper. Well, he didn't find any traces of a stranger, either in the laboratory, or in the vestibule. Both were clean as a whistle. But since they did find some footprints *outside* this window, Mademoiselle's attacker could have gone through the ceiling of the Yellow Room into the attic, then cut his way through the roof and then dropped to the ground outside the vestibule window. Except that there's no hole in the ceiling of the Yellow Room or in the roof—that's for certain! So, you see, we've got nothing—absolutely nothing! My guess is that we won't ever find out the truth! This mystery is of the Devil's own making."

Rouletabille got down on his knees again in front of the door leading to a small lavatory located at the back of the vestibule. He remained in that position for a minute or so.

"Well?" I asked him when he got up.

"Oh! Nothing very important… A small drop of blood," he replied.

Then, he turned towards Père Jacques again.

"When you were washing the laboratory and the vestibule floors, was the vestibule window open?" he inquired.

"I had just opened it because I had lit some charcoal for the Professor in the laboratory furnace, and, as I had used some old newspapers to start the fire, there was a bit of smoke, so I opened both the windows in the laboratory and this one, to create a draft. After the smoke cleared, I shut the windows in the laboratory, but I left this one open when I went out to get some rags at the Chateau.

"When I returned, it was about 5:30 p.m. as I told you. I then washed the floors. After I finished, I went back to the castle again, leaving the window open. When I returned to the pavilion for the last time, *it had been closed* and the Professor and Mademoiselle were already busy at work in the laboratory."

"So the Professor or Mademoiselle Stangerson had probably shut the window?"

"Probably, yes."

"Did you ask them?"

"No."

After a close examination of the little lavatory and the staircase leading up to the attic, Rouletabille—to whom we seemed to no longer exist—entered the laboratory. I followed him, in a state of growing excitement. Meanwhile, Darzac had closely watched all of my friend's movements.

My eyes were drawn at once to the door of the Yellow Room. It was, in fact, leaning against the door frame, having been broken off its hinges. The efforts of the two men who had crashed through it on the night of the crime had severely damaged it.

Rouletabille, who went about his business methodically, studied the laboratory in silence. It was a big and well-lit room with two very large windows—almost bays—protected by strong iron bars, looking out upon the neighboring woods.

Through an opening in the trees, one had a wonderful view of the entire valley, all the way to the town of Epinay, which must have been visible on a clear day. On that day, however, there was only mud on the ground, sooty skies—and blood waiting for us in the Yellow Room!

One side of the laboratory was entirely taken up by a large fireplace, crucibles, ovens, and other implements required for chemical experiments. Next to it was a long table loaded haphazardly with beakers, test tubes, notebooks, filing boxes, measuring instruments, batteries and some kind of an electrical apparatus, which Darzac told us, was used by the Professor "to demonstrate the dissociation of matter under the action of electrical power."

Along the other wall were cabinets, plain or with glass-doors, through which one could see microscopes, special photographic equipment, and a large quantity of crystals.

Rouletabille was now ferreting inside the fireplace. He searched the crucibles and, suddenly, drew himself up. He held up a piece of half-charred paper in his hand. He walked toward the window where we stood, chatting.

"Will you please keep this paper for me, Monsieur Darzac?" he said.

I loked at the scorched piece of paper which Darzac had just taken from Rouletabille, and read the only words that remained legible on it:

Presbytery ... lost none ... charm, nor ... gard... its glow.
And beneath that was a date: *October 23*.

This was the second time that I had seen, or heard, those apparently meaningless words, and I saw that they produced the same frightful effect on Darzac. His first reaction was to look at Père Jacques, but the old man was busy at the other window and hadn't noticed anything. Then, the Sorbonne Professor opened his wallet and, his hand shaking, put the piece of paper inside, sighing: "My God!"

Meanwhile, Rouletabille had climbed up inside the fireplace. Perched on top of the furnace, he was attentively examining the chimney flue, which grew narrower, ending in a conduit sealed by an iron grate fastened into the brickwork, and subdivided into three small pipes, each about 6 inches in diameter.

"Totally impossible to get out that way," my friend said, jumping back into the laboratory. "Besides, even if our perpetrator had tried to do it, he would have had to tear out all that metalwork. No, this is definitely a dead end."

Rouletabille then examined the furniture and opened the doors of all the cabinets. After that, he looked at the windows, an obstacle which he finally pronounced "unconquerable and unconquered." At the second window, he found Père Jacques absorbed in silent contemplation.

"Well, Père Jacques," my friend said, "what are you looking at?"

"I'm looking at that policeman who's always circling the pond outside. He isn't going to be any smarter than all the other smarties!"

"You don't know Frederic Larsan, Père Jacques, or else you wouldn't be saying that about him," said Rouletabille, shaking his head in mock sadness. "If anyone can find who attacked Mademoiselle Stangerson, it is he."

Then, he heaved a deep sigh.

"Before they can find him, they've got to discover how they lost him in the first place," said Père Jacques, stubbornly.

At last, we reached the door to the Yellow Room.

"And there is the door behind which a terrible thing took place," said Rouletabille, with a solemnity which, under any other circumstances, would have been comical.

Chapter Seven
*In Which Rouletabille Launches
an Investigation Beneath the Bed*

Rouletabille, having pushed open the door to the Yellow Room, paused on the threshold, and said with an emotion which I only understood much later:

"Ah… *The perfume of the lady in black!*"

The chamber was dark. Père Jacques was about to open the shutters when Rouletabille stopped him.

"Didn't the tragedy take place in complete darkness?" he inquired.

"No, young man, I don't think so," replied Père Jacques. "Mademoiselle always insisted on having a lamp on her night stand and I lit it every evening before she went to bed. I'm like a chambermaid to her, you see. The real chambermaid only comes in the mornings, and Mademoiselle often works late—far into the night."

"Where was the night stand? Far from the bed?"

"Some way, yes."

"Can you light the lamp now?"

"Well, the lamp is broken and the oil was spilled when the night stand was kicked over. But everything else in the room is just the way it was. Let me open the shutters and you'll see for yourself."

"Wait!"

Rouletabille went back into the laboratory, closed the two shutters and the door of the vestibule. When we were in total darkness, he lit a candle, gave it to Père Jacques and asked him to go and stand in the very same spot where the lamp had been burning that night.

Père Jacques, who was wearing slippers—he had left his clogs in the vestibule—entered the Yellow Room with the candle. Under the small, flickering light, we saw various objects lying on the floor, a bed in a corner, and, in front of us, to our left, the reflection of a mirror hanging on the wall, near the bed. It took only a glance to inventory the contents of the room.

"That will do!" said Rouletabille. "You may open the shutters now."

"Please, don't go in," begged Père Jacques. "You might leave marks with your boots, and nothing must be disturbed. That's what the Magistrate said, alhough I can't imagine what more business he's got here."

The old man pushed the shutters open. Pale daylight entered from outside, casting sinister shadows on the saffron-colored wallpaper. Unlike the floors of the laboratory and the vestibule, which were tiled, the Yellow Room had a parquet floor, entirely covered by a single piece of yellow carpet, including under the bed and the dressing-table—the only piece of furniture that remained upright. A small round table, the night stand and two chairs had been overturned. They didn't prevent us from observing a large blood stain on the carpet, which Père Jacques informed us was from the wound on Mademoiselle Stangerson's forehead. Other, smaller blood stains were visible, parallel to the large, black footprints left by the perpetrator. One might have assumed that these drops of blood had fallen from the wound of the man who had left his blood-stained handprint on the wall. There were other bloody handprints on the wall, but much less distinct. There was no doubt that that single, clearly defined handprint belonged to a robust man.

"See! See the blood on the wall!" I couldn't help exclaiming. "That man, lost in the dark, must have thought that he was pushing the door! That's why he pressed so hard, leaving that terrible clue on the yellow wallpaper. I don't think there are many hands like that around. It's large, strong and all the fingers are nearly the same length! The thumb is missing; we only have the palm; but if we follow the trail, we see that, after pressing against the wall, the man felt for the door, found it, and then felt for the lock…"

"No doubt," interrupted Rouletabille, chuckling, "except that *there is no blood on the lock or on the bolt!*"

"What does that prove?" I replied, with the common sense of which I was proud. "The perpetrator might have opened the lock with his left hand, which would have been only natural, since he'd just been wounded in his right hand."

"I told you, no one opened the door!" Père Jacques shouted. "We're not blind! The door remained locked all the time, and there were four of us here when we smashed it open!"

"It's a funny-looking hand nevertheless," I continued. "Look at it!"

"It's a very natural-looking hand," said Rouletabille. "The handprint has been *elongated by the slippage of the hand on the wall*. What you see here is the trace left by a man *who wiped his bloody hand off on the wallpaper*. That man must be about five feet eight."

"How can you know that?"

"By the height of the handprint on the wall."

My friend next occupied himself with the hole in the wall left by the bullet. It was a small, round hole.

"This bullet was fired straight," said Rouletabille. "Not from above, not from below."

And my friend drew our attention to the fact that the hole was located a few inches lower than the handprint.

Rouletabille went back to the door and carefully examined the lock and the bolt, satisfying himself that the door had been broken open from the outside, and that both the lock and the bolt were still shut on the inside of the shattered door. The two latches, their screws ripped from the wall, still hung on the side of the door, with the bolts still inside them.

The young reporter examined the lock and the bolt carefully, looked at both sides of the door again, and assured himself that it couldn't possibly have been opened from the outside. He also verified that they key had been found still in the lock, on the inside. He finally satisfied himself that, with the key in the lock inside, the door couldn't be opened with another key from outside. Then, having made sure that there was no automatic shutting mechanism, and that the door was just what it appeared to be: a simple, ordinary door, with one lock and a sturdy bolt, which had both been locked, he said:

"Very good!"

Then, sitting down on the ground, he hastily took off his boots and entered the Yellow Room in his socks. The first thing he did was to minutely examine the overturned furniture. We watched him in silence.

"Young man, you seem to be going to a lot of trouble," said Père Jacques ironically.

Rouletabille raised his head and said:

"You were right, Père Jacques. Mademoiselle Stangerson didn't have her hair in plaits that night. I was an ass to have ever thought she did."

Then, with the agility of a snake, he crept under the bed.

"I think that's where the murderer must have certainly been hiding," said Père Jacques. "He must have been there at 10 p.m. when I went in to close the shutters and light the night light, since neither the Professor, nor Mademoiselle, nor I, left the laboratory until that dastardly attack."

Presently we heard Rouletabille ask:

"Père Jacques, at what time did the Professor and Mademoiselle Stangerson arrive at the laboratory?"

"At 6 p.m."

The voice of Rouletabille continued:

"Yes, he's been under here, that's certain... In fact, there's nowhere else where he could have been hiding... When you came in—the four of you—did you look under the bed?"

"At once! We even overturned the bed."

"And between the mattresses?"

"There was only one mattress on the bed, and we placed Mademoiselle upon it. Then, the Professor and Monsieur Bernier immediately carried her into the laboratory. There was nothing under it but the metal bed frame, which could not conceal anything or anyone. Remember, Monsieur, that there were four of us and we couldn't fail to notice everything. The room is so small and so scantily furnished, and the pavilion was locked…"

I ventured a hypothesis:

"Perhaps he got away with the mattress—inside it even! Anything is possible in the face of such a mystery! In their distress, Professor Stangerson and Monsieur Bernier may not have noticed that they were carrying the weight of two people—*especially if the caretaker was part of the plot*! I throw out this hypothesis for what it's worth, but it would explain many things, particularly the fact that neither the laboratory nor the vestibule bear any traces of the footprints found inside the Yellow Room. If, in transporting Mademoiselle Stangerson on the mattress from the pavilion to the Chateau, the Professor and Bernier rested for a moment, there might have been an opportunity for our man to escape."

"Surely you must be joking!" said Rouletabille, laughing from under the bed.

I felt rather vexed and replied:

"Well, I don't know, of course, but anything seems possible…"

"The Investigating Magistrate had the same idea, Monsieur," said Père Jacques, "and he carefully examined the mattress. Finally, he was forced to laugh at the idea, just as your friend is doing right now, for whoever heard of a mattress with a double bottom? Besides, if a man had been hiding inside, we would have seen him!"

I was obliged to laugh, too, realizing that my theory was absurd after all; but, in an affair like this, one hardly knows where an absurdity begins or ends.

Only Rouletabille seemed able to speak sensibly. He called out from under the bed.

"This carpet has been moved. Who did that?"

"We did, Monsieur," explained Père Jacques. "When we couldn't find any trace of the villain, we asked ourselves if there wasn't a hole in the floor…"

"There isn't," replied Rouletabille. "Is there a cellar?"

"No, there's no cellar. But that hasn't stopped the Investigating Magistrate and his clerk from examining the entire floor, one slat of wood at a time, as if there had been a cellar under it."

The reporter reappeared. His eyes were shining and his nose quivered. He looked like a hound dog back from a successful hunt… He remained on his hands and knees. I couldn't help thinking that there was no better comparison than that of a sporting dog on the scent of some unusual quarry. And, indeed, he was hunting for a man, the prey he had sworn to bring back to his master, the editor-in-chief of *L'Epoque*. Don't forget that Rouletabille was, first and foremost, a journalist.

Thus, on his hands and knees, he made his way around the room, sniffing and examining everything—everything that we could see, which wasn't much, and, more importantly, everything that we obviously could not see, which must have been a lot.

The dressing-table was a simple table, standing on four legs. It would have been impossible to hide under it. There was no dresser, because Mademoiselle Stangerson kept her clothes at the Chateau.

Rouletabille passed his nose and hands over the walls, *which were made of solid bricks*. When he finished with the walls, having explored every inch of the saffron-colored wallpaper, he turned to the ceiling, which he was able to examine by placing a chair on top of the dressing-table, and moving that impromptu ladder from one end of the room to the other. He checked every square inch of it, including the hole made by the second bullet. After that, he approached the window, and, once again, tested the iron bars and the shutters, all of which were solid and intact. At last, he gave a grunt of satisfaction and declared:

"Now, I'm done!"

"Well, do you believe that our poor dear Mademoiselle was locked up well and good, when she was attacked by that miscreant, and called out for help?" asked Père Jacques.

"Yes," said the young reporter, mopping the sweat off his forehead. "*The Yellow Room was as tightly shut as a safe.*"

"That's why this mystery is the most intriguing that I've ever come across," I said. "In *The Murders in the Rue Morgue*, even Edgar Allan Poe didn't offer us such a puzzle. There, the scene of the crime was sufficiently closed to prevent the flight of a man, but there was a small window through which an ape could escape![10] But here, there can be no question of an opening of any kind. The door was bolted, the window and the shutters were shut—*not even a fly could have gotten in or out.*"

"True, true," acquiesced Rouletabille as he mopped his forehead, which seemed to be perspiring less from his recent efforts than from his mental agitation. "Indeed, it's a great, beautiful, and very strange mystery."

"Even if the Holy Beast itself had attacked Mademoiselle," muttered Père Jacques, "it couldn't have escaped. Listen! Do you hear it? Hush!"

Père Jacques waved at us to be quiet and, stretching his arm towards the wall nearest to the forest, he appeared to be listening to something we couldn't hear.

"It's gone," he finally said. "I should kill it. It's too wicked, but it's the Holy Beast, after all. Every night, it goes and prays on the tomb of Sainte Genevieve No one would dare harm it, less Mère Angenoux cast an evil spell on them."

"How big is the Holy Beast?"

"Nearly as big as a large basset hound. It's a monster, I tell you. Ah! I've asked myself more than once if it was not that which attacked our poor Mademoiselle, ripping her throat with its claws. But the Holy Beast doesn't wear boots, doesn't

---

[10] Conan Doyle dealt with a similar type of mystery in *The Speckled Band*. A terrible murder is committed in a locked room. What happened to its perpetrator? Sherlock Holmes finds out when he discovers in the room a small airvent big big enough to let through the eponymous "Speckled Band"—a poisonous snake. (*Note from the Author.*)

use guns—and wouldn't leave behind a handprint like that!" exclaimed Père Jacques, pointing at the bloody mark on the wall. "Besides, we would have seen it, just the same as a man, and it would certainly have been trapped inside the Yellow Room and the pavilion…"

"Obviously," I said. "Before we had a chance to inspect the Yellow Room, I confess that I'd also asked myself if, maybe, Mère Angenoux's cat might not have been…"

"Not you too!" cried Rouletabille.

"Why? Didn't you?" I asked.

"Not for a moment. After reading the article in *Le Matin*, *I knew that no animals were involved in this matter*. But now, I know that some frightful tragedy did happen here. By the way, you didn't say anything about the béret and the handkerchief that were found here, Père Jacques."

"Well, the Magistrate took them," the old man answered, hesitatingly.

"I haven't seen either of them, but I think I can tell you what they were made of," Rouletabille said gravely.

"You're a clever lad, aren't you?" said Père Jacques, coughing and looking a bit embarrassed.

"The handkerchief is rather large, blue with red stripes. The béret is a traditional basque béret, just like the one you're wearing now."

"You're a wizard!" said Père Jacques, trying to laugh but not quite succeeding. "How do you know that the handkerchief is blue with red stripes?"

"Because if it wasn't, it wouldn't have been found here."

Without paying any further attention to Père Jacques, Rouletabille then took a piece of paper and a small pair of scissors from his pocket, and, bending over the footprints, he placed the paper over one of them and began to cut. In a short time, he had made a perfect pattern which he handed to me, begging me not to lose it.

He then returned to the window and, pointing to the figure of Frederic Larsan, who walking in the woods outside near the pond, he asked Père Jacques if the detective had examined the Yellow Room too.

"No," replied Robert Darzac, who, since Rouletabille had handed him the piece of charred paper, had not uttered a word. "He claims that he doesn't need to examine the Yellow Room. He says that the murderer made his escape quite naturally, and that tonight, he will explain how he did it."

As he listened to Darzac, Rouletabille turned pale—which was quite unusual.

"Has Larsan found out the truth, which I'm only guessing at?" he murmured. "He's clever, very clever—and I admire him. But what's required here is more than the work of a policeman... better than what experience teaches us... *It is a matter of pure logic!* And by that, I mean just as logical as God Himself was when he ordered that $2 + 2 = 4$! ONE MUST GRAB LOGIC BY THE RIGHT END, AS IF IT WERE A STICK!"

The reporter rushed outside, devastated at the idea that "Frederic the Great" might beat him to the solution of the Mystery of the Yellow Room.

I managed to catch him on the threshold of the pavilion.

"Calm yourself, my dear fellow," I said. "Aren't you satisfied with what you found?"

"Yes," he confessed to me, with a deep sigh. "*I am quite satisfied.* I have discovered many things."

"Psychological or physical?"

"Several psychological, one physical. This, for example..."

And he quickly pulled from his pocket a piece of paper which he must have stored there during his investigation under the bed, and which contained *a woman's blond hair.*

Chapter Eight
The Investigating Magistrate
Questions Mademoiselle Stangerson

Five minutes later, Rouletabille was bending over the footprints discovered in the grass under the window of the vestibule. Suddenly, we saw a man—obviously a servant from the Chateau—running towards us and calling out to Monsieur Darzac, who was just coming out of the pavilion:

"Monsieur Robert, the Magistrate is questioning Mademoiselle!"

Darzac muttered a quick apology to us and rushed off towards the Chateau; the servant followed him.

"If the poor girl can speak," I said, "it might be interesting to hear what she has to say."

"I agree," said my friend. "Let's return to the Chateau."

We rushed over, but, unfortunately, a gendarme stationed in the vestibule denied us admission to the first floor, where the interrogation was taking place and we were therefore forced to wait downstairs.

From what I learned later, this is what took place in Mademoiselle Stangerson's bedroom, while we were waiting below. The family doctor, finding that his patient had been doing better, but also concerned about a relapse which might further delay the possibility of her being interviewed, thought it was his duty to inform the Investigating Magistrate. Monsieur de Marquet then decided to proceed immediately with the interview. It was attended by his clerk, Professor Stangerson, and the doctor.

Later, during the trial, I managed to obtain a transcript of this interview, which I reproduce below in all its legal dryness:

"*Question.* Mademoiselle, without exhausting yourself, are you capable of giving us some details about the frightful attack of which you were the victim?

"*Answer*. Thank you, I feel much better, Monsieur. I will tell you all that I know. When I entered my room, I didn't notice anything unusual there…

"*Q*. Excuse me, Mademoiselle, if you will allow me, I will ask the questions and you will answer them. That will be less tiring for you than making a long recital.

"*A*. As you please, Monsieur.

"*Q*. What did you do on that day? I want you to be as detailed and precise as possible. I wish to know everything that happened on that very day—if it's not too much to ask.

"*A*. I got up at 10 a.m. because my father and I had come home late the night before, having been invited to a banquet given by the French President to honor the Academy of Sciences of Philadelphia. When I left my room at 10:30 a.m., my father was already working in the laboratory. We worked together till noon. We then took a half-hour's walk in the grounds, as we often do, before having breakfast at the Chateau. After breakfast, we took another half-hour's walk, and then returned to the laboratory at 1:30 p.m. There, we found my chambermaid, who had come to clean my room. I went into the Yellow Room to give her some orders. Then, she left the pavilion and I resumed my work with my father. At 5 p.m., we went out again for another walk in the grounds and, after that, we had tea.

"*Q*. Before leaving the pavilion at 5 p.m., did you go into the Yellow Room?

"*A*. No, Monsieur, but my father did, at my request, to bring me my hat.

"*Q*. And he found nothing suspicious there?

"*Professor Stangerson*. Obviously not, Monsieur.

"*Q*. It is, therefore, almost certain that the murderer wasn't yet hiding under the bed. When you went out, was the door of the Yellow Room locked?

"*A*. No, there was no reason to lock it.

"*Q*. How long were you and your father away from the pavilion?

"*A*. About an hour.

"*Q*. It was likely during that hour that the perpetrator got inside the pavilion. But how? Nobody yet knows. We did find some footprints in the grounds, but *leading away from the vestibule window*. We've found none *going towards it*. Did you notice whether the vestibule window was open when you went out with your father?

"*A*. I don't remember.

"*Professor Stangerson*. It was closed.

"*Q*. And when you returned?

"*A*. I didn't notice.

"*Professor Stangerson*. It was still closed. I remember it very well because I remarked aloud: 'Père Jacques could have opened the window while we were out.'

"*Q*. Very strange! You might recall, Professor, that Père Jacques, in his testimony, claimed to have opened that window during your absence, before he went out... So you returned to the laboratory at 6 p.m. and resumed work?

"*A*. Yes, Monsieur.

"*Q*. And you didn't leave the laboratory from that hour up to the moment when you went into the Yellow Room?

"*Professor Stangerson*. Neither my daughter nor I left the laboratory, Monsieur. We were engaged on work that was so pressing that we didn't dare waste a minute, and neglected everything else because of it.

"*Q*. Did you dine in the laboratory?

"*A*. Yes, for the same reason.

"*Q*. Are you accustomed to dining in the laboratory?

"*A*. No, we rarely eat there.

"*Q*. Could the perpetrator have known that you would be dining there that evening?

"*Professor Stangerson*. Good Heavens! I don't think so, Monsieur. It was only when we returned to the pavilion at 6 p.m. that I decided that my daughter and I would be dining there. At that moment, our gamekeeper came and detained me for a few minutes. He wanted me to go with him to look at a section of the grounds which I've decided to thin. I told him I didn't have the time to do it then and put it off until the next day. But since he was going by the Chateau, I asked him to tell our butler that we would be dining in the laboratory. After the gamekeeper left to deliver my message, I rejoined my daughter. I had given her my key to the pavilion, and she'd gone inside, leaving the key in the lock outside. When I walked into the laboratory, she was already at work.

"*Q*. Mademoiselle, at what hour did you go into the Yellow Room while your father continued to work?

"*A*. At midnight.

"*Q*. Did Père Jacques enter the Yellow Room during the evening?

"*A*. Yes, once. To close the shutters and light the lamp, as he did every night.

"*Q*. He saw nothing suspicious?

"*A*. He would have told us if he did. Père Jacques is a good man who's very attached to me.

"*Q*. Professor, do you confirm that Père Jacques didn't leave the laboratory? That he remained with you at all times?

"*Professor Stangerson*. I'm sure of it. I have no doubt about it.

"*Q*. Mademoiselle, when you entered the Yellow Room, you immediately locked and bolted the door... Why those precautions when you knew that your father and your servant were just outside? Were you afraid of something?

"*A*. My father would be returning to the Chateau and Père Jacques would be going to bed in the atyic. But, as a matter of fact, yes, I was afraid of something.

"*Q*. You were so afraid that you borrowed Père Jacques's revolver without telling him?

"*A*. That's correct. I didn't want to alarm anyone, especially since my fears might have been foolish ones.

"*Q*. What was it that you feared?

"*A*. I'm not sure how to explain it. For several nights, I thought I'd heard unusual sounds around the pavilion, sometimes footsteps, at other times, the cracking of branches, coming from both inside and outside the grounds. The night before the attack, when I didn't go to bed until 3 a.m. because of the banquet at the Elysée palace, I stood for a moment before my window, and I'm sure I saw shadows.

"*Q*. How many?

"*A*. Two. They were moving around the pond. Then, the Moon clouded over and they vanished. Normally, at this time of the year, I've moved back into my apartment at the Chateau for the winter; but this year, I decided that I wouldn't leave the pavilion until my father had finished his paper on the Dissociation of Matter for the Academy of Sciences. I didn't want that important work, which only required a few more days to be completed, to be delayed by a change in our daily habits. So you will understand that I didn't want to share my childish fears with my father, nor did I say a word to Père Jacques whom, I knew, wouldn't have been able to hold his tongue. Knowing that he had a revolver in his room, I took advantage of his absence and borrowed it, placing it in the drawer of my nightstand.

"*Q*. Do you know of any enemies you might have?

"*A*. None.

"*Q*. You understand, Mademoiselle, that this revelation, at this stage of the investigation, is rather suprising?

"*Professor Stangerson*. I must say, my child, I, too, find such precautions astonishing.

"*A*. I understand, but as I've just told you, I had been uneasy for two nights...

"*Professor Stangerson*. You should have told me, Mathilde! It's unforgivable! We could have avoided this horrible misfortune...

"*Q*. After you locked the door of the Yellow Room, did you go to bed?

"*A*. Yes. I was very tired, I fell asleep at once.

"*Q*. The lamp was still burning?

"*A*. Yes, but it gave very little light.

"*Q*. Tell us what happened next, Mademoiselle.

"*A*. I don't know how long I'd been asleep, but, suddenly, I awoke and cried out...

"*Professor Stangerson.* Yes, a horrible cry. 'Murder!' It still rings in my ears.

"*Q.* You screamed?

"*A.* Yes. A man was in my room. He sprang at me and tried to strangle me. I was about to pass out when I was able to reach into the drawer of my night table and grasp the revolver which I had loaded and placed there. At that moment, the man pushed me off the bed and brandished some kind of bludgeon over my head. I fired. But he still had time to strike a blow, a terrible blow. All that, Monsieur, happened in the blink of an eye. I'm afraid I don't remember anything else.

"*Q.* Nothing else? Do you have any idea how your attacker might have escaped from the Yellow Room?

"*A.* None whatsoever. I don't remember anything else. Generally, one doesn't notice what's going on when one is almost dying.

"*Q.* Was your attacker tall or short?

"*A.* I only saw a shadow, which seemed formidable.

"*Q.* You don't have any idea who it might have been?

"*A.* As I said, Monsieur, I don't know anything other than that a man threw himself upon me and I shot him. Nothing else."

That was the end of Mademoiselle Stangerson's interview. While it took place, Rouletabille and I waited patiently for Monsieur Darzac to return.

The Sorbonne Professor had followed the interview from a room next to Mademoiselle Stangerson's, and eventually came to recount it to my friend with great accuracy, an excellent memory, and a docile compliance which, frankly, surprised me. Thanks to some notes which he had hastily jotted down, he was able to quote, almost word for word, the questions and the answers.

It looked as if Darzac had become Rouletabille's personal secretary and he certainly behaved as if there was nothing he wouldn't do for him, acting virtually as his proxy.

The fact of the closed vestibule window struck Rouleta-bille just as it had Monsieur de Marquet. My friend asked Darzac to repeat carefully Mademoiselle Stangerson's account of how she and her father had spent their time on the day of the tragedy, just as she had recounted it to the Magistrate. The circumstance of the dinner in the laboratory seemed to interest him in the highest degree, and he had Darzac repeat it to him twice. He wanted to be sure that only the gamekeeper knew that the Professor and his daughter were going to be dining in the laboratory, and how he had come to learn of it.

When Darzac had finished, I said:

"That interview doesn't seem to bring us closer to a solution."

"I think it's even put us back," said Darzac.

"And yet it has shined a light upon the whole case," said Rouletabille, thoughtfully.

Chapter Nine
A Journalist and a Detective

The three of us returned to the pavilion. As we were about 100 meters away from the building, Rouletabille stopped and, pointing at a small clump of trees to our right, said:

"That's where the perpetrator hid before he entered the pavilion."

As there were other, nearly identical patches of trees between the great oaks, I asked Rouletabille why he had picked that one, rather than any of the others. He responded by pointing to the path, which ran close to that thicket, all the way to the door of the pavilion.

"As you can see, this path is topped with gravel," he said. "Our man *had to* take it, since we haven't found any footprints *going towards the pavilion* elsewhere on the soft ground. Our man didn't have wings. He had to walk, but he did so on gravel in order to leave no footmarks. This gravel path has, in fact, been trodden by many other feet, since it's the most direct route between the pavilion and the Chateau. As for this clump of trees, it's the sort of vegetation that remains leafy during the winter—laurels and fuchsias—and it provided the perpetrator with a good hiding place until it was time for him to make his way to the pavilion. It was while hiding in this thicket that he saw Professor Stangerson and his daughter, and later Père Jacques, leave the pavilion. Note that the gravel path extends almost to the vestibule window. Earlier, we saw a single footprint of our man *running parallel to the wall*. That proves that he only needed one stride from the path to reach the vestibule window, left open by Père Jacques. Then, he drew himself up by his hands and entered the vestibule."

"I suppose that's possible," I said.

"Suppose? Suppose?" cried Rouletabille, suddenly angry at my innocent observation. "Why do you say, 'I suppose'?"

I begged him not to be mad at me, but he was too upset to listen and said sarcastically that he admired the cautious skepticism with which some people—he meant me!—approach even the simplest problems, never risking anything by saying things like "I agree," or "'I disagree," but instead only "I suppose." He added that 'those people' could reach the same conclusion if God had forgotten to place a brain in their heads.

As I was clearly vexed, my young friend took me by the arm and told me that he hadn't meant for me to take his last comment personally, because he had a much higher opinion of me than that.

"But, Sainclair, you must admit that it's almost criminal to not reach a certainty, *when the facts leave you no alternative*. If I didn't reason as I did with respect to this gravel path," he went on, "I would have to postulate that our perpetrator used some kind of flying device! My dear fellow, the science of balloons and dirigibles isn't advanced enough for me to entertain the supposition that a murderer might drop from the clouds! So don't say that you 'suppose' that a thing is possible, *when it can't be otherwise*!"

Then, he continued:

"We know now how our man entered by the window, and when—during the five o'clock walk of the Professor and his daughter. Further, the presence in the laboratory of the chambermaid, who had just cleaned the Yellow Room, at 1:30 p.m., when the Professor and his daughter returned from their walk, enables us to determine that the perpetrator wasn't yet in the Yellow Room under the bed at that time, unless he was working in collusion with the chambermaid. What do you think, Monsieur Darzac?"

Darzac shook his head and assured us of the chambermaid's fidelity, stating that she was a thoroughly honest and devoted servant.

"Besides," he added, "at 5 p.m., Professor Stangerson went into the Yellow Room to fetch his daughter's hat."

"There is that, too," said Rouletabille.

"I admit that our man entered by the vestibule window at the time you say," I said, "but why did he shut it afterward? It was an act which would necessarily draw the attention of those who had left it open"

"It may be the window was not shut at once," replied the young reporter. *"But if he did shut it, it was because of the bend in the gravel path, 25 yards from the pavilion, and the three oaks that grow on that spot."*

"What do you mean by that?" asked Darzac, who had followed us and was hanging on Rouletabille's every word with almost breathless attention.

"I'll explain it all to you later, Monsieur, when I think the time is right to do so, but this might well be the most important thing I've said so far about this affair, *at least if my theory is correct.*"

"And what is your theory?"

"I'll never tell you if it turns out to be false. It's much too serious to speak of it lightly, as long as it's only a theory."

"Do you have, at least, an idea as to who Mathilde's attacker might be?"

"No, Monsieur Darzac, I don't know who he is, but don't be concerned, *I will find out the truth.*"

I observed that Darzac was deeply stirred by Rouletabille's confident statement, but in a way that caused me to suspect that he wasn't pleased by it. I wondered—assuming of course that I had read his thoughts correctly—if he was worried about discovering the identity of the man who had attacked his fiancée, why was he helping my friend to catch him? Rouletabille seemed to have come to the same conclusion, for he said, rather bluntly:

"Monsieur Darzac, you do want me to find out who the attacker was, don't you?"

"Oh! I'd like to kill that man with my own hands!" cried Mademoiselle Stangerson's fiancé, with a vehemence that surprised me.

"I believe you," said Rouletabille gravely, "but you haven't answered my question."

We were walking by the thicket which the young reporter had mentioned a minute earlier. I stepped inside and, at once, noticed footprints indicating that a man had been hiding there. Rouletabille had again been proven right.

"Of course!" he said, when I pointed the footmarks out. "We're dealing with an ordinary man, made of flesh and blood, with the same resources as we. It'll get sorted out eventually."

Having said this, he asked me for the paper pattern of the footprint which he had entrusted to me earlier and applied it to one of the footmarks in the thicket.

"There we go!" he said, rising.

I thought that he was now going to follow the perpetrator's trail after he escaped through the vestibule window, but instead, he took us far to the left, saying that it was useless to trample in the mud, since he was now sure of the direction taken by the criminal.

"He went along the wall there, then jumped over that hedge and ditch. See, just in front of that little path leading to the pond. That's the quickest way out."

"How do you know he went toward the pond?"

"Because Frederic Larsan spent all morning there. There must be some important clues there."

A few minutes later, we reached the pond.

It was a pool of marshy water, surrounded by reeds, on which floated several dead water lilies. Frederic the Great must have seen us approaching, but we probably didn't interest him enough, since he took little notice of us and continued to be stirring something which we couldn't see with his cane.

"Look!" said Rouletabille, "*here are the footprints of our fugitive!* They skirt the pond and finally disappear just before this path, which leads to the main road going to Epinay. From there, the man probably traveled to Paris."

"What makes you say that?" I asked, "since there are no footprints on that path?"

"What makes me say that, you ask? Why, this other set of footprints, which I expected to find!" he cried, pointing to the clearly defined footmarks left by an expensive pair of boots.

"See!" he said. Then, he called to Larsan: "Monsieur Larsan, were these expensive bootprints already here when the crime was discovered?"

"Yes, young man," replied the detective, without raising his head. "And we've taken careful impressions of them. As you can see, there are two sets of footprints: those coming and those going."

"And I see that our man had a bicycle!" cried the reporter.

After looking at the tire tracks, which, both coming and going, paralleled the set of expensive bootprints, I thought I was ready to express an opinion.

"The bicycle tracks might explain the disappearance of the perpetrator's footprints," I said. "He, in his cheap boots, just rode away on the bicycle. His accomplice, who wears expensive boots, had come to wait for him at the edge of the pond, bringing the bike with him. One might suppose that the perpetrator was working for the man with the expensive boots."

"No, not at all!" said Rouletabille, with an indulgent smile. "I fully expected to discover these bootprints from the start. They're my find; I'm not going to let you misinterpret it. They're the footprints of Mademoiselle Stangerson's attacker!"

"What about the cheap boots then?"

"They belong to the perpetrator as well."

"So there were two perpetrators?"

"No, only one man, working alone."

"Very good! Very good!" said Frederic Larsan from where he stood.

"Look!" continued the young reporter, showing us a section of the ground which had been disturbed by big and heavy heels. "Our man sat here and took off his big, cheap boots, which he had worn only for the purpose of misleading the police. Then, *he stood up on his usual boots*. After that, taking

80

his cheap boots with him, he quietly made his way to the main road, holding his bicycle in his hand, because he couldn't ride it on this rough path. What proves it is the lightness of the impression made by the wheels despite the softness of the ground. If a man had been riding the bicycle, the wheels would have sunk more deeply into the soil. So, you see, Sainclair, there was only one man here, the perpetrator, on foot."

"Bravo! Bravo!" cried Larsan again.

Then, he came suddenly toward us and, planting himself before Monsieur Darzac, said to him:

"If we had a bicycle here, we could demonstrate the correctness of this young man's reasoning, Monsieur Darzac, *would you know if there is one at the Chateau?*"

"No!" replied Darzac. "There isn't. I took mine back to Paris four days ago, the last time I came to Glandier before the crime."

"That's a pity!" replied Larsan, rather coldly. Then, turning toward Rouletabille, he added: "If we continue at this rate, we'll both arrive at the same conclusion soon. Have you any idea as to how the murderer got away from the Yellow Room?"

"Yes," said my young friend. "I do have an idea."

"So have I," said Larsan, "and I'd bet it's the same as yours. There are no two ways of looking at this case. I'm waiting for the arrival of my superior officer before presenting my report to the Investigating Magistrate."

"Ah! Is the Chief of the Sûreté coming here?"

"Yes, this afternoon. He's coming for the reconstruction in the laboratory before the Magistrate. All those who have played any part, big or small, in this tragedy have been summoned to attend. It will be very interesting. It's a pity you won't be there."

"Oh, but I will," said Rouletabille confidently.

"Really? You're truly an extraordinary fellow—for your age, I mean!" replied the detective in a somewhat ironic tone. "You'd make a wonderful detective, if only you had a little more method, if you didn't follow your instincts and those bumps on your forehead. As I've noted several times in the past, Monsieur Rouletabille, you reason too much. You don't allow yourself to be guided by only your observations. What did you think about the blood-stained handkerchief and the bloody handprint on the wall of the Yellow Room? You have seen the handprint and I, only the handkerchief. What conclusions did you draw?"

"Easy!" said Rouletabille, somewhat surprised. "The perpetrator *was wounded in the hand* by Mademoiselle Stangerson's revolver!"

"Ah! A purely instinctual observation! Take care, Monsieur Rouletabille, you're much too logical. Logic will end up playing tricks on you if you follow it blindly. There are times when you must challenge it, almost transcend it... You're right when you say that Mademoiselle Stangerson fired her revolver, but you're just as wrong when you say that she wounded the murderer in the hand."

"I am sure of it," cried Rouletabille.

Larsan, imperturbable, interrupted him:

"That's the result of a faulty or incomplete observation! The examination of the handkerchief, the numerous small drops of blood on the floor, drops which I determined *were under the footprints of the perpetrator when he walked*, prove to me that the perpetrator wasn't wounded at all, Monsieur Rouletabille. *He bled from his nose!*"

Larsan spoke very seriously. I couldn't refrain from uttering an exclamation.

Rouletabille looked gravely at the detective, who did the same. Then, Larsan concluded:

"The man first bled into his hand and handkerchief, then he swiped that hand against the wall. The fact is very important," he added, "*because there is no need for him to be wounded in the hand in order to be guilty*."

Rouletabille seemed to be thinking deeply.

"There is something else, Monsieur Larsan," he finally said, "that is much more dangerous than following logic blindly. It is the predisposition of some detectives to twist logic to make it serve their own, preconceived notions. I know that you already have your own theory about the murderer's identity. Don't bother denying it. But it requires that the perpetrator shouldn't have been wounded in the hand, otherwise it collapses. So you've looked and found another possibility. It's dangerous, very dangerous, to start from a preconceived idea and then to find the evidence you need to back it up. That method might lead you astray. Watch out, Monsieur Larsan, you're on a path that's taking you right into the field of judicial error!"

With his hands in his pockets, an ironic smile and a malicious look in his eyes, Rouletabille was challenging Frederic the Great.

Larsan silently contemplated that young reporter who claimed to be better than he. Then, shrugging, he bowed to us and strode away, hitting the stones in his path *with his long cane.*

Rouletabille watched him walk away, and then turned toward us, his face joyous and triumphant.

"I shall beat him!" he cried. "I shall beat Larsan at his own game, clever as he is! I shall beat them all, because I, Rouletabille, am smarter than all of them! And as for Larsan, the famous, the illustrious, the wonderful Frederic the Great, excuse me, but he's got a turnip for a brain, yes, a turnip!"

And he began a small triumphant gig, but suddenly stopped right in the middle of a step. My eyes followed his gaze; they were fixed on Darzac, who was looking fearfully at the impression left on the path by his feet next to the expensive bootmarks. *They were exactly the same!*

We thought the Sorbonne Professor was about to faint. His eyes, bulging with terror, avoided ours, while his right hand, with a nervous gesture, twitched at the beard that covered his honest, gentle, and now despairing face. Finally, he regained some of his composure, bowed to us, and said, in a changed voice, that he was obliged to return to the Chateau.

"The Devil!" exclaimed Rouletabille, after Darzac had left.

My friend seemed to be deeply concerned. He tore a sheet of paper from his notebook and, as he had done earlier, cut out the shape of the perpetrator's expensive bootmarks with his scissors. Then, he fitted this new pattern over Darzac's footprints. The two were indeed exactly alike.

Rising, Rouletabille exclaimed again: "The Devil!"

I didn't dare say a word because I realized the grave turmoil that must have been brewing under "those bumps" on my friend's forehead.

"And yet, I believe Monsieur Darzac to be an honest man," said Rouletabille with finality.

He then led me on the road to the Auberge du Donjon, which we could see on the highway, by the side of a small clump of trees.

Chapter Ten
"I'd Like Some Blood Pudding"

The Auberge du Donjon didn't look very impressive, but I like old buildings with their wooden beams blackened with age and the smoke of their fireplaces. I like inns dating back to the days of the stagecoaches, half-crumbling structures that will soon exist only in our memories. They belong to the past, they're part and parcel of History, they remind us of the folk-tales of those bygone days when highwaymen roamed our countryside and wild adventures could be had just outside our city walls.

I saw at once that the Auberge du Donjon was at least two centuries old, perhaps even older. Bits of stones and mortar had come loose from the building's sturdy wood frame, the X- and V-shaped beams of which still firmly supported the aging roof, which had nevertheless slipped forward a little, like a cap on a drunkard's head. Over the front door, a signboard was swinging creakily as a result of the Autumnal wind. A local artist had decorated it with the picture of a tower with a pointed roof and a lantern, just like that of Glandier. Under it, on the threshold, stood a man with a crabby face, seemingly lost in dark thoughts, at least judging from the wrinkles on his forehead and the knitting of his furry brow.

When we approached, he deigned to take notice of us and asked, in a gruff tone, whether we wanted anything. He was obviously the unfriendly landlord of this otherwise charming inn. As we expressed the desire to have lunch, he told us that he had no food, all the while looking at us suspiciously.

"You don't have to worry about us," Rouletabille said. "We're not with the police."

"I'm not afraid of the police!" replied the man. "I'm not afraid of anyone!"

With a discreet gesture, I tried to make Rouletabille understand that maybe we should try our luck elsewhere, but my friend was determined to go into that inn, and managed to slip by the man.

"Come on," he said from the common room. "It's very nice in here."

A hearty fire was blazing in the fireplace. We held out our hands to warm them up, as one could already feel winter approaching. The room was quite large, furnished with two heavy tables, some stools, and a counter decorated with rows of bottles of wines and liqueurs. Three windows looked out onto the road. A brightly-colored poster on the wall displayed a pretty young Parisienne naughtily tipping her glass to promote the aperitive virtues of a new brand of vermouth. On the mantelpiece of the fireplace, the innkeeper had displayed an impressive collection of earthenware pots, stone jugs and ceramic dishes.

"That's a fine fire for roasting a chicken," said Rouletabille.

"I haven't got any chicken," said the innkeeper. "Not even a wretched rabbit."

"I know," said my friend in an ironic tone which surprised me. "*Then I'd like some blood pudding.*"

I confess I didn't understand what Rouletabille meant by what he had just said, nor why the innkeeper, as soon as he heard it, uttered an oath, quickly stifled it, and began to obey my friend as diligently as Monsieur Darzac had done, when he had heard the words: "*The presbytery has lost none of its charm, nor the garden its glow.*" Obviously, Rouletabille knew how to make people understand him by using utterly incomprehensible phrases. I said as much to him, but he merely smiled. I would have preferred some kind of explanation, but he put a finger to his lips, which meant not only that he had decided to remain silent, but that he was asking me to do the same.

Meanwhile, the innkeeper had pushed open a small side door and called to somebody to bring half a dozen eggs and a steak. The order was quickly delivered by a pretty young woman with beautiful blonde hair and large, soft eyes, who looked at us with curiosity.

"Get out!" said the innkeeper roughly. "And if the Green Man comes, don't let me see you!"

She disappeared. Rouletabille took the eggs, which had been brought in a bowl, and the steak, which was on a dish, placed them carefully beside him in the fireplace, unhooked a frying pan and a gridiron, and began to beat up our omelette before proceeding to grill our steak. He then ordered two bottles of cider, and seemed to take as little notice of our host as the latter had done of us earlier. But now, the man was looking at Rouletabille in wonder and at me with undisguised anxiety. He let us do our own cooking and set our table near one of the windows.

Suddenly, I heard him mutter:

"Ah! Here he comes!"

His face changed, now expressing fierce hatred. He went and glued himself to one of the windows, watching the road. I didn't need to draw Rouletabille's attention; he had already left our omelette and joined the innkeeper at the window. I went with him.

A man dressed entirely in green corduroy, his head covered with a huntsman's cap of the same color, smoking a pipe, was walking leisurely on the road. He carried a rifle over his shoulder. His movements displayed an almost aristocratic ease. He looked to be about 45, because his hair and his moustache were peppered with grey. He was remarkably handsome and wore glasses. As he passed near the inn, he seemed to hesitate, as if he was considering whether or not to enter. He gave a glance towards us, took a few puffs of his pipe, and then resumed his walk at the same nonchalant pace.

Rouletabille and I looked at our host. His flashing eyes, his clenched fists, his trembling mouth, advertised his tumultuous feelings all too well.

"He did well to not come in here today!" hissed the innkeeper.

"Who is he?" asked Rouletabille, returning to his omelette.

"The Green Man," growled the innkeeper. "Don't you know him? If so, all the better for you! He isn't a good acquaintance to make. He's Monsieur Stangerson's gamekeeper."

"You don't appear to like him very much," said the reporter, pouring his omelette into the frying pan.

"Nobody here likes him, Monsieur. He's a conceited man who must have been rich himself once, but lost it all, and now he blames everyone for the fact that he's been forced to become a servant to make a living. Because a gamekeeper is just another servant, right? Upon my word, one would say that he is the master of Glandier, and that all its lands and woods belong to him. He won't let a poor creature eat a morsel of bread on the grass—his grass!"

"How often does he come here?"

"Too often! But I'm going to make it clear to him that he isn't welcome here. Until about a month ago, he wasn't bothering me. It was as if my inn didn't exist! He had no time for it! He preferred paying court to the pretty landlady at the Auberge des Trois Lys in Saint-Michel. But when the bloom was off that rose, he had to find himself another watering hole. He's a bad fellow, a rake, a skirt chaser, a scoundrel! There isn't an honest man around who like him. Why, the caretakers at the Chateau can't stand the very sight of him!"

"The caretakers are decent people, then, Monsieur?"

"Call me Père Mathieu, Monsieur; everyone else does. And yes, they are, as true as my name's Mathieu. I believe them to be honest."

"And yet, they've been arrested?"

"What does that prove? But I don't want to get mixed up in other people's business..."

"What do you think of the attempt on Mademoiselle Stangerson's life?"

"She's a good girl that one, kind, much loved by everyone... What do I think of the attempt on her life?"

"Yes."

"Nothing… And many things besides… But that's nobody's business."

"Not even mine?" insisted Rouletabille.

The innkeeper looked at him sideways and said gruffly:

"Not even yours."

The omelette was ready. We sat down at table and were silently eating when the door was pushed open and an old woman, dressed in rags, leaning on a stick, her head doddering, her white hair hanging loosely over her wrinkled forehead, appeared on the threshold.

"Ah! Mère Angenoux! It's been a long since I've seen you," said our host.

"I've been very ill, very nearly dying," said the old woman. "Would you have any scraps for my Holy Beast, Père Mathieu?"

And she came in, followed by a cat larger than I ever thought could exist. The beast looked at us and gave such a heart-wrenching meow that I shuddered. I had never heard such a lugubrious cry.

As if he'd been drawn by the cat's meow, a man entered right behind the old woman. It was the Green Man. He saluted by tipping his cap and seated himself at the table next to ours.

"A glass of cider, Père Mathieu," he said.

When the Green Man had come in, the innkeeper had reacted violently, but he quickly regained his composure and said:

"I haven't got any cider. I served my last two bottles to these gentlemen."

"Then give me a glass of white wine," said the Green Man, without showing the least surprise.

"I haven't got any white wine either. I'm out of everything."

Then Père Mathieu repeated in a surly voice:

"I haven't got anything to drink."

"How is Madame Mathieu?"

Upon hearing this question, Père Mathieu clenched his fists and rushed towards his nemesis, looking so angry that I became concerned that he might hit him. But instead, he replied:

"She's quite well, thank you."

So the young woman with the large, soft eyes whom we'd seen earlier was the wife of this loathsome, ill-mannered brute, whose jealousy seemed only to emphasize his physical ugliness.

Slamming the door behind him, the innkeeper left the room. Mère Angenoux was still standing, leaning on her stick, the cat at her feet.

The Green Man asked her:

"Have you been ill, Mère Angenoux? We haven't seen you for a week."

"Yes, Monsieur. I've only been able to get up three times to go to pray to Sainte Genevieve, our good patroness, but I've spent the rest of my time lying on my cot, with no one to care for me but my Holy Beast!"

"She hasn't left your bedside?"

"No, neither by day nor by night."

"Are you sure of that?"

"As I am of Our Lord in Heaven."

"Then how was it, Mère Angenoux, that, during night of the attack on Mademoiselle Stangerson, everyone heard the cry of your Holy Beast?"

Mère Angenoux planted herself in front of the gamekeeper and struck the floor with her stick.

"I don't know anything about that," she said. "But shall I tell you something? There are no two cats in the world that cry like that. Well, on that night, I, too, heard the cry of the Holy Beast outside—and yet, she was there, lying on my knees, and she didn't meow once, I swear. I crossed myself when I heard that cry, just as if I'd heard the Devil himself!"

I was looking at the gamekeeper when he asked that last question, and I am much mistaken if I didn't detect an evil smile on his lips.

At that moment, the noise of a loud quarrel reached us. We even thought we heard the dull sound of blows, as if someone was being beaten. The Green Man quickly rose and hurried to the side door; but it was opened by the innkeeper who appeared, and said:

"Don't alarm yourself, Monsieur. It's only my wife. She's got a toothache." And he laughed. Then he added: "Mère Angenoux, here are some scraps for your cat."

He held out a bag to the old woman, who took it eagerly and went out, closely followed by her beast.

"Then you won't serve me?" asked the Green Man.

Père Mathieu no longer tried to contain the expression of hatred on his face.

"I've got nothing for you! Nothing! Get out!"

The Green Man quietly refilled his pipe, lit it, bowed to us, and went out. No sooner was he over the threshold than Père Mathieu slammed the door behind him. Then, he turned toward us. His eyes were bloodshot and he was frothing at the mouth. He shook his fist at the door which he had just shut on the man he so obviously hated.

"I don't know who you really are," he said, "or how you know the words '*I'd like some blood pudding*,' but if you're looking for the man who almost killed the Mademoiselle at the Chateau, you need look no further: it's him!"

After speaking these words, Père Mathieu immediately left. Rouletabille returned to the fireplace and said:

"Now we'll grill our steak. How do you like the cider? It's a little tart, but I like it that way."

We saw no more of Père Mathieu that day. Total silence reigned at the inn when we left, after placing five francs on the table in payment for our lunch.

Rouletabille at once set off on a three mile walk around Professor Stangerson's estate. He halted for some ten minutes at a crossroad where the main road from Epinay to Corbeil intersected with a smaller road, black with soot, located near some charcoal-burners' huts in the forest of Sainte Genevieve. There, he told me that the perpetrator had certainly passed that way, before entering the grounds and concealing himself in the little clump of trees because of the sooty marks he had left behind with his cheap boots.

"So you don't think that the gamekeeper was involved in this business?" I asked.

"We shall see about that later," Rouletabille replied. "For the moment, I'm not interested in what the innkeeper said. The man was obviously obsessed by his hatred. But I didn't choose to have lunch at the Auberge du Donjon because of the Green Man."

After that, Rouletabille, taking great precautions, approached the small house which stood next to the main gate and was the home of Monsieur and Madame Bernier, the caretakers who had been arrested earlier. I followed him. With the skill of an acrobat, he got into the house through an upper window which had been left open. He came out ten minutes later, saying only "Good grief!"—an expression which, in his mouth, could mean many things.

We were about to take the road leading to the Chateau, when a considerable stir at the gate attracted our attention. A carriage had just arrived and some people were coming from the Chateau to meet it. Rouletabille pointed out to me a gentleman who descended from it.

"That's the Chief of the Sûreté" he said. "Now we shall see what Monsieur Larsan has up his sleeve, and whether he is so much cleverer than everybody else."

The carriage of the Chief of the Sûreté was followed by three other vehicles containing reporters, who also sought to enter the estate. But the two gendarmes stationed at the gate had evidently received orders to refuse admission to anybody. The Chief of the Sûreté calmed their impatience by promising to give the press, that very evening, all the information he could, without interfering with the judicial investigation.

Chapter Eleven
In Which Frederic Larsan Explains How the Perpetrator Was Able To Leave the Yellow Room

Among the mass of papers, legal documents, memoirs, and newspaper cuttings which I have collected relating to the Mystery of the Yellow Room, there is one particularly interesting piece. It is a report of the reconstruction that took place that afternoon in the laboratory of Professor Stangerson for Monsieur Dax, the Chief of the Sûreté.

This report was written by Monsieur Maleine, the Investigating Magistrate's clerk and court recorder, who, like his superior, entertained literary ambitions. This piece was to be included in a book of his memoirs, to be entitled *My Investigations*, which was never published. A copy of it was handed to me by Monsieur Maleine himself some time after the astonishing conclusion of this case, surely unique in judicial history.

This memoir isn't simply a dry transcription of questions and answers, like the previous document; Monsieur Maleine often interspersed his report with his own personal reflections, which makes it even more interesting.

Monsieur Maleine's Memoirs

For the last hour, Monsieur de Marquet, the Investigating Magistrate, and I had been standing inside the Yellow Room in the company of the builder who had constructed the pavilion according to Professor Stangerson's designs. The man had brought a workman with him. Monsieur de Marquet had the walls entirely laid bare, that is to say, he had them stripped of the saffron-colored paper which had covered them. Random blows of a pick satisfied him of the absence of any kind of secret passage. The floor and the ceiling were equally thoroughly probed. We found nothing. There was nothing to be

94

found. Monsieur de Marquet appeared to be delighted by the results and never tired of telling the builder:

"What a case! What a case! Mark my words, Monsieur, we'll never find out how the perpetrator was able to get out of here!"

The Magistrate was beaming because he genuinely enjoyed the puzzle, but then, he remembered that it was his duty to try to find an answer to it. So he called the Brigadier in charge of the gendarmes.

"Brigadier," he said, "will you please go to the Chateau and ask Professor Stangerson and Monsieur Darzac to join us in the laboratory? Bring Père Jacques too, and have two of your men fetch the caretakers."

Five minutes later, everyone stood in the laboratory. The Chief of the Sûreté, who had just arrived at Glandier, joined us. I was seated at Professor Stangerson's desk, ready to take notes, when Monsieur de Marquet made the following speech—as original as it was unexpected:

"With your permission, gentlemen, since police questioning hasn't led us anywhere so far, we will, for this once, abandon that traditional method. I'm not going to have you appear before me one at a time. Instead, we'll all remain here together, just as we are: Professor Stangerson, Monsieur Darzac, Père Jacques, Monsieur and Madame Bernier, Monsieur Dax, my clerk and I. And we'll be on the same footing, as it were. The caretakers, for this occasion, may forget that they're under arrest. We're just going to have a conversation... Yes, a conversation. Since we're at the scene of the crime, what else could we talk about but that crime! So let's talk, freely, intelligently or otherwise, as long as we all speak our minds. There's no need to worry about formalities, since they've been useless so far. I'll start with a prayer to the God of Chance to inspire our conversation. Let's begin..."

Then, passing before me, he said in a low voice:

"What do you think of my speech, eh? What a scene! Could you have ever thought of something like that? I'll get an entire act out of it in my next vaudeville."

And he rubbed his hands together gleefully.

I looked at Professor Stangerson. The hope he had felt after talking with the doctor, who believed that Mademoiselle Stangerson would recover from her wounds, had not erased from his noble features the signs of the great suffering which he had endured.

That man had believed his daughter was dead, and he was still shaken over it. His soft, clear blue eyes expressed only endless sorrow. I had had many opportunities in the past to see Professor Stangerson at public ceremonies, and I had always been struck by his gaze, pure as that of a child—the dreamlike, sublime and mystical stare of geniuses and madmen.

On those occasions, his daughter had always been at his side. It was said they were inseparable and they had been sharing the same labors for many years. This virginal young woman, who was 35 at the time, although she looked not a day older than 30, had devoted her entire life to science. Many admired the beauty of her proud features which remained intact, without a wrinkle, victorious over time and passions. Who could have predicted that, one day, I would be seated at her bedside taking notes, that I would see her, on the point of death, painfully recounting the most monstrous and most mysterious crime of my entire career? Who could have predicted that I would be, that very afternoon, listening to her despairing father trying in vain to explain how his daughter's assailant had escaped? Why bury yourselves with work in an obscure retreat in the depths of woods, if it won't protect you from the vicissitudes of life and death usually reserved for those who succumb to the charms of city life?[11]

"Now, Professor Stangerson," said Monsieur de Marquet, commandingly, "would you mind placing yourself exact-

---

[11] I will remind the reader that I only copied Monsieur Maleine's memoirs and that I did not attempt to alter his emphatic and somewhat grandiloquent prose style (*Note from the Author.*)

ly where you were when Mademoiselle Stangerson left you to go to her room?"

The Professor rose and went to stand about 20 inches away from the door of the Yellow Room. He then said in an even voice, without any trace of emotion—a voice which I can only describe as a dead voice:

"I was here. At about 11 p.m., after I had conducted a small chemical experiment in the furnace, I moved my desk to this spot, because Père Jacques, who had spent the entire evening cleaning my instruments, needed the extra space. My daughter had been working at the same desk as I. When she left to go to her room, after kissing me and bidding Père Jacques good night, she had to squeeze, with some difficulty, between the desk and the door. So I was indeed quite close to the scene of the crime."

"What happened to the desk?" I asked, following my superior's orders and interjecting myself into the conversation. "When you heard the cry of 'murder,' followed by the gunshots, what did you do with the desk?"

Père Jacques answered:

"We pushed it back against the wall there, close to where it is right now, in order to get to the door."

I followed up my line of reasoning, even though I regarded it only as a weak hypothesis:

"With the desk so close to the door, might not a man coming out of the Yellow Room be able to hide under it and thus not be noticed?"

"You're forgetting," interrupted Professor Stangerson wearily, "that my daughter had locked and bolted her door, *that it had remained fastened, that we vainly tried to force it open when we heard the noise of the struggle between the murderer and my poor child, and that we heard her cries as she was being strangled by the very fingers which left their red mark upon her throat.* Quick as the attack was, we were no less quick in getting to this door which was the only thing separating us from the tragedy."

I stood up and went to take a closer look at the door, which I examined with the greatest care. Then I returned to my seat feeling disappointed.

"If the lower panel of the door," I said, "*could be removed without the whole door being necessarily opened*, our problem would be solved. But, unfortunately, I can confirm, after an examination of the door, that it's made of a single piece of oak. It's still massively strong, even after the damage inflicted upon it by those who forced it open."

"Yes," said Père Jacques. "It's an old door which we brought from the Chateau. They don't make them like that anymore. We had to use this iron bar to pry it open, the four of us. Even Madame Bernier, brave woman that she is, helped us. It pains me to see her and her husband under arrest," he added for the Magistrate's benefit.

Père Jacques had no sooner uttered these words of support and protest than tears and lamentations broke out from the two caretakers. I never saw any accused cry more bitterly. I felt quite nauseated.[12] Even if they were innocent, I couldn't understand how they could show such a lack of dignity in the face of misfortune. A composed bearing at such times is much better than tears and groans, which, more often than not, are feigned and hypocritical.

"Enough sniveling," said Monsieur de Marquet. "In your own interest, tell us what you were doing under the windows of the pavilion when your mistress was being attacked, for you were close to the pavilion when Père Jacques met you."

"We were coming to help!" they whined.

"If only we could lay hands on that villain, we'd teach him a lesson he'd never forget!" the woman gurgled between her sobs.

As before, we were unable to get a sensible statement out of them. They persisted in their denials and swore, by God and all the Saints in Heaven, that they were in bed when they heard the sound of the gunshot.

---

[12] *Sic!*

"It wasn't one, but two shots that were fired!" said the Magistrate, annoyed. "Don't you realize that you're lying? If you'd heard one shot, you would have heard the other."

"But, Monsieur, we only heard the second shot. We must've been asleep when the first shot was fired."

"I'm sure that two shots were fired," said Père Jacques. "My revolver was fully loaded. We found two cartridges, two bullets, and heard two shots behind the door. Isn't that right, Professor?"

"Yes," replied the Professor. "There were indeed two shots, one dull, the other sharp and ringing."

"Why do you persist in lying?" said Monsieur de Marquet to the caretakers. "Do you think the police are fools? Everything indicates that you were out and near the pavilion at the time of the attempted murder. What were you doing there? You don't want to answer? Your very silence is proof of your complicity. And as far as I am concerned," he added, turning to Professor Stangerson, "I can only explain the escape of the perpetrator by the fact that he was helped by these two. As soon as the door was forced open, while you were busy taking care of your wounded daughter, Monsieur Bernier and his wife facilitated the perpetrator's flight. He must have hid behind them, reached the window in the vestibule, and sprang out into the grounds. Monsieur Bernier then closed the window behind him and fastened the shutters, *because they couldn't have closed and fastened themselves*. That's my theory. If anyone here has any other idea, let him state it."

Professor Stangerson intervened:

"What you say is impossible, Monsieur. I don't believe in either the guilt or the complicity of my caretakers, even though I confess I don't understand what they were doing in the grounds at that late hour of the night. I say it's impossible, purely because Madame Bernier held the lamp and didn't move from the threshold of the Yellow Room, and also because, as soon as the door was forced open, I threw myself on my knees beside my daughter. *Therefore, no one could have left or entered the room by that door without stepping over her body and pushing me out of the way!* Finally, it's also imposs-ible because Père Jacques and Monsieur Bernier could cast a single glance around the room and under the bed, as I had done myself on entering, and see that there was nobody there, except my daughter lying on the floor."

"What do you think, Monsieur Darzac?" asked the Magi-strate. "You've said nothing so far."

Monsieur Darzac replied that he had no thoughts on this matter.

Monsieur Dax, the Chief of the Sûreté, who, until then, had only been listening and looking at the room, deigned to speak at last:

"While we look for the perpetrator, we should also find out what his motive was. Perhaps that might advance us a lit-tle?"

"Certainly," said Monsieur de Marquet. "The attempt on Mademoiselle Stangerson's life seems to me to have been motivated by strong passion. The footprints left behind by the perpetrator, the common handkerchief and the awful béret indicate that he must belong to one of the lower classes of society. Perhaps the caretakers might have more light to throw on this subject…"

Turning towards Professor Stangerson, the Chief of the Sûreté asked in that cold tone which, I think, is the mark of superior intelligences and strong characters:

"I understand that your daughter was shortly to have been married?"

The Professor looked sadly at Monsieur Darzac.

"Yes, to my friend here, whom I should have been happy to call my son, Monsieur Robert Darzac."

"I gather that Mademoiselle Stangerson is feeling much better and is recovering from her wounds. So the marriage is presumably only delayed, isn't that right, Professor?" insisted the Chief of the Sûreté.

"I certainly hope so.

"What! Do you have any doubts about it?"

Professor Stangerson did not reply. Monsieur Darzac appeared agitated. Being very observant, I noticed that his hand was trembling a little as he fingered his watch chain. Monsieur Dax coughed, as did Monsieur de Marquet, a sign that he was embarrassed.

"You understand, Professor," he said, "that in an affair as confusing as this one, we cannot neglect any fact. We must know everything concerning the victim, even the smallest and seemingly most insignificant details. So why do you doubt that this marriage will take place, now that we know that Mademoiselle Stangerson will surely recover? You expressed a hope, but hope also implies doubt. So I ask you again: why do you doubt?"

Professor Stangerson made a visible effort to regain his composure.

"You're right, of course, Monsieur," he said finally. "It is best that you should know something which, if I were to conceal it, might appear significant. Monsieur Darzac agrees with me on this."

Monsieur Darzac, whose pallor at that moment seemed altogether abnormal to me, made a sign of assent. In my opinion, he made that sign because he was unable to speak.

"I want you to know," continued Professor Stangerson, "that my daughter swore never to leave me, and has stuck firmly to her oath despite all my entreaties urging her to marry, as is my duty. We've known Monsieur Darzac for many years. He loves Mathilde, and I believed that she loves him, since she recently consented to marry him, something which I desire with all my heart. I'm an old man, Monsieur, and it was a great reassurance for to me to know that, after I had gone, my daughter would have someone at her side who loved her, and who would help her in continuing our common work. I love and esteem Monsieur Darzac, both for his greatness of heart and for his devotion to science. However, two days before the tragedy, for a reason unknown to me, my daughter told me that she would not marry him."

A long silence followed Professor Stangerson's words. It was a moment fraught with apprehension.

"Did Mademoiselle Stangerson give you any explanation? Did she tell you what her reason was?" asked Monsieur Dax.

"She told me that she was now too old to marry, that she had waited too long. She said she had given much thought to the matter and, while she had a great esteem, even affection, for Monsieur Darzac, she felt it would be better if things remained as they were. She would be happy, she said, to see the relations between ourselves and Monsieur Darzac become closer, but only on the understanding that there would be no more talk of marriage."

"That is very strange!" muttered Monsieur Dax.

"Very strange indeed!" echoed Monsieur de Marquet.

"You'll certainly not find any motive there, Monsieur Dax," Monsieur Stangerson said with a cold smile.

"In any case, the motive doesn't appear to have been a robbery!" said the Chief of the Sûreté impatiently.

"I'm entirely convinced of that!" said the Investigating Magistrate.

At that moment, the door of the laboratory opened. The Brigadier entered and handed a card to Monsieur de Marquet. The Magistrate read it and exclaimed:

"This is really too much!"

"What is it?" asked Monsieur Dax.

"It's the card of that young reporter from *L'Epoque*, Joseph Rouletabille. It has these words written on it: 'One of the motives of the crime was robbery.' "

The Chief of the Sûreté smiled.

"Ah! Young Rouletabille! I've heard of him. He's considered rather clever. Let him in."

Monsieur Rouletabille was allowed to enter. I had made his acquaintance that morning in the train to Epinay-sur-Orge. He had sneaked, against my will, into our compartment. I should say that his manners, the arrogance with which he pretended to know what was going on in an affair where even the

101

best investigators were puzzled, hadn't endeared him to me. I don't like journalists. They interfere and meddle and are the type of writers that should be avoided like the plague. They think that everything is permissible and they respect nothing. Grant them the least favor, allow them even to talk to you, and you never can tell what kind of trouble will ensue. This one appeared to be scarcely 20, and the effrontery with which he had dared to question us and discuss the case had made him particularly odious to me. Further, he had a way of expressing himself that made us feel as if he were making fun of us. I know quite well that *L'Epoque* is an influential paper, with which one must stay on good terms, but it shouldn't allow itself to be represented by such novice reporters.

Monsieur Rouletabille entered the laboratory, bowed to us, and waited for Monsieur de Marquet to ask him to explain his presence.

"You claim, Monsieur," said the Magistrate, "that you know the motive for the crime, and that, despite all evidence to the contrary, it was robbery?"

"No, Monsieur, I don't claim that. I didn't say that robbery was *the* motive for the crime, *and I don't believe it was.*"

"Then, what is the meaning of this card?"

"It means that robbery was *one of the motives* for the crime."

"What makes you think that?"

"If you will be kind enough to follow me, I will show you…"

The young man asked us to follow him into the vestibule, which we did. There, he led us towards the lavatory and asked Monsieur de Marquet to kneel beside him. This lavatory was lit through a glass door by the vestibule's lights. When that door was open, enough light went inside to light it perfectly. Monsieur de Marquet and Monsieur Rouletabille knelt down on the threshold, and the young man pointed to a spot on the tiles.

"The floor of this lavatory hasn't been washed by Père Jacques for some time," he said. "It's obvious because of the layer of dust on the tiles. Now, notice here these two large footprints and the sooty residue they left behind—the same as the perpetrator's footprints in the Yellow Room. That residue is charcoal dust from the road which one must take in order to get from Epinay to Glandier through the woods. You must know that there is a little village of charcoal-burners there, who make large quantities of charcoal. What the murderer did was to come here during the afternoon, when the pavilion was empty, and rob it."

"What robbery? Where do you see any signs of a robbery? What proves to you that a robbery was committed here?" we all said at once.

"What put me on the right track..." replied the journalist.

"...Was this!" interrupted Monsieur de Marquet, still on his knees.

"Exactly!" said Rouletabille.

And Monsieur de Marquet explained that there was on the dusty tiles, next to the footprints, the impression, freshly-made, of a heavy rectangular parcel, the string marks of which were still clearly visible.

"You have been here, then, Monsieur Rouletabille?" said the Magistrate. "I thought I had given strict orders to Père Jacques, who was in charge of the pavilion, not to allow anyone on the premises."

"Don't scold Père Jacques, I came here with Monsieur Darzac."

"Really?" said Monsieur de Marquet, unhappy. He cast a side-glance at Monsieur Darzac, who remained perfectly silent.

"When I saw the impression of that parcel next to the footprints, I had no doubt as to the robbery," replied Monsieur Rouletabille. "The thief didn't bring a parcel with him. He made it here to carry off his loot, then he put it in this corner intending to take it with him when he made his escape. *He also left his boots beside the parcel.* As you can see, there are no footprints leading to or from the boots. Further, the two footprints are next to each other, *resting on the floor, clearly made by two empty boots just placed there.* That accounts for the fact that the murderer left no footprints when he fled from the Yellow Room, not in the laboratory, nor in the vestibule. After entering the Yellow Room *in his boots*, the perpetrator took them off, either because they bothered him, or because he wished to make as little noise as possible. The marks left by him *coming through* the vestibule and the laboratory were subsequently washed away by Père Jacques. This leads us to the conclusion that the perpetrator entered the pavilion through the vestibule's open window during Père Jacques' first absence, before he washed the floors at 5:30 p.m.

"Having taken off his boots, which must have somehow impeded him, our villain then carried them in his hand to the lavatory and left them there, on the threshold, since we can't find any other footprints in the dust: no traces of bare feet, feet covered with socks, or *wearing another kind of shoes*. He left his boots next to the parcel he had prepared. By that time, the robbery had been accomplished. Our man then returned to the Yellow Room and slipped under the bed, where the mark of his body is still perfectly visible on the carpet, which is slightly creased and rumpled on that very spot. Bits of straw, recently broken, also bear witness to the perpetrator's presence under the bed."

"Yes, yes, we know all that," said Monsieur de Marquet.

"That return trip from the lavatory to hide under the bed of the Yellow Room," continued the amazing young reporter, "proves that robbery wasn't *the only motive* behind our man's visit. Don't tell me that he might have had to find refuge there in a hurry because, through the vestibule window, he might have seen or heard Père Jacques, Professor Stangerson or his daughter about to return to the pavilion. No, if that were so, it would have been much easier for him to climb up to the attic and hide there, waiting for an opportunity to get away, that is, *if his only purpose had been to escape*. No! No! *He wanted to be in the Yellow Room!*"

Here, the Chief of the Sûreté intervened:

"That's very good! Congratulations, young man! If we don't know yet how our perpetrator managed to get away, at least, we can see how he got in and committed his robbery. But what did he steal?"

"Something very valuable," replied the reporter.

At that moment, we heard a cry coming from the laboratory. We rushed in and found Professor Stangerson, his eyes rolling, his arms trembling, pointing to a cabinet which he had opened, and which, we saw, was empty.

The Professor sank into the large armchair before the desk and moaned:

"I have been robbed again!" Tears began rolling down his cheeks. "For God's sake," he added, "don't say a word to my daughter. She would be even more hurt than I am."

He sighed very deeply and concluded, in a tone that I shall never forget:

"After all, what does it matter, *as long as she lives!*"

"She will live!" said Monsieur Darzac, in a voice that was strangely touching.

"And we will find the stolen articles," said Monsieur Dax. "But what was in that cabinet?"

"Twenty years of my life," replied the illustrious professor sadly, "or rather, of our lives, the lives of myself and my daughter! Yes, our most precious documents, the records of our most secret experiments and all our labors of 20 years were in that cabinet. I stored a selection of our most valuable documents there, which are all too often spread around this room. It's an irreparable loss to us and, dare I say, science. All the processes which I carefully studied before reaching the irrefutable proof of the dissociation of matter were all in there, methodically filed, labeled, annotated, illustrated with graphs and photos. It was all kept in that cabinet! There were also the blueprints for three new inventions: one, a device to study the decrease of certain electrified bodies under the effect of ultraviolet light, another to render that electrical decrease visible by projecting particles of dissociated matter in superhot gases, and, finally, the most ingenious of all three, a new differential electroscopic condenser. There was also a binder containing all our charts recording the fundamental properties of the intermediate substance between tangible matter and intangible aether; 20 years of experiments in intranuclear chemistry and the unknown states of equilibrium in matter; my unpublished manuscript on stressed metals... And what else? What else?... The man who robbed us took everything from me: my daughter, my work, my heart and my soul."

And the great Professor Stangerson began to cry like a child.

We stood around him in silence, deeply affected by his great distress. Monsieur Darzac, leaning against the Professor's armchair, tried in vain to comfort him, which, for a moment, almost made me like him, despite the instinctive dislike I felt for this strange man's odd behavior and inexplicable nervousness.

Meanwhile, Monsieur Rouletabille, as if his precious time and the sense of his mission on Earth didn't permit him to dwell on the contemplation of human suffering, had very calmly stepped up to the empty cabinet. Pointing at it, he crudely broke our solemn silence acknowledging the Professor's great loss. The young man gave the Chief of the Sûreté some basic reasons—which we cared little about—why he had been led to believe that a robbery had been committed. These included the discovery he had made in the lavatory and the presence of the cabinet in the laboratory. He said that he had only made a cursory examination of the laboratory, but the first thing that had struck him was the unusual shape of that cabinet. It was strongly built, made of iron, fire-proofed, clear evidence that it was intended for the safekeeping of valuable objects. Then, he had noticed that the key had been left in the lock. "One does not ordinarily bother having a safe and leaving it open!" he had thought.

This little key, with its brass head and complicated wards, had attracted Monsieur Rouletabille's attention, when it had been ignored by the rest of us. To us, respectable members of society, the presence of a key in a lock made us think of safekeeping. But to Monsieur Rouletabille, who is obviously a genius (like José Dupuy says in *The Five Hundred Millions of Gladiator*, "What a genius! What a dentist!"[13]), a key in a lock instead suggests robbery! We soon found out his conclusions.

But before I share them here, I have to report that Monsieur de Marquet appeared to be greatly concerned, as if he didn't know whether he should be glad of the new direction given to the investigation by the young reporter, or sorry that he hadn't found those new clues by himself. In our profession, we have to put up with such embarrassments and bury our pride for the sake of the public good. That's why Monsieur de Marquet's better nature won out and he was soon adding his compliments to those of Monsieur Dax, who was being lavish with praise.

As for our young Monsieur Rouletabille, he simply shrugged his shoulders and said: "All in a day's work!" I would have gladly slapped him, especially when he added: "You would do well, Monsieur, to ask Professor Stangerson who normally kept that key."

"My daughter," replied the Professor. "She was never without it.

"Ah! But then, this must change Monsieur Rouletabille's conception of the crime!" said Monsieur de Marquet. "If that key never left Mademoiselle Stangerson, the perpetrator must have waited for her in her room for the purpose of stealing it. Therefore, the robbery couldn't have been committed *until after the attack on her person*. But then, after that attack, there were four persons present in the laboratory! Upon my word, I can't make neither heads nor tails of this!"

Monsieur de Marquet repeated that last sentence several times gleefully, because, as I think I have already noted, nothing pleased him more that a mystery which he couldn't solve.

---

[13] Leroux is (purposefully?) misquoting Eugène Labiche's vaudeville, *Les Trente Millions de Gladiator* (The Thirty Millions of Gladiator), whose lead character is named Dupuis, not Dupuy. (*Note from the Publisher*.)

"…Neither heads nor tails!"

"The robbery," said the reporter, "could only have been committed *before the attack upon Mademoiselle Stangerson.* That fact is incontrovertible for the very reason you stated Monsieur, *and for others, which I believe I know.* When the murderer entered the pavilion, *he already had the brass key in his possession.*"

"That's impossible," said Professor Stangerson in a low voice.

"Not at all, Professor, and here's the proof…"

And the young rascal pulled out of his pocket a copy of *L'Epoque* dated October 21 (the crime was committed on the night between October 24 and 25), and showed us a classified advertisement which read:

" '*Lost yesterday at the Grands Magasins du Louvre a black satin handbag containing, among other things, a small key with a brass head. A handsome reward will be given to the person who has found it. This person must write to M.A.T.H.S.N., Poste Restante, Bureau 40.*' Don't these letters suggest Mademoiselle Stangerson?" continued the reporter. "The *key with a brass head*—is it not this key? I always read the classifieds. In my business, as in yours, Monsieur, one should always read the classifieds. They often contain the keys to many mysteries, not always brass-headed ones, but none the less interesting. This advertisement caught my eye because of the aura of mystery with which the woman who had lost her key—normally not a compromising item—surrounded herself. Obviously, she valued that key very much, since she promised a big reward for it! And then, I considered these six letters: M.A.T.H.S.N. The first four pointed to a Christian first name; I thought M.A.T.H. stood for 'Mathilde'—obviously, the first name of the woman who had lost her handbag. But I could make nothing of the last two letters. So I threw the paper aside and busied myself with other matters.

"Four days later, when the evening papers appeared with enormous headlines announcing the attempted murder of Mademoiselle MATHILDE STANGERSON, without any conscious thought, I remembered the advertisement. But I had forgotten the last two letters. So I asked the archives to pull out another copy of that issue for me, and when I had it, I finally got my answer: S.N. When I saw it, I couldn't help exclaiming, 'STANGERSON!'

"I jumped into a cab and rushed to Bureau 40, where I asked the clerk if he had a letter addressed to M.A.T.H.S.N. He replied that he had not. As I insisted, begged and entreated him, he wanted to know if I were playing a joke on him. He then told me that he had had a letter addressed to M.A.T.H.S.N, but three days prior, he had given it to a lady who had come for it. 'Now you're here today to claim this letter, and just the day before yesterday, another gentleman did the same with similar insistence! I've had enough of this,' he said angrily. I tried to question him regarding the two individuals who had asked for the letter before me, but whether he wished to retreat behind professional secrecy—he may have thought that he had already said too much—or whether he was disgusted at the joke that had been played on him—he would not answer any of my questions."

Rouletabille paused. We all remained silent, each of us drawing their own conclusions from the strange story of the letter at the Poste Restante. It seemed that we now had a new thread which might help us unravel this amazing mystery.

"Then it's almost certain," said Professor Stangerson, "that my daughter did lose her key, but that she didn't tell me, probably to spare me any further anxiety, and that she begged whoever had found it to write to the poste restante. She evidently feared that, if she gave our address, I might have learned of her losing the key. It was quite logical, quite natural, for her to have done so—*because I have been robbed once before.*"

"Where and when was that?" asked the Chief of the Sûreté.

"Oh! Many years ago, in Philadelphia. Someone stole the blueprints of two of my inventions from my laboratory, which might have made the fortune of a nation. Not only did I never

109

learn the identity of the thief, but I never heard that these inventions were ever exploited. But that's probably because, in order to thwart the thief, I gave them away to the public, thereby making them financially worthless. From that moment, I have been very suspicious and careful to lock the doors when I'm working. The bars to these windows, the isolated location of this pavilion, this cabinet, which I had specially constructed, this special lock, this unique key, all are precautions taken against fears inspired by a sad experience."

"Very interesting!" remarked Monsieur Dax.

Monsieur Rouletabille asked about Mademoiselle Stangerson's black satin handbag. Neither the Professor nor Père Jacques had seen it for several days. A few hours later, we learned from Mademoiselle Stangerson herself that her handbag had either been stolen from her, or she had lost it. She further corroborated everything that her father had said. She had gone to the Poste Restante on October 23, where she had been given a letter which, she said, was nothing but a bad joke, and which she had immediately destroyed.

To return to our reconstruction, or rather our "conversation," I must add here that the Chief of the Sûreté, having inquired of Professor Stangerson under what conditions his daughter had gone to Paris on October 20—the day she had lost her handbag—we learned that Monsieur Darzac had accompanied her, and that he had not been seen again at the Chateau until the day after the attack on his fiancée. The fact that Monsieur Darzac was with Mademoiselle Stangerson at the Grands Magasins du Louvre when the handbag had disappeared didn't go unnoticed and, it must be said, strongly attracted our interest.

This "conversation" between Magistrates, victims, witnesses and journalists was coming to an end when a surprising new development occurred—the kind of theatrical incident that Monsieur de Marquet likes so much. The Brigadier came to announce that Inspector Frederic Larsan requested to be admitted—a request that was immediately granted.

The detective came in, holding in his hand a pair of heavy, muddy boots, which he threw on the floor of the laboratory.

"Here," he said, "are the boots worn by the murderer. Do you recognize them, Père Jacques?"

Père Jacques bent over the appalling footwear and, quite astonished, recognized a pair of old boots which he used to wear, some years ago, and which he claimed to have thrown into a corner of his attic. He was so taken aback by that discovery that he couldn't hide his distress and had to blow his nose.

Then, pointing to the handkerchief in the old man's hand, Monsieur Larsan said:

"That's a handkerchief amazingly like the one found in the Yellow Room."

"I know," said Père Jacques, trembling, "they're almost the same."

"Lastly," continued Monsieur Larsan, "the old Basque béret also found in the Yellow Room might, at one time, have been Père Jacques'... Don't be alarmed," he said at once to the old man who was almost fainting. "In my opinion, gentlemen," he continued, "all this proves that the murderer wished to disguise his real identity, and did so rather clumsily—or so it seems, *because we're certain that the perpetrator isn't Père Jacques, who never left Professor Stangerson's side.* But think about what might have happened if Professor Stangerson hadn't carried on working that night and had returned to the Chateau after saying good night to his daughter. If she had been murdered when there was no one else in the pavilion, except for Père Jacques sleeping in his attic. *Then no one would have doubted for an instant that he was the murderer!* He owes his safety only to the fact that the attack on Mademoiselle Stangerson occurred too soon. The perpetrator must have thought, from the silence in the laboratory, that it was empty, and that the moment for action had come. The man who was able to enter this pavilion so mysteriously and leave so many clues accusing Père Jacques, must be—without a

111

doubt—familiar with this house. When did he enter the pavilion exactly? In the afternoon or in the evening? I can't say. *But someone so familiar with the habits and the routine of the people living and working in this pavilion could choose his own time to go into the Yellow Room.*"

"But he couldn't have gone into it when there were people in the laboratory," said Monsieur de Marquet.

"How do we know that?" replied Monsieur Larsan. "There was the dinner being served in the laboratory, the coming and going of the servants. There was a chemical experiment being carried on between 10 and 11 p.m., which kept Professor Stangerson, his daughter and Père Jacques busy near the furnace in a corner of the fireplace. Who can say that the perpetrator—an intimate!—a friend!—didn't take advantage of that moment to slip into the Yellow Room, after having taken off his boots in the lavatory?"

"That's very improbable," said Professor Stangerson.

"Perhaps, but it isn't impossible either. I assert nothing yet. As to the escape from the pavilion, that's another thing. How could the perpetrator have left? *Why, the most natural way in the world.*"

Here, Monsieur Larsan paused for a moment, that seemed to us to last a very long time. You can easily imagine how eager we were to hear the rest of what he had to say.

"I haven't been inside the Yellow Room," the detective continued, "but I take it for granted that you've satisfied yourselves that *the only way out is through the door.* So it's through the door, then, that the perpetrator left. Since it's impossible for him to have done otherwise, then that must be the truth. He committed the crime, then left through the door. But when? The answer is: when it was the easiest for him to do so, *when it is the easiest to explain,* so completely explainable in fact, that there can't be any other explanation. Let us go over the various events which immediately followed the attack on Mademoiselle Stangerson. Event No. 1 was when Professor Stangerson and Père Jacques stood in front of the door to the Yellow Room, in the laboratory, ready to bar the way of the perpetrator if he came out. Event No. 2 was when Père Jacques left to check the window of the Yellow Room outside and Professor Stangerson found himself alone in front of the door. Event No. 3 was when the Professor was joined by Monsieur Bernier, the caretaker. Event No. 4 was when Père Jacques returned with Madame Bernier and five people now stood in front of the door. Event No. 5 was when the door was forced open and the Yellow Room entered. *The moment when the escape took place is obviously when there were the least number of people in front of the door. That's Event No. 2 when there was only one person standing alone—Professor Stangerson.* Unless, of course, we assume the complicity of Père Jacques—which I don't, because he wouldn't have gone out of the pavilion to check the window of the Yellow Room if he had seen the door open. *Therefore, the door was opened when Professor Stangerson was alone and that's how our man escaped.*

"Here, we must further assume that the Professor had some powerful reason for not stopping the perpetrator, or at least reporting him to the police later. Instead, he allowed him to leave through the vestibule window and even closed it after him! Once that was done, as Père Jacques was about to return, *everything had to look exactly the same.* So, Mademoiselle Stangerson, though horribly wounded, still had enough strength, no doubt following her father's orders, to refasten the door of the Yellow Room from the inside, with both the bolt and the lock, before sinking down to the floor.

"We don't know who committed the crime. We don't know of what villain Professor and Mademoiselle Stangerson are the victims, but there's no doubt that they both know! It must be a dreadful secret, since the father didn't hesitate to leave his daughter to die behind a door which she had shut upon herself, dreadful enough for him to have allowed the man who had just attacked her to escape. *But there is no other way in the world to explain how the perpetrator was able to leave the Yellow Room!*"

The silence which followed this dramatic and enlightening explanation was terrible. All of us felt sorry for the illustrious Professor, who had been backed into a corner by the merciless logic of Monsieur Larsan, forced either to confess the truth of his martyrdom, or to keep silent, and thus make an even more dreadful admission.

We saw the Professor stand up. Like the very incarnation of despair, he raised his hand with a gesture so solemn that we bowed our heads as if we were at a religious service. He then uttered these words in a voice so forceful that it seemed to exhaust him:

"I swear upon the head of my suffering child that I never, not for an instant, left the door of the Yellow Room unattended after hearing her cries for help; that that door was not opened while I was alone in the laboratory; and that, finally, when we entered the Yellow Room, my three servants and I, the perpetrator was no longer there! I also swear that I do not know his identity!"

Need I say that, despite the solemnity of Professor Stangerson's words, we didn't believe his denial. Monsieur Larsan had shown us the truth and we weren't so easily ready to give it up.

Monsieur de Marquet then announced that our "conversation"—the reconstruction—was over. As we were about to leave, Joseph Rouletabille approached Professor Stangerson, took him by the hand with the greatest respect, and I heard him say:

"I believe you, Professor."

Here ends the excerpt which I selected from the memoirs of Monsieur Maleine, court recorder at the Tribunal of Corbeil. I don't need to tell the reader that all that went on in the laboratory was immediately and faithfully reported to me by Rouletabille himself.

Chapter Twelve
Frederic Larsan's Cane

I was planning to leave Glandier at 6 p.m., taking with me an article that had been hastily written by Rouletabille in the little sitting room, which Monsieur Darzac had placed at our disposal. The reporter was to sleep at the Chateau, taking advantage of the inexplicable hospitality offered him by Monsieur Darzac, upon whom Professor Stangerson relied, in that tragic time, to take care of all his domestic affairs. Nevertheless, my friend insisted on accompanying me to the station at Epinay. As we crossed the grounds, he said to me:

"Larsan is really very clever and deserves his reputation. Do you know how he found Père Jacques' boots? Near the spot where we noticed the traces of the expensive pair of boots that replaced the cheap ones, he found the impression of a squarish hole that had been freshly made into the damp soil, where a stone had obviously been removed. Larsan searched for that stone and, not finding it, theorized that it had been used by the perpetrator to sink the boots into the pond and get rid of them that way. His theory was excellent, as the success of his search proves. That fact escaped me, but in my defense, I must say that my mind was already occupied in another direction, that of *the great many false clues left by the perpetrator to incriminate Père Jacques.* Earlier, I'd noticed that the size of the sooty footprints in the Yellow Room matched the old man's boots, a fact which I kept to myself, but was further proof, in my eyes, that the perpetrator sought to direct our suspicions onto the old servant. That's what enabled me, if you remember, to describe the béret and the handkerchief found in the Yellow Room, by assuming that they must have been just like the ones I'd seen Père Jacques use. Up to that point, Larsan and I are in agreement, but no further. *It's going to create a terrible conflict*, because he's making an honest mistake and I'm going to have to fight him all the way, with nothing to support my side!"

I was surprised by the somber tone in which my young friend delivered these last words.

He repeated:

"Yes, *it's going to create a terrible conflict!* But is it really fighting with nothing, when one already has a plan…"

At that moment, we were walking alongside the back of the Chateau. Night had fallen. A window on the first floor was partially open and a feeble light came from it, as well as a noise, which drew our attention. We approached until we reached a side door located just beneath that window. Rouletabille, in a low tone, told me that this was the window of Mademoiselle Stangerson's bedroom. The sounds which had attracted our attention suddenly stopped, then started again. They were stifled sobs. We could only catch three words, which reached us distinctly:

"My poor Robert!"

Rouletabille leaned on my shoulder and whispered in my ear:

"If we could only know what's being said in that room, our investigation would soon be over."

He looked around; the darkness of the evening enveloped us. We couldn't see much beyond the narrow lawn bordered by trees which ran behind the Chateau. Meanwhile, the sobs had stopped again.

"If we can't hear, at least we might try to see," said Rouletabille.

Instructing me to me to muffle the sound of my steps, he dragged me across the lawn to a tall beech tree, the white trunk of which was visible in the darkness. This tree grew exactly in front of the window that interested us, and its lower branches were level with the first floor of the Chateau. From there, one would be able to spy on what was happening in Mademoiselle Stangerson's bedroom. Obviously, that was Rouletabille's idea, because, enjoining me to remain silent, he clasped the trunk with his two strong arms and started climbing. I soon lost sight of him in the foliage, and then, there was a long silence.

In front of me, the open window remained lit. I saw no shadows move across it. All was silence. I waited. Suddenly, I heard the following words come from directly above me:

"After you!"

"No, please, after you!"

Two people above my head were talking, exchanging courtesies. I was amazed to see two men slide down the slippery trunk of the tree and quietly set foot on the ground. Rouletabille had climbed up the tree alone; he had returned in the company of another man.

"Good evening, Monsieur Sainclair!"

It was Frederic Larsan. The detective had already been watching in the tree when my young friend had climbed it. Neither man commented upon my surprise. I was told that they had witnessed a tender and sorrowful scene between Mademoiselle Stangerson, lying in her bed, and Monsieur Darzac, on his knees by her side. But I surmised that each man was drawing a different, if cautious, conclusion from what they had just seen. It was clear that the scene had strongly impressed Rouletabille in favor of Monsieur Darzac, while, to Larsan, it showed nothing but the consummate hypocrisy and fine acting talents of Mademoiselle Stangerson's fiancé.

As we reached the gate, Larsan stopped us.

"My cane!" he cried.

"You forgot your cane?" inquired Rouletabille.

"Yes," replied the detective. "I left it near the tree."

He left us, saying he would soon catch up with us.

"Have you noticed Monsieur Larsan's cane?" asked the young reporter, as soon as we were alone. "It's quite new. I've never seen him use it before. He seems very attached to it; it never leaves his side. One would think he was afraid it might fall into the wrong hands. Before today, *I never saw Larsan with a cane.* Where did he find it? *It isn't normal that a man who never used a cane before should, the day after the crime, never take a step without one.* When we arrived at the Cha-

117

teau, as soon as he saw us, he put his watch back in his pocket and picked up his cane. Perhaps I was wrong not to attach some importance to that gesture..."

We were now out of the estate. Rouletabille was silent. His thoughts were certainly still occupied with Larsan's cane. I had proof of that when, as we neared Epinay, he said:

"Larsan arrived at Glandier before me. He began his investigation before me. He had time to find out things which I don't know. Where did he find that cane?" Then he added: "It's likely that his suspicions—more than mere suspicions, his deductions—have led him to Robert Darzac, and they must be based on something tangible, which nevertheless remains intangible to me. Has this cane anything to do with it? Where the Devil could he have found it?"

As I had to wait 20 minutes for the train to Paris, we went into a café. Almost immediately, the door opened and Larsan made his appearance, brandishing his famous cane.

"I found it!" he said laughing.

The three of us sat at a table. Rouletabille never took his eyes off Larsan's cane. He was so absorbed that he didn't notice a sign that the detective made to a railway employee, a young man with a small, blond, ill-kept beard. Upon seeing that gesture, the man rose, paid for his drink, bowed, and went out. I wouldn't have attached any importance to this event, if later it hadn't resurfaced when the man with the beard reappeared during one of the most tragic moments of this case. I then learned that that young man was one of Larsan's agents who the detective had been assigned the job of watching the comings and goings of the travelers at Epinay station. Decidedly, Larsan left no stone unturned.

I again turned my eyes to Rouletabille.

"Ah, Monsieur Larsan," he said, "when did you start using a cane? I've always seen you walking with your hands in your pockets!"

"It's a present," replied the detective.

"A recent one?" insisted Rouletabille.

"No, it was given to me in London."

"Ah, yes, I remember, you've just returned from London. May I look at it?"

"Certainly!"

Larsan handed his cane to Rouletabille. It was a large bamboo cane with a crutch handle decorated with a gold ring. Rouletabille examined it carefully.

"It seems you were given a French cane in London!" he said in a jovial tone.

"Possibly," said Larsan, imperturbably.

"Read the mark there, in tiny letters: *Cassette, 6b, Opera*."

"There are wealthy Parisians who have their laundry pressed in London. Why couldn't an Englishman buy his cane in Paris?"

Rouletabille returned the cane to the detective. Later, when saw me into the train, he said:

"You remember the address?"

"Yes, Cassette, 6b, Opera. You can count on me. You'll get a report tomorrow morning."

That evening, in Paris, I visited Monsieur Cassette, dealer in canes, walking-sticks and umbrellas, and wrote to my friend:

"A man unmistakably answering to the description of Monsieur Darzac—same height, slightly stooping, putty-colored coat, bowler hat—purchased a cane similar to the one in which we are interested, on the evening of the crime, at about 8 p.m. Monsieur Cassette has not sold another such cane during the last two years. Larsan's cane is new. It is quite clear that it's the same cane. He did not buy it at Cassette's, since he was in London. So, like you, I think that he found it, somewhere near Monsieur Darzac. But if, as you suppose, the perpetrator was in the Yellow Room since 5 or 6 p.m., and the attack on Mademoiselle Stangerson didn't take place until close to midnight, the purchase of this cane provides an indisputable alibi for Monsieur Darzac."

Chapter Thirteen
"The Presbytery Has Lost None of Its Charm, Nor the Garden Its Glow"

Eight days after the events I have just recounted—on November 2, to be exact—I received the following telegram at my home in Paris: "*Come to Glandier by earliest train. Bring guns. Best. Rouletabille.*"

I have already mentioned, I think, that, at that point in my life, being a young attorney with only a few cases, I frequently visited the Palais de Justice, more for the purpose of familiarizing myself with my professional duties than for defending widows and orphans. I wasn't surprised, therefore, by Rouletabille taking advantage of me in such a cavalier fashion. Further, he knew how keenly interested I was in his adventures in general, but especially so in the Yellow Room. The only news I'd read about the case during the past week were the various bits of gossip printed at length by some newspapers, and the very brief articles filed by Rouletabille in *L'Epoque*. The latter had mentioned the existence of the sheep-bone, and reported that traces of human blood had been found on it—the most recent coming from Mademoiselle Stangerson, while the old stains belonged to other crimes, probably dating from several years ago.

By then, the so-called "Mystery of the Yellow Room" had captured the attention of the world press. No crime had ever fascinated so many people before. However, it seemed to me that the investigation was making little progress. Normally, I would have been very glad to have received my friend's invitation to return to Glandier, if it hadn't contained the rather ominous words: "*Bring guns.*"

That puzzled me greatly. If Rouletabille was asking me to bring guns, it meant that he foresaw that we might need them, perhaps even have to use them. Now, I confess without shame that I'm no hero. But here was a friend, obviously in danger, who was asking for my help. So I didn't hesitate. After making sure that the only revolver I owned was properly loaded, I rushed to the Gare d'Orléans. On my way, I remembered that Rouletabille had asked for *guns*—plural. So I stopped at a gunshop and bought a fine revolver, which I intended to offer to my friend as a gift.

I had hoped to find Rouletabille waiting for me at the Epinay station, but he wasn't there. However, a cab was, and soon, I arrived at Glandier. Nobody was at the gate. It was only at the threshold of the Chateau that I met my young friend. He greeted me warmly, hugging me and inquiring about the state of my health.

Once we were in the small sitting room, which I've mentioned before, Rouletabille asked me to sit down.

"It's going rather badly," he said.

"What's going rather badly?" I asked.

"Everything."

He came closer to me and whispered in my ear:

"Frederic Larsan is hell-bent on convicting Monsieur Darzac."

This didn't surprise me. I had seen Mademoiselle Stangerson's fiancé's face grow pale when we had discovered his footprints by the pond. However, I asked:

"What about Larsan's cane?"

"It is still in his hands. *He never lets go of it.*"

"But doesn't it provide an alibi for Darzac?"

"Not at all. I gently questioned him, and he denied having ever bought a cane at Cassette's, on that evening or any other. However," added Rouletabille, "I wouldn't swear to that, because Monsieur Darzac *has such strange silences* that one never knows exactly what to think of what he says."

"That cane must be a significant piece of evidence against Darzac for Larsan," I said. "But why? The time when it was bought shows that it couldn't have been in the murderer's possession."

"That doesn't bother Larsan," said Rouletabille. "He doesn't have to follow my timeline, which assumes that the perpetrator got into the Yellow Room sometime between 5 and 6 p.m. There's nothing to stop him from postulating that it happened between 10 and 11 p.m. At that time, Professor Stangerson, assisted by his daughter and Père Jacques, was conducting a delicate chemical experiment in the furnace by the fireplace. Larsan is going to claim, as unlikely as it seems, that the perpetrator managed to slip past them unnoticed. He's already said as much to the Investigating Magistrate. When you think about it, his reasoning is absurd. His so-called 'intimate'—*if there is one*—would have known that the Professor would shortly leave the pavilion, and that his own safety required that he waited until after the Professor's departure to proceed with his plans. Why would he have risked crossing the laboratory while the Professor was still there? And when did he get inside the pavilion?

"There are many points that need to be cleared up before I can accept *the products of Larsan's imagination*. I won't waste my time worrying about them because I've got *a perfect theory* that ignores them altogether. However, for the moment, as I am obliged to remain silent, while Larsan keeps talking, events could go badly for Monsieur Darzac—unless I intervene, of course," added the young reporter proudly. "There is, in fact, some superficial evidence against him, far more damning than that cane, which remains incomprehensible to me— all the more so since Larsan doesn't hesitate to let Darzac, who's supposed to have bought it, see him parading around with it! I understand much of Larsan's theory, but I can't make anything of that cane."

"Is he still at the Chateau?" I inquired.

"Yes! He hardly ever leaves it! He sleeps here, as I do, at Professor Stangerson's request. The Professor has extended him his hospitality, just as Monsieur Robert Darzac has done for me. Accused by Larsan of knowing the perpetrator's identity and having facilitated his escape, the Professor wishes to afford the detective every facility for arriving at the truth—again, just like Darzac with me."

"But I thought you were convinced of Darzac's innocence?"

"I am now, but at one time I did believe in the possibility of his guilt. That was after we'd just arrived here... In fact, the time has come for me to tell you what transpired between Monsieur Darzac and me then..."

Here Rouletabille paused and asked me if I had brought the guns. I showed them to him. Having examined both closely, he declared them excellent, and handed them back to me.

"Will we have to use them?" I asked.

"Very likely this evening. You'll spend the night here. You don't mind, do you?"

"On the contrary," I said with an expression that made Rouletabille laugh.

"Excuse me," he said, "this is no time for laughing. Do you remember that phrase that became our 'open sesame' to this Chateau?"

"Of course, I do," I said. "Perfectly. It was '*The presbytery has lost none of its charm, nor the garden its glow.*' It was the same phrase which you found on the half-burned piece of paper in the ashes of the fireplace in the laboratory."

"That's correct, and at the bottom of that paper was a date: *October 23*. Remember it! It's very important. I'm now going to tell you the origins of that curious phrase. On the evening before the crime, that is to say, on October 23, Professor Stangerson and his daughter attended a banquet at the Elysée Palace. They stayed for the reception afterward. I know this because I was there myself, on duty, interviewing some of the scientists from Philadelphia who were being feted that evening. Until that day, I had never met either the Professor or his daughter. I was sitting in the sitting room next to the Salon des Ambassadeurs, tired of being pushed around by so many celebrities, and had fallen into a vague reverie, when I suddenly smelled, close to me, *the perfume of the lady in black!*

"You may well ask me what *the perfume of the lady in black* is... Suffice it to say that it's a perfume of which I'm very fond, because it was that of a woman, always dressed in black, who was very kind to me when I was a child. The woman who, that evening, wore *the perfume of the lady in black* was, however, dressed in white. She was wonderfully beautiful. I couldn't help rising and following her—and her perfume. An old man gave her his arm and, as they walked by, I heard voices say: 'It's Professor Stangerson and his daughter.' That's how I found out who it was I was following.

"They met Monsieur Darzac, whom I knew by sight. Professor Stangerson, accosted by Mr. Arthur William Rance, one of the American scientists, sat in the Salon, while Monsieur Darzac took Mademoiselle Stangerson to the gardens. I followed. The weather was very mild that evening. Mademoiselle Stangerson threw a shawl over her shoulders and I could saw that it was she who was begging Monsieur Darzac to go with her into the then-deserted gardens. I continued to follow them, interested by the turmoil plainly displayed on Monsieur Darzac's face. They slowly walked alongside the wall abutting the Avenue Marigny. I took the central aisle, walking parallel to them, then stepped across the lawn in order to get closer. The night was dark. The grass muffled the sound of my steps. They had stopped under the bright light of a lamp post and appeared to be looking at a paper held by Mademoiselle Stangerson, reading something which interested them both deeply. I stopped as well. I was surrounded by darkness and silence, so neither of them noticed me. Then I distinctly heard Mademoiselle Stangerson say, as she was refolding the paper: '*The presbytery has lost none of its charm, nor the garden its glow!*'

"It was said in a voice that was at once scornful and desperate, and was followed by a burst of such hysterical laughter that I think these words will never be erased from my memory. Then Monsieur Darzac replied: '*Must I then commit a crime to win you?*' He was in an extraordinarily agitated state. He took Mademoiselle Stangerson's hand and held it to his lips for a long time. From the movement of his shoulders, I thought that he might have been crying. After that, they walked away.

"When I returned to the Salon," continued Rouletabille, "I saw no more of Monsieur Darzac, whom I didn't meet again until the day after the attack, but I saw Mademoiselle Stangerson and her father in conversation with the American scientists. Mademoiselle Stangerson was standing near Mr. Rance, who was talking to her animatedly, his eyes glowing with a singular brightness. Mademoiselle Stangerson, I thought, wasn't even listening to what he was saying, her face was expressing perfect indifference. Mr. Rance's face was the red face of a drunkard—a man fond of gin, I thought. When the Professor and his daughter left, he went to the bar and remained there.

"I joined him and helped him order in the midst of the pressing crowd. He thanked me and told me that he would be returning to America three days later, that is to say on October 26, the day after the crime. I mentioned Philadelphia. He told me that he'd lived in that beautiful city for 25 years, and that it was there that he had met the renowned Professor Stangerson and his daughter. He drank a great deal of champagne, so much that I thought he'd never stop. When I left him, he was quite drunk.

"Such were my experiences on that evening. During the rest of the night, I couldn't clear my mind of the twin images of Robert Darzac and Mathilde Stangerson. So I leave you to imagine what effect the news of her attempted murder produced on me. How could I not remember Monsieur Darzac's words, '*Must I then commit a crime to win you?*' However, it was not that phrase which I said to him when we met him at the gate. It was the one about the presbytery and the garden which he had read on the piece of paper held by his fiancée. And as you recall, it was sufficient for us to gain entrance to this Chateau. Did I believe, then, that Monsieur Darzac was the perpetrator? I don't think I really did. At the time, I don't think I really believed anything yet. I had so little evidence to go on... But I needed to make sure that he hadn't been wounded in the hand.

"When the two of us were alone, later that morning, I told him how I had chanced to overhear a portion of his conversation with Mademoiselle Stangerson in the gardens of the Elysée. When I repeated to him the words, '*Must I then commit a crime to win you?*' he became greatly troubled, but much less so than he had been when he'd heard me repeat the phrase about the presbytery. What threw him into a state of great consternation, however, was to learn from me that, earlier that day, Mademoiselle Stangerson had gone to Bureau 40 of the Post Office to claim a letter from the Poste Restante. It was that letter which they had read in the gardens of the Elysée, and which contained the words: '*The presbytery has lost none of its charm, nor the garden its glow.*'

"My theory about the contents of the letter was later confirmed by my finding its remains in the ashes of the laboratory. It was dated October 23, having been written and picked up from the Post Office the same day. There can be no doubt that, upon returning from the Elysée that night, Mademoiselle Stangerson tried to destroy that compromising letter. Monsieur Darzac pointlessly tried to deny that the letter had anything to do with the crime. I told him that, in such a mysterious affair, he had no right to hide this letter from the police, and further, that I was persuaded of its great importance because of the desperate tone in which Mademoiselle Stangerson had pronounced the fateful phrase, of his own, subsequent tears, and of the threat he had made after reading it. The combination of these facts left no room for doubt.

"As Monsieur Darzac became increasingly agitated, I determined to take advantage of his distress.

" 'You were about to be married, Monsieur,' I said nonchalantly and without looking at him, 'but, suddenly your marriage becomes impossible *because of that letter*. As soon as you've read it, you speak of the necessity of a crime to win Mademoiselle Stangerson's hand. *Therefore, there is someone between you and her, someone who's forbidden her to marry you, someone who tried to kill her in order to stop her from marrying you!*'

"And I concluded with these words:

" 'Now, Monsieur, you must tell me in confidence the name of the man who attacked your fiancée!'

"The words I uttered must have had some secret meaning unknown to me, for when I next looked at Monsieur Darzac, his face was haggard, his forehead shiny with perspiration, and his eyes gleamed with fear.

" 'Monsieur Rouletabille,' he said to me, 'I'm going to ask you something which may seem insane, but for which *I would gladly trade my life!* You mustn't tell the Magistrate what you saw and heard in the gardens of the Elysée, nor tell the police or anyone else. I swear to you that I am innocent, and I know, I feel, that you believe me. But I'd rather be taken for guilty than see the Law look into the meaning of the phrase, "*The presbytery has lost none of its charm, nor the garden its glow.*" The police must never learn of it! My entire case is in your hands, Monsieur, I'm entrusting it to you, but *you must forget the evening at the Elysée.* For someone like you, I'm sure there will be 100 other avenues that will lead you to the perpetrator. I will open them for you myself. I will help you. Will you agree to stay here? You may do as you please, eat, sleep, watch my actions, everyone else's actions. You will be the virtual master of Glandier, but please, Monsieur, *forget the evening at the Elysée!*' "

Rouletabille stopped to catch his breath. I now understood what had seemed so inexplicable in Monsieur Darzac's behavior towards my friend, and the facility with which the young reporter had been able to install himself at the scene of the crime. My curiosity couldn't fail to be excited by all I had just heard. I asked Rouletabille to satisfy it further. What had happened at Glandier during the past eight days? Had he not told me that there was some superficial evidence against Monsieur Darzac which was much more incriminating than the cane found by Larsan?

"Yes, I'm afraid everything seems to accuse him," replied my friend, "and the situation is becoming exceedingly serious. Monsieur Darzac appears not to mind, but he's wrong. Nothing seems to interest him other than Mademoiselle Stangerson's health, which is improving daily. But while you were gone, *something strange and extraordinary occurred here that is even more puzzling than the Mystery of the Yellow Room!*"

"That's impossible!" I cried. "What could be more mysterious than that?"

"Let's first return to the case of Monsieur Darzac," said Rouletabille, calmly. "As I've just told you, everything seems to be accusing him. The footprints left by the expensive boots found by Larsan appear to be really his. The tiremarks may have been left by his bicycle. The police checked it out. Monsieur Darzac usually left his bike at the Chateau; why did he, that day, take it to Paris? Was it because he wasn't planning on returning? Was it because of his break-up? Did he believe that his relations with the Stangersons were over? Everyone involved claim that those relations were to continue as before, but Larsan believes they were over. From the day Monsieur Darzac accompanied Mademoiselle Stangerson to the Grands Magasins du Louvre until after the attack on his fiancée, he hadn't been seen at Glandier. Remember that Mademoiselle Stangerson lost her handbag containing the key with the brass head while she was with him.

"From that moment until the evening at the Elysée, Monsieur Darzac and Mademoiselle Stangerson didn't see each other—but they might have corresponded! Later that day, Mademoiselle Stangerson went to Bureau 40 to collect a letter from the Poste Restante. Larsan thinks that letter was written by Monsieur Darzac. Not knowing what happened in the gardens of Elysée, unlike me, Larsan believes that it was Monsieur Darzac who stole the handbag with the key, intending to blackmail Mademoiselle Stangerson into marrying him by getting possession of her father's precious documents, which, of course, he would have returned after their marriage.

"All that would still make for a rather dubious, even absurd, theory—as Larsan himself was the first to admit to me—if it weren't for another, even more serious set of circumstances. First—and this is something that even I haven't yet been able to explain—it would appear that it was Monsieur Darzac himself who went to the Post Office the next day, October 24, to ask for the letter which Mademoiselle Stangerson had picked up the day before. *The description of the man who asked for that letter matches that of Monsieur Darzac in every respect.* When the Investigating Magistrate asked him about it, he vehemently denied having gone there. Now, even if one was prepared to believe that he wrote that letter—which I don't—*he knew that Mademoiselle Stangerson had picked it up, since he read it with her in the gardens of the Elysée.* Therefore, it can't have been Darzac who went to the Post Office on October 24 to pick up a letter which he knew was no longer there!

"To me, it seems clear that someone else, who impersonated Monsieur Darzac, stole Mademoiselle Stangerson's handbag. In the letter, that person must have asked something of her, which she obviously refused to do. Our man must then have been surprised by his failure to get what he wanted, which is why he went to the Post Office to check whether his letter had been picked up or not by 'M.A.T.H.S.N.,' to whom it had been addressed. Finding from the clerk that it had indeed been picked up, our man then became angry. His letter had been delivered, and yet, what he had asked for hadn't happened. What was he demanding? Nobody but Mademoiselle Stangerson knows...

"Then, the following day, we find out that Mademoiselle Stangerson has been attacked during the night. The next day, I discover that the Professor has, at the same time, been robbed by means of the key that was in his daughter's handbag. So it would seem, logically, that the man who went to the Post Office to inquire about the letter must be our elusive perpetrator. Larsan followed the same logic, but assumes it points to Monsieur Darzac. You may be sure that the Investigating Magistrate, Larsan, and myself, have done our best to get a precise description of the man who came, on October 24, to ask for the letter addressed to 'M.A.T.H.S.N.' from the Post Office clerk, but we still don't know where he came from, nor where he went. Beyond his description, which resembles that of Monsieur Darzac, we know nothing.

"I had an advertisement published in all the major newspapers promising a handsome reward to any cab driver who might have dropped our man at Bureau 40 at about 10 a.m. on October 24, and asked that replies be sent to 'J. R.' at *L'Epoque*, but no one has responded so far. Perhaps our man may have walked, but, as he was most likely in a hurry, he might have taken a cab... I purposefully didn't give a description of our suspect in my ad so that any cabdriver that might have dropped anyone at that time and that location might come forward. But no one has. I keep asking myself, night and day, who is this man who so strangely resembles Monsieur Darzac, and who also bought the cane which is now in Frederic Larsan's hands?

"Finally, the most incriminating fact is this: *Monsieur Darzac was scheduled to deliver a lecture at the Sorbonne at the very same time that his lookalike presented himself at the Post Office, but did not do so*. Instead, he was replaced by one of his colleagues. When I asked him where he was at that time, he said that he had gone for a stroll in the Bois de Boulogne. What do you think of a Professor who, instead of giving a lecture, goes for a stroll in the Bois de Boulogne?

"You should also know that, if Monsieur Darzac confesses to having gone for a stroll in the Bois de Boulogne on the morning of October 24, *he is unable, or unwilling, to tell us where he was or what he was doing on that very same night*, when Mademoiselle Stangerson was being attacked! When Larsan asked him for that information, he quietly replied that it was none of the police's business how he spent his time in Paris. Upon which Larsan swore aloud that he would find out, without anyone else's help.

"All of this seems to fit nicely with Larsan's theory. If Monsieur Darzac is indeed the perpetrator from the Yellow Room, that would explain why Professor Stangerson allowed him to escape: to avoid a scandal. I myself believe that theory to be false, and I think that Larsan is mistaken, something that wouldn't normally displease me, but in this case, an innocent man's life is at stake... *But is Larsan truly mistaken? That is the question...*"

"Perhaps he's right," I said, interrupting Rouletabille. "Are you sure that Monsieur Darzac is really innocent? It seems to me that these are extraordinary coincidences..."

"Coincidences," replied my friend, "are truth's worst enemies."

"What does the Investigating Magistrate think of all this?"

"Monsieur de Marquet hesitates to charge Monsieur Darzac in the absence of incontrovertible evidence. Not only would public opinion be against him, to say nothing of the Sorbonne, but Professor Stangerson and his daughter still adore Monsieur Darzac. As little as Mademoiselle Stangerson remembers about her attack, it would be hard to get the jury to believe that she wouldn't have recognized Monsieur Darzac if he'd been the perpetrator. Yes, the Yellow Room was dimly lit, but there was a night light, however small.

"Here, my friend, was how things stood when, three days, or rather three nights ago, the strange and extraordinary incident which I mentioned earlier occurred..."

Chapter Fourteen
"Tonight, I'm Expecting the Perpetrator!"

"I must take you to the scene of the incident," said Rouletabille, "so that you can understand what happened, or rather so I can convince you of why it's impossible to understand.

"I now believe that I have found what everyone else has been looking for, that is, how the perpetrator was able to escape from the Yellow Room, without any accomplices, and without Mademoiselle Stangerson having had anything to do with it. But as long as I'm not certain of the identity of the perpetrator, I can't divulge my theory, except to say that I believe it to be true and, in any event, quite natural and simple.

"As for what happened here at the Chateau three nights ago, I must confess that, for an entire day, I thought that it defied belief. Even now, the theory that I've come up with to explain it seems so outlandish that I sometimes wonder if I wasn't better off in the dark..."

The young reporter invited me to go out and walk around the Chateau with him. The only sound was that of the dead leavescrunching under our feet. The silence was so overpowering that one might well have believed that Glandier had been abandoned. The old stones, the stagnant water of the moat surrounding the tower, the bleak grounds strewn with the remains of a long-gone summer, the dark, skeleton-like silhouettes of the trees, everything contributed to give that desolate place, filled with its strange mysteries, a funereal look. As we walked around the tower, we met the 'Green Man,' Professor Stangerson's gamekeeper, who didn't greet us, but walked by as if we weren't there. He was looking the same as when we had met him at the Auberge du Donjon. He still carried his rifle over his shoulder, his pipe was in his mouth, and his eyeglasses on his nose.

"There goes a strange man," said Rouletabille, in a low voice.

"Have you spoken to him?" I asked.

"Yes, but I couldn't get anything out of him. His only answers were grunts and shrugs. He sleeps on the first floor of the tower, in a big room that once served as a prayer room. He lives there like a hermit, never goes out without his gun, and is only pleasant with girls. He uses the excuse of chasing after poachers to come and go at all times of the night, but I suspect him of having several affairs. Mademoiselle Stangerson's chambermaid, Sylvie, is one of his mistresses. Right now he seems to be pursuing the wife of Père Mathieu, the innkeeper of the Auberge du Donjon, but Mathieu watches over his wife like a hawk, and I think it's his inability to seduce her that's making our 'Green Man' even surlier than usual. Otherwise, he's a handsome man who takes good care of himself. All the women in the region are infatuated with him."

After going around the tower, which was located at the end of the Chateau's left wing, we found ourselves at the back of the property. Rouletabille pointed to a window, which he identified as belonging to Mademoiselle Stangerson's apartment.

"If you'd been standing here two nights ago at 1 a.m.," he said, "you would have seen your humble servant climbing a ladder and about to enter the Chateau by that very window."

As I expressed some surprise at these nocturnal acrobatics, Rouletabille asked me to carefully memorize the outside lay-out of the grounds. We then went back into the building.

"I must now take you to the first floor of the right wing, where I'm staying," said my friend.

To enable the reader to better understand what happened next, and the strange and extraordinary incident which I mentioned earlier, the details of which I'm about to relate, I'm including here a plan drawn by Rouletabille himself the day after that incident:

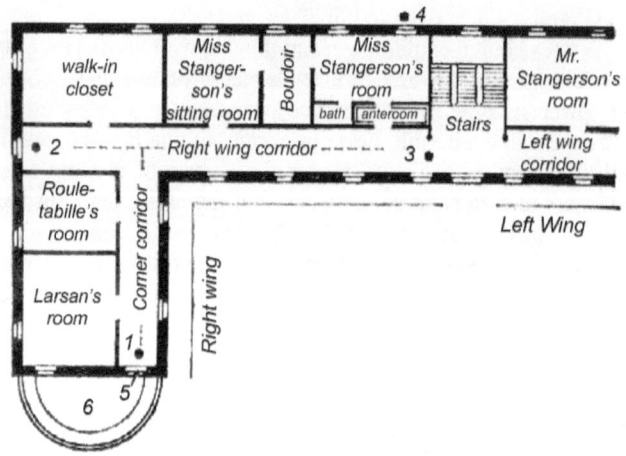

Chateau Glandier – 1st Floor – Right Wing

1. Place assigned by Rouletabille to Larsan.
2. Place assigned by Rouletabille to Père Jacques.
3. Place assigned by Rouletabille to Professor Stangerson.
4. Window used by Rouletabille to enter.
5. Window found opened by Rouletabille when he came out of his room. (He closed it. All the other doors and windows remained shut.)
6. Roof terrace over a ground floor oval room.

Rouletabille motioned me to follow him up a magnificent flight of stairs which ended on the first floor landing. From there, one could turn right or left to go into the Chateau's wings, which were connected through a grand hallway or corridor. This corridor, high and wide, extended along the whole length of the building and was lit from the front of the Chateau, facing the north. The rooms, the windows of which looked to the south, opened out on the corridor. Professor Stangerson lived in the Chateau's left wing, while his daughter had her apartment in the right wing.

We turned right at the top of the stairs. A narrow carpet, laid on the polished oak floor of the corridor, shone like a mirror and muffled our footsteps. Rouletabille asked me, in a low voice, to walk carefully as we passed the door of Mademoiselle Stangerson's apartment. He told me that it consisted of her bedroom, an anteroom, a small bathroom, a boudoir, and a sitting room. Naturally, one could go from one room to the other without having to go out into the corridor. The sitting room and the anteroom were the only rooms with doors opening onto the corridor.

The corridor continued straight to the western end of the building, where it was lit by a high window (No. 2 on the plan). At about two-thirds of its length, it branched out at a right angle into another, smaller corridor which followed the course of the right wing.

The better to follow this narrative, I will call the corridor leading from the landing at the top of the stairs to the eastern window, the "left-wing corridor;" the corridor leading from the landing at the top of the stairs to the western window, the "right-wing corridor;" and the smaller corridor branching out from the right-wing corridor at a right angle, the "corner corridor." It was at the meeting point of the right-wing corridor and the corner corridor that Rouletabille's room was located, next to Frederic Larsan's, the doors of each opening onto the corner corridor. As I have stated, the doors of Mademoiselle Stangerson's apartment opened into the right-wing corridor.

Rouletabille opened the door of his room and, after we went in, carefully drew the bolt. I didn't have time to look around when he uttered a cry of surprise and pointed to a pair of eye-glasses on a table.

"What are these doing here?" he asked.

I was, of course, entirely unable to answer him.

"Unless…" he said, "Unless this is what I've been looking for…"

He seized them eagerly, his fingers caressing the lenses.

"*These are farsighted spectacles!*" he said. Then looking at me with a frightful expression, he added: "Hmmm!"

He kept maniacally repeating "Hmmm!" again and again and I wondered briefly if he'd gone mad.

Finally, he put his hand on my shoulder, giggled inanely, and said:

"These spectacles will drive me mad! You see, Sainclair, logically speaking, what I'm thinking is possible, of course, but humanly speaking, it isn't... Unless... Unless..."

Suddenly, there were two light knocks on the door. Rouletabille opened it and a woman entered. I recognized Madame Bernier, the caretaker's wife, whom I had met when she was taken to the pavilion for the reconstruction. I was surprised to discover that she wasn't under lock and key anymore.

"*In the groove of the parquet,*" she said to Rouletabille in a low voice.

"Thank you," replied the reporter.

The woman left. After carefully relocking the door behind her, Rouletabille turned to me and, looking deranged again, began muttering some incomprehensible sentences:

"But if that thing is logically possible, then why shouldn't it be humanly possible as well? But if it is humanly possible, then it'd mean... No, that would be too dreadful to contemplate..."

I interrupted his crazy soliloquy:

"I see that the caretakers have been released," I said.

"Yes," replied the reporter. "I had them freed. I need people I can trust. That woman is thoroughly devoted to me, and her husband would do anything I'd ask of him. And *since the farsighted spectacles,* I've got to be surrounded by people ready to lay down their lives for me."

"Uh-ho!" I said. "You're not joking! And when should we be ready for that sacrifice?"

"Tonight, my friend! *I'm expecting the perpetrator tonight!*"

"Really? You're expecting the perpetrator tonight? Truly? The man who attacked Mademoiselle Stangerson... Here? Tonight? ...But then, this means you know who he is!"

"Well, I *might* know who he is… But I would be crazy if I were to say categorically that I do know him. The logical theory I have of the murderer's identity is so frightful, so monstrous, *that I hope that I might still be wrong! Oh! I hope so with all my heart!*"

"But if five minutes ago you weren't sure the identity of the perpetrator, how can you be sure that he's coming here tonight?"

"*Because he must!*"

Rouletabille slowly filled his pipe and lit it. That meant an interesting story. Suddenly, we heard someone walking in the corner corridor, past our door. Rouletabille listened. The sound of the footsteps died away in the distance.

"Is Frederic Larsan in his room?" I asked, pointing to the wall.

"No," my friend replied. "He went to Paris this morning, still after Darzac, who's also left for the capital. This case is going to end very badly. I expect that Monsieur Darzac will be arrested within the week. The worst thing, as I said, is that everything seems to be accusing him: circumstances, things, people... Not an hour passes without some new evidence surfacing against him. The Investigating Magistrate is overwhelmed—and blinded—by it. Which is quite understandable, under the circumstances."

"Frederic Larsan, however, isn't a novice," I said.

"I thought so," said Rouletabille, with a slightly contemptuous smile. "I thought he was a lot smarter… Of course, he isn't just any policeman… He's a capable one. Indeed, I felt a great admiration for him, before I got to know his methods. They're deplorable. He owes his reputation solely to his perseverance, but he lacks intelligence… The logic behind his ideas is very poor."

I looked closely at Rouletabille and couldn't help smiling at this boy of a mere 18 chastising a man in his 50ies who had proved himself one of Europe's finest detectives as if he were a schoolboy.

"You're smiling?" he said? "You're wrong! I swear I'll outwit Larsan, unquestioningly… But I must hurry, because he's got an enormous headstart on me, given to him by Monsieur Darzac, who is, this very evening, going to increase it still further. Think of it! *Every time the perpetrator comes to the Chateau*, Monsieur Darzac, by some strange twist of fate, absents himself and refuses later to give any account of his time."

"*Every time the perpetrator comes to the Chateau?*" I said. "You mean, he has returned?"

"Yes, during that famous night when that strange and extraordinary incident occurred."

I was finally going to find out about that astonishing incident which Rouletabille had kept mentioning for the last half-hour without any further explanation. But I had learned never to press my friend when he was telling a story. He spoke when the fancy took him, or when he judged it useful. He was less concerned about my curiosity than he was about drawing for himself a full picture of an important event in which he was interested.

At last, in short rapid phrases, he acquainted me with the nature of that incident, which plunged me into a state of total bewilderment. Indeed, the results attributed to the science of mesmerism, which is still largely unknown, seemed just as inexplicable to me as the "dissociation of the matter" of the perpetrator that happened when four persons were within touch of him. I'm using mesmerism here as an example, just as I would electricity, because we happen to be ignorant of the fundamental nature of either and know little about the laws they follow. At that moment, the strange and extraordinary incident seemed to me explicable only by the inexplicable, that is to say, by an event outside the known laws of Nature. And yet, if I had had Rouletabille's brain, I should have had, like him, an intuition of its natural explanation—because the most peculiar thing about all of Glandier's mysteries was the natural manner in which my friend eventually explained them.

But who could flatter himself that he has a brain as powerful as that of Rouletabille? I have never seen the same rather unappealing bumps on anyone else's forehead—except, perhaps, but in a far less pronounced fashion, on Frederic Larsan's. But you had to look closely to see Larsan's bumps, while Rouletabille's were obvious to everyone.

I have, among the papers that were sent me by my young friend after the Yellow Room affair was over, one of his notebooks in which he wrote a detailed account of the "strange and extraordinary incident of the dissociation of the matter of the perpetrator," and the thoughts which it provoked in his mind.

It is better, I think, to give the reader this account *verbatim* rather than continuing to reproduce my conversation with Rouletabille, for in such an important case, I'm concerned there should be no extraneous content that is not in accordance with the strictest truth.

Chapter Fifteen
The Trap

Excerpts from Joseph Rouletabille's notebook:

Last night—the night of October 29-30—I woke up around 1 a.m. Was it caused by sleeplessness, or some noise from outside? I don't know. I heard the sinister cry of the Holy Beast coming from the other end of the estate.

I got up and opened the window. Outside, there was only rain, cold wind, darkness and silence. I closed the window. Again, I head a weird cry in the distance. I dressed quickly. The weather was too ghastly, I thought, for even the Holy Beast to be out. So who could be imitating Mère Angenoux' cat so close to the Chateau? I grabbed a good-sized stick, the only weapon I had, and, silently, I opened the door.

The corridor outside my room was well lit by a reflector lamp. Its flame, however, was trembling; I felt a draft. I turned around and saw that the window at the end of the corridor was open. Both Larsan's and my room opened onto the corner corridor. Mademoiselle Stangerson's apartment, on the other hand, opened onto the central, right-wing corridor. Who might have left that window open? Or perhaps, who came upstairs and opened it? I went to the window and leaned out. Five feet below me was a semi-circular terrace built over the roof of an oval-shaped room located on the ground floor. One might, if one wanted to, jump from the window onto that terrace, and from there, drop into the courtyard of the Chateau. Obviously, whoever had entered through this window didn't have a key to the main door. But why was I picturing such nocturnal gymnastics in my mind? Was it solely because of that open window? Perhaps it had been inadvertently left open by a servant? I reclosed it, smiling at myself because of the ease with which I had built a full-length drama at the mere suggestion of an open window…

Suddenly, I heard the cry of the Holy Beast again, followed by a long silence; the rain had stopped beating on the window. Everyone in the Chateau was asleep. I walked warily along the carpet of the corridor. Upon reaching the corner, I looked around cautiously. There was another reflector lamp lighting up the sparse furnishings of the right-wing corridor: three chairs and a few pictures hanging on the wall. I asked myself what I was doing there... Never had the Chateau seemed so quiet. Everyone was in bed. What strange instinct, then, compelled me to move towards Mademoiselle Stangerson's door? Why did a voice within me shout: 'Go to her apartment!' I looked down upon the carpet and saw that my steps were unconsciously following another set of footprints. Yes, there were definitely muddy footprints on the carpet, heading towards Mademoiselle Stangerson's room! Horror! Horror! I recognized those footprints! They were the same as those left by the perpetrator's expensive boots! So he had returned from outside during that awful night. If one could leave the Chateau by the corner corridor through the window and the terrace, then one could get inside it by the same means.

I realized that the perpetrator was still inside, for *there were no returning footprints*. He had come in through the open window at the end of the corner corridor. He had walked by Frederic Larsan's door and mine, turned right, *and had entered Mademoiselle Stangerson's room*.

I now stood before the door of her anteroom. It was open. I pushed it silently. I immediately noticed a streak of light coming from under the door of her bedroom. I listened, but there were no sounds, not even of that of breathing! Ah! If I only I could find out what was going on in the silence behind that door! I looked at the door and saw that it had been locked from the inside. I thought that the perpetrator might still be in there. He had to be... Would he escape again? It all depended on me! I had to be calm, and, above all, make no mistakes. I had to look into that room. I could try to go in through Mademoiselle Stangerson's sitting room, but in order to do so, I would have to cross her boudoir and, during that time, the perpetrator might escape into the corridor, through the very the door before which I now stood.

I became certain that no other crime was being committed, because there was complete silence from Mademoiselle Stangerson's bedroom. I knew that two nurses slept in the boudoir, taking care of their mistress until she was recovered.

Since I was almost certain that the perpetrator was in the bedroom, why didn't I give the alarm? Yes, he might escape again, but Mademoiselle Stangerson's life would be saved. But what if he hadn't come to murder her? The bedroom door had to be opened in order to allow him to enter. By whom? And it was locked behind him. Again, by whom? Mademoiselle Stangerson locked herself in every night. So who turned the key to allow the perpetrator to enter? The nurses? They were two faithful family retainers. The old chambermaid, or her daughter, Sylvie? Improbable. Besides, they all slept in the boudoir. Monsieur Darzac had told me that Mademoiselle Stangerson, worried and cautious, had seen to her own security since she'd been well enough to move about in her room, which I hadn't yet seen her leave. This concern of hers, which had struck Monsieur Darzac, had also given me food for thought. During the night of the events in the Yellow Room, there was no doubt that Mademoiselle Stangerson *had been expecting her attacker*. Was she also expecting him to return tonight? Had she herself opened her door to him? Since she could—or should—fear him, did she have some other compelling reason for letting him in? Was she forced to do it? What was the dreadful purpose of their meeting? Was it some kind of criminal conspiracy? Certainly, it couldn't be a lover's meeting, for I believe Mademoiselle Stangerson was genuinely in love with Monsieur Darzac. All these thoughts ran through my brain like flashes of lightning through the darkness. What would I not have given to know the truth!

If there was such an awful silence behind that door, there must have been a good reason for it. My intervention might do more harm than good, I thought. But how could I tell? How could I be sure that, if I intervened, I might not trigger another crime? If only I could only see and find out what was going on without breaking that ghastly silence!

I left the anteroom and walked down the central staircase. Once in the downstairs vestibule, I ran as silently as possible towards the small room where Père Jacques had been sleeping since the attack at the pavilion.

I found him already dressed, his eyes wide open, quite agitated. He didn't seem surprised to see me. He told me that he had gotten up because he had heard the cry of the Holy Beast and heard footsteps outside his window. He had looked out and seen a black shadow go by. I asked him if he had a gun. He replied that he didn't since the Magistrate had confiscated his revolver. We went out together by a back door. We walked alongside the walls until we reached a point just below Mademoiselle Stangerson's bedroom.

I pushed Père Jacques against the wall, instructing him not to move. Then, taking advantage of a moment when the Moon was hidden by a cloud, I stepped back to try to look through   Mademoiselle Stangerson's half-opened window, careful to stay outside the patch of light emanating from it! Why was it half-opened, I asked myself? Was it a precaution to enable the intruder to leave the room more quickly if someone walked in through the door? Anyone jumping out of that window risked breaking his neck! But perhaps the perpetrator had a rope with him? He must have planned for everything. Ah, if only I could find out what was going on in that silent bedroom, and understand the reasons for that very silence!

I returned to Père Jacques and whispered the word "ladder" in his ear. At first, I had thought of using the same tree which, a week earlier, I had used as a watching post. But I had noticed that the window was opened in such a way that I wouldn't be able to see anything inside from that vantage point. Besides, I didn't want just to see, but also to hear—and possibly to act.

Greatly agitated, almost trembling, Père Jacques disappeared for a moment and returned without a ladder, but waving at me with his arms, asking me to come quickly. When I got there, he gasped:

"Come with me!"

We walked around the tower until we reached its entrance. There, he said:

"I went to the tower looking for my ladder, which I normally keep in the lower room that the gardener and I use for storage. But when I got there, I found the door open and the ladder gone. When I came out, I caught sight of it by the moonlight."

He pointed to the far end of the Chateau, where a ladder stood resting against the stone brackets supporting the terrace, under the window which I had found open earlier. The terrace had prevented me from seeing it before.

Thanks to that ladder, it was quite easy to get into the corner corridor of the first floor. I no longer doubted that this was the path taken by the perpetrator.

We ran to the ladder, but as we were about to grab it, Père Jacques drew my attention to the half-open door of the small oval room located just under the terrace, at the extremity of the right wing of the chateau. The old man pushed the door open a little further and looked in.

"He's not there!" he whispered.

"Who?"

"The gamekeeper."

With his lips to my ear, he added:

"Didn't you know that he's been sleeping in this room since they started renovating the tower?"

And with the same gesture, he pointed to the half-open door, the ladder, the terrace, and the window in the corner corridor which I had reclosed earlier.

What were my thoughts then? I had no time to think. I felt more than I thought.

Obviously, I felt that if the gamekeeper was up there, in Mademoiselle Stangerson's bedroom—I said "if," because at that time, I had no evidence that it might be him, except for the presence of the ladder and his vacant room—if he was up there, he had to use the ladder, because the ground floor rooms lying between his oval room and the stairs were occupied by the butler and his wife, the cook, and the kitchens, thereby barring his way to the vestibule and the rest of the Chateau. If it was the gamekeeper who was up there, it would have been easy for him, during the evening, on any pretext, to go to the corner corridor and see that the window there could be opened by a simple push from the outside, thereby facilitating his later access into the first floor. That window, unfastened from the inside, narrowed my field of research regarding the identity of the perpetrator. He had to belong to the household, unless he had an accomplice inside, which I didn't believe... Unless... Unless Mademoiselle Stangerson had opened that window herself! But then, what could be the frightful secret forcing her to remove the obstacles separating her from her would-be murderer?

I grabbed the ladder, and we returned to the back of the Chateau. Mademoiselle Stangerson's bedroom window was still lit and half-open. The curtains had been drawn, but not completely, allowing a bright stream of light to fall upon the lawn at our feet.

I positioned the ladder under the window. I was careful to not make any noise. While Père Jacques remained at the foot of the ladder, I mounted it, very quietly, my stout stick in my hand. I held my breath as I lifted my feet one at a time with the greatest care. Suddenly, a heavy cloud dropped a fresh downpour of rain upon us. I considered that lucky.

Then, I heard the sinister cry of the Holy Beast again, as if it had come from just behind me, only a few yards away. Could that be a signal? Had some accomplice of the perpetrator spotted me climbing on the ladder? Was that cry meant to bring the man to the window? Perhaps! Yes! There he was, at the window! I felt him above me. I heard the sound of his breath! But I couldn't look up. The least movement on my part and I might be lost. Would he see me? Would he look down and peer into the darkness? No! He went away. He had seen nothing. I felt him, rather than heard him, moving on tip-toe inside the bedroom. I carefully climbed a few more steps. My head now reached the bottom of the windowsill. My forehead rose just a little above it. My eyes looked between the opening in the curtains...

I saw a man seated at Mademoiselle Stangerson's desk, *writing*. His back was turned toward me. A candle was lit before him. As he bent over the flame, its light cast distorted shadows. I could see nothing but his monstrous, stooping back.

The most amazing thing was that Mademoiselle Stangerson herself didn't seem to be present! Her bed hadn't been turned down! Where, then, was she sleeping that night? Probably in the boudoir with the nurses... But this was only a guess... I was happy to find the man alone, the better to prepare my trap.

Who, then, was that man, writing before my eyes, seated at that desk as if he were in his own home? If there hadn't been those footprints on the carpet in the corridor, that open window, that ladder under it, I could well have believed that that man had a right to be there, that he was there as a matter of course and for reasons which I didn't as yet understand... But there was no doubt that this mysterious person was the man from the Yellow Room, the same man who had attacked Mademoiselle Stangerson, who had done nothing but fend off his murderous blows... Ah, if only I could have seen his face! If only I could have surprised and captured him!

But if I sprang into the room, he would escape by the anteroom or the boudoir. There, by crossing the sitting room, he would reach the corridor and I would lose him. Now, I had him; in another five minutes, he would be trapped, better than if he'd been in a cage.

What was he doing there, alone in Mademoiselle Stangerson's room? What was he writing?

I finally decided to climb down the ladder. Having placed it back on the ground, I asked Père Jacques to follow me. We went back to the Chateau. There, I sent the old man wake up Professor Stangerson, but told him to wait for me there and say nothing to the scientist until I returned. In the meantime, I planned to go and wake up Larsan. It was a shame, because I would have preferred to work alone and reap all the glory, right under the detective's very nose, but Père Jacques and the Professor were both old men, and I, well, I wasn't very strong... Larsan was used to wrestling villains to the ground and handcuffing them as they struggled.

Larsan opened his door, looking surprised to see me, his eyes still swollen with sleep. I could tell that he was ready to send me to the Devil, without believing any of my reporter's fancy notions. I had to assure him that our man was indeed here!

"That's strange!" he said. "*I thought I'd left him in Paris this afternoon.*"

He dressed himself quickly and took his service revolver. We walked silently into the right-wing corridor.

"Where is he?" asked the detective.

"In Mademoiselle Stangerson's room."

"What about Mademoiselle Stangerson?"

"She isn't there."

"Let's go then!"

"No! At the first sign of trouble, the perpetrator will escape. He's got three ways by which to do it: the door, through the anteroom, the window, and the boudoir, where the women are sleeping."

"I'll shoot him..."

"But what if you miss? Or even if you only wound him? Then he'll escape again. Besides, he might be armed too... Please, let me manage the situation and I'll answer for everything."

"As you wish," he replied, with fairly good grace.

Then, after satisfying myself that all the windows of the corridors were thoroughly secure, I placed Larsan at the end of the corner corridor, in front of the window which I had found open and had reclosed.

"Under no circumstances," I said to him, "must you leave this post until I call you. There's a 100% probability that our man, once the chase begins, will return to this window and try to escape that way, because that's how he got in here and prepared for his eventual flight. You have the most dangerous position."

"Where will you be?" asked Larsan.

"I'll run into the room and chase him your way."

"Then take my revolver," said the detective. "I'll take your stick."

"Thank you," I replied. "You're a brave man."

So I took his gun. I was now going to be alone with the man in the room and I was really thankful to have that weapon with me.

I left Larsan at the window (No. 1 spot on the plan) and, with the greatest precaution, walked towards Professor Stangerson's apartment in the left wing of the Chateau. I found him with Père Jacques, who had faithfully followed my directions, confining himself to asking his master to dress as quickly as possible.

In a few words, I explained the situation to the Professor. He armed himself with a revolver and followed me and Père Jacques back into the corridor. Since I had first seen the perpetrator seated at the desk, barely ten minutes had gone by. Professor Stangerson wished to spring upon the man and kill him there and then. I made him understand that, if he did that, *he might not only not shoot him dead, but also miss him alive.*

When I had sworn to him that his daughter was not in the room, and therefore not in danger, he relented and let me direct the operations. I told the two men that they must come to me as soon as I called to them, or when I fired my revolver. I then sent Père Jacques to stand before the window at the end of the right wing corridor (No. 2 spot on my plan). I had chosen that position for the old man because I thought that the perpetrator, once the chase began, would run towards the window he had left open, but seeing that it was guarded by Larsan, would then continue his flight along the right-wing corridor. There, he would come across Père Jacques, who would prevent him from using that window to jump into the grounds below. I believed the perpetrator was familiar with the premises of Glandier, and therefore, must have known that, under that window, was a kind of buttress. Jumping from any of the other windows in the corridors was impossible, at least without risking breaking one's neck, because they were too high, and were above ditches. All the doors and windows, including those of the large walk-in closet at the end of the right-wing corridor, were securely fastened, as I had rapidly assured myself.

Having shown Père Jacques his post, and having seen him take up his position, I placed Professor Stangerson on the landing at the head of the stairs. My plan was that, as soon as I would spring onto the perpetrator, he would attempt to flee through the anteroom, rather than the boudoir, where the women were, the door of which must have been locked by Mademoiselle Stangerson herself if, as I thought, she had taken refuge there in order to avoid the perpetrator who had come to see her. In any event, he would find himself in the corridor, where people were waiting for him at every possible exit.

Upon leaving Mademoiselle Stangerson's apartment, on his left, he would see the Professor. He would turn right, towards the corner corridor—the way he had come and planned to leave—but there, at the intersection of the two corridors, he would see Larsan on his left, at the end of the corner corridor, Père Jacques in front of him, at the end of the right-wing corridor. The Professor and I would then catch up with him, and he would be captured! This time, he would not, could not escape!

This plan seemed to me the best, the safest, and the simplest. It would, no doubt, have been easier still if we could have placed someone directly behind the door of Mademoiselle Stangerson's boudoir, which opened into her bedroom. It might have seemed to make more sense to block the only two doors leading into the bedroom where our man was: that of the boudoir, and that of the anteroom. But we could only get into the boudoir by going through the sitting room, the door of which had been locked on the inside by Mademoiselle Stangerson. Thus, that plan, which might have appealed to the simpler mind of an ordinary policeman, was in this instance impractical. But even if I had had free access to the boudoir, I still would have stuck to my original plan, because any other mode of attack would have separated us during the struggle with our man, while my plan gathered us all for the attack at the very spot which I had selected with almost mathematical precision: the intersection of the two corridors.

Having thus placed my three helpers, I went out again, rushed to the ladder, and, replacing it against the wall, climbed up, revolver in hand, towards the window of Mademoiselle Stangerson's bedroom.

If some people might be inclined to smile at my taking so many precautionary measures, I can only refer them to the earlier Mystery of the Yellow Room, which provided plenty of evidence of the perpetrator's devilish cunning. Also, if some people find my observations needlessly detailed, when they believe that priority should be given to rapidity of movement, quick decisions and action, I will say that I only wished to report here, at length and completely, all the details of a plan of attack that was conceived very rapidly. It is only the slowness of my pen that gives an appearance of delay in its execution.

I have wished, by this slowness and precision, to be certain to omit nothing from the conditions under which the strange and extraordinary incident occurred, an incident which, until a natural explanation was found, seemed to me to validate Professor Stangerson's theories on the Dissociation of Matter—I would even add, the *instantaneous* Dissociation of Matter.

Chapter Sixteen
The Strange and Extraordinary Incident of the Dissociation of Matter

Excerpts from Joseph Rouletabille's notebook (con'td.):

I found myself back at the windowsill, and again about to raise my head above it. Through the opening in the curtains, the disposition of which had remained the same, I was anxiously ready to take note of the position in which I expected to find the perpetrator. Would his back still be turned toward me? Would he still be seated at the desk writing? Perhaps he might no longer be there! But how could he have fled? Hadn't I taken away his ladder? I forced myself to be calm. I raised my head a little higher. I looked inside. He was still there! I saw his monstrous back, distorted by the shadows thrown by the candle. He was no longer writing, but bending over the candle, now on the floor. That position served my purpose.

I held my breath. I climbed up the ladder. I now stood on its uppermost rung. My left hand grabbed the windowsill. In this moment of approaching success, I felt my heart beating wildly. I put the gun between my teeth. Now my right hand grabbed the windowsill too. If I pulled myself up, after a quick jump, I would be standing on the window ledge. But what about the ladder? I was right to be concerned, because I was forced to lean on it a little too heavily, and as soon as my foot left it, I felt it sway beneath me. It scraped against the wall and fell down to the ground. But, my knees were already touching the windowsill and, with matchless speed, I managed to stand on the ledge.

However, the perpetrator had been even quicker than me. He had heard the scraping sound made by the ladder against the wall. I saw his monstrous back turn around. He stood up. Briefly, I saw his face—or thought I did. The candle on the floor only lit his legs. Above the height of the table, the room was only darkness and shadows. I thought I'd seen a man with long hair, a full beard, wild eyes, a pale face, framed in large whiskers. Their color, as much as I could see color during that dark second, was red. Or so it seemed... Or so I believed... I didn't know that face. That was, in short, the brief impression I received from a face seen briefly in the dim half-light. I didn't know it—*or, at least, I didn't recognize it!*

Now was the time to act quickly! I had to be like the wind! The storm! The lightning! But alas, alas! It took a minimum of a few gestures to extricate oneself from the position in which I stood... As I was about to drop through the window, the man leaped to his feet and rushed toward the door of the anteroom, just as I had foreseen. He had time to open it and flee. But I was already behind him, revolver in hand, shouting "Help!"

I crossed the room like an arrow, noticing a letter on the table as I rushed past. I almost caught up with the perpetrator in the anteroom because it'd taken him almost a minute to open the door onto the corridor. I nearly had him, but he slammed the door in my face. I had wings. I found myself in the corridor barely three meters behind him. The perpetrator had turned right, as I had supposed he would, following the path he had prepared for his escape.

"Help, Père Jacques! Larsan!" I cried.

He couldn't escape! I let out a shout of joy, of savage victory... The man reached the intersection of the two corridors barely two seconds ahead of me. Then, the encounter which I had planned, the fateful confrontation that was inevitably to take place at that very spot, happened! We all met at the intersection of the right-wing and the corner corridors: Professor Stangerson and I, coming from one end of the right-wing corridor, Père Jacques from its opposite end, and Larsan from the corner corridor. We almost bumped into each other.

But the perpetrator was not there!

We looked at each other stupidly, with terror in our eyes, because of the unreality of the scene. The perpetrator was not there!

"Where is he? Where is he?" we all asked.

"It's impossible for him to have gotten away!" I shouted, my anger being then more powerful than my fear.

"I touched him!" exclaimed Larsan.

"He was there! I felt his breath on my face!" cried Père Jacques.

"We all saw him! I almost touched him too!" said Professor Stangerson.

"Where is he? Where is he?" we all cried.

We raced like madmen along the two corridors. We checked all the doors and windows—they were closed, hermetically closed. They hadn't been opened since we had found them all fastened. Besides, the opening of a door or window by the man whom we were hunting, without us noticing anything, would have been even more inexplicable than his disappearance.

Where was he? Where was he? He couldn't have escaped through a door or a window, nor by any other way. He could not have passed through our bodies![14]

I confess that, at that moment, I felt utterly annihilated. The two corridors were well lit; there were no trapdoors, no secret door in the walls, nor any kind of hiding-place. We moved the chairs and lifted the pictures. Nothing! Nothing! We would have looked into flower pots, if there had been any in which to look!

---

[14] When this mystery, thanks to Rouletabille, was eventually solved, through only the resource of his prodigious mind, we were able to realize that the perpetrator had indeed escaped not through a door, a window, nor the stairs—a fact which the police refused to accept. (*Note from the Author.*)

Chapter Seventeen
The Unfathomable Corridor

Excerpts from Joseph Rouletabille's notebook (con'td.):

Mademoiselle Stangerson appeared from her anteroom. By then, we were standing near her door in the corridor where the strange and extraordinary incident had just taken place. There are moments when one feels as if one's brain is about to burst. A bullet in the head, a fracture of the skull, and the seat of reason is shattered, one's mind murdered. I can only compare the sensations I felt, which left me exhausted and devoid of thought, with those. I had just experienced the end of everything rational; I no longer thought like a man. The destruction of my physical sight wouldn't have been worse than that of my intellectual vision, which I had just experienced like a hammer's blow to the skull!

Fortunately, Mademoiselle Stangerson appeared. I saw her, and that helped to calm my chaotic state of mind. I breathed her scent, again I inhaled *the perfume of the lady in black*... That dear, dear lady in black, whom I would never see again. My God, I would have gladly given ten years of my life—more than half of it—to see her again! Alas! Nowaday, I only encountered—and very rarely at that!—her perfume, the same scent that I had just inhaled, and which, to me alone, evoked the parlor of my schooldays, back when I was young.[15]

---

[15] When he wrote these lines, Rouletabille was only 18, and yet he spoke of his "youth." I haven't changed what my friend wrote, but I feel obliged to point out to the reader that the Mystery of the Yellow Room bears no relation to that of the Perfume of the Lady in Black. It is not my fault if, in his note-books, Rouletabille often likes to refer to events from his childhood. (*Note from the Author.*)

It was this sharp reminder of my youth, that beloved perfume of the lady in black, which made me step toward Mademoiselle Stangerson. She stood there, dressed entirely in white, so pale and so beautiful, on the threshold of that unfathomable corridor. Her beautiful golden hair, gathered in a bun at the back of her neck, left visible the red scar on her temple which had so nearly been the cause of her death.

When I first grabbed what I called *the right end of logic* in this case, I had thought that, on the night of the tragedy in the Yellow Room, Mademoiselle Stangerson had worn her hair in plaits. But how could I have thought otherwise when I hadn't yet seen the Yellow Room!

But since the strange and extraordinary incident of the unfathomable corridor, I had stopped thinking at all! I could only stand there, dumb, before the apparition, so pale and so beautiful, of Mademoiselle Stangerson. She was, as I said, clad in a dressing-gown of dreamy white. One might have taken her for a ghost, a lovely phantom. Her father took her in his arms and kissed her with great relief, as if he was finding her again after having lost her once more. He dared not ask her any questions. He took her into her bedroom and we followed, because we had to know the truth!

The connecting door to the boudoir was now open. The terrified eyes of the two nurses stared at us. Mademoiselle Stangerson inquired about the meaning of such a great disturbance. The reason why she hadn't been in her room was quite simple indeed—or so she made it sound. She said she'd had a fancy not to sleep in her bedroom that night, but in her boudoir with her nurses, locking themselves in as usual. Since the attack in the Yellow Room, Mademoiselle Stangerson often experienced feelings of terror and sudden fears... It all sounded quite understandable, didn't it?

But, who could claim to understand why, on that particular night, when the perpetrator was sure to return, Mademoiselle Stangerson decided, apparently by mere chance, to lock herself in the boudoir with her nurses? Who could understand why she would ignore her father's wish to spend the night in her sitting room, since she felt so afraid? Who could understand why the letter written by the perpetrator, which I'd seen earlier lying on top of the desk in her bedroom, was no longer there?

Someone who could understand all this would have to conclude that Mademoiselle Stangerson knew that her attacker would be returning. She couldn't stop him. She couldn't alert anyone because his identity had to remain hidden from everyone—except Monsieur Darzac. The Sorbonne Professor must know the perpetrator's identity, I thought. Perhaps he even knew it when I talked to him! What was it that he had said in the gardens of the Elysée? "*Must I then commit a crime to win you?*" A crime against whom, if not the man who stood between them and happiness, a crime against the perpetrator?

When I asked Darzac: "Do you want me to find out who the attacker was?" he had replied: "Oh! I'd like to kill that man with my own hands!" to which I had said: "I believe you, but you haven't answered my question." That was the very essence of truth! Darzac knew who the perpetrator was, but while he wished to kill him, he was also afraid that I should find out who he was! There were two reasons why he offered to help me in my investigation. One was because I forced him to do so; two was so he could better protect his fiancée.

I stood in Mademoiselle Stangerson's bedroom. I looked at her, then at the place where the letter had been earlier. It was obvious that she had taken it; that the letter was clearly intended for her... It was all too evident... How the poor woman trembled! She was terrified by the story her father was telling her of the presence of the strange man in her room, and of the pursuit which had ensued. But I could plainly see that she truly felt safe only when she heard that the perpetrator, by some incomprehensible means, had once again escaped.

After that, there was a long silence. And what a silence it was! We all stood there, looking at Mademoiselle Stangerson: her father, Larsan, Père Jacques and I. What thoughts were brewing during that silence? After the events of that night, the mystery of the unfathomable corridor, the astonishing fact of the presence of the perpetrator in her bedroom, it seemed to me that our thoughts, from the unformed notions agitating Père Jacques to the more sophisticated ideas inside Professor Stangerson's head, could all be boiled down in a simple request to Mademoiselle Stangerson: "You, who know the answer to this mystery, please explain it to us, and then we might be able to save you." Oh! How I longed to save her, from herself and that mysterious man! So much misery so poorly hidden brought tears to my eyes.

But she only stood there, wearing the perfume of the lady in black. At last, I thought, I'm seeing her in her bedroom, where she has refused to see me so far, where she has remained obdurately silent... Since that fateful hour in the Yellow Room, we have all circled around this mysterious, silent woman, trying desperately to find out what she knows. Our desires, our desperate curiosity, must be one more torment for her. Who knows if, by learning her secret, we might not precipitate a tragedy even more terrible than that which she had already endured? Who knows if it might not mean her death? She had come close to dying once already, and yet we knew nothing. Or, rather, most of us knew nothing... For there was Darzac, who knew something... If only I knew the "who," I would know everything. Who? Who? But not knowing that, I had no choice but to remain silent for her own sake. I had no doubt that she knew how HE had escaped from the Yellow Room, and yet she remained silent... Why should I speak anyway? When I know who the "who" is then I will speak—to him!

Mademoiselle Stangerson gazed at us now, with a faraway look in her eyes, as if we were not even in the room. The Professor broke the silence. He declared that, from now on, he wouldn't leave his daughter's apartments. She tried to convince him otherwise, but failed. He would brook no objections. He would stay here this very night, he said. Then, concerned for his daughter's health, he reproached her for having left her bed too soon. He suddenly began talking to her as if she were a small child. He smiled and seemed not to know what he said or what he did. The illustrious Professor Stangerson was in danger of appearing to be senile. He repeated the same meaningless words of affection, indicating his state of mental distress. But our own mental state wasn't much better, to tell the truth...

"Father... Father, please, stop..." Mademoiselle Stangerson said in a tone of great sorrow.

Père Jacques blew his nose. Even Larsan felt obliged to turn away to hide his emotions. As for me, I was exhausted. I was unable to think or reason. I felt utterly depressed, even disgusted with myself.

It was the first time that Larsan, like me, had met Mademoiselle Stangerson since her attack in the Yellow Room. Like me, he had insisted on being allowed to question the unfortunate woman but he hadn't had any more luck than I. The same answer had always been given to us both: Mademoiselle Stangerson was too weak to see us. The Investigating Magistrate's interview had exhausted her. I was convinced that this was done purposefully to hamper our investigations. Larsan had been surpriserd by such lack of cooperation. I hadn't been. But it's true that he and I had very different conceptions of the crime...

Both the Professor and his daughter were now in tears... I caught myself thinking with deep emotion: "You must save her! From herself and from that mysterious man! But without compromising her, without making him talk!" Who was he, our elusive perpetrator? How could I capture him and yet force him to remain silent? That's what Darzac must have meant: in order to for the perpetrator to remain silent, he must be killed. That was the only logical conclusion based on what he'd said. Did I have the right to kill Mademoiselle Stangerson's persecutor? No, I did not. But if he only gave me an opportunity, how I would seize it! Let me find out whether he really was a creature of flesh and blood! Let me see his dead body, since we weren't able to take him alive!

If only I could make this woman, who didn't even look at us, who was so overcome by her fears and her father's distress, understand that I was capable of anything to save her! Yes, I would grab logic by the right end again and perform miracles for her!

I moved towards Mademoiselle Stangerson. I wanted to talk to her, to beg her to trust me... I would have liked to convince her, with but a few words that only she and I alone would have understood, that I knew how her enemy had escaped from the Yellow Room, that I had guessed half of her secret, and that I felt sorry for her with all my heart. But her gestures begged us to leave her alone, expressing her weariness and exhaustion.

Professor Stangerson asked us to go back to our respective rooms and thanked us. Larsan and I bowed and, followed by Père Jacques, we went out in the corridor.

There, I heard Larsan murmur: "Strange! Strange!"

He gestured me to come to his room. On the threshold, he turned towards Père Jacques and asked:

"Did you see him?"

"Who?"

"The perpetrator."

"Did I see him? He had a big red beard and red hair."

"That's how he appeared to me," I said.

"And to me too," said the detective.

After that, Larsan and I spent some time alone in his room, discussing the case. We talked for an hour, turning the matter over and looking at it from every angle. From his questions, and his explanations, it was clear that, despite the evidence of our senses, he was convinced that our man vanished by some secret passage known to him alone.

"He knows the Chateau," he said. "He knows it very well."

"He was rather tall and well-built," I said, returning to the topic of the perpetrator's identity.

"He's as tall as he wants to be," said Larsan.

"I understand what you mean," I said, "but how do you account for his red hair and beard?"

"Too much beard, too much hair... They must be false."

"That's too easy. You're still thinking of Robert Darzac, aren't you? Can't you get rid of that notion? I'm telling you, I'm certain that he is innocent."

"Bully for him then! I hope so for his sake. But everything condemns him. Did you notice the footprints on the carpet? Come and look at them."

"I've seen them already. They're the same prints as those left by the expensive boots, which we saw near the pond."

"Can you deny that they belong to Darzac?"

"Of course, I can! There's always room for error."

"But have you noticed that the footprints only go in one direction? That there are no outgoing prints? When the man came out of Mademoiselle Stangerson's bedroom, chased by all of us, he left no traces behind him."

"He might have been in her room for hours. The mud on his boots had dried. Plus, he ran with such speed that only his toes touched the floor. We saw him running, but we didn't hear his steps."

I decided to put an end to this idle chatter, devoid of any logic, unworthy of men like us, and gestured to Larsan to be quiet and listen.

"Downstairs! Someone has just shut a door."

I stood up. Larsan followed me. We walked down to the ground floor of the Chateau. I took him to the small oval room located under the terrace beneath the window of the corner corridor. I pointed at the door, which had been opened a while ago, but was now closed. Under it, a shaft of light was visible.

"The gamekeeper!" said Larsan.

"Let's go!" I whispered.

Prepared—I don't know why—I wouldn't even have admitted it—to believe that the gamekeeper might have been our perpetrator after all, I walked to the door and knocked loudly on it.

Some might think that we were rather late in thinking of the gamekeeper, since our first business, after the perpetrator had escaped us upstairs, should have been to search for him everywhere, inside and outside the Chateau, on the grounds, etc.

Had this criticism been made at the time, I could only have answered that the perpetrator had vanished in such a way that we thought he was no longer anywhere! He had escaped us when we all had our hands stretched out, ready to grab him, when we were almost touching him. We no longer had any reasonable hopes of finding him during that mysterious night in or out of the Chateau.

After I had knocked, the door opened and the gamekeeper asked us calmly what we wanted. He was undressed and preparing to go to bed. His bed hadn't yet been turned down.

We entered and I affected surprise.

"Not gone to bed yet?"

"No," he replied roughly. "I've been making the rounds of the grounds and in the woods. I've just come back—and I feel sleepy. So a good night to you!"

"Listen," I said. "About an hour or so ago, there was a ladder next to your window..."

"Really? I didn't see any ladder. Good night, I said!"

And he put us out. Once outside, I looked at Larsan. His face was impenetrable.

"Well?" I said.

"Well?" he repeated.

"Does that give you any new ideas?"

There was no mistaking Larsan's bad temper. On returning to the Chateau, I heard him mutter: "It would be strange, very strange, if I had made such a mistake!" And it seemed to me that he had said this more for my benefit than his. Then he added: "In any event, we shall soon find out what's what. *It will be light tomorrow.*"

Chapter Eighteen
Rouletabille Draws a Circle Between the Two Bumps on His Forehead

Excerpts from Joseph Rouletabille's notebook (con'td.):

Larsan and I separated on the thresholds of our rooms with a melancholy handshake. I was glad to at least have sown some doubt in his mind. His was an original brain, very intelligent but without logic.

After our conversation, I didn't go to bed. I waited for the first light of dawn and went down to the front of the Chateau. I then made a complete tour of it, examining every footstep coming towards or going away from it. These, however, were so mixed and confusing that I could make nothing of them. I might as well note here that normally I don't attach too much importance to the physical clues left in the wake of a crime. The method which consists in identifying a criminal by his footprints is altogether too primitive for my taste. Too many footprints are identical, and clues like these should, in no instance, be considered sufficient to convict someone.

However, in my disturbed state of mind, I had gone to the deserted courtyard and had examined all the footprints I could find, seeking some indication that could have been the basis for a theory to solve the mystery of the unfathomable corridor. But I found nothing! Nothing!

If only I could find *the right end of logic*! I thought. In despair, I sat on a stone. I reflected that, for the last hour, I had busied myself like a common, ordinary policeman. Like the least intelligent of detectives, I had gone blindly looking for footprints to tell me either something I already knew or anything I wanted them to say!

I came to the conclusion that I was a fool, lower on the scale of intelligence than the many Sûreté inspectors who prided themselves in applying the methods of Lecoq or followed in the footsteps of Dupin and Sherlock Holmes. Those policemen would erect mountains of stupidity out of the simple molehills of a footprint in the sand or the impression of a hand on a wall. I recognized all too well Frederic Larsan's method. Trying to imitate Sherlock Holmes would cause Frederic the Great to make mistakes bigger than any recorded in the great British detective's casebooks, blunders that would send an innocent to prison, or to the scaffold... Playing Sherlock Holmes had served Larsan well so far. He had succeeded in convincing the Investigating Magistrate and the Chief of the Sûreté of the validity of his theory. Now, he said he was waiting only for the last piece of evidence before arresting Darzac... The last piece! The fool! He didn't even have the first piece to begin with! All his mountain of clues didn't offer a single, real piece of hard evidence. I, too, had looked at the handprint on the wall of the Yellow Room, and examined the footprints left by the expensive boots, but only to ask them *to enter into a circle of logic which I had drawn in my mind!*

Yes, that circle might seem small at first, too small sometimes—and yet, it was immense, *because it contained only the truth!* The footprints left by the expensive boots and all the other physical clues we had gathered had to be the slaves of logic, not its masters! They hadn't been allowed to turn me into the one thing that's worse than a blind man: a man who sees falsely. And that's why I thought I would triumph over Frederic Larsan's blunders born from his unreasoning and illogical mind.

Take heart, Rouletabille, I said to myself. It's not because, for the first time, last night, in that unfathomable corridor, a strange and extraordinary incident occurred that didn't fit within your circle of logic that you should lose all confidence in yourself and start behaving like a pig, its snout in the mud, looking for truffles. Come on, Rouletabille, get your head up. It was impossible for the incident of the unfathomable corridor to be outside my circle of logic. I knew that! Then lift your head high, I said, put your hands on those two bumps on your forehead, and start thinking! Remember that when you drew that circle of logic in your mind, like with a compass on a piece of paper, you did it *by grabbing logic by its right end!*

Well, now, continue to do so! Go back to the unfathomable corridor and use *the right end of logic* for support, just as Frederic Larsan uses his cane, to figure out the answer.

And if I know you, Rouletabille, it won't be long before you prove that Frederic the Great is nothing but a fool!

Joseph Rouletabille
October 30, Noon

Excerpts from Joseph Rouletabille's notebook (con'td.):

That was what I thought then, and that was what I did. With my brain on fire, I returned to the unfathomable corridor, and, without finding anything more than I had already seen on the previous night, *the right end of logic* showed me something so momentous that I was forced to cling to it to prevent myself from falling.

Now, I was going to need great strength and patience to find the physical clues that would fit—nay, that must fit—within the circle of logic that I drew there, in my mind, beneath the two bumps on my forehead!

Joseph Rouletabille
October 30, Midnight

Chapter Nineteen
Rouletabille Invites Me to Lunch
at the Auberge du Donjon

It was not until later that Rouletabille sent me the note-book in which, the following day, he had written down in great detail the story of the unfathomable corridor.

When I arrived at Glandier and joined him in his room, he told me everything which I have now related, plus how he had spent several hours back in Paris where he had learned nothing that could be of any help.

The events of the unfathomable corridor had occurred on the night between October 29 and October 30, three days before my return to the Chateau. It was now November 2, the day I had been summoned back by my friend's telegram, asking me to bring a couple of guns with me.

I sat quietly in Rouletabille's room while he finished his story.

While he had been talking, I had noticed that he was continually fingering the lenses of the spectacles he had found on his night stand. From the obvious pleasure he was taking in handling these farsighted glasses, I understood that they must have been one of the clues he intended to place inside *the circle of logic* which he had drawn in his mind.

That strange and unique way he had of expressing himself, using terms that perfectly described his thoughts, no longer surprised me. However, it was often necessary to know what his thoughts were in order to understand the terms he used—and it was never easy to divine Rouletabille's thoughts.

This young man's mind was one of the most curious things I had ever observed. Rouletabille went along, never suspecting the astonishment and bewilderment that his way of thinking caused in others. People were so much in awe of his mind that they turned around after he'd gone and looked at him as if they'd just crossed paths with some kind of colorful character on the road. And, just as one might say, "Who is he? Where does he come from? Where is he going?", they would say, "What is Rouletabille thinking? What is he going to do next?" Since he was entirely unaware of the unique nature of his mind, he wasn't in the least concerned by his public behavior, going around just like everyone else, a little like the way someone who doesn't realize that he's dressed eccentrically feels no embarrassment no matter where he is. This young man, gifted with such an extraordinary brain, was, in a similar fashion, expressing naturally the most amazing ideas born out of his prodigious leaps of logic, so prodigious, in fact, that most us couldn't follow them until he took the time to reduce them into a series of smaller, more easily graspable, increments before our astonished eyes.

When Rouletabille had finished his story, he asked me what I thought. I replied that I was completely mystified by what had happened in the unfathomable corridor. Then he begged me to try *to grasp logic by its right end*, just as he had done.

"Very well," I said. "It seems to me that the starting point of trying to explain what happened should be this: there can be no doubt that the perpetrator you were pursuing was, in fact, in the corridor."

I paused.

"After making such good a start," said Rouletabille, "it would be a shame to stop so soon. Come on, continue with your reasoning."

"I'll try. Since he vanished from the corridor without passing through any known doors or windows, then he must have escaped through some other, as yet unknown, opening."

My friend looked at me with pity, sighed wistfully and remarked that I was dumb as a doorknob.

"What am I saying, a doorknob! You're dumber than Larsan himself!" he added.

Rouletabille seemed to alternate between fits of admiration and contempt for Frederic the Great. Sometimes, he exclaimed, "He's really brilliant!" while at others, he complained, "He's such an idiot!", depending or not on whether the detective's discoveries tallied with Rouletabille's own theories. It was a small, petty side of his otherwise noble character.

We finally got up and left his room. Rouletabille led me back outside. As we crossed the courtyard, and were proceeding towards the main gate, we heard the sound of shutters being thrown back against the wall. We turned around and saw, at a window on the first floor of the left wing of the Chateau, the ruddy and clean shaven face of a person whom I did not recognize.

"Hello!" muttered Rouletabille. "That's Arthur Rance!"

He lowered his head, quickened his pace, and I heard him mutter to himself between his teeth:

"So he was at the Chateau last night? What is he doing here?"

When we had gone some distance from the Chateau, I asked him who this Arthur Rance was, and how he knew him. He reminded me of the story he had told me of his evening at the Elysée Palace. Arthur W. Rance was the American from Philadelphia with whom he had had so many drinks.

"But wasn't he about to return home?" I asked.

"Indeed! That's why I'm surprised to find him not only still in France, but at Glandier. He didn't arrive this morning or last night. He must have gotten here before dinner then, and I missed him. Why didn't the caretakers tell me?"

Speaking of the Berniers, I reminded Rouletabille that he hadn't yet told me what he had done to get them released.

We were close to the caretakers' lodge. Monsieur and Madame Bernier saw us coming. A frank smile lit up their happy faces. They seemed to harbor no ill-feeling over their preventive detention. My friend asked them at what time had Mr. Rance arrived. They replied that they didn't know that he was staying at the Chateau. They said that he must have come during the evening of the previous night, but they didn't have to open the gate for him, because, being a great walker, and not wishing that a carriage be sent to meet him at the station, he was accustomed to getting off at the hamlet of Saint-Michel, from which he came to the Chateau through the woods. He got into the estate by going through the grotto of Sainte Genevieve, and there, climbed over a low gate which separated Glandier from the neighboring countryside.

As the caretakers explained all this, I saw Rouletabille's face cloud over and exhibit disappointment—no doubt, with himself. Obviously, he was a little upset that, after having spent so much time at Glandier, and having conducted such a thorough investigation of its people and events, he hadn't discovered until now that Arthur Rance was a regular visitor to the Chateau.

"You say that Monsieur Rance is *a regular visitor*," he asked somberly, trying to clarify what the caretakers had said. "When did he come here last?"

"I can't tell you exactly," replied Monsieur Bernier. "Because of our having been locked up. Besides, when the gentleman comes, he doesn't use the main gate, so we don't see him arrive or leave."

"But surely, you must know when he came *for the first time?*"

"Oh yes, Monsieur! That was nine years ago."

"So he was in France nine years ago," said Rouletabille. "Since that time, as far as you know, how many times has he been at Glandier?"

"Three times."

"When did he come for the last time, as far as you know?"

"A week before the attack in the Yellow Room."

Rouletabille asked another question, this time addressing Madame Bernier:

"*In the groove of the parquet?*"

"Yes. *In the groove of the parquet*," she replied.

"Thank you!" said Rouletabille. "Be prepared for to-night."

He spoke the last words with a finger on his lips as if to advise silence and discretion.

We left the estate and took the road to the Auberge du Donjon.

"Have you eaten there often?" I asked.

"Sometimes."

"But you also took meals at the Chateau?"

"Yes," said Rouletabille. "Larsan and I were sometimes served in our rooms."

"Hasn't Professor Stangerson ever invited you to his table?"

"No, never."

"Does your presence at the Chateau displease him then?" I asked.

"I don't know, but if it does, he's shown no signs of it."

"Does he ever question you?"

"Never. He is in the same frame of mind as he was when he stood outside the Yellow Room when his daughter was being attacked, and after he broke open the door and couldn't find her attacker. He is convinced that, since he couldn't find anything that night, we won't either. But he has felt obliged, since Larsan came up with his theory implicating him, to not oppose our efforts."

Rouletabille spent some time absorbed in his own thoughts, then told me of how he had arranged the release of the caretakers.

"I went to see Professor Stangerson. I had him write the following on a piece of paper: 'I hereby promise, notwithstanding anything that I might learn, to keep my two loyal servants, Monsieur and Madame Bernier, in my employ.' I told him that, by signing that document, he would enable me to persuade the Berniers to talk, and that I was certain that they were innocent of any involvement in the crime. That was also his opinion, so he signed. The Investigating Magistrate then showed the document to the Berniers, who did begin to talk. They said, as I was sure they would, that they'd been too afraid of losing their jobs before.

"They confessed to poaching on the Professor's estate, and it was while poaching, on the night of the attack, that they

169

found themselves near the pavilion when Mademoiselle Stangerson was being assaulted. They sold the various game, ducks and rabbits, that they caught to the landlord of the Auberge du Donjon, who served them to his customers in the form of much appreciated pâtés and terrines, and sold the rest to the markets in Paris. That was what I had guessed earlier. Do you remember what I said when we walked into the Auberge du Donjon? *I'd like some blood pudding*—a type of sausage made of pig or cattle blood.

"You see, I'd heard the same words on the morning when we arrived at Glandier. You probably heard them too, but didn't attach any importance to them. As you remember, when we reached the main gate, we stopped to look at a man who was running alongside the wall of the estate, constantly checking his watch. That was Larsan who was already at work. Well, not too far from there, the landlord of the Auberge du Donjon was standing on his doorstep, and I heard him say to someone inside: '*Now, you'll have to be content with blood pudding.*'

"What did he mean by *now*? When you're searching, as I always am, for the hidden meanings of things, you can't afford to ignore anything you see or hear. You've got to understand everything. We were in a backwater part of the country which had just been turned upside down by a ghastly crime. Logic told me that every phrase I might hear would likely reflect it. So I took that '*now*' to mean, '*since the crime.*' During my initial investigation, I kept looking for a connection between that harmless-sounding phrase and the attack upon Mademoiselle Stangerson, but I found none. However, when we went to the Auberge du Donjon for lunch, I repeated it and saw, by the surprise and trouble on Père Mathieu's face, that I had not exaggerated its importance, at least as far as he was concerned.

"I had just learned that the caretakers had been arrested. Père Mathieu spoke of them as of dear friends, people for whom he felt sorry. In a wild burst of inspiration, I put two and two together and said to myself that what he had meant was: '*Now* that the caretakers have been arrested, *you'll have to be content with blood pudding.*' No more caretakers, no more game, no more pâtés! The reason I made that connection was because of the hatred Père Mathieu expressed towards Professor Stangerson's gamekeeper—a hatred which he claimed was also shared by the caretakers! That easily led me to think of poaching. Since all the evidence showed that the caretakers hadn't been in their bed at the time of the attack, what were they doing outside that night? Were they parties to the crime? I didn't think so. I had already arrived at the conclusion, for reasons which I will tell you later, that the perpetrator had worked alone, and that the entire tragedy was based on a mysterious connection between Mademoiselle Stangerson and said perpetrator, a mystery which didn't involve the caretakers.

"Poaching was the key to explaining everything, *at least as far as the caretakers were concerned.* With that theory in mind, I searched for some proof in their lodge, which, as you remember, I entered. I found it under their bed: collars and copper wire. 'Ah-ah!' I thought, 'this explains what they were doing outside at night!' I was no longer surprised by their stubborn silence and their refusal to answer the Investigating Magistrate's questions, even when they were being accused of complicity in the matter of the attack on Mademoiselle Stangerson. Confessing to poaching would have saved them from the Court of Assize, but would have cost them their jobs. Since they were perfectly certain of their innocence in the matter of the attack, they hoped that the true perpetrator would soon be caught, and that everyone would forget about the poaching. Besides, they could always confess to it later if things turned out badly.

"I hastened their confession by means of the document signed by Professor Stangerson. They gave all the evidence necessary, were released at once, and now are extremely grateful to me. Why didn't I get them released sooner? Because I wasn't sure that poaching was their only crime. I needed to learn more. But, as the days went by, my conviction became a certainty. Then, the day after the events of the unfathomable corridor, I needed help that I could rely on, so I resolved to have them released at once. And there we are!"

That's how Rouletabille explained the situation. Once again, I was astonished by the simplicity of the reasoning which had brought him to the truth in the matter of the two caretakers. Certainly, this was a minor side issue, but I couldn't help thinking that, someday soon, that young man was going to explain the formidable Mystery of the Yellow Room, as well as that of the unfathomable corridor, with the same simplicity.

While talking, we had reached the Auberge du Donjon and went inside.

This time, we didn't see the innkeeper, but were greeted with a pleasant smile by his wife. I have already described the room in which we found ourselves, and I have given a description of the charming blonde woman with the gentle eyes who immediately began to prepare our lunch.

"How's Père Mathieu?" inquired Rouletabille.

"Not much better, Monsieur. He's still confined to his bed," replied the woman.

"His rheumatisms are still tormenting him, then?"

"Yes. Last night, I had to give him a morphine shot again. That's the only medicine that gives him any relief."

She spoke in a soft voice. Everything about her expressed gentleness. She was, indeed, a beautiful woman, with an air of indolence, great, sorrowful blue eyes—the eyes of a lover. Père Mathieu, when he wasn't suffering from rheumatisms, must have been a happy man. But could a woman like her ever be happy with a foul-tempered, rheumatic husband? The domestic dispute which we had witnessed earlier didn't lead me to believe so. And yet, there was something about her that did not suggest despair or hopelessness.

She disappeared into the kitchen to prepare our meal, leaving a bottle of excellent cider on the table. Rouletabille filled our mugs, lit his pipe, and quietly explained to me his reason for asking me to come to Glandier with guns.

"Yes," he said, contemplatively looking at the clouds of smoke he was puffing out, "yes, my friend, *I'm expecting the perpetrator tonight.*"

A brief silence followed, which I took care not to interrupt, and then he went on:

"Last night, just as I was going to bed, Monsieur Darzac knocked at my door. I let him in and he told me that he had to go to Paris the next day, that is to say, this morning. The reason the journey was necessary was both peremptory and mysterious; peremptory because he absolutely had to go; mysterious because he wouldn't tell me the reason. 'I must go," he said, "and yet, I would give half my life not to leave Mademoiselle Stangerson right now.' He didn't try to hide the fact that he believed her to be in danger again. 'I wouldn't be surprised,' he added, 'if something happens tomorrow night, and yet I must go. I can't be back at Glandier until the morning of the day after tomorrow.'

"I asked him to explain himself, but that's all he would tell me. His fear of a new threat had come to him solely from observing the coincidence that his fiancée had been attacked twice, at both times when he had been absent. On the night of the incident of the unfathomable corridor, he had been obliged to be away from Glandier. On the night of the tragedy in the Yellow Room, he had also not been able to be at the Chateau, at least according to his own statements. For a man with such a clear understanding of a threat, to still be compelled to leave meant that *he was being forced to obey a will stronger than his own.* That was how I reasoned, and I told him so. He replied: 'Perhaps.' I asked him if the will was that of Mademoiselle Stangerson. He said that it was not, and that his decision to go to Paris had been taken without any consultation with her. In short, he repeated that his belief in the possibility of a new attack was based entirely on that extraordinary coincidence which he had observed—and upon which the Investigating Magistrate had also commented.

" 'If anything happens to Mademoiselle Stangerson,' he said to me, 'it will be terrible for us both. For her, because her life will be in danger again; for me, because I shan't be able to defend her, nor tell anyone *where I've spent the night*. I'm perfectly aware of the suspicions that weigh on me. The Investigating Magistrate and Monsieur Larsan both believe me guilty. Larsan tailed me the last time I went to Paris, and I had all the trouble in the world of getting rid of him.'

" 'Why don't you tell me the name of the perpetrator now, if you know it?' I exclaimed.

"Darzac appeared extremely troubled by my question, and replied in a hesitating tone:

" 'I? You think I know the name of the murderer? But how could I know his name?'

"I replied at once:

" 'Because Mademoiselle Stangerson told it to you.'

"He became so pale that I thought he was about to faint. I saw that I had hit the nail right on the head. *Mademoiselle Stangerson and he knew the perpetrator's name!*

"When he recovered himself, he said to me:

" 'I am going to leave you, Monsieur Rouletabille. Since you've been here, I've learned to appreciate your exceptional intelligence and your unequalled ingenuity. I would now like to ask this service of you. Perhaps I'm wrong to fear another attack tomorrow night, but I must plan for that possibility and I would like to count on you to thwart any attempts that may be made on Mademoiselle Stangerson's life. Take every step required to protect her. Keep a very careful eye on her room and make sure no one goes inside. Be her watchdog. Don't go to sleep, don't allow yourself one moment of repose. The man we fear is remarkably cunning, with unequalled craftiness. *That very cunning might save her* if you keep watch, because our man will know that you're watching, and because of his cunning, he won't try anything.'

" 'Have you told all this to Professor Stangerson?'

" 'No.'

" 'Why not?'

" 'Because I don't wish him to ask me the same thing that you did just now, the name of the perpetrator. If you were surprised by what I told you, imagine what the Professor might say! He might question the fact that my prediction of the perpetrator's return in my absence is based on a series of coincidences that he, too, might find rather questionable... If I tell you all this, Monsieur Rouletabille, it's because I have great, very great, confidence in you. I know that you do not suspect me.'

"The poor man spoke in hiccups, as if he could hardly breathe. It was obvious that he was in pain. I felt sorry for him, the more so because I felt certain that he would prefer to be killed himself rather than to tell me who the perpetrator was, just as Mademoiselle Stangerson would rather die than reveal the identity of the man of the Yellow Room and the unfathomable corridor. That man must have been controlling her, or both of them, through some terrible secret, and it was clear that they lived in fear that the Professor would learn that his daughter was being manipulated by her assailant. I told Monsieur Darzac that he had said enough, since he couldn't tell me anything. I further promised him I would stay awake and keep watch all night. He insisted that I should establish a truly impenetrable barrier around Mademoiselle Stangerson's bedroom, her boudoir where the two nurses slept, and her sitting room where, since the affair of the unfathomable corridor, the Professor had been spending his nights. In short, I was to cordon off the whole apartment.

"From his insistence, I understood that Monsieur Darzac intended not only to make it impossible for the perpetrator to reach Mademoiselle Stangerson's bedroom, but also to make such a goal so obviously impossible that, realizing that he was being expected, he wouldn't even try. At least, that's how I interpreted his final words when we parted: 'After I'm gone, you may share my suspicions with Professor Stangerson, Père Jacques, Monsieur Larsan, and everyone else at the Chateau, but make it look like the idea or organizing such insurmountable defense, at least until I return, was entirely yours.'

"The poor fellow left me, hardly knowing what he was saying. My silence and my eyes told him that I had guessed three quarters of his secret. And, indeed, he must have been at his wits' end to have come to me at such a time, and to abandon Mademoiselle Stangerson despite his dreadful fear of another *coincidental* attack.

"After he'd gone, I began to think hard. I knew that I had to outsmart our foe's own smartness, so that if the perpetrator were to return that night, he shouldn't for a moment suspect that he was being expected. I had to bar his way, under pain of death, and yet let him in far enough so that, *dead or alive, I might see his face clearly!* I had to put an end to this! *Mademoiselle Stangerson had to be freed from this murder in installments.*

"Yes, my friend," concluded Rouletabille, after placing his pipe on the table, and emptying his mug of cider, "I must see his face distinctly, *in order to make sure that it can fit inside that circle which I've drawn inside my head with the right end of logic.*"

The landlady reappeared at that moment, bringing in the traditional bacon omelette. Rouletabille flirted a little with her, and she took it in stride with a most charming smile.

"She is much nicer when Père Mathieu is in bed with his rheumatisms," Rouletabille observed.

However, I wasn't thinking about Rouletabille or the landlady's smiles. I was entirely absorbed by my friend's last words and Monsieur Darzac's strange behavior.

When he had finished his omelette, and we were again alone, Rouletabille continued his tale:

"When I sent you my telegram this morning," he said, "I had only the word of Monsieur Darzac that, perhaps, the perpetrator might return tonight. I can now say that he will certainly come. In fact, I'm planning for it."

"What made you feel so certain? Could it be...?"

"Quiet!" interrupted Rouletabille, smiling. "Please. You're going to say something stupid. I've been sure that the perpetrator would return tonight *since 10:30 a.m.* I knew it *before we saw Arthur Rance at the window in the courtyard.*"

176

"Ah!" I said. "Really? But then... I don't understand... What made you so sure? And why at 10:30 a.m.?"

"Because, at 10:30 a.m., I had proof that Mademoiselle Stangerson was making as much of an effort to allow the perpetrator in as Monsieur Darzac had made to stop him."

"How can that be?" I cried. Then, in a sotto voice, I added: "Didn't you tell me that Mademoiselle Stangerson is in love with Monsieur Darzac?"

"I told you that because it's true."

"Then don't you think it's strange that..."

"Everything in this business is strange, my friend; but take my word for it, the strangeness you've seen until now is nothing compared to the strangeness that's coming!"

"Then," I said, hesitantly, "we should assume that Mademoiselle Stangerson and her attacker are talking to each other, or at least corresponding..."

"Assume away, my friend! Where's the problem? I told you about the letter left on Mademoiselle Stangerson's desk on the night of the unfathomable corridor, a letter which later disappeared into her pocket... Who could say if, in it, the perpetrator wasn't asking Mademoiselle Stangerson for another rendezvous? A rendezvous that might take place as soon as Monsieur Darzac left the Chateau? The night following his departure, for example?"

My friend laughed silently. There were moments when I asked myself if he wasn't having fun at my expense.

Suddenly, the door of the inn opened. Rouletabille was on his feet so suddenly that one might have thought he had received an electric shock.

"Mr. Rance!" he cried.

It was indeed Mr. Arthur William Rance who stood before us and calmly saluted us.

Chapter Twenty
Mademoiselle Stangerson's Ominous Gesture

"Do you remember me, Monsieur?" asked Rouletabille.

"Perfectly!" replied Mr. Rance. "You're the boy I met at the bar at the Elysée." (Here, Rouletabille went red in the face at being called *boy*) "I came down to shake hands with you, because you're a bright little fellow aren't you?"

The American extended his hand and Rouletabille, now laughing in spite of himself, shook it and introduced Mr. Rance to me. He invited him to share our meal.

"No, thanks. I'll be having lunch later with Professor Stangerson."

Mr. Rance spoke perfect French, almost without an accent.

"I didn't expect to have the pleasure of seeing you again, Monsieur," said my friend. "I thought you were planning to return to America the day after the banquet at the Elysée."

Rouletabille and I, outwardly indifferent, listened intently for the American's answer.

The man's purplish red face, his heavy eyelids, his nervous twitching, all spoke of his addiction to drink. How could such a sorry specimen of a man be intimate with Professor Stangerson?

I was to find out the answer a few days later from Frederic Larsan who, like ourselves, had been surprised and mystified by Rance's appearance and reception at the Chateau, and had had the American investigated. It turned out that Mr. Rance had been an alcoholic only for the last 15 years, that is to say, since the Professor and his daughter had left Philadelphia. During the time the Stangersons had lived in Pennsylvania, they had become friends with Rance, who was one of America's most distinguished phrenologists. Thanks to some bold, new experiments he had conducted, he had made enormous progress since the discoveries of Gall and Lavater.[16] The friendliness with which he was received at Glandier was explained by the fact that he had once rendered Mademoiselle Stangerson a great service by stopping, at the peril of his own life, the runaway horses of her carriage. The immediate consequence of that act of bravery had been a close and friendly association with the Stangersons, but by no stretch of the imagination a love affair.

Larsan didn't tell me from where he had gathered his information, but he seemed to be quite sure of his facts.

Had we known all this when Arthur Rance met us at the Auberge du Donjon, his presence at the Chateau might not have seemed so puzzling, but they wouldn't have decreased our interest in the man himself. The American must have been at least 45 years old. He responded to Rouletabille's question very naturally.

"I put off my return to America when I heard of the attack on Mademoiselle Stangerson. I wanted to be certain that she hadn't been harmed, and I shan't leave until she is perfectly recovered."

Mr. Rance then took the lead in our conversation, simply ignoring some of Rouletabille's questions. He gave us, without any prompting, his views on the matter of the tragedy, which, as far as I could tell, were not far from those held by Frederic Larsan. The American also thought that Robert Dar-

---

[16] Phrenology is the science which studies the relationships between a person's character and the morphology of their skull. The analysis of the face, or physiognomy, was particularly studied by the 18th century Swiss author Johann Kaspar Lavater (1741-1801). True scientific phrenology, which established a direct link between the morphology of the skull and the human character, was discovered by the Austrian physician Franz Joseph Gall (1758-1828). It was Gall who established the foundations for an anatomic caracteriology. He was also one of the first scientists to consider the brain as the home of all mental activities. (*Note from the Publisher*)

zac had something to do with the attack on Mademoiselle Stangerson. He didn't mention him by name, but there was no doubt about whom he meant. He told us that he was aware of Rouletabille's efforts to untangle the Mystery of the Yellow Room. He explained that Professor Stangerson had also related to him what had taken place in the unfathomable corridor. Listening to Mr. Rance, it was clear that, to him, the answer to all these mysteries was one and the same: Robert Darzac. Several times, he remarked that Monsieur Darzac had been away from the chateau just when all those mysterious occurrences had taken place, and we understood all too well what he was implying. Finally, he thought that Monsieur Darzac had been very smart in allying himself with Rouletabille, who wouldn't fail, sooner or later, to catch the perpetrator. He uttered that last sentence with undisguised irony. Then he rose, saluted us again, and left.

Rouletabille watched him through the window.

"A rather odd character, that man!" he said.

"Do you think he'll spend the night at Glandier?" I asked.

To my amazement, the young reporter answered that it was a matter of entire indifference to him whether Mr. Rance did or not.

I won't bother recounting here how we spent the rest of the afternoon. All I need to say is that Rouletabille took me for a walk through the forest; there, we visited the grotto of Sainte Genevieve. During all that time, my friend talked of every subject except the one in which I was the most interested.

As evening arrived, I was surprised to find Rouletabille making none of the preparations I had expected him to make. I mentioned it to him when, at nightfall, we found ourselves back in his room. He replied that all his arrangements had already been made, and that this time, the perpetrator wouldn't get away.

I expressed some doubts, reminding him of the man's earlier disappearance in the corridor, and suggested that the same phenomenon might occur again. He replied that he hoped that it would, and desired nothing more. So I didn't insist, knowing from experience how useless that would have been. Rouletabille told me that, with the caretakers' help, the Chateau had been watched since dawn in such a way that no one could approach it without his knowing. No one could come from the outside, and he felt no concern about those who were already inside.

Rouletabille pulled out his pocket watch. It was 6:30 p.m. Rising, he gestured me to follow him outside. Without trying in the least to conceal our movements or the sound of our footsteps, he led me through the corridor. We reached the right-wing corridor, turned right and came to the landing, which we crossed. We then continued our way in the left-wing corridor, passing Professor Stangerson's apartment.

At the far end of that corridor, before the tower, was the room occupied by Arthur Rance. We knew that because we had seen him at the window looking onto the courtyard earlier that morning. The door of that room opened at the very end of the corridor, exactly facing the east window at the far end of the right-wing corridor where Rouletabille had positioned Père Jacques during the night of the unfathomable corridor. When one left Mr. Rance's bedroom, one had an uninterrupted view of the entire corridor from one end to the other of the Chateau, except of course for the corner corridor where Rouletabille's room was.

"I'll take care of the corner corridor," said Rouletabille. "You, when I tell you, come and stand right there."

And he showed me a small dark, triangular closet, built into a bend of the wall, to the left of the door to Mr. Rance's room. From this recess, I could see all that occurred in the corridor just as well as if I had been standing in front of the American's room, and I could watch his door, too. The door of that closet, which was to be my place of observation, was fitted with panels of clear glass. All the lamps in the corridor were lit, it was quite bright. In the closet, however, it was dark. It was a splendid place from which to observe while remaining unobserved.

I was to play the part of a spy or an ordinary policeman. It wasn't something which I enjoyed, and I also thought that it might compromise the dignity of my profession. What would my colleagues from the Paris Bar say if they ever found out what I was doing? It never occurred to Rouletabille that I might refuse him my assistance, and indeed I did not. I wanted to oblige him because, first, I didn't wish him to think me a coward, second because I could always say that I was searching for the truth as an amateur detective, and finally, because it was too late for me to back out. Why I had not experienced such scruples sooner, or at all, was because my curiosity had simply gotten the better of me. Lastly, I could also say that I was helping to save a woman's life, and there can be no nobler purpose, even for a lawyer.

We walked back along the corridor. As we reached Mademoiselle Stangerson's apartment, the sitting room door was pushed opened by the butler who had been serving dinner. The Professor had, for the last three days, dined there with his daughter. As the door remained open, we distinctly saw Mademoiselle Stangerson, taking advantage of the butler's absence, while her father was stooping to pick up something he had let fall, pour the contents of a phial into the Professor's glass.

Chapter Twenty-One
Lying In Wait

That ominous gesture, which upset me greatly, didn't seem to surprise Rouletabille. We went back to his room and, without even referring to what we had just seen, he gave me my final instructions for the night. First, we were to go to dinner; after dinner, I was to take my position in the corridor closet and wait there as long as it was necessary to see what might happen.

"If you see anything before I do," he explained, "you must let me know. If our man enters the right-wing corridor by any other way than the corner corridor, you will see him before I do, because you have a view along the whole length of the corridor, while I can only see the corner corridor. To alert me, all you need to do is to untie the cord holding up the curtain of the window nearest to your closet. It will fall and, since the entire corridor is well lit, it will immediately create a square of shadow where before there had been a square of light. To do this, you only need to reach out of the closet with your hand. From the corner corridor, I can see all the windows of the left-wing gallery. When I see one go dark, I'll know what it means."

"And then?"

"Then you will see me coming around the corner."

"What am I to do then?"

"You will immediately come towards me, behind the perpetrator. I shall soon be upon him, and at last, I shall see *if his face fits inside my circle*."

"That circle which you've drawn with your *right end of logic*?" I said smiling.

"Why do you smile? It's not funny. Enjoy yourself while you can, because I swear to you, you won't feel like it later."

"What if our man escapes again?"

"*So much the better!*" said Rouletabille, coolly. "I don't want to capture him. After all, he might still have time to rush down the stairs and leave via the groundfloor vestibule, since you'll be coming from the far end of the left-wing corridor. Let him go, if it comes to that, *but I want to see his face*. That's all I want. Then, I'll know what to do afterwards so that, as far as Mademoiselle Stangerson is concerned, *it will be as if he was dead*, even though he might still be alive. Mademoiselle Stangerson and Monsieur Darzac might never forgive me if I took him alive, and I wish to retain their respect. They're good people.

"If Mademoiselle Stangerson was prepared to pour a narcotic into the Professor's glass, as we have just seen, so that he might not be awake to interrupt the conversation she is planning to have with her attacker, can you imagine how she would feel *if I brought the man of the Yellow Room, bound and gagged, to her father*? We were lucky, in fact, that the perpetrator managed to escape mysteriously during the night of the unfathomable corridor. I realized that when I saw Mademoiselle Stangerson's great relief *when she found out that the perpetrator had managed to flee*. I understand now that, to save that unhappy woman, I mustn't capture this man, but silence him—forever. But to kill a human being! To commit a murder! It's no small thing. Unless, of course, the man himself gives me a reason to do so... Besides, her concerns are not really my business... Still, to render him forever silent without Mademoiselle Stangerson's trust and confidence, means that I have to guess everything, without the first bit of knowledge. Fortunately, my friend, I have guessed, or rather, I have reasoned it all out. All that I now ask of the man who is coming here tonight is to show me his face, so that I may see if it fits..."

"Into your *circle of logic*?"

"Exactly! And his face won't surprise me!"

"But I thought you'd already seen his face during the night when you ran into Mademoiselle Stangerson's bedroom?"

184

"Only partially. The candle was on the floor. And with that beard…"

"Will he wear his beard this evening?"

"I think I can say for certain that he will. But the corridor is well lit and, now, I know... Or at least, my brain knows… And my eyes will see…"

"If we're here only to see him and let him escape, why are we armed?"

"Because, my dear Sainclair, *if the man of the Yellow Room and the unfathomable corridor knows that I know his secret, he is capable of anything!* We might have to defend ourselves."

"And you're sure that he will come tonight?"

"As sure as that you're standing there! This morning, at 10:30 a.m., Mademoiselle Stangerson, in the cleverest way possible, got rid of her two nurses. She gave them a leave of absence for 24 hours, under some plausible pretext, and while they're gone for the night, she said she didn't want anyone but her father to stay with her. The Professor gladly agreed, and made arrangements to sleep in the boudoir. Darzac's *coincidental* departure, and what he told me, as well as the extraordinary precautions taken by Mademoiselle Stangerson to be alone and undisturbed tonight, leaves no room for doubt. *She has prepared the way for the man whom Darzac dreads to come.*"

"That's awful!"

"Yes it is!"

"And what we saw her do was done to send her father to sleep?"

"Yes."

"So there are only the two of us for tonight's work?"

"Four; the Berniers will be watching as well. I don't think they'll see anything *beforehand*, but their testimony might be useful *afterward, if there is a murder!*"

"Then you think there might be a murder?"

"*If our man wishes it*, yes."

"Why haven't you brought in Père Jacques? Have you made no use of him today?"

"No," replied Rouletabille sharply.

I kept silent for awhile, then, anxious to know his thoughts, I asked him point blank:

"Why not tell Arthur Rance? He could be of great assistance…"

"I see!" said Rouletabille crossly. "You want to let everybody into Mademoiselle Stangerson's secrets? Come, let's go to dinner; it's time. Tonight, we'll dine in Frederic Larsan's company, unless he's tailing Monsieur Darzac again. He sticks to him like glue. But, anyhow, if he isn't here now, I'm quite sure he'll be here later! He's the one I'm going to surprise tonight!"

At that moment, we heard a noise in the room next to us.

"Speak of the Devil," said Rouletabille.

"I forgot to ask you," I said. "I'm not to make any allusions to tonight's business before Larsan, right?"

"Obviously! Tonight, we'll be operating alone, on our own personal account."

"So that all the glory will be ours?"

Rouletabille laughed, and concluded:

"Of course!"

We dined with Frederic Larsan in his room; he told us he had just come in and invited us to eat with him. We were in the best of spirits, which I attributed to the fact that both Rouletabille and Larsan felt that they each had solved the Mystery. Rouletabille told the detective that I had returned on a whim, and that he had asked me to stay and help him with a lengthy article which he had to write this very night for *L'Epoque*. I was supposed to return to Paris, he said, by the 11 p.m. train, taking the article back with me. It was meant to be a serialized overview of the various episodes of the mysteries of Glandier. Larsan smiled at that explanation like a man who wasn't fooled, but was politely refraining from making the slightest remark on matters which didn't concern him.

With infinite precautions, carefully choosing the words they used, even down their intonations, for several minutes, Larsan and Rouletabille discussed Mr. Rance's presence at the Chateau and his past in America, which they would have liked to know better, at least insofar as his relations with the Stangersons were concerned. At one time, Larsan, who seemed to me to be somewhat unwell, said, with a noticeable effort:

"I think, Monsieur Rouletabille, that we don't have much left to do at Glandier, and my guess is that neither of us will sleep here many more nights."

"I think so, too, Monsieur Larsan," said my friend.

"Then you think that *the case is over?*"

"Yes, I believe so. There's nothing more to find out."

"Have you found your perpetrator?" asked Larsan.

"Have you?"

"Yes."

"So have I," said Rouletabille.

"Are they the same man?"

"I don't think so, *unless you've changed your mind*," said the young reporter. Then, he added, with emphasis: "Monsieur Darzac is an honest man!"

"Are you certain?" asked Larsan. "Well, I am sure of the contrary. So we'll being doing battle, then?"

"Yes, and I will beat you, Monsieur Larsan."

"Youth never doubts anything," said Frederic the Great laughing. He held out his hand to me by way of conclusion.

Rouletabille's answer came like an echo:

"Never doubt anything!"

Suddenly Larsan, who had risen to wish us goodnight, pressed both his hands to his chest and staggered. He was obliged to lean on Rouletabille for support and to save himself from falling.

"Oh! Oh!" he cried. "What's the matter with me? Have I been drugged?"

He looked at us with dazed eyes. We questioned him in vain; he didn't answer us. He had sunk into an armchair and we couldn't get word out of him. We were extremely distressed, both on his account and on our own, for we had partaken of all the same dishes that he had eaten. His pain finally seemed to ebb, but his heavy head had fallen on his shoulder and his eyelids were tightly closed. Rouletabille bent over him, listening for the beatings of his heart.

My friend's face, when he stood up, was as calm as it had been agitated only a moment ago.

"He's asleep," he said.

He took me back to his room, after closing Larsan's door.

"Is it Mademoiselle Stangerson's narcotic?" I asked. "Does she wish to put everybody to sleep, tonight?"

"Perhaps," replied Rouletabille, but I could see his mind was elsewhere.

"What about us?" I exclaimed. "How do we know that we haven't been drugged?"

"Do you feel indisposed?" Rouletabille asked me coolly.

"Not in the least."

"Do you feel sleepy?"

"Not at all."

"Well, then, my friend, I suggest that you smoke this excellent cigar."

And he handed me a choice Havana, one which Monsieur Darzac had given him, while he lit his briar pipe—his perennial briar pipe.

We remained in his room until about 10 p.m. without a word passing between us. Buried in an armchair Rouletabille sat and smoked steadily, his brow furrowed in thought and a far-away look in his eyes. On the stroke of 10, he took off his boots and signaled to me to do the same. As we stood in our socks, he said, in such a low tone that I guessed, rather than heard, the word:

"Revolver."

I drew my gun from my jacket pocket.

"Cock it!" he said.

I did as he directed.

Then moving towards the door of his room, he opened it with infinite precaution; it made no sound. We were in the corner corridor. Rouletabille made another sign to me. I understood that he wanted me to take up my post in the closet.

As I was walking away, he caught up with me and silently hugged me. Then, with the same precaution, he went back to his room. Astonished by this gesture of affection, and somewhat worried because of it, I arrived at the right-wing gallery, turned right, crossed the landing, and reached the small closet without any difficulties.

Before entering the closet, I examined the curtain cord of the window and found that I had only to release it from its fastening with my fingers for the curtain to drop due to its own weight and hide the square of light from Rouletabille—the signal agreed upon. A sound of footsteps made me stop in front of Arthur Rance's door. He wasn't yet in bed, then! How was it that, being in the Chateau, he hadn't dined with Professor Stangerson and his daughter? At least, I hadn't seen him at their table when we had looked in earlier and caught Mademoiselle Stangerson's ominous gesture.

I retired to the closet. I found myself perfectly situated. I could see along the whole length of the corridor. Nothing, absolutely nothing, could happen there without my seeing it. But what was going to happen tonight? Perhaps something very dangerous... Rouletabille's hug came back to my mind. Friends don't part from each other that way unless they're on an important or dangerous mission. Was I then in danger?

My hand closed on the butt of my revolver and I waited. I am no hero, but neither am I a coward.

I waited for about an hour, and during all that time, I saw nothing unusual. The rain, which had begun to come down strongly around 9 p.m., had now stopped.

My friend had told me that probably nothing would occur before midnight or 1 a.m. It was only 11:30 p.m., however, when I heard Arthur Rance's door open. The slight creak of its hinges indicated that it was being opened very slowly and carefully. It remained open for a minute, which seemed a very long time. As it opened outwards into the corridor, I couldn't see what was happening inside the room.

At that moment, I noticed a strange mewling sound coming from outside. It was repeated three times. Ordinarily, I wouldn't have paid any more attention to it than I would to the noise of cats on the roof. But the third time, the mewling was so sharp and penetrating that I remembered what I had heard about the cry of the Holy Beast. As it had accompanied all the tragic events at Glandier before, I couldn't repress a shudder.

Then I saw a man appear outside of the door and close it after him. At first, I could not see who it was because his back was turned toward me and he was bending over a rather bulky package. After he had closed the door and picked up his package, he turned toward the closet, and then I saw who he was. It was the game keeper, the "Green Man." He was wearing the same costume that he had worn when we had first met him at the Auberge du Donjon, and earlier that day when Rouletabille and I had seen him outside. There was no doubt about it. It was the gamekeeper. I saw him very distinctly. He seemed rather anxious. As the cry of the Holy Beast resounded for the fourth time, he put down his package and went to the corridor's second window, counting from the closet. I dared not make any movement, fearing that I might betray my presence.

Arriving at the window, he stuck his face against the glass and peered out. He remained like that for half a minute. Outside, the night was bright, the Moon showing at intervals between clouds. The Green Man raised his arms twice, making signs which I didn't understand. Then, leaving the window, he picked up his package again and moved along the corridor towards the landing.

Rouletabille had instructed me to drop the curtain if I saw anything. Was this what Rouletabille had been expecting? It wasn't my business to question. All I had to do was obey my instructions. I unfastened the cord. The curtain dropped. My heart was beating as if it would burst. Meanwhile, the gamekeeper had reached the landing, but, to my utter surprise—I had expected him to continue along the corridor—I saw him walks down the stairs toward the groundfloor vestibule.

What was I to do? I looked stupidly at the heavy curtain which had shut the light from the window. The signal had been given, but I didn't see Rouletabille appear at the corner corridor. Nobody happened. I was exceedingly perplexed. Half an hour passed, which seemed like an age. What was I to do now, even if I saw something? The signal, once given, couldn't be given a second time. Also, to venture into the corridor now might upset Rouletabille's plans. On the other hand, I had nothing to reproach myself for. If something had happened that my friend had not expected, he could only blame himself. Unable to be of any further assistance to Rouletabille by means of a signal, I decided to leave the closet after all, and, still in my socks, made my way to the corner corridor.

There was no one there. I went to the door of Rouletabille's room and listened. I could hear nothing. I knocked gently. There was no answer. I turned the handle and the door opened. I went in. I saw Rouletabille lying there, on the floor.

Chapter Twenty-Two
The Unbelievable Body

I immediately leaned over my friend's body, fearing the worst. I was exhilarated to find out that he was only deeply asleep—the same unnatural sleep that had affected Frederic Larsan earlier. I thought that the young man had succumbed to the effects of the same narcotic that must have been mixed with our food. But how was it that I had not been overcome by sleep too? I reflected that the drug must have been put into either our wine or water, which explained why I had escaped its effects. I never drink when eating. Naturally inclined to being overweight, I am restricted to a dry diet.

I shook Rouletabille, but didn't succeed in waking him. I was certain that this was Mademoiselle Stangerson's handiwork. She must have deemed it necessary to protect her secret from this very clever young man, who saw everything, who guessed everything, who was far more perceptive, and therefore dangerous, than her father. I remembered that the butler who had served us had recommended an excellent Chablis which, very likely, had come from the Professor's table.

A good 15 minutes went by. I resolved, under the pressure of circumstances, to resort to extreme measures. I threw a pitcher of cold water over Rouletabille's face. He opened his eyes, but they were dull and lifeless. So I slapped him good a few times and propped him up. I felt him come awake in my arms and heard him murmur: "Again, but don't make as much noise." To continue slapping him in silence was impossible, so I pinched him hard and shook him until he was able to stand up. We were saved!

"I've been drugged," he said. "Ah! I passed an awful moment before giving up to sleep. But I feel better now. Don't leave me."

He had no sooner uttered those words than we heard a dreadful scream that rang through the Chateau—a veritable death cry.

"Curses!" roared Rouletabille. "We're too late again!"

He tried to rush to the door, but was still too dazed and fell against the wall. However, I was already in the corridor, gun in hand, rushing like a madman towards Mademoiselle Stangerson's rooms. As I reached at the intersection of the corner and right-wing corridors, I saw a figure leaving her apartment. In a few strides, the man reached the landing.

I couldn't control myself and fired. The gunshot made a deafening noise. Nevertheless, the man continued his flight down the stairs. I ran behind him, shouting:

"Stop! Stop, or I'll kill you!"

As I rushed after him, I came face to face with Arthur Rance, coming from the left wing of the Chateau.

"What's going on?" he yelled.

The American was armed too, as is their custom.

We arrived almost at the same time at the foot of the stairs. The window of the vestibule was open. We distinctly saw the shape of a man running away. Instinctively, we both fired in his direction. Our target was barely 40 feet ahead of us. He staggered and we thought he was about to fall. We jumped through the window, but when the man saw us, he found some new vigor and dashed away.

I was in my socks, and the American was barefooted. As there was no hope of catching up with him, we fired our last cartridges. But he kept on running, going along the right side of the courtyard, towards the end of the right wing of the Chateau, which abutted on a ditch and a tall fence, and had no other practical outlet than the door of the small oval room occupied by the gamekeeper.

The man, though he had obviously been wounded by our shots, was now 70 feet ahead of us. Suddenly, behind us, above our heads, a window in the first floor corridor opened and we heard Rouletabille's voice crying out desperately:

"Fire, Bernier! Fire!"

At that moment, the night was lit by a flash of lightning. We saw Monsieur Bernier with his hunting rifle standing on the threshold of the tower.

His aim was good. The shadowy figure fell. But as our man had reached the end of the right wing, he fell on the other side of the Chateau, behind its corner; that is to say, we saw him just as he was about to fall, but we didn't see him actually touch the ground.

Bernier, Rance and myself turned the corner 20 seconds later and we saw the shape of a man lying dead on the ground.

Then, we heard Frederic Larsan, who must have been awakened from his lethargy by our cries and the gunshots. He had opened his window and was calling to us in the same fashion as Mr. Rance earlier:

"What's going on?" he yelled.

The three of us were shrouded in darkness, bending over the dead body of the mysterious perpetrator

Rouletabille, quite awake now, joined us at that moment. I cried out to him:

"He's dead!"

"So much the better," he said. "Take him into the vestibule of the Chateau." Then, as if on second thought, he said: "No! Let's put him in the gamekeeper's room."

Rouletabille knocked at the door. Nobody answered. Somehow, this didn't surprise me.

"He is evidently not there, otherwise he would have come out," said the reporter. "Let's carry him into the vestibule then."

Since reaching the dead man, a thick cloud had covered the Moon and darkened the night, so that we were unable to make out his features despite our mutual eagerness to find out his identity.

Père Jacques, who had now joined us, helped us to carry the body into the vestibule, where we laid it down on the lower step of the stairs. On the way, I felt my hands become wet from the warm blood that still seeped from the man's wounds.

Père Jacques ran to the kitchen and returned with a lantern. He held it close to the face of the dead man, and at last we saw the face of the gamekeeper, the man whom the landlord of the Auberge du Donjon had nicknamed the "Green Man."

An hour earlier, I had seen that same man come out of Arthur Rance's room carrying a parcel. But I could only tell that to Rouletabille later, when we would be alone.

I shouldn't fail to report that both Rouletabille and Larsan were bitterly disappointed by the result of the night's adventure. They could only look in consternation and stupefaction at the body of the Green Man. They touched the corpse, felt his uniform, searched his pockets, each muttering:

"That's impossible!"

Rouletabille even added:

"Well, knock me down with a feather!"

Père Jacques showed a great deal of sorrow and, between inane lamentations, kept repeating that we were mistaken, that the gamekeeper couldn't the man who had attacked Mademoiselle Stangerson. Finally, we were forced to tell him to be quiet. He couldn't have shown greater grief if the body had been that of his son. I explained this overflowing of sentiment by the fact that he must have been afraid that we might think that he derived some joy from the gamekeeper's death, because everyone knew he hated the man. I also noticed that, while all the rest of us were more or less undressed and barefooted, he was fully clothed.

Rouletabille had not left the body. Kneeling on the flagstones, he was undressing the corpse by the light of Père Jacques's lantern. He laid bare its chest, which was covered in blood.

Then, snatching the lantern from Père Jacques' hands, he brought it closer and discovered a gaping wound. Rising suddenly, he exclaimed in a voice filled with savage irony:

"The man you believe to have been shot was in fact killed by the stab of a knife through his heart!"

I thought Rouletabille had gone mad, but, bending over the body, I discovered that the young reporter was right.

There was not a sign of a bullet anywhere. The wound, evidently, had been made by a sharp blade, and had pierced the heart.

Chapter Twenty-Three
The Double Trail

I had barely recovered from the surprise caused by this new, astounding discovery, when Rouletabille touched me on the shoulder.

"Come with me!" he said.

"Where to?" I asked.

"To my room."

"What are we going to do there?"

"Think."

I confess that I was in no condition for doing much thinking. I could hardly imagine how, on this tragic night, in the midst of events the horror of which was only equaled by their unbelievability, with the gamekeeper's body still lying at his feet and Mademoiselle Stangerson perhaps on the brink of death, Rouletabille could bring himself to sit down calmly and think. And yet, that is just what he did, with the cold-bloodedness of the greatest generals during a battle. Closing the door of his room, he motioned me to a chair and, seating himself before me, took out his pipe. I looked at him sitting there, in silence, thinking; then I fell asleep.

When I awoke, it was daylight. It was 8 a.m. by my watch. Rouletabille was no longer in the room. His chair, in front of me, was empty. I rose to stretch my arms and legs when the door opened and my friend walked in. Judging by his face, I saw at once that he must have been busy.

"How is Mademoiselle Stangerson?" I asked.

"Her condition, though serious, isn't life-threatening."

"When did you go out?"

"Towards dawn."

"You've been working?"

"Very hard!"

"Have you found out anything?"

"Two sets of footprints—an interesting discovery that might have bothered me..."

"But it doesn't bother you anymore?"

"Not in the least."

"Do they explain anything?"

"Yes, they do."

"With respect to the gamekeeper's unbelievable body?"

"Yes. That body is entirely believable now. This morning, walking around the Chateau, I found two distinct sets of footprints, made simultaneously last night. I'm saying 'simultaneously' because it can't have been otherwise. If the second set of prints had come after the first, following the same path, it would have flattened them out, yet that wasn't the case. They were made by two persons walking side by side. One set of prints was almost parallel to the other. That double trail separated from all the other footprints in the center of the courtyard, then moved in the direction of the oak grove.

"I was leaving the courtyard, following those footprints, when Larsan joined me. He was at once interested by my discovery, because that double trail was clearly worth further investigation. These were the same kind of footprints we'd seen in the Yellow Room—one from cheap boots and the other from the expensive ones, except that, before, the expensive bootprints had taken over from the cheap ones at the pond, leading both Larsan and I to conclude that they belonged to the same person who had just switched footwear. Here, on the contrary, the two sets of prints were side by side. Such a discovery could only upset all my previous theories. Larsan was as confused as I was. So we bent over and examined these footprints more closely, like a hunting dog searching for a scent.

"I took the paper cut-outs I made of the previous footprints out of my notebook. The first cut-out was that of the cheap boots, which Larsan identified later as an old pair owned by Père Jacques. It matched perfectly the first set of new footprints left by those cheap boots. The second cut-out, which was that of the expensive boots, also matched the second set of prints, but with one small difference: the point of the boot seemed slightly larger. So we couldn't conclude with absolute certainty that the expensive prints had been made by the same man—but we couldn't rule it out either. Our suspect might simply have switched boots.

"Still following the double trail, Larsan and I came out of the oak grove and reached the pond again. This time, the trail didn't stop there, but carried on to the path leading to the main road going to Epinay. There, we lost the trail because of the tarred surface of the road, so we came back to the Chateau in silence.

"We parted company in the courtyard. But as our thoughts were running along the same lines, we met again in Père Jacques' room. We found the old servant still in bed. His clothes, hanging on a chair, were soaking wet and his boots— which looked remarkably like the cheap boots whose prints we'd just been studying—were muddy.

It certainly wasn't by helping us carrying the body of the gamekeeper from the courtyard to the vestibule, or going to the kitchen to fetch a lantern, that he had gotten them in such a state. Besides, it hadn't been raining then. His face showed extreme fatigue and he looked at us with fearful eyes.

"Upon questioning, he first told us that he had gone to bed straight after the doctor had arrived. (We had the butler go out and fetch a doctor after finding the body the night before.) After proving to him that he was lying, he finally confessed that he had gone out and left the estate. When we asked him why, he explained that he had had a headache and had gone out looking for fresh air, but he claimed he hadn't gone further than the oak grove. When we then described the trail we had just followed, *almost as if we'd been walking by his side*, he sat up in bed trembling.

" 'You weren't alone!' accused Larsan.

" 'Did you see him?' gasped Père Jacques.

" 'Who?' I asked.

" '*The dark phantom!*'

"And Père Jacques began telling us that, for several nights already, he had seen something ,or someone, whom he called the *dark phantom,* walking through the grounds at the stroke of midnight, gliding stealthily through the trees—in fact, it seemed to the old man that the phantom was literally walking *through* the trees. Twice, Père Jacques had seen that wraith from his window, by the light of the Moon, and had gotten up to try to catch him. The night before last, he had almost overtaken him, but the phantom had vanished at the corner of the tower. Last night, he had gone out, his mind obsessed by the new crime which he had just witnessed. Suddenly, he'd seen the phantom rush out from the center of the courtyard. He had followed him, carefully at first, then more energetically, through the oak grove and all the way to the pond, but the wraith had vanished on the main road to Epinay.

" 'Did you see his face?' asked Larsan.

" 'No! I saw nothing but black robes.'

" 'And after what had happened in the corridor upstairs, you didn't think to try to grab him?'

" 'No! I was too terrified. I had barely enough strength to follow him'

" 'Père Jacques,' I said in a threatening voice, 'you didn't *follow* him, as you just said. You and the phantom were going together, virtually arm in arm! You must have gone on the main road with him.'

" 'No!' he cried, 'I didn't. It began to pour and I turned back. I don't know what became of the phantom.'

"But as he said this, he refused to look me in the eye.

"So we left the old man. When we were outside, I turned to Larsan.

" 'Is he an accomplice?' I asked, looking at his eyes, trying to divine what he really thought

" 'How can I tell?' the detective replied, raising his arms in disbelief. 'You can't be sure of anything in a case like this. Twenty-four hours ago, I would have sworn that there were no accomplices!'

"He left me, saying he was off to Epinay."

Rouletabille had finished his story.

"Well, what do you think?" he asked.

"Personally, I'm utterly confused. I can't make head or tails out of it. But obviously, you do. What do you know?"

"*Everything!*" he exclaimed. "*Everything!*"

I had never seen him happier. He got up and pulled my hand forcefully.

"Can you explain it to me then?" I said.

"Not yet. First, let's find out how Mademoiselle Stangerson is feeling," he said abruptly.

Chapter Twenty-Four
Rouletabille Knows the Two Halves of the Perpetrator

Mademoiselle Stangerson had almost been murdered a second time. Unfortunately, this latest attempt on her life had been much worse than the first. The perpetrator had had time to stab her three times in the chest during that tragic night. As a result, she spent a long time lingering between life and death. When finally her will to live proved the strongest, and we had good reasons to hope that she would escape her grim fate, we found out that, even though she had recovered physically from her wounds, her mental condition had been seriously damaged. The least mention of the dreadful attack sent her into fits of delirium, and the arrest of Robert Darzac, which took place at Glandier on the day after the gamekeeper's tragic death, only seemed to sink her further into a deep depressive state.

Darzac arrived at the chateau around 9:30 a.m. I saw him running through the courtyard, his hair and clothes in disarray, his boots covered in mud, his face deadly pale. Rouletabille and I were looking out of a window in the upstairs corridor. He saw us and gave a despairing cry:

"Am I too late?"

"No! She still lives!" Rouletabille shouted.

A minute later, Darzac had gone into Mademoiselle Stangerson's bedroom and, through the door, we heard his heart-rending sobs.

"There's a curse attached to this place!" growled Rouletabille. "Some demons from Hell must be causing the misfortunes of this family! If I hadn't been drugged, I could have saved Mademoiselle Stangerson. I could have silenced her enemy forever, *and the gamekeeper wouldn't have lost his life!*"

Darzac came out to speak with us. He was in tears. Rouletabille told him everything: his preparations for Mademoiselle Stangerson's safety; his plans for disposing of her assailant forever *if only he had seen his face*; and how he would have succeeded had it not been for him being drugged.

"If only you had trusted me!" said the young man, in a tone of reproach. "If only you had begged Mademoiselle Stangerson to confide in me! But, then, everybody here distrusts everybody else: the daughter distrusts her father, the fiancée her lover... While you were asking me to protect her from her attacker, *she was doing everything in her power to facilitate her own murder!* That's why I arrived too late, still half awake, groggy, dragging myself to her bedroom where she lay in a pool of blood!"

At Darzac's request, Rouletabille described the whole scene. Leaning on the wall, to prevent himself from falling, he had made his way to Mademoiselle Stangerson's bedroom, while we were running after the perpetrator through the vestibule and the courtyard. The anteroom door was open. When he entered the bedroom, he found Mademoiselle Stangerson lying unconscious over the desk, her dressing-gown red with the blood flowing from her chest. Still under the influence of the drug, the young reporter felt he had just fallen prey to a horrible nightmare.

Mindlessly, he returned to the corridor, opened a window, and shouted his order to fire. Then, he went back to Mademoiselle Stangerson's room. He crossed the deserted boudoir, entered the sitting room, and tried to rouse Professor Stangerson who was lying on a sofa. He woke him up just as I had awakened him earlier. The Professor got up and, still dazed, let Rouletabille drag him up to the bedroom where, upon seeing his daughter's body, he uttered a heart-rending cry. Now fully awake, the Professor helped Rouletabille and, despite their feeble strength, the two men managed to carry Mademoiselle Stangerson to her bed.

Once that was done, Rouletabille's first thought was to join us, so eager he was *to know the face of the perpetrator*.

But as he walked by the desk, he noticed a bulky package on the floor. What was it doing there? he asked himself. He quickly knelt down and untied its string. Inside was an enormous quantity of papers and photographs. One was marked: "New differential electroscopic condenser." Another: "Fundamental properties of the intermediate substance between tangible matter and intangible aether." Rouletabille pondered at the mysterious irony of fate that had returned the Professor's precious scientific documents just as an attempt had been made to kill his daughter! As a matter of fact, the Professor was so grief-stricken that he found no joy in such restitution, and ended up burning most of the papers in the fireplace the next day!

The morning following that awful night, the Investigating Magistrate, Monsieur de Marquet, his clerk and the gendarmes, returned to the Chateau. Of course, we were all questioned thoroughly, except for Mademoiselle Stangerson who was nearly comatose. Rouletabille and I had already agreed on what we would say. I withheld any information about my being in the closet and said nothing about the drugging. In short, we didn't say anything that might have led the Magistrate to find out that we were anticipating some kind of attack, or that Mademoiselle Stangerson was, in fact, expecting her nocturnal attacker. The poor woman might, perhaps, pay with her life for the secret which bound her to her would-be murderer, and we wouldn't have wished to render her sacrifice useless.

Arthur Rance told everybody, in a manner so natural that it astonished me, that he had last seen the gamekeeper around 11 p.m. that fateful night. The man had come to his room to pick up a package that he was to take to Saint-Michel station early the next morning, and they had spent some time chatting about game and poachers. Mr. Rance had, indeed, intended to leave Glandier that morning and, according to his habit, planned to walk to Saint-Michel station. Not wanting to be burdened with excess luggage, he had asked the gamekeeper to take a package there for him. It was that parcel I had seen him carry when he had left Mr. Rance's room the night before.

At least, I thought so when Professor Stangerson confirmed what Mr. Rance had just said, adding that he had not asked him to dine with them because the American had already said his good-byes to his daughter and him at about 5 p.m. Mr. Rance was feeling midly indisposed and, instead, had ordered tea to be served in his room.

The caretaker, Monsieur Bernier, testified as instructed by Rouletabille. He said that the gamekeeper had requested his assistance that night to go after some poachers. (Clearly, the dead gamekeeper wasn't in a position to contradict his testimony.) They had been supposed to meet at a spot near the oak grove, but when the gamekeeper failed to show up, he, Bernier, had gone looking for him. He was almost at the tower, having taken a short-cut through a small door that led directly into the courtyard, when he saw a figure running swiftly from the opposite direction, towards the right wing of the Chateau. Then, he heard gunshots from behind the man, and saw Rouletabille at one of the gallery windows. Rouletabille saw him too, and recognized him. He heard the young reporter call out to him to fire, and he had done so. He believed that he had hit the man, possibly even killed him, until Rouletabille had undressed the body and shown that the man had died from a knife wound. He had not the faintest idea about what might have happened. If the body they had found wasn't that of the man who had been running and whom he had shot, when, then, was that other body? In the confined area where they were, all gathered looking at a body, there was no room for any other body, *dead or alive*.

Thus spoke Monsieur Bernier. But when the Investigating Magistrate reminded him that the spot where the body was found was very dark, and that he himself had not been able to recognize the gamekeeper until after he had been carried away to the vestibule, the caretaker replied that, even if they had missed the other body, *dead or alive*, they would have at least stepped on it, so narrow was the place where they stood. With five people standing there, it was impossible for another body to have escaped their notice. The only door that opened into that courtyard was that of the gamekeeper's oval room, but it was locked, and its key was found in the man's pocket.

However, as Bernier's testimony, no matter how impeccably logical it had been, led unerringly to the conclusion that *a man had been shot to death with a knife*, the Investigating Magistrate refused to take it into account. Instead, it became clear to us later that he was convinced that, somehow, we had missed the man we were chasing and had come upon the gamekeeper's body by accident, in a matter wholly unrelated to the present affair.

To Monsieur de Marquet, the murder of the gamekeeper belonged to another murder investigation, and he sought to prove it without further delay. It probably fitted with some of the conclusions he had already arrived at with respect to the gamekeeper's personality, his scandalous life and numerous affairs, including with the wife of Père Mathieu, the landlord of the Auberge du Donjon. The various death threats issued by Mathieu toward the gamekeeper had been widely reported. So, at about 1 p.m., despite his rheumatism, his whining and the loud protests of his wife, Père Mathieu was arrested and taken into custody. No evidence was found against him at the inn, but new threats against the gamekeeper's life, which he had uttered only the day before, and which had been reported by some carters, condemned him more than if the police had found the bloody murder weapon under his bed.

We were all stunned by the many incomprehensible and dreadful facts uncovered by the investigation so far when, to add to our surprise, Frederic Larsan returned to the Chateau. He had left Glandier soon after talking to the Magistrate, and was now back, with one of the railway employees.

At that moment, Mr. Rance and I were in the vestibule arguing about Père Mathieu's guilt or innocence. Rouletabille stood apart, seemingly lost in his thoughts and paying no attention at all to our conversation. The Investigating Magistrate and his clerk were in the green sitting room, where Darzac had taken us when we had first arrived at Glandier. Père Jacques, summoned by the Magistrate, had just walked into the sitting room. Monsieur Darzac was upstairs, in Mademoiselle Stangerson's bedroom, with her father and the doctors. As Frederic Larsan entered the vestibule with the railway employee, Rouletabille and I recognized the man at once by his small blond beard.

"That's the station employee from Epinay-sur-Orge," I said, looking at Larsan.

"You're correct, that's him indeed," the detective replied, smiling.

Larsan asked the gendarme stationed at the door of the sitting room to announce him to the Investigating Magistrate. At once, Père Jacques was asked to leave and Larsan went in with the employee. Some ten minutes went by during which Rouletabille seemed extremely impatient. The door of the sitting room opened at last and we heard the Magistrate calling to the gendarme who entered. Presently, he came out, went upstairs, but returned quickly. Entering into the sitting room, but leaving the door open, the gendarme said:

"Monsieur Darzac refuses to come down, Monsieur!"

"What do you mean, he refuses to come down?" cried Monsieur de Marquet.

"He says he can't leave Mademoiselle Stangerson's bedside in her present state."

"Very well," said Monsieur de Marquet. "Then we'll go to him."

Monsieur de Marquet and the gendarme mounted the stairs. He made a sign to Larsan and the railroad employee to follow. Rouletabille and I went along too.

Upon reaching the door of Mademoiselle Stangerson's bedroom, Monsieur de Marquet knocked. A chambermaid appeared. It was Sylvie, with her blond hair all in disorder and consternation showing on her face.

"Is Professor Stangerson within?" asked the Magistrate.

"Yes, Monsieur."

"Tell him that I wish to speak to him."

Sylvie went to fetch the Professor. He came out. He had been crying. He inspired great pity.

"What do you want?" he asked the Magistrate. "Can't I be left in peace in such a tragic moment, Monsieur?"

"Professor," said the Magistrate, "I absolutely have to talk to Monsieur Darzac at once. Could you persuade him to come out? Otherwise, I shall be compelled to cross this threshold and arrest him with all the force of the Law behind me."

The Professor made no reply. He looked at the Magistrate, the gendarme, and all of us like a victim looking at his torturers. Then, he went back inside.

Almost immediately, Monsieur Darzac came out. He was very pale and distraught. But when his eyes fell on the railway employee, standing behind Larsan, his features sagged, his eyes went wild and he couldn't repress a groan.

We all grasped the meaning of his painful realization. We couldn't help but let out a sigh of compassion for that tragic figure. We knew that what was about to happen would decide Monsieur Darzac's fate. Larsan's face alone was beaming, showing the joy of a hunting dog that has at last gotten its prey.

Monsieur de Marquet, pointing to the railway employee, asked Monsieur Darzac:

"Do you recognize this man, Monsieur?"

"I do," said Darzac, in a tone which he vainly tried to make firm. "He works at the railway station at Epinay-sur-Orge."

"This young man," continued Monsieur de Marquet, "says that he saw you get off the train at Epinay..."

"Last night," said Monsieur Darzac, interrupting, "at 10:30 p.m. That's correct."

A silence followed.

"Monsieur Darzac," the Magistrate went on in a tone of deep emotion, "what were you doing last night in Epinay, a few miles away from the place where Mademoiselle Stangerson was being assaulted?"

Darzac remained silent. He didn't lower his head, but just closed his eyes, either to hide his pain, or because he was afraid we might read some part of his terrible secret in them.

"Monsieur Darzac," insisted Monsieur de Marquet, "can you tell me what you did in Epinay last night?"

Darzac opened his eyes. He seemed to have recovered his self-control.

"I cannot, Monsieur."

"Think, Monsieur! For, if you persist in your strange refusal, I shall be under the painful necessity of placing you into custody."

"I cannot tell you."

"Then, you leave me no choice. Monsieur Robert Darzac, in the name of the law, you are under arrest!"

No sooner had the Investigating Magistrate uttered those words that I saw Rouletabille move quickly towards Darzac. He was almost certainly going to say something, but Darzac, with a sharp gesture, ordered him to remain silent. As the gendarme approached his prisoner, we heard a despairing cry from the bedroom:

"Robert! Robert!"

We recognized Mademoiselle Stangerson's voice and the sheer pain in it made us all shudder. Larsan himself turned pale. Darzac, in response to her cry, rushed back into the bedroom.

The Magistrate, the gendarme, and Larsan followed him. Rouletabille and I remained on the threshold. We witnessed a heart-wrenching scene. Mademoiselle Stangerson, her face deathly pale, had risen on her bed, despite the efforts of the two doctors and her father who had tried to restrain her. She was holding out her trembling arms towards Darzac, whom Larsan and the gendarme had grabbed. Her eyes were wide open and she saw—worse, *she understood*—what was happening. Her mouth seemed to form a word, a single word which expired on her lips and which nobody heard... Then, she collapsed and fell back unconscious.

Darzac was hurried out of the room and held in the vestibule, waiting for the vehicle that Larsan had gone to fetch. We were all overcome by emotion and even Monsieur de Marquet had tears in his eyes. Rouletabille took advantage of the opportunity to say to Monsieur Darzac:

"Are you going to say anything in your defense?"

"No!" replied the prisoner.

"Very well, then I will, Monsieur."

"You can't do it," said the unhappy man with a faint smile. "You can't succeed at what Mademoiselle Stangerson and I failed to achieve."

"Not only I can, but I will." Rouletabille's voice was strong and strangely confident. "I will succeed, Monsieur Darzac, because *I know much more than you do!*"

"Come on!" murmured Darzac, almost angrily.

"But fear not! I shall *know* only what will enable me to save you."

"If you want me to be grateful, you must seek to *know* nothing, young man."

Rouletabille shook his head, and walked very close to Darzac.

"Listen to what I am about to say," he said in a low tone, "and hopefully, it'll give you some confidence in me. You only know the name of the perpetrator. That's half of the secret. *Mademoiselle Stangerson knows the other half. But I... I now know the two halves! I know the whole man!*"

Robert Darzac opened his eyes wide, with a look that showed he had not understood a word of what Rouletabille had said to him.

At that moment, the conveyance arrived, driven by Larsan. Darzac and the gendarme entered it, Larsan remaining on the driver's seat. The prisoner was then taken to Corbeil.

Chapter Twenty-Five
Rouletabille Goes on a Journey

That same evening, Rouletabille and I left Glandier. We were very glad to get away, and there was no longer any reason for us to stay there. I declared my intention to give up trying to solve the whole matter. Rouletabille, with a friendly tap on my shoulder, told me that he had nothing more to learn at Glandier because the Chateau had told him everything there was to know.

We reached Paris at about 8 p.m., had dinner together, then, tired, we separated, agreeing to meet the next morning at my apartment.

The next day, Rouletabille arrived at the appointed time. He was dressed in a suit of English tweed, with an ulster on his arm, a cap on his head and a suitcase in his hand. Evidently, he had prepared himself for a journey.

"How long shall you be gone?" I asked.

"A month or two," he said. "It all depends."

I didn't dare ask him any more questions.

"Do you know," he asked, "what the word was that Mademoiselle Stangerson tried to say while looking at Monsieur Darzac before she fainted?"

"No. Nobody heard it."

"I did!" replied Rouletabille. "She said 'Speak!' "

"Do you think Darzac will speak?"

"No. He never will."

I was about to make some further observations, but he shook my hand warmly and wished me good health. I only had time to ask him one more question before he left:

"Aren't you concerned that other attempts on Mademoiselle Stangerson's life may be made while you're gone?"

"No," he replied. "I fear nothing of the kind now that Monsieur Darzac is in prison."

With this strange remark, he left. I was not to see him again until the day of Darzac's trial at the Court of Assize, when he finally showed up to explain the unexplainable.

Chapter Twenty-Six
In Which Joseph Rouletabille
Is Eagerly Expected

On January 15, that is to say, two and a half months after the tragic events which I have narrated, *L'Epoque* printed the following sensational article on its front page:

The jury of the Seine-et-Oise district has been summoned today to render its verdict in one of the most mysterious affairs in the annals of crime. Never before has a criminal trial been filled with so many obscure, incomprehensible, and unexplainable mysteries. And yet, the Public Prosecutor has not hesitated to drag into the dock and charge with attempted murder a man who is respected, esteemed, and loved by all who know him, a young scientist, the hope of French Science, whose entire life has been devoted to knowledge and truth.

When Paris heard of Monsieur Robert Darzac's arrest, a unanimous cry of protest arose from all sides. The University of the Sorbonne, its collective honor besmirched by this unprecedented action by an Investigating Magistrate, has asserted its belief in Mademoiselle Stangerson's fiancé's innocence. Professor Stangerson himself has been vociferous in his denunciations of this miscarriage of justice. There is no doubt in the mind of anybody that if the victim herself could speak to the 12 jurors of Seine-et-Oise, she would beg them to acquit the man whom she wishes to marry, but whom the prosecution would send to the scaffold.

One hopes that Mademoiselle Stangerson will soon recover her sanity, which was severely shaken by the horrible attack she suffered at Glandier. How could anyone wish for her to lose her precious senses again when she finds out that the man whom she loves has perished on the scaffold? That is a question for the jury, to whom we have decided to appeal directly through this article.

For we are determined to not let 12 worthy, decent men commit an abominable miscarriage of justice. We freely admit that there have been terrible coincidences, accusatory evidence, the unfathomable silence on the part of the accused, refusing to account for his time, as well as his absence of an alibi, in short, there have been more than enough reasons for the prosecution, which has tried fruitlessly to find the truth elsewhere, to finally arrest Monsieur Darzac.

The evidence against him appears so overwhelming that one understands how even a detective as experienced, intelligent, and usually successful as Monsieur Frederic Larsan, could have been misled. Until now, everything the investigation has uncovered has pointed a finger at Monsieur Darzac. Today, however, we shall defend him before the jury, and we shall bring such a light to the court that it will illuminate the entire mystery of Glandier. For we know the truth!

If we have not spoken sooner, it is because the very interests of the parties we are trying to protect demanded it. Our readers may remember the articles we published in the past on the affair of the "Left Foot of the Rue Oberkampf," the Crédit Universel robbery, and the famous case of the theft of the gold bullion from the Hôtel de la Monnaie. In all those instances, we were able to discover the truth long before even the excellent ingenuity of detective Frederic Larsan. Those articles were written by our youngest reporter, 18-year-old Joseph Rouletabille, whose name, we predict, will soon become a household word.

When the Glandier case first made the headlines, our intrepid young reporter was first on the spot; he overcame all obstacles and succeeded in staying at the Chateau when every other member of the press was denied admission. He worked side by side with Frederic Larsan, searching for the truth. He was terrified by the grave mistake the celebrated detective was about to make, and tried to pull him back from the false leads he was following; but "Frederic the Great" refused to take instructions from a young journalist. We know now what his stubbornness has done to Monsieur Darzac.

But now, France—the whole world—must know that, on the very evening of Monsieur Darzac's arrest, Joseph Rouletabille entered our editorial office and informed us that he was about to leave on a journey.

*"How long I shall be away," he told our editor-in-chief, "I cannot say; perhaps a month, perhaps two, perhaps three, perhaps I may never return. But here is a letter. If I am not back on the day when Monsieur Darzac appears before the judges in the Court of Assize, have this letter opened and read to the court, after all the witnesses have been heard. Arrange it with Monsieur Darzac's lawyer. Monsieur Darzac is inno-*cent. This letter contains the name of the perpetrator, *and I won't say the proof of his guilt, since that's exactly what I'm leaving to get,* but the irrefutable explanation of what truly happened at Glandier."

Our reporter then left. We were without news from him for a long time; but, a week ago, a stranger called our editor-in-chief and said: "Act in accordance with Rouletabille's instructions, if it becomes necessary to do so. *The truth is inside that letter." The gentleman who delivered that message would not give his name.*

Today, January 15, is the day when Monsieur Darzac's trial starts. Joseph Rouletabille has not returned. It may be that we shall never see him again. The press also counts its heroes, its martyrs to duty, the most important of all duties: freedom of the press. It may be that Joseph Rouletabille is no longer living. We shall then know how to avenge him. Our editor-in-chief will be, this afternoon, at the Court of Assize in Versailles, with Rouletabille's letter—the letter containing the name of the perpetrator!

The article was illustrated with a large photo of Rouletabille.

Those Parisians who flocked to the Court of Assize in Versailles that day in order to attend the trial of what was now called "*The Mystery of the Yellow Room*" certainly remember the terrible crush at Saint-Lazare station. The regular trains were so full that special ones had to be chartered. The article from *L'Epoque* had provoked so much discussion, excited so many passions, stirred up so many emotions, that even blows were exchanged. The partisans of Rouletabille fought with the supporters of Frederic Larsan. Curiously enough, all that excitement was due less to the fact that an innocent man might be wrongly convicted than to the interest taken by the readers in their own theories of the Mystery of the Yellow Room. Everyone had their own explanation for it, which they all thought was the only one that was valid. Those who agreed with Frederic Larsan's theory refused to entertain any challenge to the perspicacity of the popular detective. Others, who had arrived at a different solution, naturally insisted that this must be Rouletabille's explanation, although they obviously didn't know as yet what that was.

With the day's copy of *L'Epoque* in their hands, the pro-Larsans and the pro-Rouletabilles fought and shoved each other on the steps of the Palais de Justice, right into the courtroom itself. An extraordinary display of police had been arranged by the city of Versailles to calm everyone's spirits. Those who couldn't get inside the courtroom remained in the neighborhood until the evening and were, with great difficulty, kept back by the police. They became hungry for news, welcoming the most absurd rumors. At one point, the rumor spread that Professor Stangerson himself had been arrested, having confessed to being the perpetrator. This was pure madness. Nervous excitation reached a fevered pitch. Rouletabille was still expected. Some claimed to have seen him or recognized him. When a young man with a "pass" crossed the open space which separated the crowd from the Court House, a scuffle took place. Cries were heard of "Rouletabille! There's Rouletabille!" Other people who vaguely resembled the photograph published by *L'Epoque* were similarly greeted. The arrival of the editor-in-chief of the newspaper was the signal for a great demonstration. Some applauded, others hissed. There were many women in the crowd.

Inside the courtroom, the trial was presided over by Monsieur de Rocoux, a judge imbued with the prejudices of his class, but an honest man at heart. The witnesses had been summoned. I was there, of course, as were all who had, in any way, been involved in the mysteries of Glandier: Professor Stangerson, looking ten years older and almost unrecognizable, Frederic Larsan, Arthur Rance, with his face as ruddy as ever, Père Jacques, Père Mathieu, who was brought into court handcuffed between two gendarmes, Madame Mathieu, in tears, the two Berniers, the two nurses, the butler, all the servants of the Chateau, the employee of the Poste Restante of Bureau 40 of the Paris Post Office, the railway employee from Epinay, some friends of the Stangersons, and all of Monsieur Darzac's character witnesses. I was lucky enough to be called early in the trial, so I was then able to watch and be present during the entire proceedings.

The courtroom was so crowded that many lawyers were compelled to sit on the steps. Representatives from other local benches had come to take their honorific positions behind the main bench where the three judges in their solemn red robes sat. Monsieur Darzac stood in the prisoner's dock between two gendarmes, tall, handsome, and calm. A murmur of admiration rather than compassion greeted his appearance. He leaned forward toward his lawyer, Maître Henri Robert, who, assisted by his chief secretary, Maître Andre Hesse, was busily doing a last review of his brief.

Many expected that Professor Stangerson was going to go over to Monsieur Darzac and publicly shake hands with him; but the witnesses were called out and they left the courtroom without that sensational gesture taking place. After the jurors were seated, someone observed that they appeared to be deeply interested in a conversation that Maître Henri Robert was having with the editor-in-chief of *L'Epoque*. The editor then went to sit in the front row of the public seats. Some were surprised that he wasn't asked to go with the other witnesses in the room that had been reserved for them.

The reading of the indictment went, as it always does, without any incident. I shall not here report the long examination to which Monsieur Darzac was subjected. He answered all the questions with a natural ease, and yet with an aura of mystery. Everything he revealed seemed entirely natural; but everything he refused to divulge seemed to hurt his cause dreadfully, even in the eyes of those who believed him to be innocent. His silence on the important points which we already know worked against him, and it seemed that his reticence to tell the truth might prove fatal. He resisted the exhortations of the Public Prosecutor, and the Judges' entreaties, even when told that his silence might mean death.

"Very well," he said; "I will submit to it; but I am innocent."

With the splendid oratory skill which has made him famous, Maître Robert took advantage of the incident to try to show his client's noble character, arguing that only true heroes could remain silent for moral reasons in face of such a peril. The eminent attorney, however, succeeded in persuading only those who already believed in Darzac's innocence; the others remained unconvinced. There was an adjournment, then the witnesses began to be heard. Meanwhile, Rouletabille had not yet arrived. Every time a door opened, all eyes turned towards it, then back to the editor of *L'Epoque*, who sat impassive in his seat. At one point, he was seen feeling in his pocket and pulling out an envelope. A loud murmur of expectation followed. Surely, that was Rouletabille's letter!

It isn't, however, my intention to report in detail the course of the trial. My readers are sufficiently acquainted with the mysteries surrounding the Glandier case to enable me to go on to the truly dramatic denouement of this ever-memorable day.

It took place when Maître Robert was questioning Père Mathieu who, on the witness stand, between two gendarmes, was denying any part in the death of the "Green Man," the gamekeeper. His wife was brought in to confront her husband. She burst into tears and confessed that she had been the gamekeeper's mistress, and that her husband had indeed suspected it. However, she swore again that he had nothing to do with

218

her lover's murder. Maître Robert thereupon asked the court to hear Frederic Larsan on this point.

"In a short conversation which I have had with Monsieur Larsan during the adjournment," declared the lawyer, "he hinted that the gamekeeper's death might have been caused by someone other than Monsieur Mathieu. I would be interested to hear Monsieur Larsan's theory at this stage."

The Judges agreed. Larsan was brought in. His explanation was quite clear.

"I see no reason," he said, "to bring Père Mathieu into this. I said so to Monsieur de Marquet, but the innkeeper's repeated threats against the gamekeeper had already, understandably, prejudiced the Investigating Magistrate against him. To me, the attempted murder of Mademoiselle Stangerson and the death of the gamekeeper are the work of one and the same person. Several shots were fired at Mademoiselle Stangerson's murderer when he was fleeing through the courtyard. All the shooters believed they had hit him, perhaps even killed him. In truth, he only stumbled just he vanished behind the corner of the right wing of the Chateau. There, he came across the gamekeeper who, undoubtedly, tried to capture him. The murderer already had in his hand the knife with which he had stabbed Mademoiselle Stangerson. With it, he killed the gamekeeper."

This simple explanation appeared even more plausible because many people following the Glandier case had already made the same reasoning. A murmur of approbation was heard.

"And the murderer? What became of him?" asked the President of the Court.

"He obviously hid in a dark corner at the end of the courtyard. After the witnesses had left the courtyard carrying the body of the gamekeeper with them, the murderer quietly made his escape."

At that moment, a youthful voice arose from the back of the courtroom and shouted:

219

"I agree with Frederic Larsan as to the death of the gamekeeper; but I don't agree with him as to the way the murderer escaped!"

Everybody turned round, astonished. The ushers rushed towards the man who had just spoken, calling out silence. The President angrily asked who had dared raise his voice and ordered the intruder's immediate expulsion.

The same clear voice, however, was again heard to respond:

"It is I, Monsieur. I, Joseph Rouletabille!"

Chapter Twenty-Seven
In Which Joseph Rouletabille
Appears In All His Glory

The crowd suddenly got very excited. Women fainted; shouts were heard; there was a great deal of hustle and bustle. The "majesty of the law" was totally forgotten. Everyone tried to catch a sight of Rouletabille. The President kept shouting that he was going to have the courtroom cleared, but no one paid any attention to him.

Meanwhile, the young reporter nimbly jumped over the railing that separated the seated spectators from the ones standing up at the back, elbowed his way though and finally reached his editor, who greeted him cordially. Rouletabille took back his famous letter, pocketed it, and then managed to find his way to the witness box. He was smiling and looked happy; his face was like a ruddy ball illuminated by two large, shiny round eyes. He was dressed exactly as on the day he had left me—but showed much more wear and tear!—even to the ulster over his arm and the cap in his hand.

Turning to the President of the Court, he said:

"I beg your pardon, Monsieur, but the steamer was late. I have just returned from America. My name is Joseph Rouletabille!"

The silence which had followed his stepping into the witness box was suddenly broken by laughter as his words were heard. Everybody seemed relieved and glad that he was here at last. People were literally breathing more easily. They now knew they were certain to hear the truth.

But the President was still incensed.

"So you are Joseph Rouletabille," he said. "Well, young man, I'll teach you to turn my courtroom into a circus! I'll review your case later, but in the meantime, I'm holding you in contempt and remanding you in the court's custody."

"But I ask nothing more than to be in this court's custody, Monsieur," replied Rouletabille. "I have come here with the specific purpose of assisting this court, and I humbly beg the court's pardon for the disturbance which I have unwittingly caused. I ask you to believe me, Monsieur, when I say that no one has a greater respect for this court than I, but I had no choice but to rush here as fast as I could. I didn't even have time to change."

He laughed and the courtroom laughed with him.

"Take him away!" ordered the President.

Maître Robert intervened at once. He began by apologizing profusely for this young man, who, he said, was moved only by the very best of intentions. He made the President understand that they could hardly ignore the evidence of a witness who had slept at Glandier throughout the entire eventful week, especially that of a witness who had come ready to prove the accused innocent and name the real murderer.

"You're going to tell us who the murderer is?" asked the President, somewhat shaken but still skeptical.

"I have come for that very purpose, Monsieur!" replied Rouletabille.

An attempt at applause from the crowd was immediately silenced by the ushers.

"Monsieur Rouletabille," said Maître Robert, "has not been technically summoned as a witness in this case, but since he is here, and has placed himself freely at the disposition of this court, I hope that the court will allow him to testify."

"Very well!" said the President, "we will hear him. But first, he should be sworn in and..."

The Public Prosecutor rose:

"May it please the court," he said, "the State has no objections to dispensing with the usual formalities. It would be, perhaps, better if the young man were to tell us straight away whom he suspects."

The President nodded ironically:

"Very well. If the Public Prosecution attaches so much importance to Monsieur Rouletabille's testimony, then I see no reason why this witness should not identify the murderer right away."

A pin could have dropped and been heard in the courtroom. Rouletabille stood silent, looking sympathetically at Darzac, who, for the first time since the start of the trial, showed some fear and concern.

"Well," said the President, "we're waiting."

Rouletabille, pulled out a watch from his waistcoat pocket and, looking at it, said:

"Monsieur, I'm afraid that I can't name the murderer before 6:30 p.m.! *We still have four hours to go.*"

Loud murmurs of surprise and disappointment filled the room. Some of the lawyers were heard to mutter: "He's making fun of us!"

The President looked rather pleased. Maître Robert and his chief secretary, on the other hand, looked embarrassed.

"This joke has gone far enough" said the President in a curt tone. "Monsieur Rouletabille, you may retire into the witnesses' room. The other charges against you will remain pending."

Rouletabille protested:

"I swear to you, Monsieur," he cried in his sharp, clear voice, "that, when I do name the murderer, *you will understand why I couldn't identify him until 6:30 p.m.* I swear this on my honor; I give you my sacred word. But I can, however, provide an explanation for the murder of the gamekeeper. Monsieur Larsan, who has seen me at work at Glandier, can tell you with what care I studied this case. Even though I disagreed with him arresting Monsieur Darzac, because I know he's innocent, Monsieur Larsan knows my good faith and knows that some importance may be attached to my discoveries, which have often corroborated his own."

Larsan rose and said:

"I agree. It will be interesting to hear what Monsieur Rouletabille has to offer, especially if it differs from what I've said."

A murmur of approbation greeted the detective's speech. He showed himself to be a good sportsman in accepting the challenge. The struggle between the two men promised to be exciting.

As the President remained silent, Larsan continued:

"We both agree that the man who killed the gamekeeper was also Mademoiselle Stangerson's attacker, but we disagree as to how the perpetrator escaped. I'm curious to hear Monsieur Rouletabille's explanation."

"I have no doubt you are," said my friend.

General laughter followed this remark. The President angrily repeated that, if such an outburst occurred again, he would have the courtroom cleared.

"Really," concluded the President. "I don't see what there is to laugh about in a case like this."

"Neither do I," agreed Rouletabille with a disarming look of sincerity, which caused some spectators in front of me to chew on their handkerchiefs in order to keep themselves from laughing hysterically.

"Now, young man," said the President, "you've heard Monsieur Larsan. How did the perpetrator get away from the courtyard?"

Rouletabille looked at Madame Mathieu, who smiled back at him sadly.

"Since Madame Mathieu," he began, "has freely admitted her relationship with the gamekeeper…"

"She's a tramp!" shouted Père Mathieu.

"Remove that man!" ordered the President.

Père Mathieu was instantly removed from the courtroom. Rouletabille went on:

"Since she has made this confession, I'm at liberty to tell you that she often met the gamekeeper at night on the first floor of the tower, in the room that was once an oratory. These trysts became more frequent as her husband was laid up by his rheumatism. She gave him morphine to ease his pain and to have more time to spend with her lover. Madame Mathieu went to the Chateau at night, enveloped in a large black shawl, which served as a disguise. She was the 'dark phantom' that disturbed Père Jacques so much. She had learned how to imitate the sinister mewing of a cat belonging to Mère Angenoux, an old witch-woman living in the forest of Sainte Genevieve. Madame Mathieu would imitate its cries to inform the gamekeeper of her arrival. Then he would come down from the tower to let his mistress in. Despite the recent renovation of the tower, their meetings continued to take place in the gamekeeper's old room there, since the new oval room assigned to him at the end of the right wing of the Chateau was only separated from the servants' rooms by a thin partition wall, rendering it unsuitable for a romantic evening.

"On the night in question, Madame Mathieu had just left the gamekeeper when the tragedy in the courtyard occurred. As a matter of fact, they had just exited the tower together. I learned this from my examination of the footprints in the courtyard the following morning. I had stationed Monsieur Bernier, the caretaker, behind the tower—*as he will explain himself*—so he couldn't see what was happening in the courtyard. He didn't enter it until he heard the gunshots, and then he fired. So the gamekeeper and Madame Mathieu were alone in the courtyard in the silent night. They said their good-byes, and then she left, walking towards the open gate, while he returned to the oval room located at the end of the right wing.

"He had almost reached its door when he heard the gunshots. He turned around anxiously. He walked back to see what was going on. As he reached the corner, a shadow jumped on him and stabbed him through the heart. He died instantly. Within minutes, his body was surrounded by various people who thought they had just shot the murderer, but in reality were only looking at his latest victim!

"Meanwhile, Madame Mathieu, surprised by the gunshots and by the arrival of the people in the courtyard, crouched in the darkness. The courtyard is large and she, being near the gate and dressed in her black robes, went entirely unnoticed. From her vantage point, she saw a body being carried away. In great distress, she approached the vestibule and there, lying on the stairs, lit up by Père Jacques' lantern, she recognized her lover's dead body! She started to flee, but somehow, she had caught Père Jacques' attention. So he ran after the 'dark phantom' which had kept him awake for so many nights.

"That same night, before the murder occurred, Père Jacques had been awakened by the phony cat's cry, and, looking through his window, he had seen the 'dark phantom' go by. He had hastily dressed himself and gone out, which is why he was already fully dressed when we asked him to help us carry the gamekeeper's body to the vestibule. This time, he was keen to identify the 'dark phantom' once and for all. So he gave chase and, by a stroke of luck, managed to recognize Madame Mathieu. Now, Père Jacques is an old friend of the Mathieus. When she saw she'd been identified, Madame Mathieu had no choice but to confess the truth to Père Jacques, telling him of her liaison with the gamekeeper and begging for his help. Having just seen the body of her dead lover, she must have been nearly hysterical. Père Jacques, who is a good man, took pity on her and accompanied her through the oak grove, out of the estate, past the pond and onto the road to Epinay. From there, it was but a short distance to her home.

"Père Jacques then returned to the Chateau, but realizing how important it might be for Madame Mathieu's presence in the courtyard that night to remain secret, he did the best he could to try to hide the incident, the latest in a series of already dramatic events. I need not ask Père Jacques and Madame Mathieu to corroborate my story, because *I know* this is exactly what happened. I shall only appeal to Monsieur Larsan, who understands how I came to learn all this, because he saw me, the next morning, examine the two sets of footprints paralleling each other, which turned out to be those of Madame Mathieu and Père Jacques."

Here, Rouletabille turned towards Madame Mathieu, who was still in the witness box, and with a gallant bow, added:

"Your footprints, Madame, bear an uncanny resemblance to the expensive boots worn by the murderer."

Madame Mathieu trembled and looked at the young reporter with frightened awe. What had he meant by that? What would he say next?

"Madame Mathieu," continued Rouletabille, "has a shapely foot, long and perhaps a trifle large for a woman. Its imprint is very much like that of the murderer's boots, except for its tip."

There was some agitation in the courtroom, which Rouletabille calmed with a simple gesture. It now truly looked as if it was he, and not the President, who was in full control of the trial.

"I rush to add," he went on, "that this fact means very little. Any detective who would arrest someone based purely on such clues, *without a general theory explaining the nature of the crime*, would commit a terrible judicial mistake. After all, Monsieur Darzac's footprints are also like the perpetrator's, and *yet he is not the perpetrator!*"

There was more agitation in the courtroom. The President, turning to Madame Mathieu, asked:

"Is what Monsieur Rouletabille just told us what truly happened that night, Madame?"

"Yes, Monsieur," she replied. "It is just as if Monsieur Rouletabille had been behind us all the time."

"Did you see the perpetrator running towards the end of the right wing of the Chateau?"

"Yes, just as clearly as I saw the other people afterward carrying away the gamekeeper's body."

"What became of the perpetrator then? You were alone in the courtyard. You should have been able to see what he did next. He wasn't aware of your presence. You could easily have seen how he escaped."

"But I saw nothing, Monsieur," replied Madame Mathieu, whining. "It was too dark, too confusing..."

"Then Monsieur Rouletabille," said the President, "must still explain how the perpetrator managed to escape."

227

"Naturally!" replied Rouletabille, with such winning confidence that even the President couldn't repress a thin smile.

"It was impossible for the perpetrator to escape the way he had come without our seeing him," continued the young reporter, "and even if we couldn't see him, we certainly would have felt him, since that section of the courtyard is very narrow and enclosed between the ditches on one side and high iron railings on the other. In order to leave, the perpetrator would have had to step on us, or us on him. This small square of ground was as hermetically closed as the Yellow Room itself, *and we were the locks!*"

"Then, if the man was trapped in that narrow square," said the President in frustration, "please tell us why didn't you catch him? I've been asking you that question for the last half-hour!"

Rouletabille again pulled out his watch and checked the time.

"I'm truly very sorry, Monsieur," he replied, "but I can't answer that question until 6:30 p.m.!"

This time, the whispers in the courtroom were neither hostile nor disappointed. People were beginning to trust Rouletabille. They had faith in him. And they were amused by his pretention in setting up a time with the President just as if he was setting up an appointment with a friend.

As for the President, after asking himself if he should be angry at the young man, it looked as if he, too, had made up his mind to accept Rouletabille's peculiarities. The reporter's charm was contagious and there was no doubt that it had begun to mollify even the learned judge. Further, Rouletabille had explained Madame Mathieu's role in the case so well that Monsieur de Rocoux now felt almost obliged to take him more seriously.

"Very well, Monsieur Rouletabille," he sighed. "As you wish. But don't let me see any more of you before 6:30 p.m."

Rouletabille bowed to the President and made his way to the witnesses' room.

I could see that he was looking for me, but couldn't find me. So I quietly made my own way through the crowd and left the courtroom at almost the same time. When we finally connected, he greeted me heartily, shaking my hands repeatedly, looking very glad indeed to see me.

"I'm not going to ask you, my dear fellow," I said, smiling, "what you've been doing in America, because I've no doubt you'll say you can't tell me until 6:30 p.m."

"Not at all, my dear Sainclair!" he replied. "I'll tell you right now why I went to America, because you're my friend. I went looking *for the name of the perpetrator's other half!*"

"His *other half?*"

"Precisely! When we left Glandier, I knew there were *two halves* to the perpetrator, and I knew the name of only one. So I went to America to find the name of the other half."

Just then, we entered the witnesses' room. Rouletabille was immediately surrounded. He was very friendly toward all, except Arthur Rance to whom he showed a marked coldness. Frederic Larsan also arrived. Rouletabille went up and shook his hand with one of his patented handshakes that left you with bruised fingers. His manner toward the detective showed that he must have felt that he had now gained the upper hand in their battle. Larsan smiled, very sure of himself, and asked my friend what he had been doing in America. Rouletabille, very amicably, took him by the arm and began telling him anecdotes about his trip. Then, they walked to a corner, presumably to discuss more serious and confidential matters, and I felt it more proper to leave them alone. In any event, I was eager to return to the courtroom to hear the evidence being given by the other witnesses. I returned to my seat and noticed right away that the public was only mildly interested in what was happening, because of their impatience for Rouletabille's return at the appointed time.

On the stroke of 6:30 p.m., Rouletabille was again brought in. It is impossible for me to describe the powerful emotions that ran through the crowd, which followed him with hungry eyes. The young man made his way to the witness box. Darzac rose to his feet. He was deathly pale.

The President, addressing Rouletabille, said gravely:

"I will not ask you to take the usual oath, Monsieur, because you have not been properly summoned; but I trust that I don't need to emphasize the gravity of the statement you are about to make, and the importance of being truthful..." And he added, threateningly: "...*For your sake* as well as others'."

Rouletabille, showing no visible emotions, replied:

"Of course, Monsieur."

"Then, let us continue where we left off," said the President. "We had reached the point where we were discussing that narrow section of the courtyard where the perpetrator had been trapped, and from which he had nevertheless managed to escape. And you had stated that, at 6:30 p.m., you would tell us not only how had the perpetrator escaped, but also his name. It is 6:35 p.m. now. Monsieur Rouletabille, we await your explanations."

"Very well, Monsieur," began my friend amidst such a profound silence that I don't recall having ever felt one like it before. "I told you how that section of the courtyard was virtually closed off and how impossible it was for the perpetrator to get away without being seen by those chasing him. That's the God-given truth. If so, then the only logical answer is: *when we stood in that narrow courtyard, the perpetrator was still with us.*"

"But you said no one saw him? Or at least, that's what the prosecution claims."

"That's incorrect, Monsieur!" replied Rouletabille. "*We all saw him!*"

"Then why didn't you arrest him?"

"Because no one, besides myself, knew that he was the perpetrator! And for my plans to work, I needed the perpetrator to remain free a little while longer. Besides, I had no proof, other than my own logic. Yes, only my logic told me that the perpetrator was there, among us, that we were looking at him. But I needed more time to find *some irrefutable, material*

230

proof that I could bring before this Court of Assize and which, I swear to God, will satisfy everyone."

"Speak out, Monsieur! Tell us the perpetrator's name."

"You will find it on the list of names who were present in the courtyard on the night of the tragedy," replied Rouletabille, who seemed to be in no hurry to share his unformation.

The people in the courtroom began showing some impatience.

"The name! Tell us the name!" some of them even called out.

Rouletabille continued in a tone of voice that would have gotten him slapped in the face had he been in a less solemn place.

"If I'm dragging my feet a bit, Monsieur, it's because I've got good reason, as you'll soon find out…"

"Tell us the name!" roared the crowd.

"Silence!" shouted the usher.

"You must tell us that name, Monsieur Rouletabille," said the President, looking at his notes. "The list of those present in the courtyard that night consists of… the dead gamekeeper… Was he the perpetrator?"

"No, he wasn't, Monsieur."

"Père Jacques?"

"Not at all."

"Monsieur Bernier the caretaker?"

"Not him."

"Monsieur Sainclair?"

"Absolutely not."

"Mr. Rance, then? The only ones left are Mr. Rance and yourself. Are you the perpetrator, Monsieur Rouletabille?"

"Of course not!"

"So are you accusing Mr. Rance of being the perpetrator?"

"No, Monsieur!"

"Then, I confess I do not understand… What you are driving at? There were no other persons in the courtyard."

231

"That's not the case, Monsieur. While it's true that there were no persons in the courtyard, or below it, *there was someone above it, who was leaning out of his window, looking down on us*."

"Do you mean, Frederic Larsan?" exclaimed the President.

"Yes, Frederic Larsan!" replied Rouletabille in a loud, ringing tone. Then, turning towards the public, who had already started to protest, he shouted with a vehemence I wouldn't have believed him capable of: "*Frederic Larsan is the perpetrator!*"

The courtroom exploded with loud cries of astonishment, indignation, incredulity and, for some, enthusiasm for the young man who had dared to utter such an inconceivable accusation. The President himself was so astonished that he didn't attempt to quiet the crowd. The racket died down by itself under the hushes of those eager to find out more.

In the relative calm that followed, Robert Darzac was heard to distinctly whisper:

"It's impossible! He's mad!"

"You dare to accuse Frederic Larsan, Monsieur Rouletabille?" said the President. "Even Monsieur Darzac himself believes you are mad. But if you're not, you'd better have some solid proof!"

"Proof, Monsieur? You want proof? Well, I'll give it to you," said Rouletabille shrilly. "Let Frederic Larsan be called!"

"Usher, call Frederic Larsan," ordered the President.

The usher hurried to the side door, opened it, and disappeared. The door remained open, while all eyes turned expectantly towards it. The usher reappeared and, stepping forward, said:

"Monsieur Larsan is gone. He left at 4 p.m. and no one has seen him since."

"That's my proof!" said Rouletabille triumphantly.

"What proof? I don't understand! Explain yourself!" demanded the President.

"The *irrefutable* proof that I mentioned earlier—Larsan's flight!" said the young reporter. "He won't be back. You will never see Frederic Larsan again."

"Unless you're making fun of this court, Monsieur Rouletabille, why didn't accuse Monsieur Larsan when he was here, in this box, looking him in the eye? He could then have answered you."

"But what answer could be less equivocal than the one he's just given me, Monsieur? *He won't answer. He can't answer!* I accuse Larsan of being the perpetrator, *and he takes flight!* Don't you think that's answer enough?"

"I won't, no, I can't believe that Monsieur Larsan has fled, as you've just said. There was no reason for him to do so. How could he have known that you were going to accuse him anyway?"

"Because I told him so earlier, in the witnesses' room."

"You did that! But why? If you knew that Larsan was the perpetrator, why did you give him an opportunity to escape?"

"Because, Monsieur," replied Rouletabille, proudly, "I'm not a judge or a policeman, but a simple reporter. My business is not to arrest people; it's to serve the truth, and I serve it as I see fit. It's what I do. Your job is to protect society as best as you can, but that's not mine. I'm not going to deliver a man to the scaffold. If you're fair, Monsieur—and I know that you are—you will see that I was right. Didn't I tell you earlier that I couldn't reveal the perpetrator's name until 6: 30 p.m.? I'd calculated that it would give me enough time to warn Larsan, and enable him to catch the 4:17 p.m. train for Paris, where he would know where to hide and leave no traces.

"Now, you won't find Frederic Larsan," continued Rouletabille, staring at Darzac, "because he's too cunning. He is the man *who has always escaped you* and for whom you have long searched in vain. Even though he couldn't outwit me," continued the young reporter, laughing heartily, and laughing alone, because no one else in the courtroom felt like laughing, "he will easily outwit all the police forces in the world. For this man who, four years ago, managed to join the Sûreté and become famous under the name of Frederic Larsan, is also notorious under another name, well known to all the students of crime. Frederic Larsan, Monsieur, *is also Ballmeyer!*"

"Ballmeyer!" cried the President.

"Ballmeyer!" exclaimed Darzac, springing to his feet. "Ballmeyer! *It was true, then!*"

"Ah! Monsieur Darzac, you don't think I am so mad now, eh?" said Rouletabille smiling.

Ballmeyer! Ballmeyer! No other word could be heard in the courtroom. The President ordered an immediate adjournment.

You can imagine how eventful was the break which followed! The crowd had something new to chew. Ballmeyer! Everyone was impressed by Rouletabille's sagacity! Ballmeyer indeed! The rumor of his death had obviously been greatly exaggerated, as the saying went. He had managed to cheat death, just as he had succeeded in escaping from the police.

Is it really necessary, at this point, to remind my readers of the highlights of Ballmeyer's notorious criminal career? For 20 years, the man's villainous exploits had been a regular feature of judicial chronicles and newspaper headlines alike. If some of my readers may have forgotten the "Mystery of the Yellow Room," I doubt that they forgot the name of Ballmeyer!

Ballmeyer exemplified that class of high society criminals known as "gentlemen burglars." There was no gentleman more gentlemanly than Ballmeyer. There was no stage magician more adept at sleight of hand than he. There was no "apache" (as we call crooks today) deadlier or craftier than he. He had been received in the best society, and had been a member of some of the most exclusive clubs. He had stolen the honor of young girls and the fortunes of their fathers with a gusto never since equaled. Yet, when cornered, he had not hesitated to use a knife or swing a sheep-bone, like the most common of criminals. Ballmeyer never hesitated and no operation was too dangerous for him. He had been caught once, but had escaped on the morning of his trial by throwing pepper into the eyes of his guards. Later, we learned that, while the best detectives of the Sûreté were hunting for him all over Paris, he had been attending the premiere of a new play at the Théâtre Français, without the slightest disguise.

Ballmeyer had later left France to go to America. There, the police of the State of Ohio had managed to capture him, but he had escaped again the next day. Ballmeyer! I would need an entire tome to recount all the adventures of this master-criminal, this man who had chosen to hide under the guise of Frederic Larsan!

And it was a mere lad of 18 who had exposed him! It was Rouletabille who, knowing Ballmeyer's long and sinister career, had allowed him to thumb his nose at society again and escape! I couldn't help but admire the young reporter's bold move, because I felt certain that his overriding motivation had been to protect both Mademoiselle Stangerson and Monsieur Darzac, and rid them of their enemy at the same time.

The crowd had barely recovered from the effect of Rouletabille's astonishing revelation when the trial was resumed.

The question on everybody's mind was: Even if one accepted that Larsan was the perpetrator, how had he escaped from the Yellow Room?

Rouletabille was immediately called to the witness bar and his examination (for it was more an examination than a testimony) continued.

"Monsieur Rouletabille," said the President, "you have told us that it was impossible to escape from the end of the courtyard. I'm willing to accept, as you suggested, that since Monsieur Larsan was leaning out of his window just above your heads, he was technically *in* the courtyard. But if he was the man you'd been chasing, in order to reach that window, he first had to leave the courtyard. How did he manage that?"

"He escaped in a most unusual way Monsieur," replied Rouletabille. "I said that this section of the courtyard was as hermetically closed as the Yellow Room itself. That's not entirely true. One can't climb the walls of the Yellow Room to go anywhere; whereas, there, Larsan climbed the wall, sprang

235

onto the terrace, and, while we were busy looking at the gamekeeper's body, entered the first floor corridor through an open window. After that, it was easy for him to rush to his room, open his window, and call out to us, as if he'd just woken up. It would have been child's play for a man of Ballmeyer's strength and skills. And here, Monsieur, is the proof of what I'm saying."

Rouletabille pulled a small bag from his pocket and produced an iron spike from it.

"This, Monsieur," he said, "is a spike which will perfectly fit into a hole we have yet to discover in the cornice supporting the terrace. Larsan, who planned and prepared for every contingency—something necessary in his line of work—had planted this spike into the cornice. All he had to do to escape was to plant one foot on a stone at the corner of the Chateau, another on this spike, one hand on the cornice of the gamekeeper's door and the other on the terrace, and he was clear of the ground. The rest was easy for someone as nimble as he. We had dined together that night, and afterward, he acted as if he had just been drugged. He needed to appear drugged so that no one would be surprised that I had been drugged too! To the extent that we shared the same misfortune, no suspicion would fall on him. Because, you see, Larsan was the one who drugged me! If he hadn't done so, he could never have gone into Mademoiselle Stangerson's bedroom that night and tried to kill her."

A groan came from Darzac, who appeared to be unable to control his suffering.

"You can understand," added Rouletabille, "that Larsan felt handicapped by the fact that my room was next to his. He knew, or at least had guessed, that I would be watching. Naturally, he couldn't bring himself to believe that I suspected him! But I could have caught him leaving his room or as he was about to go into Mademoiselle Stangerson's. So I had to be put out of commission. He waited until I was asleep, when my friend Sainclair was busy trying to rouse me, to enter Mademoiselle Stangerson's bedroom. Barely ten minutes later, she was crying out in agony!"

"How did you come to suspect Larsan?" asked the President.

"*By grabbing logic by its right end*," replied Rouletabille. "That's why I was watching him! But I didn't foresee the drugging. He's very cunning indeed. Yes, grabbing logic by its right end allowed me to discover his true nature, but I still needed some material evidence, so that my eyes could see his guilt *just well as my mind already did*."

"What do you mean, *grabbing logic by its right end*?"

"Well, Monsieur, logic is like a walking stick; it's got two ends: the right one and the wrong one. But there's only one end upon which you can lean and rely to walk straight: the right end! You can tell the right end because no amount of pressure will break it, no matter what happens or what anyone says. The day after the strange and extraordinary incident of the unfathomable corridor, when I felt so miserable, like an imbecile who can't think logically because he can't tell which end is which, when I was bent over the ground looking at some misleading evidence, I suddenly came to my senses and, *leaning on the right end of logic*, returned to the unfathomable corridor.

"There, I realized that the perpetrator whom we'd been chasing couldn't have left the corridor. So *I drew a circle inside my mind* using the right end of logic. Inside that circle was the mystery of the perpetrator's escape. Outside, in flaming letters, I mentally wrote the words: '*Since the perpetrator can't be outside the circle, he must still be inside it.*' So who was inside that circle? The right end of logic showed me that, in addition to the perpetrator who was still trapped in the circle, there was Père Jacques, Professor Stangerson, Frederic Larsan, and myself. Five persons in total, counting the perpetrator. Yet, when I looked inside the circle, or the corridor if you will, I only saw four people. Now, since I had proved to my satisfaction that the fifth person couldn't have escaped, couldn't have left the circle, *logic dictated that there was a person in my circle who was in reality two persons!* Meaning that that person *was both himself and the perpetrator!* Why had I not realized this before? Simply because the phenomenon of that person splitting into two persons had not taken place before my eyes.

"Now, who out of the four persons present in the corridor could have split into himself and the perpetrator without my noticing it? It certainly couldn't be a person whom I had seen *simultaneously and separately* from the perpetrator. For example, in the corridor, I had seen both Professor Stangerson and the perpetrator *simultaneously*, Père Jacques and the perpetrator *simultaneously*, and even myself and the perpetrator *simultaneously*. So the perpetrator couldn't be Professor Stangerson, Père Jacques, or myself. Besides, if I'd been the perpetrator, I would have known, wouldn't I? However, had I seen Frederic Larsan and the perpetrator *simultaneously*? No! *Two seconds* had passed, during which I had lost sight of the perpetrator, for, as I have noted in my papers, he had reached the meeting-point of the two corridors *two seconds* before the Professor, Père Jacques, and myself arrived there. That would have given the perpetrator enough time to turn into the corner corridor, take off his false beard, change back into Larsan, turn around, and collide into us, just as if he, like ourselves, had been in pursuit of the perpetrator! Ballmeyer has managed to successfully pull off more difficult tricks than that before!

"It was child's play for him to disguise himself in order to appear as a bearded stranger to Mademoiselle Stangerson, or with a small, chestnut-colored beard to make him look like Monsieur Darzac, whom he had sworn to destroy, to the Postal employee at Bureau 40.

"Yes, by leaning on the right end of logic, I was able to bring together two persons, or rather *two halves of the same person*, whom I had never seen *simultaneously*: Frederic Larsan and the man I had been chasing, the perpetrator!

"That discovery almost overwhelmed me. I tried to regain my balance by going over all the material clues previously gathered, which now had to fit inside my circle of logic.

"What were the clues which, that night, could have led me away from realizing that Larsan was the perpetrator?

"No.1: I had seen the perpetrator in Mademoiselle Stangerson's bedroom. On rushing to Larsan's room, I had found him sound asleep.

"No.2: The ladder.

"No.3: I had placed Larsan at the end of the corner corridor and had told him that I was planning to run into Mademoiselle Stangerson's bedroom to try to capture the perpetrator. When I returned to her bedroom, I saw that the perpetrator was still there.

"No.1 didn't bother me very much. It's likely that, when I got off the ladder, after having seen the perpetrator in Mademoiselle Stangerson's bedroom, Larsan had already finished what he was doing there. Then, while I was re-entering the Chateau, he'd had time to return to his own room. There, he must have quickly undressed and, when I knocked at his door, he only pretended to have been asleep.

"Nor did No.2, the presence of the ladder, trouble me much. It was obvious that, if Larsan was the perpetrator, he had no need of a ladder to get inside the Chateau, since he slept there, next to my room. I believe he positioned the ladder to make everyone believe that the perpetrator was coming from the outside, which was essential to his plan to frame Monsieur Darzac, who was absent from the Chateau that might. Besides, having the ladder there might have also facilitated his flight in the event of something going amiss.

"But No.3 puzzled me more. Having placed Larsan at the end of the corner corridor, I couldn't explain why he would have taken advantage of the brief time during which I had gone into the left wing to fetch Professor Stangerson and Père Jacques, *to return to Mademoiselle Stangerson's bedroom.* It was a very dangerous thing to do. He risked being captured, and he knew it. And as a matter of fact, he very nearly was captured, not having had the time to regain his post, as he had certainly hoped to do. So he must have had a very compelling reason to go back to Mademoiselle Stangerson's bedroom, a reason which must have occurred to him only after I had left him, *because otherwise he wouldn't have loaned me his gun!*

"As for me, when I sent Père Jacques take his place at the end of the right wing corridor, I naturally thought that Larsan was still occupying his at the end of the corner corridor. It didn't occur to Père Jacques, walking to his post, to look to see whether Larsan was there or not. He was preoccupied with executing my instructions faithfully. And it didn't occur to me to ask him to check!

"So, what then could have been the compelling reason forcing Larsan to return to Mademoiselle Stangerson's bedroom for a second time? I guessed that it had to be some kind of evidence of his earlier presence which he had left there by mistake. What could it have been? And had he successfully recovered it during his second trip? Then, I remembered the candle on the floor and the perpetrator bent over, *as if he were looking for something he'd just lost.* I asked Madame Bernier, who was accustomed to cleaning the room, to search it thoroughly for me, and she found a pair of spectacles—this very pair, Monsieur!"

And Rouletabille pulled the pair of spectacles, which I'd seen him study before, from his bag.

"When I saw these spectacles," he continued, "at first, I was aghast. I had never seen Larsan wearing any spectacles before. If he didn't wear any, it was because he didn't have to. So why would he have worn spectacles at a time when every minute counted? What did these spectacles mean? How could I fit them into my circle of logic? Then, I noticed they were *farsighted spectacles* and I asked myself: 'What if Larsan is farsighted?' I had never seen him writing or reading. He might, then, be farsighted. Certainly, his colleagues at the Sûreté would have known if that was the case... So if the spectacles were Larsan's, they could be identified... To find Larsan's very own spectacles in Mademoiselle Stangerson's bedroom after the mystery of the unfathomable corridor would be damning... So that explained Larsan's return! I know now

240

that Larsan-Ballmeyer is indeed farsighted and that these spectacles did belong to him.

"You now understand, Monsieur, the basis of my system," continued Rouletabille. "I'm not asking material clues to tell me the truth; I'm only asking them to not contradict the truth already shown to me by the right end of logic.

"In order to be totally certain of Larsan's guilt—because, let's face it, accusing someone like Frederic the Great required some exceptional proof—I made one mistake. I wished to see his face. I was punished for this. You might say that the right end of logic took revenge on me because it had shown me the truth in the matter of the unfathomable corridor, and yet I had stopped leaning on it, reliably, definitively and trustingly. Had I refrained from seeking that additional evidence, the second, terrible attack on Mademoiselle Stangerson might have been prevented…"

Rouletabille paused here and blew his nose, obviously moved.

"But," asked the President, "why should Larsan go to Mademoiselle Stangerson's bedroom, at all? Why should he twice attempt to murder her?"

"Because he loved her passionately, Monsieur."

"I suppose that's a motive…"

"That's the only motive, Monsieur. He was madly, insanely in love with her, and because of that, and… other things… he was capable of committing any crime."

"Did Mademoiselle Stangerson know this?"

"Yes, she did, Monsieur. But she was, of course, ignorant of the fact that the man who was pursuing her was Frederic Larsan of the Sûreté, otherwise, obviously, he wouldn't have been allowed to stay at the Chateau. In fact, I noticed that, when we were all in her room after the incident of the unfathomable corridor, he kept himself in the shadow, his head bent down. He was probably looking for the lost spectacles. Mademoiselle Stangerson was stalked and persecuted by Larsan under another name which we don't know, but which she evidently did."

241

"Monsieur Darzac," asked the President, "did Mademoiselle Stangerson tell you anything about this? Why did she never speak of this to anyone? This might have helped the police to find the perpetrator. And if you're innocent, to spare you the pain of being arrested."

"Mademoiselle Stangerson told me nothing," replied Darzac.

"Does what this young man say seem likely to you?" the President asked.

"Mademoiselle Stangerson has told me nothing," Darzac repeated stolidly.

"How do you explain that, on the night of the murder of the gamekeeper," the President asked, turning to Rouletabille again, "the perpetrator brought back the papers he had stolen from Professor Stangerson? How do you explain how he gained entrance into Mademoiselle Stangerson's locked bedroom?"

"The last question is easily answered, Monsieur," replied the young reporter. "For a man like Larsan-Ballmeyer, making a set of duplicate keys would have been easy. As to the documents, I think Larsan hadn't intended to steal them at first. He had been closely watching Mademoiselle Stangerson, wanting only to prevent her marriage to Monsieur Darzac. One day, he followed the two of them into the Grands Magasins du Louvre. There, he stole her handbag, or perhaps grabbed it after she left it behind somewhere. In it was a key with a brass head. He didn't learn of its importance until he saw the advertisement placed in the newspaper by Mademoiselle Stangerson. He then wrote to her in care of the Poste Restante, as instructed. He probably asked her to meet him, informing her of the fact that he was the same man who'd been pursuing her. He received no reply. So, he went to the Post Office and ascertained that his letter had, indeed, been collected. *But he went disguised as Monsieur Darzac, because he had already decided to attack Mademoiselle Stangerson, no matter the consequences, and he planned that Monsieur Darzac, her fiancé,*

his hated rival whom he sought to destroy, would be the man
accused of his crimes.

"I said *no matter the consequences,* because I don't believe that Larsan was, at that stage, clearly determined to murder Mademoiselle Stangerson. But whatever he might do, he would make sure that Monsieur Darzac would be blamed for it! Larsan was very nearly the same height as Monsieur Darzac and had almost the same sized feet. It wasn't difficult, after taking an impression of Monsieur Darzac's footprints, to have similar boots made for himself. Again, such tricks were child's play for someone like Ballmeyer.

"So, having receiving no reply to his letter, no offer of rendezvous being forthcoming, Larsan, furious, determined that, since Mademoiselle Stangerson would not come to him, he would go to her. He still had the brass headed key in his possession. His plan had long been formed. He had carefully researched Chateau Glandier and its pavilion. One afternoon, while Professor Stangerson and his daughter were out for a stroll, while Père Jacques was away, he entered the pavilion by the vestibule window.

"Being alone, and in no hurry, he began examining the furniture. One of the pieces, resembling a safe, had a small keyhole. That interested him! He had the brass headed key on him, and, associating the two, he tried it in the lock. The door opened. He saw nothing but papers. They must have been very valuable to have been stored away in a safe, and for that key to be so important. Perhaps the thought of blackmail occurred to him as a useful possibility in helping him crush Mademoiselle Stangerson's resistance? So he quickly made a parcel of the papers and took it to the lavatory next to the vestibule. Between that day and the night of the murder of the gamekeeper, Larsan had plenty of time to find out what those papers contained. He realized that he could do nothing with them, and further, they were compromising if found in his possession. So that night, he took them back to the Chateau. Perhaps he hoped that, by returning the papers which represented 20 years of hard, pioneering work, he might find some gratitude from

Mademoiselle Stangerson? Everything is possible with a mind as twisted as his. But whatever his reasons, he took the papers back *and was glad to be rid of them*."

Rouletabille coughed. It was obvious to me that he was embarrassed. He had arrived at a point in his story where he had to withhold his knowledge of Larsan's *true motive* for his frightful attacks on Mademoiselle Stangerson. The explanations he had given to the Court were a trifle too simplistic to satisfy everyone, and the President would certainly have remarked on it if Rouletabille, smart as a fox, hadn't immediately said:

"And now, we come to the explanation of the Mystery of the Yellow Room!"

There was a movement of the chairs in the courtroom, a general agitation and an energetic whispering of "Hush!" showing that the public's curiosity had reached its peak.

"It seems to me, Monsieur Rouletabille," said the President, "that the Mystery of the Yellow Room was explained by Frederic Larsan, except of course that, according to your theory, he misled us as to the true identity of the perpetrator by substituting himself with Monsieur Darzac. It's obvious that the door of the Yellow Room was open when Professor Stangerson was alone, and that he allowed the man who was coming out of his daughter's room to leave without arresting him, *perhaps at her entreaty to avoid a scandal*."

"No, Monsieur," protested the young man. "You appear to have forgotten that, stunned by her attack, Mademoiselle Stangerson was in no condition to make such an entreaty, nor could she have locked herself back in her room. You must also remember that Professor Stangerson has sworn on his daughter's head *that the door remained closed at all times*."

"But, Monsieur Rouletabille," said the President, "that is the only way we can explain the mystery. *The Yellow Room was as closely shut as a safe*. It was impossible for the perpetrator to make his escape through natural means or otherwise. When the room was broken into, he wasn't there! Therefore, he must have escaped."

"Not necessarily, Monsieur."

"What do you mean?"

"There was no need for him to escape, *if he wasn't there in the first place!*"

The public became agitated.

"Not there?"

"*Since he couldn't have been there, it obviously means that he wasn't.* One must always grasp logic by the right end, Monsieur!"

"But… what about all the evidence of his presence?" asked the President.

"That, Monsieur, is precisely the wrong end of logic! The right end tells us this: from the time Mademoiselle Stangerson locked herself in the Yellow Room to the time its door was broken open, it was impossible for the perpetrator to escape from that room. Since we can't find him there, *it means that he wasn't there during that time.*"

"But what about all the clues?"

"Again, Monsieur, they're the type of material clues which cause judicial mistakes, *because they tell you whatever you want them to say!* They have led us astray. One must first use logic to reason out a solution, and then see if the clues fit within that circle of logic. In this case, we begin with a very small circle: *The perpetrator wasn't inside the Yellow Room when it was locked.* Why did everyone conclude that he had been? Because he left traces of his passage inside the room? But he could have left these traces *before*! Nay! He *must* have left these traces before! Logic dictates it! Let us look into the matter of these clues in light of what we now know, and see if they contradict the notion of the perpetrator being in the Yellow Room *before Mademoiselle Stangerson locked herself in, in front of her father and Père Jacques.*

"After the publication of the article in *Le Matin* and my conversation with the Investigating Magistrate in the train from Paris to Epinay-sur-Orge, I became certain that the Yellow Room had been hermetically sealed, and that consequently, the perpetrator had escaped *before* Mademoiselle Stangerson had gone into the room at midnight.

"Then, all the material clues seemed to argue against such a theory. After all, Mademoiselle Stangerson couldn't have assaulted herself, and the evidence ruled out a suicide attempt. If her would-be murderer had come into the Yellow Room *before*, how was it possible then for Mademoiselle Stangerson to be attacked *after*? Or maybe it only *seemed* that way... It was necessary for me to reconstruct the attack in two stages, each clearly separated from the other by several hours. The first stage was when someone genuinely tried to kill Mademoiselle Stangerson who, for some reason, then hid that attempt; the second stage was when she was alone in the Yellow Room and, probably waking up from a nightmare, screamed and caused the people outside the room, her father and Père Jacques, to believe that she was being murdered within!

"At the time, I hadn't yet visited the Yellow Room. I asked myself what the marks left by her attacker on Mademoiselle Stangerson were. There were two: signs of strangulation and a wound from a hard blow to the temple. The signs of strangulation didn't bother me much. If they'd been made *before*, Mademoiselle Stangerson could have easily concealed them under a collar, a scarf or any similar article of apparel. Because you understand that, from the moment I assumed that there were two separate incidents in this affair, I also had to assume that *Mademoiselle Stangerson had taken steps to hide all the visible clues left by the attack during the first one!* She obviously had compelling reasons to do so, since she had told her father nothing, and told the Investigating Magistrate that the attack, *which she could no longer deny*, had taken place during the second incident, *which was a lie*. She was forced to lie, because otherwise her father would have asked her: 'Why did you keep this a secret? What is the meaning of your silence after such an aggression?'

"If I could easily explain hiding the signs of strangulation, I couldn't understand how Mademoiselle Stangerson might have done the same with the blow on her temple. I understood it even less when I learned that a bloody sheep-bone had been found in the Yellow Room. She couldn't materially hide the fact that she had been struck on the head, and yet, according to my theory, that wound had to have been inflicted during the first incident, since it required the perpetrator's effective presence. At first, I thought the wound might be less serious than it had been reported—which, as I found out later, was not the case. Then, I supposed that Mademoiselle Stangerson might have hidden it *by wearing her hair in plaits*.

"As to the bloody handprint left on the wall of the Yellow Room, it had obviously been made *before*, during the first incident, *when the perpetrator had really been there*. All the traces of his presence had naturally been left during that first attempt: the sheep-bone, the sooty footprints, the Basque béret, the handkerchief, the blood on the wall, on the door, and on the floor... If those traces were still all there, it was obviously because Mademoiselle Stangerson, who desired nothing more than to hide the entire affair, hadn't had time to clear them away.

"This led me to the conclusion that *the first attack must have taken place shortly before the second one*. If after the initial attack, after the perpetrator had escaped, Mademoiselle Stangerson, after returning to the laboratory where her father found her pretending to be working, had had the time to go back into the Yellow Room, she would have at least removed the sheep-bone, the beret and the handkerchief which were lying on the floor. But she couldn't do so because her father was with her all the time, working. So, after the first attack took place, she couldn't go back to the Yellow Room until midnight. Now we know that Père Jacques did go in the Yellow Room, as he did every night, at 10 p.m., to close the shutters and light the nightlight. At that time, owing to her great distress, Mademoiselle Stangerson, still pretending to work in the laboratory, had forgotten that routine. When she realized that Père Jacques was about to enter the Yellow Room, she immediately begged him not to trouble himself, not to go into

247

the Yellow Room. All this was clearly reported in the article from *Le Matin*. Père Jacques, however, did go in, but, because of the dim light of the room, saw nothing.

"I'm sure that Mademoiselle Stangerson must have experienced some terrible anxiety when the old man went into the Yellow Room, but I think she also wasn't aware that the perpetrator had left so many clues behind. After the first part of the attack, she only had time to hide the traces of the man's fingers on her neck and to rush back to the laboratory. Had she known that the sheep-bone, the béret, and the handkerchief were still there, she would have thrown them away, or picked them up when she returned to the Yellow Room at midnight. But she, too, didn't see them when she undressed by the inadequate glimmer of the nightlight. She went to bed, worn-out by anxiety and terror, the same terror that had made her remain in the laboratory as late as possible.

"My reasoning thus *logically* brought me to the second part of the tragedy, *when Mademoiselle Stangerson was alone in the Yellow Room, and the perpetrator was long gone*. Now, I had to fit the remaining material clues inside my circle of logic. What were they?

"I had to explain the two gunshots heard during that second incident and Mademoiselle Stangerson's cries of *'Murder! Murder! Help!'* What was the right end of logic saying? First, the cries. Since the perpetrator was gone, and Mademoiselle Stangerson was alone in the Yellow Room, *then those cries could only result from a nightmare!*

"The witnesses stated that they heard the sounds of furniture being overturned. I suppose… No, I'm *logically* compelled to assume that Mademoiselle Stangerson fell asleep, still haunted by the terrible attack that she'd experienced earlier in the afternoon. The nightmare made her terror even more vivid… In her dream, she saw the murderer about to spring upon her and she cried: *'Murder! Murder!'* Her hand wildly looked for the gun she had placed within her reach on the night table by the side of her bed, but instead, she hit the table and overturned it. When it fell, the gun discharged. A bullet struck the ceiling. That bullet always seemed to me to have been the result of an accidental shot. Its very position suggested so, and supported my theory of a nightmare. That's why I began to feel certain that the real attack had taken place *before* Mademoiselle Stangerson had retired for the night, and that she had hidden it with her unusual strength of character.

"So, we have a nightmare, followed by a gunshot... Mademoiselle Stangerson was now awake, but in a terrible state... She tried to get up, but fell to the ground, dragging more furniture down with her. She uttered her final scream, *'Help!'* before fainting.

"However, *two gunshots* had been heard that night. For my theory—which looked increasingly like the truth to me—to work, it required that one gunshot was fired during the first part of the attack, and not two during the second part. One gunshot to wound the perpetrator *before*, one gunshot caused by the nightmare *after*. So, were we certain, in fact, that two shots had been fired after midnight? First, the alleged gunshots were heard among the fracas of the overturned furniture. Professor Stangerson said he had heard a dull shot first, followed by a sharp ringing one. What if the dull shot had been caused by the falling of the marble-topped table? Then the ringing shot was that of the actual gunshot that had struck the ceiling. It was absolutely *necessary* that this be the case for my theory to be true. I became convinced that I was indeed correct when the two caretakers, the Berniers, who were up and about poaching near the pavilion, *testified that they'd heard only one gunshot.* That's exactly what they told the Investigating Magistrate.

"So I had already virtually reconstructed the two parts of the attack when I stepped into the Yellow Room for the first time. However, I still had to fit the serious wound on Mademoiselle Stangerson's temple in my circle of logic. That wound was too severe to have been inflicted by the perpetrator with the sheep-bone during the first stage. Further, Mademoiselle Stangerson couldn't have kept it hidden, and indeed had not tried to do so by rearranging her hair. So *logically*, it had to have been inflicted during the second part, that of the nightmare. It was to find out what had happened exactly that I went into the Yellow Room, and I did find my answer there."

Rouletabille drew a piece of white folded paper from his bag, and out of it, an almost invisible object which he held between his thumb and forefinger. He showed it to the President.

"This, Monsieur," he said, "is a hair, a blond hair stained with blood. It is a hair from the head of Mademoiselle Stangerson. I found it stuck to one of the corners of the overturned table. The corner of the table was itself stained with blood, a tiny stain, hardly visible, but very important, because it told me that, when she tried to rise from her bed, Mademoiselle Stangerson fell heavily and struck her head on the corner of the marble top, which retained some of her blood and hair stuck to it. The doctors said that Mademoiselle Stangerson had been hit by a *blunt object*, and since the sheep-bone was there, the Investigating Magistrate just assumed that it was the weapon that had caused the blow. *But the marble-top corner of a table is also a blunt object,* one that neither the doctors nor the Investigating Magistrate considered, and that I might have missed too *if the right end of logic hadn't pointed me toward it!*"

The courtroom exploded with cheers, but Rouletabille continued his story and silence returned at once.

"I still had to find out, in addition to the perpetrator's name, which I only discovered later, the time of the original attack. I learned it from the Investigating Magistrate's questioning of Mademoiselle Stangerson and her father, even though the answers she gave were designed to deceive Monsieur de Marquet. Mademoiselle Stangerson provided a detailed account of how she had spent her time during that fateful day. We had otherwise established that the perpetrator had entered the pavilion between 5 and 6 p.m. Let's assume it was 6:15 p.m. when the Professor and his daughter resumed their work. Logically, therefore, the attack had to have taken place between 5 and 6:15 p.m. Not even 5 p.m. because Professor

Stangerson was with his daughter then, and the attack could only have occurred in his absence. Therefore, I had to find out exactly when he had left her.

"I found the answer in the transcript of the interview that took place in Mademoiselle Stangerson's bedroom, in her father's presence. It stated that the Professor and his daughter returned to the pavilion at 6 p.m. Professor Stangerson declared: '*At that moment, our gamekeeper came and detained me for a few minutes.*' The Professor then became involved in as conversation with the gamekeeper about '*a section of the grounds which he had decided to thin.*' Mademoiselle Stangerson was nowhere in sight. She had gone into the pavilion. The Professor further stated: '*After the gamekeeper left... I rejoined my daughter. I had given her my key to the pavilion, and she'd gone inside, leaving the key in the lock outside. When I walked into the laboratory, she was already at work.*'

"Therefore, it was during that short interval of time that the tragedy took place. *It is logical.* I imagine Mademoiselle Stangerson entering the pavilion, going to her room to take off her hat, and finding herself face-to-face with the man who had been pursuing her. The perpetrator had been in the pavilion for some time, waiting for her. He had presumably planned to wait for nightfall. He had already taken off Père Jacques's old, muddy boots, as I pointed out to the Investigating Magistrate. And he had already removed the Professor's scientific papers from the safe, as I described. Then, he had slipped under the bed of the Yellow Room to hide when Père Jacques had returned to wash the floors of the laboratory and the vestibule. After the old man had left, finding the time long, he had gotten up, wandered off to the laboratory, then to the vestibule. There, he had looked into the garden, and had seen, in the twilight, coming towards the pavilion, *Mademoiselle Stangerson, alone.*

"He would never have dared to attack her at that hour, if she hadn't been alone. In order to seem that way, the conversation between Professor Stangerson and the gamekeeper had to have taken place at a spot along the path hidden from sight,

251

such as a small clump of trees, or a thicket, blocking the per-
petrator's view.

"His mind was now made up. He would be less disturbed alone with Mademoiselle Stangerson in the pavilion than in the middle of the night, with Père Jacques sleeping in the attic. *So he shut the vestibule window.* That explains, by the way, why neither the Professor, nor the gamekeeper, who were at some distance from the pavilion, heard the first gunshot later.

"So the perpetrator went back to the Yellow Room. Mademoiselle Stangerson came in. What happened then must have taken place very quickly. Mademoiselle Stangerson called, or rather tried to call, for help, but the perpetrator seized her by the throat. He was about to strangle her... Her hand sought and grasped the revolver which she had been keeping in the drawer of her nightstand, since she had come to fear the threats of her stalker. The perpetrator was about to strike her on the head with the sheep-bone—a terrible weapon in the hands of a Ballmeyer—but she fired, just in time, and her shot wounded the perpetrator in the hand. The sheep-bone fell to the floor, *covered with the blood of the perpetrator*, who staggered, clutched at the wall for support, leaving his red handprint behind. Then, fearing another bullet, the man fled.

"Mademoiselle Stangerson saw the perpetrator run through the laboratory, and listened. It took several minutes for him to get out of the pavilion by the vestibule window. At last, she heard him jump out. She ran to the window and shut it. Now that the danger was past, all her thoughts turned to her father. Had he either seen or heard anything? With superhuman energy, she planned to keep all this from him to the best of her abilities. Thus, when Professor Stangerson returned, he found the door of the Yellow Room closed, and his daughter in the laboratory, at her desk, *apparently at work!*"

Turning towards Darzac, Rouletabille cried:

"You know the truth! Tell us, then, if that is not how things happened."

"I don't know anything about it," replied Darzac.

252

"You're a true hero, Monsieur Darzac," said Rouleta-bille, folding his arms, "but if Mademoiselle Stangerson knew your situation, she would release you from your oath. She would beg you to tell all that she confided to you. She would be the first here to defend you!"

Darzac made no movement, nor uttered a word. He looked at Rouletabille sadly.

"Still," said the young reporter, "since Mademoiselle Stangerson isn't here, *I must do that job myself*. But, believe me, Monsieur Darzac, the only means to save Mademoiselle Stangerson and to restore her sanity is to secure your acquittal."

A thunder of applause greeted that last statement. The President didn't even try to stop the cheering. It was clear that Darzac had just been saved from the scaffold. Looking into the eyes of the jurors was evidence enough. Their body language reflected their conviction of his innocence.

"But, Monsieur Rouletabille," said the President, "what is this secret motive compelling Mademoiselle Stangerson to hide her near-murder from her father?"

"That, Monsieur, I do not know," said Rouletabille. "It's none of my business."

The President, turning to Monsieur Darzac, tried again to make him tell what he knew.

"Do you still refuse, Monsieur, to tell us how you employed your time during the attempts on Mademoiselle Stangerson's life?"

"I cannot tell you anything, Monsieur."

The President turned to Rouletabille as if appealing for an explanation.

"We must assume, Monsieur," the young reporter said, "that Monsieur Darzac's absences were indeed closely connected with Mademoiselle Stangerson's secret, and that Monsieur Darzac feels himself honor-bound to remain silent. But let's suppose that Larsan, who, during his three attempts on Mademoiselle Stangerson's life, did everything he could to frame Monsieur Darzac, had arranged, on just those occasions, a meeting with Monsieur Darzac at a compromising spot, a meeting where Mademoiselle Stangerson's secret would be discussed. That would explain why Monsieur Darzac would rather be condemned than reveal his fiancée's secret. And Larsan was cunning enough to have arranged such a trap."

The President seemed somewhat convinced, but, still curious, he asked:

"So what is Mademoiselle Stangerson's secret?"

"That, I cannot tell you, Monsieur," said Rouletabille. "I think, however, that you now know enough to order Monsieur Darzac's acquittal! Unless Larsan should return, but I don't think he will," he added, with a laugh.

Everyone laughed with him.

"One more question," said the President. "Accepting your explanation, we understand why Larsan wished to cast suspicion on Monsieur Darzac, but what interest did he have in doing the same to Père Jacques?"

"The interest of the detective, Monsieur," replied Rouletabille. "Larsan liked to prove himself as a superior investigator, a first-class solver of mysteries, which meant being able to see through false clues which he had planted himself! As I said, he is a very cunning man, and that trick often served to deflect suspicion from himself. He proved the innocence of one man, before accusing another. You can easily believe, Monsieur, that such a complicated scheme must have been carefully planned in advance. I'm telling you that Larsan had made a careful study of Glandier and its residents beforehand. If you care to learn how he had gathered such information, you will find out that he had, on several occasions, impersonated a messenger dispatched by the forensic laboratory of the Sûreté to Professor Stangerson, who had been asked to run some tests. In this way, he was able, before the crime, to visit the pavilion twice. He was so well disguised that Père Jacques didn't recognize him, but he, Larsan, used that opportunity to steal an old pair of boots and a Basque béret which the old man had tied in a handkerchief, with the intention of giving them to one of his friends, one of the charcoal-burners on the road to Epinay. When the crime was discovered, Père Jacques immediately recognized these objects as his, but as they made him appear guilty, he lied to us when we asked him about them, and was extremely distressed.

"In the end, it was all very simple, and Larsan proudly confessed all these details to me, because if he's a criminal—which, I hope, no one here any longer doubts!—he is also something of an artist. It's his trademark... He used a similar bag of tricks in the affair of the Crédit Universel, and that of the gold bullion robbery of the Hôtel de la Monnaie.

"Because, if I may be so bold, Monsieur, I think those cases should be reopened at once. Since Ballmeyer-Larsan joined the Sûreté, a number of innocent persons have been sleeping in jail."

Chapter Twenty-Eight
In Which It Is Proved That
One Can't Always Think of Everything

Great excitement, applause and cheers erupted when Rouletabille had finished.

Maître Robert immediately called for an adjournment pending further investigation, and was supported in his motion by the Public Prosecutor. The case was thus adjourned. The next day, Monsieur Darzac was released on bail, while Père Mathieu was acquitted of all charges and freed. The police searched everywhere for Frederic Larsan, but in vain. The proof of Monsieur Darzac's innocence was firmly established, and the Sorbonne Professor escaped the awful fate that, at one time, might have been in store for him. After a visit to Mademoiselle Stangerson, he hoped that she might, someday, with some careful nursing, recover her full mental faculties.

As for Rouletabille, naturally, he became the "man of the hour." On leaving the Palais de Justice, the crowd carried him in triumph. The world press published his exploits and his photos. He, who had interviewed so many famous personalities, had himself become famous and the subject of interviews. I'm glad to say that his enormous success in no way turned his head.

We left Versailles together, after having dined at the notorious Chien Qui Fume restaurant. In the train, I started to ask him a number of questions which, during our meal, had been on the tip of my tongue, but which I had refrained from asking, knowing that he didn't like to talk shop while eating.

"My friend," I said, "that Larsan case was wonderful. It was worthy of you and your phenomenal brain."

There, he stopped me and urged to me use less aggrandizing adjectives to describe him, humorously pretending that he would never console himself if a brilliant mind such as mine would fall into an abyss of stupidity just because I felt an undeserved admiration for him.

"I'll come to the point, then," I said, somewhat miffed. "None of what you revealed tell me why you went to America. If I understood what happened correctly, when you left, you already knew that Frederic Larsan was the perpetrator, and you knew how he had tried to murder Mademoiselle Stangerson?"

"That's correct. What about you?" he said, trying to turn the conversation around. "Did you suspect anything?"

"Nothing!"

"Amazing!"

"Since you took great pains to conceal your thoughts from me, my friend, I don't see how I could have suspected anything. When I arrived at Glandier with the revolvers, did you already suspect Larsan?"

"Yes! I had just reasoned my way through the incident of the unfathomable corridor. But Larsan's return to Mademoiselle Stangerson's room was only cleared up, however, by the discovery of the spectacles. In any event, my suspicions of Larsan were purely logical; the idea of him being the perpetrator seemed so extraordinary that I'd resolved to wait for material proof before venturing to act. Nevertheless, that suspicion was never far from my mind, and I sometimes spoke to you about Larsan in a way that should have opened your eyes.

"First, I no longer credited him for making a good faith mistake; indeed, I no longer said that he was making a mistake at all. I described his approach as some kind of 'system' that deserved our contempt. That contempt, which you thought I felt for the detective, was, in fact, directed at the criminal!

"Remember that when I was enumerating all the evidence gathered by Larsan against Monsieur Darzac, I said: 'All of this seems to fit nicely with Larsan's theory... I myself believe that theory to be false, and I think that Larsan is mistaken,' and then, I added in an ominous tone that should have surprised you: '*But is Larsan truly mistaken? That is the question!*'

"That '*That is the question!*' should have given you food for thought. My entire suspicions were in there. *Because, if Larsan wasn't mistaken, then the logical deduction was that he was trying to make us commit a mistake!* I was looking straight at your eyes when I said this, but I could tell you didn't get my meaning. In a way, I wasn't too unhappy about it, because until Madame Bernier found those spectacles, I could only consider Larsan-as-the-perpetrator as a rather far-fetched hypothesis. But remember how my mood changed after the discovery of the spectacles *in the groove of the parquet* of Mademoiselle Stangerson's bedroom. After that, I became elated, full of joy. Remember when I told Larsan at dinner: "Yes, we'll be doing battle and I will beat you." Obviously, I was thinking of Larsan-the perpetrator, not Larsan-the-detective.

"And when, that same evening, Monsieur Darzac had begged me to watch over Mademoiselle Stangerson, I undertook no efforts until after we had dined with Larsan, at about 10 p.m. I was certain nothing would happen *because he sat right there, in front of me*. That, my friend, should have told you that he was the only man I feared. And when we were discussing the perpetrator's arrival, I said to you: 'I'm quite sure Larsan will be here!'

"But I confess that there was one important clue that we both missed. It was the one thing which should have opened our eyes with respect to Larsan's true nature. *Do you remember the matter of his cane?*

"Leaving aside for a moment the right end of logic that accused Larsan, there was the matter of his cane that should have exposed him to any observing mind!

"I was surprised—as you may not have realized—to find that Larsan had made no use of that potential clue against Darzac during his investigation. Had the can not been purchased the night of the first attack by a man whose description tallied exactly with that of Darzac?

"Well, when I saw Larsan off during the recess, I asked him why he hadn't used the cane as evidence against Darzac.

He replied that he never had any intention of doing so, and that our discovery in Epinay *that he had lied to us* had greatly bothered him. If you remember, he told us that his cane had been given to him in London, just before we realized that it had, in fact, been purchased in Paris. Why, then, instead of saying: 'Larsan is lying. He was in London. He couldn't have received a Parisian cane there,' didn't we say: 'Larsan is lying. He wasn't in London. He bought that cane in Paris'?

"Larsan lying! Larsan in Paris at the time of the crime! That should have been the beginning of our suspicions! And when, after your visit to Cassette's, you found out that the cane had been bought by a person who looked just like Darzac, even though we had Mademoiselle Stangerson's fiancé's word that he hadn't made that purchase, and we already knew from the employee at the Poste Restante *that there was a man in Paris who looked just like Darzac*, why didn't we logically assume that that man was, in fact, Frederic Larsan?

"The way I see it, Larsan went to Cassette the evening of the crime to buy his cane, still disguised as Darzac. Once we saw that same cane in Larsan's hands, we should have been asking ourselves: '*What if the man dressed as Darzac who purchased Larsans's cane was none other than Larsan?*'

"Of course, his position as a Sûreté detective worked in his favor, but when we saw his obvious eagerness to convict Darzac, the passion which he displayed in pursuit of the man, we should have been struck by another question just as important as *the lie in which he claimed to have received a cane purchased in Paris while in London*. That one only proved that he wasn't really in England, as his superiors and everyone else believed, but in France. That other question was: *Why did Larsan buy that cane if he didn't intend to use it as additional proof against Darzac*? since the cane could have been easily manipulated to incriminate Mademoiselle Stangerson's fiancé?

"The answer is simple, so simple that we never even thought of it. Larsan bought the cane after having been wounded in the hand by Mademoiselle Stangerson, *in order to always keep his hand on it and avoid showing the palm of his hand with the incriminating wound!* You understand now? That's what Larsan himself told me. I remember asking you several times *why we never saw Larsan without his cane.* And when we dined together, he always held a knife in his right hand, never letting go of it. All these details came back to me after I had determined that Larsan was the perpetrator. By then, of course, they were too late to be of any practical use.

"The night when Larsan pretended to be drugged, I managed to take a sneak look at his hand, without him suspecting anything. I saw a thin silk bandage covering the signs of a slight healing wound. I thought that he might be able to claim that that wound had been caused by something other than a bullet. Still, it was yet another material clue I could fit in my circle of logic. Larsan told me earlier that Mademoiselle Stangerson's bullet had only grazed his palm, but caused a significant amount of bloodletting.

"Had we been more alert when Larsan lied to us about the cane, and thus more dangerous to him, it's still possible that he might have tried to divert suspicions by using *the fable we had concocted about Darzac buying the cane.* But events kept happening at a frantic pace, and we didn't give a second thought to the cane business. All the same, we had greatly worried Larsan-Ballmeyer without our knowing it."

"But," I interrupted, "if Larsan had no intention of using the cane as evidence against Darzac, why was he disguised as Darzac when he bought it? The same overcoat, bowler hat…"

"He wasn't disguised as Darzac *to buy the cane*; he had come straight to Cassette's immediately after he had attacked Mademoiselle Stangerson and was still wearing his Darzac disguise, which he used throughout to frame her fiancé. *His wound was bothering him* and, as he was passing along the Avenue de l'Opera, the idea of the cane came to him and he acted on it. It was then 8 p.m. A man looking like Darzac bought a cane, which I later found in Larsan's hands. And I, who had already discovered *that the attack had occurred ear-*

260

lier, I, who was convinced of Darzac's innocence, never suspected Larsan! There are times..."

"There are times," I said, "when even the greatest intellects..."

Rouletabille motioned me to be quiet. I continued to ask him questions, but I realized that he'd fallen asleep. I had the greatest difficulties in waking him when we reached Paris.

Chapter Twenty-Nine
Mademoiselle Stangerson's Secret

During the days that followed, I had several more opportunities to ask Rouletabille the reason for his trip to America, but I received no better answers than those he had given me in the train from Versailles on the evening of the trial. More often than not, he found ways to steer the conversation away onto other aspects of the case.

One day, however, he said:

"Can't you understand that I had to know Larsan's true identity?"

"Certainly," I replied, "but why did you have to go to America to find it?"

He kept smoking his pipe and turned his back on me. Obviously, I was getting closer to Mademoiselle Stangerson's secret. Rouletabille must have thought that that dread mystery which bound together Mademoiselle Stangerson and Larsan couldn't be solved in France, and must have originated during her time in America. So he had embarked for the United States, believing that there, he would learn more about Larsan and even find information that would give him power over him. So he had gone to Philadelphia.

What was that secret which had so effectively silenced Mademoiselle Stangerson and Monsieur Darzac? Now that the publicity around the case has died down, and since Professor Stangerson knows and has forgiven everything, the truth may at last be revealed. It is, in any event, very simple and will enable me to set the record straight, since some envious people have accused Mademoiselle Stangerson of being a manipulator, when, in fact, throughout this sinister affair, she was nothing but the victim.

It all started back when she was a young girl, living with her father in Philadelphia. There, at a reception given by one of her father's business friends, she met one Jean Roussel, a

Frenchman, who quickly seduced her using his wit, charm and persistent attentions. He was said to be rich and asked the Professor for her hand in marriage.

After making some discreet inquiries about Monsieur Roussel, Professor Stangerson, who, at first, had thought him to be a captain of industry, discovered that Roussel was, in fact, nothing but a swindler and an adventurer. He was, as we know now, the notorious Ballmeyer, a fugitive from French justice having found refuge in America, and operating there under many aliases, but neither Professor Stangerson nor his daughter knew this.

The Professor not only refused to give his consent to the marriage, but denied Roussel admission into his house. Young Mathilde Stangerson, however, had already fallen head over heels in love with the villain and, to her, he was the best and brightest man in the world. She became indignant at her father's attitude and didn't conceal her feelings.

So the Professor sent her away, to stay with an old aunt in Cincinnati in the State of Ohio. But Roussel caught up with her and, despite the respect Mathilde felt for her father, she outwitted her old relative and eloped with Roussel, intent on taking advantage of the laxity of U.S. laws in that respect to get married as soon as possible.

After their marriage, they settled in Louisville, Kentucky, but one morning, a week or so later, there was a knock on the door. It was the police who had come to arrest Roussel, despite his protests and Mathilde's tears. It was then that Mathilde learned from the police that her husband was none other than the infamous criminal Ballmeyer!

After a failed suicide attempt, the young woman, in despair, returned to her aunt in Cincinnati. The old relative was overjoyed to see her. She had been anxiously searching for her niece and hadn't dared tell Professor Stangerson of her disappearance. Mathilde swore her to secrecy, so that her father would never learn of her marriage. He aunt was happy to swear, since she felt extremely guilty for not having properly supervised her niece.

A month later, Mathilde returned to her father, repentant, her heart crushed, hoping for only one thing: to never again see or hear from her husband, the terrible Ballmeyer. In order to atone for her disobedience, she swore to spend the rest of her life dutifully assisting her father in his work.

She was true to her word. She eventually shared her story with Robert Darzac, her most trusted friend, because she believed that Ballmeyer had been killed at last. Finally, she decided she deserved to have some joy in her life and agreed to marry Darzac. Then, an evil fate resurrected Ballmeyer who took steps to let her know that he still loved her—which, alas! was true—and would never allow her to marry Darzac, even if it meant killing her.

Mademoiselle Stangerson didn't hesitate to confide the truth to Darzac. She showed him the letter in which Roussel-Larsan-Ballmeyer reminded her of their wedding ceremony in a beautiful little church near Louisville. "*The presbytery has lost none of its charm, nor the garden its glow*," he had written. The scoundrel pretended to be rich and said he wanted to take Mathilde back to America. She told Darzac that, if her father ever learned of her dishonor, she would kill herself. Darzac swore to silence her persecutor, even if it meant killing him. However, he was outmatched and would probably have been killed, had it not been for Rouletabille's genius.

As for Mademoiselle Stangerson, she was helpless against such a villain. After Roussel-Larsan-Ballmeyer had first threatened her in his letters, when he attacked her in the Yellow Room, she tried to kill him. Unfortunately, she failed. She then became the constant victim of that merciless villain who was continually blackmailing her, who lived near her, invisibly, almost by her side, and demanded her presence at clandestine interviews in the name of their old passion. When she had initially refused to see him, after he had written to her in care of the Poste Restante, the result was the tragic attack of the Yellow Room.

The second time he wrote, still asking for a meeting, the letter reached her in her bedroom, but that time, she managed to avoid her persecutor by sleeping in the boudoir with her nurses. In that letter, the wretch had warned her that, since she was apparently *too ill* to come to him, he would instead come to her, and would be in her bedroom at a particular hour on a particular night. He left it up to her to take steps to avoid a public scandal. Knowing that she had everything to fear from Roussel-Larsan-Ballmeyer, Mathilde left her room that night. It was then that the incident of the unfathomable corridor occurred.

The third time, Mathilde resolved to keep the appointment. Larsan had asked for it in a letter he had written on her desk during the night of the earlier incident. In that letter, he threatened to destroy her father's papers if she didn't meet him at the appointed time. It was to rescue these papers that she made up her mind to see him. It wasn't the first time, in fact, that Ballmeyer had pilfered the Professor's papers. Mathilde suspected that, with her unwitting help, he had already plundered her father's research once before in Philadelphia. She didn't doubt for one moment that the wretch would carry out his threat if she persisted in avoiding him. In that case, the labors of her father's lifetime would be reduced to ashes and forever be lost.

Since their meeting was inevitable, she resolved to face her former husband and appeal to his better nature. It was for this interview that she had prepared herself on the night the gamekeeper was killed. We can guess what happened. We can imagine Mathilde's supplications, his brutal refusal... Ballmeyer insisted that she renounce Darzac. She affirmed her love for him. He stabbed her in anger, determined to send Darzac to the scaffold for the crime, for he was very clever. He knew that his Larsan identity would protect him, while Darzac would never be able to explain how he spent his time away from the chateau. Ballmeyer's precautions in that respect were cunningly taken, as Rouletabille had guessed.

Larsan had blackmailed Darzac just as he had blackmailed Mathilde, with the same weapon, the same threats. He wrote Darzac urgent letters, declaring himself ready to go away, to surrender their old love letters, if only Darzac would pay his price. Like Mathilde, Darzac was forced to submit. He was obliged to go to those rendezvous at the time and place chosen by Larsan, or else the truth about Mathilde's marriage would be made public.

When Darzac went to Epinay, expecting to find Ballmeyer there, he was met by one of his accomplices, a strange being, *a creature from another world*, whom I shall discuss another time, who kept him waiting until such time as the "coincidence" of his absence, which he would be unable to explain, and of the attack on Mathilde could be established, sending him straight to the guillotine. It was all done with Machiavellian cunning, but Ballmeyer had reckoned without Joseph Rouletabille.

Now that the Mystery of the Yellow Room has been cleared up, I can briefly describe Rouletabille's adventures in America. Knowing the young reporter as we do, we can imagine with what acumen he retraced, step by step, the story of Mathilde Stangerson and Jean Roussel.

In Philadelphia, he quickly gathered information on the subject of Mr. Arthur William Rance. There, he learned of the American's act of devotion, but also of the reward he thought himself entitled to receive for it. A rumor of his marriage with Mademoiselle Stangerson had once found its way into the sitting rooms of Philadelphia, because of Rance's lack of discretion and modesty. He also learned of Rance's persistent attentions toward Mathilde, and of his regular and unwelcome visits to Glandier. Rance took to drink, or so he claimed, to drown his grief at his unrequited love. We now understand why Rouletabille was so cool toward him when they met in the witnesses' room during the trial. In any event, the young reporter had quickly determined that Rance had nothing to do with the affair.

Rouletabille learned of the passion that had brought together Jean Roussel and Mathilde Stangerson. But who was this Jean Roussel? Rouletabille traced him from Philadelphia to Cincinnati. In Cincinnati, he met the old aunt, and found a way to make her talk. Finally, the story of Ballmeyer's arrest threw a new light on the whole case. He went to Louisville and visited the "presbytery"—a small and pretty church in the old colonial style—which had, indeed, "lost none of its charm." Then, abandoning Mathilde's trail, he picked up that of Ballmeyer.

He followed it from prison to prison, from crime to crime. At last, as he was about to return to France, he learned on the seedy wharves of New York that Ballmeyer had, five years before, also gone back to France with, in his pocket, the identification papers of an honorable merchant from New Orleans named "Frederic Larsan" whom he had just murdered.

And now, do you feel that you have learned the whole secret of Mademoiselle Stangerson? You would be wrong! *Because Mademoiselle Stangerson had a child by her husband—a son.* The infant was born in the old aunt's house in Cincinnati. No one knew of it, because the aunt managed to conceal the event well.

What became of that son? That's another story which I shall relate another day.

About two months after these events, I came upon Rouletabille sitting on a bench in the Palais de Justice. He looked very depressed.

"What's the matter, my friend?" I asked. "You look sad. How are your friends getting on?"

"Apart from you," he said, "I don't really have any friends."

"What about Monsieur Darzac?"

"I suppose..."

"And Mademoiselle Stangerson. How is she?"

"Better, much better."

"Then, you shouldn't feel sad."

"I'm sad," he said, "because I'm thinking of *the perfume of the lady in black*."

"*The perfume of the lady in black!* I've often heard you refer to it. Can you tell me at last why it troubles you so much?"

"Someday perhaps… Someday," said Rouletabille.

And he heaved a profound sigh.

THE END

This short story, originally published in our edition of Arsène Lupin vs. Sherlock Holmes: The Blonde Phantom, *purports to explain what happened to Larsan (Ballmeyer) between the ending of* The Mystery of the Yellow Room, *and his return in* The Perfume of the Lady in Black, *which takes place three years later. It is enough to know that, in December 1903, Arsène Lupin, using the alias of Paul Daubreuil, saved the life of Jeanne Darcieux from her stepfather, Baron Maupertuis' diabolical schemes...*[17]

The Return of Ballmeyer, or Arsène Lupin Arrives Too Late

by Jean-Marc & Randy Lofficier

Excerpt of a letter from Jeanne Darcieux to Paul Daubreuil, Tuesday, January 12, 1904:

Dear Paul,

As you have surely heard, the Belgian Police arrested my step-father, Paul Darcieux, in Brussels. Last week, I received a communication from a Belgian policeman named Poirot, who confirmed that he would soon be extradited to France. Oh, how I shudder when I remember the horrible events that took place at Maupertuis. I still see my stepfather's evil face as he prepared to plunge his dagger into my body that terrible night. I don't think I shall ever be able to banish that image from my mind... I will never have the right words to thank you for all that you did for me, my dearest friend. (...) I have followed Dr. Gueroult's sage advice and come to London to start my life afresh. Thank you for recommending a good solicitor in Versailles to oversee the management of the Maupertuis estate, but all that is now a part of the life that I left behind...

---

[17] "La Mort Qui Rôde" in *The Confessions of Arsène Lupin.*

Excerpt of a letter from Jeanne Darcieux to Paul Daubreuil, Monday, February 1, 1904:

Dear Paul,

Your letter filled me with joy. Since you were kind enough to inquire as to my progress here, I shall report news that, I am sure, will please you greatly. Yesterday, I found a position as a tutor teaching French to Lord Strongborough's 12-year-old son, Anthony. Lord Strongborough is a charming widower who is very much involved with the Jockey Club, of which I understand he is one of the stewards. I am expected to live in his beautiful estate in Surrey. My duties will include...

Excerpt of a letter from Jeanne Darcieux to Paul Daubreuil, Friday, May 6, 1904:

Dear Paul,

Edward and I are just back from the Riviera, where he has a house near Saint Paul de Vence. We had the grandest time. Upon our return, Edward decided to announce our formal engagement. A wonderful party was held at the Manor. I so wish that you could have been there. The entire Jockey Club attended. Dr. Taylor regaled us with stories of when he and Edward used to race horses in America, in Kentucky, I believe. Major Roland told us of his service in India...

Announcement published in The Times *of London, Friday, July 1, 1904:*

The forthcoming marriage is announced between Sir Edward, 31st Lord Strongborough, Baron of Cuthbert, and Mademoiselle Jeanne Darcieux de Maupertuis of Vendôme, France. The ceremony will take place at Strongborough Hall, Surrey, later this month.

Excerpt of a letter from Jeanne Darcieux to Paul Daubreuil, Thursday, September 8, 1904:

Dear Paul,

I cannot believe that I am writing this to you, but the nightmare has returned. Death again surrounds me, creeping over me, casting an invisible shroud over my life. As I wrote to you in my last letter, young Anthony passed away of gastric fever two weeks ago. Edward was, understandably, devastated by the death of his only son, who was the light of both our lives. Major Roland, Dr. Taylor and the other stewards of the Jockey Club have all tried to console him and shake him out of his dark mood, but nothing seems to work. He had the most terrible row with Dr. Taylor, and has simply refused to see Major Roland. He now spends most of his time alone, barricaded in his room, just like my stepfather once did. That is a most horrible reminder of the evil days at Maupertuis...

Excerpt of a letter from Jeanne Darcieux to Paul Daubreuil, Tuesday, September 20, 1904:
Dear Paul,
My life is now worse than it has ever been, if such a thing is possible. There have been foul words spread about Anthony's death. Hushed whispers about poison. I see the way the staff now looks at me. I am the foreign Jezebel who has taken the place of their beloved mistress...

Excerpt of a letter from Jeanne Darcieux to Paul Daubreuil, Monday, October 3, 1904:
Dear Paul,
Last night, Major Roland called to see Edward. They spent some time together in his office. The Major looked quite unhappy when he left. We talked a bit afterwards. He mentioned that Mister Sherlock Holmes himself had agreed to come out of retirement and travel to Paris to tackle the affair of the Blue Diamond and give a sound thrashing to "that wretched braggart, Lupin," as he called you. He does not know what happened between us at Maupertuis, of course. I am so worried about you, my dearest friend. They say that Mister Holmes has no equal. Please, be careful. Here, even Edward, when I do see him, which is not often these days, has started to regard me

with suspicion. I do not know to whom to turn. I feel as if an invisible noose is tightening around my neck and I am utterly powerless to stop it...

Excerpt of a letter from Jeanne Darcieux to Paul Daubreuil, Tuesday, November 1, 1904:
Dear Paul,
The news is too horrible for words. Edward died last night. He succumbed to the same gastric fever as Anthony. He had been complaining of stomach pains, then fell prey to nausea and much vomiting. He was taken to the hospital yesterday. Dr. Taylor rushed to his side but it was too late.

Excerpt of a letter from Jeanne Darcieux to Paul Daubreuil, Thursday, November 17, 1904:
Dear Paul,
There is now talk of an inquest. The Police were here and questioned me and the staff... That man of yours whom you mentioned in your last letter never arrived. I hope nothing befell him. I feel as if I am being watched. In your last letter, you said you were *en route* to Uruguay. I so wish you could be here. I am certain you would untangle the mystery of what happened in no time. I have made a note of the lawyer you recommended, Sir Edward Leithen, should the need arise...

Article published in The Times *of London, Tuesday, December 6, 1904:*
Lady Strongborough was arrested today on suspicion of having poisoned her husband. The Home Secretary ordered that the bodies of Lord Strongborough and that of his son, Anthony, deceased August 25 last, be exhumed and checked for poison...

Excerpt of a letter from Jeanne Darcieux to Paul Daubreuil, Monday, December 12, 1904:
Dear Paul,

Dr. Taylor does not trust the Police; he insisted on supervising the removal of the organs for analysis. I think he is afraid of the scandal. I am being treated as if I had the plague. No one will see me or talk to me. I have written to Sir Edward to retain his counsel, although I pray every day that his assistance will not be required and I will awaken from this nightmare...

Article published in The Times *of London, Thursday, December 15, 1904:*
Traces of a poison called cadmium were found in both bodies. Cadmium is soluble in acid foods and the Police suspect it was administered to the victims in lemonade prepared by Lady Strongborough. Traces of cadmium were also found in medicine being taken by Lord Strongborough...

Article published in The Times *of London, Monday, December 19, 1904:*
Today, at the inquest into the death of Lord Strongborough, Constable Barnaby presented evidence that bottles containing cadmium compounds were found in the photographic laboratory set up for Lady Strongborough by her late husband in what used to be the conservatory...

Article published in The Times *of London, Wednesday, December 21, 1904:*
Today, at the inquest into the death of Lord Strongborough, the jury recorded a verdict of willful murder against person or persons unknown...

Excerpt of a letter from Jeanne Darcieux to Paul Daubreuil, Thursday, January 12, 1905:
Dear Paul,
It has now been two months since your last letter and I am still without news of you. I continue to write to the safe address you gave me in Paris, hoping that my letters are reaching you, wherever you might be. I pray every day for your safe return, for I believe you, and you alone, can put an end to this awful

nightmare I am living. I did not poison my husband, Paul, upon my soul, and neither did I poison young Anthony, who was as dear to me as if he had been my own son. The Press has reported that serious irregularities have been discovered in the accounts of the Jockey Club. Apparently, Edward had a secret life about which I knew nothing. They say I killed him because I wanted to get my hands on his fortune before he was irremediably disgraced and ruined, but this is ridiculous, for I am wealthy too in my own right. I have property in France and I could have helped poor Edward had he but asked. They also say that I was the only one who could have poisoned him because I have access to cadmium, even though I was always careful to lock up my laboratory and none of the chemicals were ever missing...

Article published in The Times *of London, Wednesday, Febuary 1, 1905:*
Lady Strongborough's trial began today at the Old Bailey. As the prosecuting counsel, Mister Erskine-Brown, laid out his case, everyone present was silent and somber. Lady Strongborough appeared vulnerable, seemingly on the verge of tears and, at one stage, she shook her head in grief as she heard some of the agonizing details of her husband's last moments. Sir Edward Leithen, counsel for the defense, made a remarkable opening statement in which he urged the jury to look beyond the circumstantial evidence that he called a "web of deceit." Right from the outset, the jury was left in no doubts as to the magnitude of the case. The judge, Mister Justice Wargrave, warned them that a case of this length, lasting possibly up to three months, was physically strenuous and advised them not to be swayed by the oratorical tricks of the defense and to look at "nothing but the facts"...

Excerpt of a letter from Jeanne Darcieux to Paul Daubreuil, Tuesday, March 14, 1905
Dear Paul,

I am still without news of you. I fear the worst. Sir Edward Leithen is mounting what I believe they call a "vigorous defense," yet the autopsy results speak against me. No one, certainly not I, can explain the presence of the fatal cadmium in the bodies. The Judge seems prejudiced against me. They call him a "hanging judge." I fear the worst...

Article published in The Times *of London, Monday, April 3, 1905:*
Lady Strongborough Found Guilty... Lady Strongborough burst into tears as Mister Justice Wargrave delivered the ritual sentence: "The sentence of the court upon you is that you be taken from this place to a lawful place of execution and that you be hanged by the neck until you are dead. And may God have mercy on your soul."

Excerpt of a letter from Jeanne Darcieux to Paul Daubreuil, Wednesday, April 5, 1905:
Dear Paul,
This is my last letter to you and I can only pray that it will find you in good health, even if comes too late to alter my fate, which now seems sealed. I am innocent, but I have reconciled myself to my destiny. Tomorrow, I shall walk to the gallows praying only that nothing evil has befallen you, my dearest friend...

Report from Lt. Colonel Venables, Governor of the Prison of Pentonville, Thursday, April 6, 1905:
The execution was set for 8 a.m. The night before, Lady Strongborough was visited by her counsel, Sir Edward Leithen. I was told that she had accepted her fate and that, apart from a slight nervous twitch at the corner of her mouth, she was calm. After Sir Edward had left, she was given brandy and water and at 11 p.m. she slept. She was awakened at 5 a.m. to prepare herself for a visit from the Prison Chaplin, Reverend Fergusson. The Reverend stayed with Lady Strongborough until 7 a.m. and tried to get her to confess that she

was guilty, but she steadfastly denied that she had poisoned either her husband or his son and categorically maintained her innocence. At 7:30 a.m., Lady Strongborough was given a cup of tea with more brandy and water. At 7:40 a.m., she was joined in the condemned's cell by Under Sheriff Regan and myself. We told her that the time had come to carry out the sentence and she was quietly led to courtyard where the gallows had been erected the day before. Here, we were joined by William Billington, the hangman, who was introduced to Lady Strongborough, who showed no emotion. Mister Billington tied her hands and she asked that he not draw the rope too tight before the drop. She was extremely calm at this point. She was then taken to the chapel where she received the final sacraments. At 7:55 a.m., the prison's death bell tolled, which marked the start of the procession to the gallows. Reverend Fergusson read extracts from the burial service. We were joined by the Head Turnkey, Mister Daley, and two warders, George Bulman and Derek Willis. As we walked across the yard to the gallows, a man was suddenly ushered in by warder Kavanagh. He shouted that the execution be stopped and indicated that he was holding a reprieve signed by Mister Akers-Douglas, the Home Secretary himself. "It's him!" screamed Lady Strongborough. "I knew he would not abandon me. I knew he would not be too late! It's Arsène Lupin!" "Shut up, you little git," said Mister Daley. "Don't you recognize Mister Sherlock Holmes?"

Excerpt from the Private Notebooks of John H. Watson, M.D., undated, but likely written in late April 1905:
My friend Mister Sherlock Holmes asked me to pen a few notes on the strange case of Lady Strongborough in which he was so fortunate as to be able to save her from the hangman's noose with but minutes to spare.

For reasons that will become clear to my reader, I seriously doubt that I will ever write, even less publish, a full account of this case, but it is sufficiently worthy for me to record some of the bare facts in this Journal.

As I have recorded in my account entitled "The Reigate Puzzle," Holmes had already crossed the path of, and thwarted Paul Darcieux, Baron Maupertuis, in the Spring of 1887. It was, therefore, the most amazing coincidence that he was called upon to save the life of the man's stepdaughter 18 years later, during his retirement in the South Downs.

On referring to my notes, I see that I made a copy of the cable which Holmes received on March 22, and that started his investigation. It came from some God-forsaken city called Malatya, deep inside the Ottoman Empire, and had been relayed through the British Embassy in Constantinople. It merely read: "STRONGBOROUGH MURDER STOP DEADLY COURT STOP SIGNED AL."

Under normal circumstances, Holmes would have ignored the message, as he receives many such nonsensical correspondences from various benighted souls all around England and even from other parts of the Empire. But there was the signatory: "AL."

At Holmes' request, his brother, Mycroft, called on some of his associates in Turkey and, two days later, we learned that Malatya was deep inside hostile territory held by a mad warlord known locally as the "Red Sultan." As the report went, a single westerner, a man in his thirties, had fought and defeated 40 of the Red Sultan's warriors to invade a telegram office and, there, had held a small army at bay during the time it took to relay that cable via Constantinople. Apparently, no more could be sent. The report labeled the man "clearly insane" while praising his bravery. When he read this, Holmes no longer had any doubts as to the identity of "AL."

Of all the enemies Holmes has fought during his tumultuous career, none, not even the nefarious Professor Moriarty or Charles-Augustus Milverton, have ever been able to get under my friend's skin as much as the Frenchman. "The Frenchman" or *He* or *Him* was, in fact, how he most often referred to *him* when we discussed *him*, which was a rare occurrence at best. Perhaps it was a habit unconsciously borrowed from Chief Inspector Ganimard. All of Holmes' other foes had, in effect, played the game according to the same rules. But with *him*, there were no rules. It was like grappling with quicksilver.

Having ascertained that the cable from Malatya came from *him*, my friend set to work immediately.

In just under a week, he had untangled the mystery. However, it took all of his considerable influence to convince the Home Secretary of Lady Strongborough's innocence and get him to sign the reprieve which, thank God, he was able to deliver just in time to spare the poor woman's life.

I shall now jot down the conversation that ensued later that selfsame day between Sherlock Holmes and Lady Strongborough, which I had the privilege of attending.

"I owe you my life, Mister Holmes," said Lady Strongborough, who was still understandably shaken by her ordeal.

At that point, my friend pulled out the cablegram and showed it to her.

"This is not entirely true, Madam," said Holmes, thoughtfully. "Your guardian angel came through, I believe."

Lady Strongborough read the cable and began crying, silently, without sobs; tears rolled gently down her cheeks as if the weight of the grim fate she had just been spared had suddenly crushed her gentle soul. We gave her time to recover. Then, she said:

"I am most grateful that you showed me this, Mister Holmes. And naturally thrilled that it made sense to you. But I confess that I do not understand. What does 'deadly court' mean? Is it a reference to Judge Wargrave?..."

"It is not 'deadly court,' Lady Strongborough–that was likely an error in the transmission–but 'deadly cort,' also known as deadly galerina or *cortinarius speciosissimus*, one of the deadliest brown-capped fungi, found commonly throughout the American Northwest, and the symptoms of which could easily be mistaken for cadmium poisoning."

"But the autopsy said..."

"This was a most unusual case. The man who strived to engineer your doom had a diabolical mind. Your husband,

Lady Strongborough, was in fact murdered after all of you thought he had been poisoned. The evidence was then retroactively tampered with to make the facts fit the theory formulated by the Police."

"So cadmium is not what killed Edward?"

"No. I will tell you the story as I reconstructed it. Your husband, I am sorry to say, Lady Strongborough, had been involved in some unpleasant business while in America 20 years ago. The sins of youth, some would say. A woman died in childbirth and so did the child. Much cause for scandal, if it were revealed publicly. Two years ago, the man whom you knew as Dr. Taylor appeared in London. He had known your husband in America and was well-acquainted with his past. He blackmailed him, first to get a position on the board of the Jockey Club, then to embezzle funds. But after his marriage to you, Lord Strongborough began to rebel; I believe he threatened to report Taylor to the Police.

"I have no doubt that Taylor decided to murder your husband at once, but I believe what gave him the idea on how to do it was young Anthony's death, which was, in fact, completely natural and due to gastric fever, as had been correctly diagnosed at the time.

"Taylor knew of your photographic laboratory and saw how Anthony's death could retroactively be made to look like cadmium poisoning. The criminal carried with him some finely ground deadly cort that, no doubt, he had collected while in America. He merely waited for Lord Strongborough to be afflicted with gastroenteritis, as Anthony had been, and perhaps did as much he could to inflame the condition. When your husband was taken to the hospital, he rushed to his side and there, he administered the poison. Deadly cort is instantly fatal and would mimic the symptoms of cadmium poisoning, which is slower and more painful. Since everyone later assumed that your husband had been poisoned at the Manor, when he was initially taken ill, no one bothered to look at the hospital records.

"Then, the only thing left for Taylor to do was to fool the medical examiners by lacing the samples with carefully measured traces of cadmium. If you recall, he insisted on supervising the autopsies. All the evidence against you was retroactively fabricated to fit the case that he wanted the Police to make against you. As I said, it was one of the most diabolically ingenious murder schemes I have ever come across."

"Have they arrested Dr. Taylor?" asked Lady Strongborough.

"I'm afraid that, as soon as he got wind of my involvement, he fled the country. That was, in fact, how I was able to persuade the Home Secretary that he was the murderer and that he should immediately grant your reprieve. I heard he's fled back to France."

"Fled back to France?"

"My investigation showed that he arrived from Paris in 1902. But I could find no more about him. He obviously is a most remarkable criminal. Perhaps *he*, I mean, your friend, will be able to shed more light on this... But, at least, you no longer have anything to fear, Lady Strongborough."

And thus did my friend Sherlock Holmes solve the murder of Lord Strongborough and save the life of a most gracious Lady. I have recorded this as an appendix to the case of Baron Maupertuis in the event that I ever decide to write it in full. But as Holmes mentioned, the case still contains some loose ends, and besides I know that my friend does not like me to write about *him*, so it is probably best to let it lie for the time being...

The village of Saint Paul de Vence in Provence was a jewel located in the hills above Nice. It was bright and beautiful this sunny afternoon of June. The sky was a deep penetrating blue and the quality of the light made every object stand out in sharp relief.

Lady Strongborough waited at the terrace of the single café that serviced the village, sipping on a *grenadine*. He had told her that he would be there precisely at 5 p.m. and she knew that he would not betray his word.

The village clock in the church tower tolled five.

"I deeply apologize for not being able to make it back in time," said a voice from behind her.

He had appeared as if by magic. She had seen no car, heard no engine, yet there he was, looking very much like the Paul Dubreuil she had met 18 months earlier. He pulled out a chair and sat down. He gestured to the *garçon* to bring him a *pastis*.

"When did you get back?" she asked.

"Two months ago. I lost the lives of a couple of good men trying to reach Constantinople in time, but the Red Sultan barred my way. I knew, however, that if I could send that cable to Sherlock Holmes, he, of all people, would have both the mental abilities and the power to rescue you. I was thrilled to discover upon my return to Marseilles that I hadn't been mistaken. I never would have forgiven myself if..."

She put her hand on his to dispel the ghastly image of the fate that they knew had almost been hers.

"Mister Holmes said that you knew more about this case than he had uncovered," Lady Strongborough said.

"How perceptive of him," he smiled. "His mind is as penetrating as ever. Yes, the trick that the so-called Dr. Taylor used, that bit of misdirection, of sleight of hand, reminded me of another case, one that was much covered in the Press, three years ago. *The Affair of Chateau Glandier a.k.a. The Mystery of the Yellow Room*. The murderer was exposed as Ballmeyer, an international criminal of the first order. We never met but I like to keep an eye on the competition. I knew that he had been in America, at the same time as your late husband, and that he would have been familiar with poisons found on that Continent. He also had been in London in 1901 and was implicated in a murky business of stolen bonds... But more to the point, when he was finally unmasked by a young reporter from *L'Epoque* at the end of the Yellow Room case, we discovered that Ballmeyer had had the prodigious idea of masquerading as an Inspector of the Sûreté, Frederic Larsan! What a stroke of genius! Ballmeyer, a man wanted by half the police forces of Europe and America, was hiding in plain sight in the French Sûreté! You have to admire that inventiveness! Why, I was almost jealous!"

"So Dr. Taylor was Ballmeyer?"

"Yes. And Ballmeyer was Frederic Larsan, and I knew that Larsan had been involved in the famous case of the gold bullion robbery of the Hôtel de la Monnaie, in which, if you recall, your stepfather, Paul Darcieux, Baron Maupertuis, was one of the suspects."

"Yes, that's true... I remember. He was one of the Trustees, but was cleared of all suspicion."

"By Frederic Larsan, his accomplice, the man who likely devised the whole scheme and used his position as Inspector of the Sûreté to frame an innocent man. You see, it all ties together. So, I asked myself, what if Ballmeyer-Larsan was up to his old tricks again, seeking to kill two birds with one stone: he murders your husband to cover his tracks with the Jockey Club, and he pins the blame on you to have you hung afterwards. If Lord Strongborough had been the only intended victim, I have no doubt that Ballmeyer could have dispatched him quickly and easily. Why resort to such a complicated scheme? Because he wanted you dead as well. Why? Ask yourself: who would have profited from your death?"

"My stepfather! He's the only family I have."

"Indeed. We're drawn back to the Ballmeyer-Darcieux connection. So, one of the first things I did upon my return to this country was to check your stepfather's fate. And I wasn't surprised to discover that someone had organized his escape soon after his extradition to France."

"Oh my God! He's free?"

"Don't fear, Jeanne. I would have taken steps, but I had no need. They say there's no honor among thieves, you know... They found an unidentified body not far from here, which I know to be Paul Darcieux. There is no doubt in my mind that when Holmes exposed Ballmeyer, and his plans to have you hung failed, Ballmeyer killed your stepfather."

"And Ballmeyer?"

"My inquiries lead me to believe that the same young journalist who exposed him the first time is back on his case. He has a brilliant mind, almost as good as Sherlock Holmes, to tell the truth. And he can be quite ruthless, under his college boy manners. I hope we never cross swords. I have no doubt he'll deal with Ballmeyer—definitively."

"You see, Sainclair, I had only condemned Larsan to life in prison, but he killed himself! It was God's will. May God have mercy on his soul!"

Joseph Rouletabille revealing Ballmeyer's fate
to his friend Sainclair at the conclusion of
The Perfume of the Lady in Black,
Summer 1905.

Gaston Leroux

Le
mystère
de la
chambre
jaune

folio
junior

Afterword

Rouletabille: A Genius for Good

*"It was as if Nature, in its infinite wisdom, after having
created a Father who was a Genius for Evil,
had created a Son who was a Genius for Good."*
(*The Perfume of the Lady in Black*–Chapter 4)

The leading *feuilletoniste* of the Belle Epoque was Gaston Leroux (1868-1927), a writer best known for his classic *Le Fantôme de l'Opéra* [*The Phantom of the Opera*] (1910),[18] the tragic yet murderous man-ape *Balaoo* (1911) and the adventures of *Chéri-Bibi*, a man unjustly pursued by a hostile fate (1913, 1919).[19]

Trained as a lawyer, Leroux was a renowned investigative journalist who even travelled to, and reported from, Russia just before the Communist Bolshevik Revolution.

His journalistic skills helped French *fantastique* literature to emerge from the melodramatic, overly romantic style of the end of the 19th century, and, by

---

[18] Available from Black Coat Press, ISBN 9781932983135.
[19] Stage play adaptation available from Black Coat Press, ISBN 9781934543436.

making it more real and contemporary, gave it a new lease on life.

Leroux's literary idols being Alexandre Dumas and Paul Féval, it was no surprise that he felt equally comfortable chronicling extravagant tales of murder, revenge, masked men, swooning women, mysterious dwarves and secret societies meeting in underground caverns, with or without fantastic elements, not unlike American pulps and serials of the 1930s.

Today, Gaston Leroux is best remembered in France as the author of a series of mystery novels starring the character of dashing young journalist, Joseph Rouletabille (initially named "Boitabille"), clearly an idealized projection of the author, and conceived as a direct challenge to Conan Doyle. Like C. Auguste Dupin, Monsieur Lecoq, Sherlock Holmes and Hercule Poirot, Rouletabille solved his cases by pure deductive reasoning, what he called the "good bit of reason." He drew a figurative circle around the facts that were known, and excluded everything that was not part of that circle, even if, to others, they appeared to be.

In the first Rouletabille novel, *Le Mystère de la Chambre Jaune* [*The Mystery of the Yellow Room*], the hero solved an attempted murder in a locked room. In that book, Leroux revealed that "Rouletabille" was the nickname of 18-year-old journalist Joseph Josephin, who was raised in a religious orphanage in Eu, a small town on the western coast of France, near Fecamp.

It turned out that Rouletabille's father was none other than Ballmeyer, an international criminal of great repute and many identities. As Jean Roussel, Ballmeyer had married a rich American heiress, Mathilde Stangerson, the "Lady in Black," who was, therefore, Rouletabille's mother.

In a tragic twist of fate, Rouletabille unmasked Ballmeyer, who was hiding under the guise of French Sûreté detective Frederic Larsan, in 1902, and saved his mother from his father's evil designs.

Ballmeyer returned in *Le Parfum de la Dame en Noir* [*The Perfume of the Lady in Black*]. At the end of the story, which took place in a castle by the sea in Southern France, Ballmeyer died, freeing Rouletabille from the evil shadow of the past.

Soon afterwards, in *Rouletabille chez le Tsar* [*Rouletabille and the Czar*], Rouletabille was summoned to Russia by the Czar, where he solved a murder at the Imperial Court.

Then, there is a break in continuity. In *Rouletabille à la Guerre* [*Rouletabille at War*], which takes place contemporaneously, i.e.: circa 1914, the fearless journalist married the beautiful Ivana Vilitchkov and defeated the mad Turk warlord Gaulow, Lord of the Black Castle.

There is an irreconcilable dating problem with the first Rouletabille novels: *Yellow Room* was stated by Leroux as taking place in 1892, and its sequel, *Perfume*, "a little over two years later," i.e.: in 1895. Yet, the subsequent novels refer to contemporaneous events, and Rouletabille has not aged ten years between *Perfume* and *Tsar*. So 1902 has therefore become the accepted dating for *The Mystery of the Yellow Room*. And 1905 for *The Perfume of the Lady in Black*.

In *Rouletabille chez Krupp* [*Rouletabille at Krupp's*], Rouletabille became a French secret agent and infiltrated the Krupp factories. Aside from John Buchan's Richard Hannay novels, this was one of the first, modern treatments of the espionage thriller. In the end, like a proto-James Bond, Rouletabille saved Paris from being annihilated by a German super-missile.

In *Le Crime de Rouletabille* [*The Crime of Rouletabille*], the detective was almost framed for Ivana's murder. Then, in *Rouletabille chez les Bohémiens* [*Rouletabille and the Gypsies*], Rouletabille helped recover a sacred book stolen from the gypsies and managed to thwart the evil schemes of the deadly Madame de Mayrens, a.k.a. *La Pieuvre* [*The Octopus*], the secret identity of whom we shall not spoil here.

There is a literary connection between *The Phantom of the Opera*, *The Double Life of Théophraste Longuet* and *The Crime of Rouletabille* in that all these novels feature a police official named Mifroid. There is a reference in *The Double Life...* (which begins in 1899) that Mifroid joined the police after the events of *Phantom* "ten years ago," yet *Phantom* takes place in 1880, so there is an inconsistency. Finally, *The Crime of Rouletabille* takes place 20 years after *The Double*

Life... (40 years after *Phantom*), so it is unlikely that it could be the same Mifroid...

Jean-Marc Lofficier

Bibliography:
1. *Le Mystère de la Chambre Jaune* [*The Mystery of the Yellow Room*] (serial. in *L'Illustration*, 1907; rep. Lafitte, 1908)
2. *Le Parfum de la Dame en Noir* [*The Perfume of the Lady in Black*] (serial. in *L'Illustration*, 1908; rep. Lafitte, 1909)
3. *Rouletabille chez le Tsar* [*Rouletabille and the Czar*] (serial. in *L'Illustration*, rep. Lafitte, 1913)
4. *Rouletabille à la Guerre* [*Rouletabille at War*] (serial. in *Le Matin*, 1914; rep. as 2 vols.: *Le Château Noir* [*The Black Castle*] and *Les Etranges Noces de Rouletabille* [*The Strange Wedding of Rouletabille*], Lafitte, 1916)
5. *Rouletabille chez Krupp* [*Rouletabille at Krupp's*] (serial. in *Je Sais Tout*, 1917; rep. Lafitte, 1920)
6. *Le Crime de Rouletabille* [*The Crime of Rouletabille*] (serial. in *Je Sais Tout*, 1921; rep. Lafitte, 1923)
7. *Rouletabille chez les Bohémiens* [*Rouletabille and the Gypsies*] (serial. in *Le Matin*, 1922; rev. Lafitte, 1923)
Authorized Sequels by Noré Brunel:
8. *Rouletabille contre la Dame de Pique* [*Rouletabille vs. The Queen of Spades*] (serial. in *Le Soir*, 1947)
9. *Rouletabille Joue et Gagne* [*Rouletabille Plays and Wins*] (serial. in *Le Soir*, 1947)

BLACK COAT PRESS

M. Allain & P. Souvestre. *The Daughter of Fantômas*
Anicet-Bourgeois. *Rocambole*
Guy d'Armen. *Doc Ardan: The City of Gold and Lepers*
Aloysius Bertrand. *Gaspard de la Nuit*
A. Bisson & G. Livet. *Nick Carter vs. Fantômas*
Félix Bodin. *The Novel of the Future*
Lucien Dabril. *Rocambole*
V. Darlay & H. de Gorsse. *Lupin vs. Holmes: The Stage Play*
C.I. Defontenay. *Star (Psi Cassiopeia)*
Charles Derennes: *The People of the Pole*
Alexandre Dumas. *The Return of Lord Ruthven*
J.-C. Dunyach. *The Night Orchid: Conan Doyle in Toulouse*
J.-C. Dunyach. *The Thieves of Silence*
Paul Féval: *Anne of the Isles*
Paul Féval. *The Blackcoats: The Companions of the Treasure*
Paul Féval. *The Blackcoats: The Invisible Weapon*
Paul Féval. *The Blackcoats: The Parisian Jungle*
Paul Féval. *The Blackcoats: 'Salem Street*
Paul Féval. *Captain Phantom*
Paul Féval. *Gentlemen of the Night*
Paul Féval. *John Devil*
Paul Féval. *Knightshade*
Paul Féval. *Revenants*
Paul Féval. *Vampire City*
Paul Féval. *The Vampire Countess*
Paul Féval. *The Wandering Jew's Daughter*
Paul Féval, *fils*. *Felifax, the Tiger-Man*
Emile Gaboriau. *Monsieur Lecoq*
Arnould Galopin. *Doctor Omega*
V. Hugo, Foucher & Meurice. *The Hunchback of Notre-Dame*
O. Joncquel & Theo Varlet. *The Martian Epic*
Jean de La Hire. *The Nyctalope on Mars*
Jean de La Hire. *The Nyctalope vs. Lucifer*
Jean de La Hire. *Enter the Nyctalope*
Steve Leadley. *Sherlock Holmes - The Circle of Blood*
Maurice Leblanc. *Lupin vs. Holmes: The Hollow Needle*
Maurice Leblanc. *Lupin vs. Holmes: The Blonde Phantom*
G. Le Faure & H. de Graffigny. *The Extraordinary Adventures of a Russian Scientist Across the Solar System* (2 vols.)

Gustave Le Rouge. *The Vampires of Mars*
Jules Lermina. *Panic in Paris*
Gaston Leroux. *Chéri-Bibi*
Gaston Leroux. *The Phantom of the Opera*
Jean-Marc Lofficier. *The Katrina Protocol*
Jean-Marc & Randy Lofficier. *Edgar Allan Poe on Mars*
Jean-Marc & Randy Lofficier. *Robonocchio*
Lofficier. *Tales of the Shadowmen 1: The Modern Babylon*
Lofficier. *Tales of the Shadowmen 2: Gentlemen of the Night*
Lofficier. *Tales of the Shadowmen 3: Danse Macabre*
Lofficier. *Tales of the Shadowmen 4: Lords of Terror*
Lofficier. *Tales of the Shadowmen 5: The Vampires of Paris*
Xavier Mauméjean. *The League of Heroes*
William Patrick Maynard. *The Terror of Fu Manchu*
Frank J. Morlock. *Sherlock Holmes: The Grand Horizontals*
Marie Nizet. *Captain Vampire*
C. Nodier, Beraud & Toussaint-Merle. *Frankenstein*
Charles Nodier. *Lord Ruthven the Vampire*
G. de Pawlowski. *Journey to the Land of the 4th Dimension*
Henri de Parville. *An Inhabitant of the Planet Mars*
John William Polidori. *Lord Ruthven the Vampire*
P.-A. Ponson du Terrail. *The Vampire and the Devil's Son*
Albert Robida. *The Clock of the Centuries*
Eugène Scribe. *Lord Ruthven the Vampire*
Brian Stableford. *The Germans on Venus*
Brian Stableford. *News from the Moon*
Brian Stableford. *The New Faust at the Tragicomique*
Brian Stableford. *The Shadow of Frankenstein*
Brian Stableford. *Sherlock Holmes - The Vampires of Eternity*
Brian Stableford. *The Stones of Camelot*
Brian Stableford. *The Wayward Muse*
Villiers de l'Isle-Adam. *The Scaffold*
Villiers de l'Isle-Adam. *The Vampire Soul*
Philippe Ward. *Artahe: The Legacy of Jules de Grandin*
P. de Wattyne & Y. Walter. *Sherlock Holmes vs. Fantômas*
David White: *Fantômas in America*

www.ingramcontent.com/pod-product-compliance
Lightning Source LLC
Chambersburg PA
CBHW030350020726
4749 3CB00003B/766